KEEP NO SECRETS

ALSO BY JULIE COMPTON

Tell No Lies

Rescuing Olivia

KEEP NO SECRETS

_____

JULIE COMPTON

Fresh Fork Publishing
Longwood, Florida

This book is a work of fiction. Names, characters, places, and incidents are product of the author's imagination or are used fictitiously. Any resemblance to actual events, locales, or persons, living or dead, is coincidental.

Cover photograph © rnl/Shutterstock.com

Cover design © Jessie Compton

ISBN-13: 978-0-9887932-2-4

First edition: March 2013

For my girls

EARLY WINTER

CHAPTER ONE

JACK WAKES TO the slam of the front door. It's Michael, home from a party down the street. For a moment, he's perturbed at his older son for the noise, for not considering anyone else in the house. It's the type of thing Claire shrugs off as typical teenage behavior, but still, it irks Jack.

He glances at the digital clock on the nightstand. It's Saturday night for one more minute; at least Michael got Celeste home and made his curfew. He must have realized the noise he made, because afterwards, the dark house falls silent once again. Jack rolls closer to a sleeping Claire and drifts back to sleep.

The second time, he doesn't look at the clock right away because he's so focused on listening for what woke him again. Voices. Not one, but two distinct voices. Michael's, and Celeste's—Celeste, who shouldn't be there. It's the whispers and giggles that did it. Had they carried on at a normal volume, Jack probably would have slept right through it. But somehow, the fact that they're trying *not* to be heard has guaranteed that they will be.

He grabs his robe and at the top of the stairs, stops to listen. They're in the family room, that much is clear. It's also clear from the sway in their speech that they're drunk. Even as he starts to fume about that, he's grateful that at least Michael had the common sense not to drive Celeste home. And even as he prepares to interrupt them and read them the riot act, he's already thinking about the logistics of the rest of the night—whether to wake Claire or do this alone, whether to call Celeste's dad now and have him pick her up, or whether to drive her home himself and talk to her dad once he gets there.

He starts down, but stops when he hears Celeste, "Shh, shh, I think I hear someone." Michael doesn't respond, at least not loud enough to hear. "Mike, stop!" she says, and giggles. "I mean it. I think someone's coming."

"I hope so," his sixteen year old son mumbles, and Jack's about to freak. Suddenly the drinking seems like the least of his concerns. His next footstep is purposely a loud one, and now they're scrambling, repositioning themselves and grasping for discarded clothes. It's all Jack can do not to go down right away. But he has no idea what state of undress they're in, and though he'd love to embarrass Michael—he deserves it and so much more right now—he doesn't want to do that to Celeste.

All he can think is, *what the hell are you thinking, Michael?* He thought his son was smarter than this. He really believed Michael would make it to adulthood without doing something too stupid. Now he realizes how naïve he was, how easily anything could happen on his watch. He's ready to lock Michael in the house until he's eighteen. Or twenty-one would be even better. Yet even as he has these thoughts, he can hear Claire: "This is the age *most* people do the stupid stuff." She'd leave the rest unsaid.

"Are you decent?" he calls down, voice level. Michael responds with a cold, "Yeah."

In the family room, Jack flips on a light and takes in the scene. Celeste's long hair looks as if she just stepped out of bed and her blouse is buttoned wrong. Michael's T-shirt covers the waist of his jeans but Jack is pretty sure they're unzipped. Celeste's dark eyes are wide with fear. As much trouble as Michael's in at this moment, her Catholic dad is ten times stricter than Jack and Claire. She's not so worried about what Jack will say or do; she's already thinking about what will happen when she gets home.

Jack glares at Michael, and Michael glares back, making Jack even angrier.

He turns to Celeste. "Go in the bathroom and put yourself together, and then I'm taking you home." She nods apologetically and jumps up. When she does, an earring falls to the floor. She sheepishly bends down for it and then takes off, staggering, for the half-bath in the front hall. To Michael, Jack says, "Don't you move. I'll be back in a minute and then we're having a little talk. You got it?"

Michael regards him without answering, still defiant.

"Did you hear me?" Louder this time.

Slowly, Michael nods, and Jack leaves the room to put on some real clothes and find his keys.

"I'm sorry, Mr. H," Celeste says as soon as she stumbles into the car. Jack picks up the smoky scent of burning oak, smells liquor on her breath. Whiskey, he thinks, and this floors him even more because he assumed they would have drunk only beer.

He doesn't answer her, for fear of what he'll say. Even though she's come to feel like family, he's not sure it's his place to scold her. He's not sure what's safe to say and what might cross a line that only her dad is entitled to cross.

So for now, as he waits for the heater to warm the car, he simply asks, "Do you have everything? All your stuff?"

She nods.

He puts the car into reverse.

Jack glances over at Celeste as he pulls out of the neighborhood. He remembers the day Michael first brought her home, how he and Claire were left speechless when the two of them came into the house from the door to the garage, dumping their backpacks on top of the clothes dryer. Only a few weeks into the current school year, it was Claire's fortieth birthday. Jack had left the DA's office early to get home in time to make dinner and help his younger son bake the cake—just one of many things he did differently since Claire had allowed him back into their home.

When Michael and Celeste stepped into the kitchen, Jack almost dropped the cake that Jamie had just finished decorating.

The resemblance to Jenny Dodson was remarkable. The long, straight black hair. The dark, smoky eyes. The copper skin. The perfectly contoured face. Much younger, of course. But still, Michael had to have known. And as much as Jack understood Michael's desire to stick it to his father, he simply couldn't believe he'd do this to his mother—on her birthday, no less.

Claire recovered first. She greeted Celeste warmly, and even invited her to stay for dinner. To Jack's relief and, he suspected, Claire's too, she politely declined.

But in the weeks that followed, Celeste quickly ingratiated herself into the Hilliard household. Jack could do nothing about it, and Michael knew it. On the days he didn't have basketball practice and she had neither volleyball nor ballet, they came to the house right after school to do homework together. Michael insisted that they needed his computer, which was in his bedroom. Claire made them keep the door open and though Michael complained, she held her ground.

On Friday nights, Celeste sat with Jack, Claire and Jamie at Michael's games. Then, without fail, she'd come back to the house afterwards for pizza. At first Jack was uncomfortable at how she clung to his family as if it was her own. And he'd be lying, too, if he didn't admit his fear that other parents at the school might also see the resemblance and wonder. No one ever brought up what had happened four years ago, how he'd betrayed Claire and his family, how he'd betrayed St. Louis, even, the city that had only just elected him, but he knew it was a shadow that followed him wherever he went.

But Celeste proved easy to have around. She adored eight-year-old Jamie. If he became restless during the games, she'd take him from the stands and play with him in the hallway outside the gym. Michael rolled his eyes the first time she offered to babysit for real, but he eventually gave in. Now Jack understands why. Michael obviously realized the benefits before Jack and Claire realized the risks: after putting Jamie to bed, he and Celeste would effectively be alone in the house. It never occurred to Jack or Claire not to trust him. They'd come home from a restaurant or the movies to find Jamie sleeping soundly, the toys put away and the dishes washed and drying in a rack next to the sink. He wonders now how long they've been carrying on.

"Mr. H?" At a stop sign closer to her home than Jack's, Celeste's soft voice breaks his thoughts. "I'm really, really sorry. We haven't done anything like that before, I swear." She tries to keep her voice even, tries to sound sober. She's only partly successful.

Until this moment Jack has directed most of his anger at Michael, but in the face of this bold lie he starts to see her as a temptress who's seducing his vulnerable son. Does she think Jack's an idiot? He didn't hear much at the top of the stairs, but what he did hear certainly wasn't the conversation of two teenagers experimenting with sex for the first time.

"Celeste," he begins, trying to pay attention to the curves in the road as he crafts a response that won't accuse her of lying but won't let her off the hook, either. It's dark here, on the way to her house. When they moved from Florida to St. Louis over the summer, her dad rejected the typical suburban choices and instead chose a home on several wooded acres far west of the city near Rockwoods Reservation. "I heard enough to know better. If you're going to engage in adult behavior, then—"

"Can we pull over?" she asks suddenly.

"Why?"

"Just . . ." In the glow of the dashboard lights he sees she's started to tear up. "Please? I think I'm going to be sick."

He sighs. Against his better judgment, he pulls into one of the small parking lots for the conservation area. The gravel crunches under the tires as he circles the car around to face the road. He puts the car in Park but leaves the headlights on and the engine running. She opens her door and swings her legs out. Leaning over, she spits a bit, but Jack's certain she's not vomiting. She's stalling.

"Are you done?" He tries to check his impatience, but he's supposed to be in bed sleeping right now, not out on some dark road with a sixteen-year-old girl he doesn't entirely trust anymore and who bears too much of a resemblance to another female he doesn't entirely trust anymore either. Whom he doesn't trust at all, really.

She nods and closes herself back in. She sets her hands in her lap and plays with a loose button of her long sweater coat. His eyes are drawn to her left pinky, which ends in a stub just after the last joint. He's never noticed it before, but the nails on her other fingers have been bitten to the quick. "I can't go home yet. He'll know I'm wasted."

Jack knows she means her father, even though she never says "my dad" or even uses his first name. It's always "he" or "him." It's impossible to handle the types of cases he's handled, first as an assistant prosecutor, now as DA, and not suspect a psychological reason for a habit like that. Jack once asked Michael about it. Michael looked at him as if he was crazy, but when Jack finally met the man, he had an inkling. At a minimum—and he hoped there wasn't more—the guy kept an unusually tight rein on his only daughter that guaranteed her close physical proximity but also, Jack thought, ensured rebellion in one form or another.

"He needs to know, Celeste. Even if he doesn't figure it out on his own, I plan to tell him."

"You can't," she pleads. "Please! I knew I'd be in trouble for breaking curfew, so I texted him and told him Mike had car trouble and I'd be late. He's okay with that. But if he finds out I was drinking—"

Jack can't believe she's made the situation worse. "It's not just the drinking I need to tell him about."

"Oh, God!" She starts breathing rapidly as if she's having a panic attack. "Please don't tell him. We really didn't do anything, Mr. H. We were just fooling around. He likes Mike so much. If you tell him, he won't let me see Mike anymore. He won't let me come over to your house." Jack might put the brakes on that, anyway, but he doesn't say this. "The only reason he even let me date Mike in the first place is because of you."

"What are you talking about?"

She shrugs bashfully and keeps tucking her hair nervously behind her ears. She combed it when he sent her to the bathroom, and looking at it now, he still can't get over how it hangs the same way as Jenny's. Heavy and sleek.

"He never let me date before," she says. "He wasn't going to let me until I was eighteen. But he made an exception for Mike. He figured a DA's son has gotta be pretty straight." She shrugs again, and something about her words and her gesture strike Jack as disingenuous.

"Well, I don't know about that, but I'm sure he trusts me to tell him if there are any problems, and that's what I have to do." He reaches down to put the car into gear. "We're telling him everything."

Before he even moves the gearshift, she grabs his arm with both hands. One hand is on his coat sleeve, but the other claws at the bare skin of his wrist. She tightens her grip. "Please, Mr. H! I'm begging you! You don't understand what will happen!"

Something in the desperate tone of her last words makes him turn and regard her differently. Where before he felt as if everything she said was orchestrated to manipulate him, he now senses her words were spontaneous and her fear is genuine.

"What do you mean?" he asks gently. She still hasn't released his arm and her close proximity makes him uncomfortable. The car windows are fogging up, and in the warm, enclosed space, he easily detects the lingering scent of her body spray, the type that all the kids use nowadays. Too sweet and slightly fruity, the scent of a girl on the cusp of womanhood. *Please, not Michael's girlfriend. Please let it be something other than what I think it's going to be.* He just wants to be home, sleeping. For an instant, he wonders if Claire has woken up to find the bed next to her empty.

Celeste tucks both lips in, trying not to cry. She reaches up with one hand, still holding his wrist with the other, and wipes under both eyes. The tears and the wiping have smeared her mascara and they make raccoon shadows on her bottom lids. He's always wanted to tell her she doesn't need all the make-up, but of course he never did.

"What do you mean?" he asks again.

She lowers her eyes and shakes her head. "Nothing." Jack barely hears her.

He wonders how much to push her. If his gut is right, she needs to tell someone, and someone needs to protect her.

"Celeste?" She looks up for just an instant. "What will happen? Are you afraid of him?"

"No," she says quietly, averting her eyes again. "As long as you don't tell him anything, as long as you wait a bit before dropping me off, then he won't do anything."

He takes a deep breath. Either she doesn't get it, or she does and she's trying to protect her father. "And if I *do* tell him, what will happen? What will he do?"

She shrugs.

Repositioning himself as a means of getting his arm back, Jack looks out the front windshield at the beams of gold coming from the headlights. When he and Claire were still in law school, they used to drive out here on the weekends, hike deep into the woods, and pitch a tent for the night. It was against park rules, but no one ever caught them. He wonders if they patrol the area better now, but as soon as he has that thought, he thinks, *as DA, I should know the answer.* If someone were to come along just now, how would he explain it? Being here—he glances at the dashboard clock—at one fifteen in the morning with his son's girlfriend. And she's got alcohol in her system. And she bears a striking resemblance to another woman he wasn't supposed to be with.

What a headline that would make.

"Will he hurt you somehow?"

She straightens up in the seat and stares forward for a long time. She's still crying, though. He waits, because he thinks she's about to confide everything. He starts thinking of his next step. If it's bad enough, does he take her back to his house and call the hotline immediately? If it's not, does he give her the time she wants, and then drop her off at her own home, but still call the hotline in the morning? And if it's the latter, what would he say? That he wants to report a sixteen-year-old girl who's afraid to go home after getting caught drinking and having sex? He can just imagine the look on the police officer's face assigned to investigate that report.

Given her intoxicated state, she almost manages to keep her voice level and composed as she speaks the next words. She still doesn't look at him. "Mr. H, I shouldn't have said what I did, okay? You're misunderstanding. I just don't want to get in trouble. That's all."

She reminds Jack of all the abused women who call the cops in the heat of the moment but then refuse to testify when the case comes to trial. But maybe he's blown things out of proportion. Maybe she's just a kid who said things to get him to do what she wanted.

Before Jack responds, her shoulders slump and she adds, "Just take me home. I'll deal."

And this is when Jack makes his first mistake. With a sigh, he cuts the lights and turns off the ignition. These actions cause her to finally turn to him, her brow furrowed in confusion.

"We'll just let you sober up some more," he explains. He prays no one comes along in the meantime.

She speaks a soft "thank you" and resumes playing with the button on her sweater. He switches on the radio for lack of anything better to do.

After a while, the two of them start talking. Just idle conversation. He asks about school and her teachers and what she wants to do after graduation, where she wants to attend college. She asks him what it's like to be the DA and whether he likes being a lawyer and if law school was hard. He keeps thinking that eventually he'll segue to talking about the drinking, about her relationship with Michael, but she's opening up so much and he doesn't want to cause her to shut down again.

"What's the worst case you've ever been involved in?" she asks.

He tries to read the meaning of the question. It's an innocent question; after all, her family didn't even live in Missouri back when the Barnard case—and then Jenny's case—was news. But still, he wonders how much she knows, if Michael has told her anything.

"Um . . ." He takes a long time to answer. He can't think about the Barnard case without thinking about everything else that happened afterwards. Jenny charged with the murder of Maxine Shepard, a prominent client at the law firm where Jenny practiced law. Jack her alibi, because he happened to make the worst decision of his life on the same night Maxine was murdered. This fact set Jenny free, but it changed Jack's life forever.

He shakes his head as if to dust the cobwebs away and tells Celeste about the Barnard case. "It was this case, a little girl named Cassia Barnard had been abducted and murdered. I mean, I've seen a lot of bad things happen to kids, but . . . I don't know . . . this one was harder for some reason."

"Why?"

"A lot of reasons, I guess. For one, we were pretty certain she suffered a lot. He'd raped her, really hurt her. Then he left her in the woods to freeze to death." Celeste winces. "But we didn't ask for the death penalty, and a lot of people thought we should have and were angry that we didn't. Angry at me. At the end of it all, *I* almost thought we should have, too, and I'm opposed to capital punishment. That's how bad it was."

She looks down at her hands. "I'd like to do what you do, I think."

"Really? Why?"

"I don't know." She shrugs. "What you do makes a difference, you know?"

Jack tenses, remembering a conversation between Claire, Jenny and his brother Mark, back when Jack was an assistant prosecutor. He was trying to decide whether to run for DA. The three of them had been discussing whether Jack should run despite his opposition to the death penalty. What had Jenny argued? *To get into a position to make any difference, you sometimes have to compromise.* The comment had made Claire mad, though she'd restrained her anger. *He makes a difference now,* she'd said. The conversation now seems as if it took place in another lifetime.

Jack laughs a little, regretfully. "I did make a difference in that case, I guess. I'm just not too sure it was the difference people wanted."

"But it seems like you really care about what you do," Celeste argues. She doesn't understand. Can't understand. "I don't think many adults care much about what they do."

"Yeah," he agrees, softly. "I do care about what I do."

They're both quiet for a moment, and then he asks, "Do you really mean it, that you'd like to be an attorney?"

"Yes, but not the kind that sits at a desk all day. I'd like to be a prosecutor, like you, and be in a courtroom all the time."

Jack grins, suppressing a laugh. He's about to tell her that even prosecutors often sit at a desk and some other types of attorneys also go to court, but then she adds, "I want to protect people."

The statement gives him pause. He thinks again of the fear she expressed earlier. Maybe the two are unrelated, but his instinct tells him otherwise.

And this is when he makes his second mistake. In that instant, almost without realizing it, he decides he's going to cover for her, just as she's asked.

"Celeste?" Her big eyes look up at him. "If you mean what you say, don't make it harder on yourself, okay?"

"What do you mean, Mr. H?"

"College and law school are tough enough without a kid in tow."

It takes her a minute, but then he sees it sink in. She's silent for a long time. Then, so softly he has to strain to hear her, she says, "Okay." She nods vehemently and says it again. "Okay."

CHAPTER TWO

WHEN JACK GETS home, Michael is flat on his back, asleep on the couch. The clock on the microwave in the kitchen announces that it's almost three a.m. Jack sits on the coffee table and studies Michael's sleeping face. It's one of the few times he sees it in a relaxed state, free of the pent-up anger Michael normally wears in his father's presence.

Michael's eyelashes are unusually long. Both his and Jamie's are. Jamie still has the rounded cheeks of a baby, but Michael's face has grown strong and angular as he left childhood behind. Peach fuzz still covers his jaw and chin—it'll be a while before he needs to shave—but still, he's more man than child. Claire says he looks just like Jack; everyone says that, really. Michael chafes at the comparison.

Jack wonders if Michael will ever let it go, if he'll ever forgive him. When Jack first moved back into the house—after a four month absence during which he hadn't seen his son but for one miserable Christmas visit—he tried to talk to him. Even Claire tried to talk to him. He claimed he wasn't mad, but anyone can see that he is. He carries his resentment like an invisible shield, always holding Jack at arm's length.

For a brief moment, Jack considers waiting until morning, letting both of them get some sleep before they have this conversation, but he decides it shouldn't wait.

He touches Michael's shoulder once, lightly, and then a second time, giving him a little shake. He can't remember the last time he touched his oldest son, and just thinking about it makes his throat tighten. Two more years and Michael will be gone. Jack resolves right then and there to start hugging him again whether he likes it or not.

When Michael opens his eyes and sees him, he rolls to his side, giving Jack his back.

"Michael, wake up. Sit up." He doesn't say it harshly.

Reluctantly, Michael complies. He keeps his head down, though, his elbows resting on his thighs. He rubs his face with his hands.

"I want to talk to you about tonight."

Suddenly Michael jerks his head toward the clock in the kitchen as if he just remembered why he's sleeping on the couch and his father has a coat on.

"Where have you been?" Michael asks, finally meeting Jack's eye. He says it as if he's the parent and Jack's the child.

"I took Celeste home, remember?" Jack regards him warily. Maybe he hasn't slept off his buzz; maybe he's disoriented. He's been known to sleepwalk. Jack wonders now if he's even fully awake yet.

Michael grunts and rolls his eyes. "She doesn't live in Wentzville."

Jack leans back slightly, understanding now that, yeah, he's awake, and his comment was an accusation. Wentzville, on the opposite side of the Missouri river, is nowhere near their home in West County. The calming effect of the talk with Celeste in the car quickly begins to erode.

"What's your point, Michael?"

Michael lowers his eyes and doesn't respond. Maybe he's realizing he's already in enough trouble.

"How much did you two drink tonight?" When Michael just shrugs, Jack adds, "You must have an idea."

"I don't know, a few shots each, I guess." He still won't look at Jack.

"What's 'a few?'"

"Two or three."

Jack is certain it was more. "Where'd you get it?"

Michael is silent.

"Were Jason's parents home?" Jack asks, trying another route.

"Yeah, they were home." Jack is about to express disbelief that Jason's parents would let kids drink at their house—he *knows* these particular parents—when Michael adds, "We didn't drink it at Jason's house."

Jack is silent. Michael understands he's waiting for more.

"About six of us left early. We went on the trail. We built a fire and partied out there for a while."

He's referring to one of the trails in the woods at the top of the street. The developer didn't raze that part of the land when he built the neighborhood because the bluffs in the middle made it impossible to build on. The bluffs split the woods into two, one upper level and one lower level, and the neighborhood kids have forged winding trails throughout, even a treacherous one that leads from top to bottom and requires a hiker to hold onto tree trunks and boulders on the way down. By day, the young kids play hide and seek and ride their dirt bikes on the upper trails; at night the teenagers hang out on the lower level, out of sight and under cover of the noise of the bubbling creek that runs alongside the bottom trail.

Michael knows he's not supposed to be there, but Jack has enough issues to deal with tonight to bust him for that, too.

"Where'd you get the whiskey?" he asks again, coming back to the earlier question that Michael avoided.

Michael fidgets on the couch. He's no longer looking down, but he's not looking at Jack, either. He stares into space.

"Michael."

"I'm not one of your frickin' witnesses," he mumbles.

Fed up, Jack stands quickly. Michael flinches as if he's about to be hit. Jack has never hit either of his kids and he never would. Yet Michael believes, after what he's done tonight, Jack might.

In the kitchen Jack throws his coat over a barstool. He turns on the small light over the stove and opens the cabinet where Claire keeps the liquor. He paws through the bottles—vodka, tequila, gin, the rum that she uses in recipes—most of them have been untouched for months, some even years. The only liquor Jack ever drinks, in the rare instances when he drinks something other than beer or wine, is Jack Daniel's. The bottle is gone.

He turns back toward the family room. The kitchen and the family room form one big space, and the stove light allows Michael a clear shot of Jack.

"What? You figured we'd never notice? Is that it?"

"No. I just didn't really care."

Jack is glad for the distance between them, because at that moment he feels as if he just might violate the "no hitting" policy. He wants to ask Michael if he knows how lucky he is, if he realizes how many fathers would break their sons' jaw if spoken to like that, or take a belt or worse to them. But he doesn't. Michael knows. No matter how much he provokes his father, he knows Jack would never lay a finger on him.

"Well, I care." Jack returns to the family room and sits on the arm chair at the end of the couch. "And Mom will care. And she'll care even more about what's going on with Celeste." It might not matter to Michael what Jack thinks, but he most definitely cares about what Claire thinks.

Michael laughs sarcastically. "Yeah, Mom *will* care. She's gonna want to know why it took almost two hours to take Celeste home."

Celeste's resemblance to Jenny has never been directly acknowledged by any of them. Not by Jack. Not by Claire. Not by Michael. Michael's statement is the closest anyone has come to saying it out loud. If Jack takes the bait, if he tries to turn it back on Michael, match his sarcasm and ask "Why would you say that?", then he'll start down a road he's not sure he wants to travel—a road where there'd be no going back. But does Michael really think the resemblance between the two women—the woman and the *girl*—would cause Jack to do something even more stupid than what he's already done? Because if Michael really thinks this, if he honestly thinks his dad would mess with a sixteen-year-old girl, then Jack might as well give up now.

"It took two hours because she begged me to give her time to sober up. She'd already texted her dad, told him your car had broken down and that she'd be late."

"Oh, right. And you agreed?"

Michael's skepticism is justified. Jack's still a little surprised that he agreed, too.

"Yeah, I did. You know why? Because she was deathly afraid to arrive home even a little tipsy. It wasn't just that she didn't want to get yelled at or grounded. It was something more."

Michael's shoulders relax slightly; he believes this. Maybe he knows what Celeste wouldn't tell.

"Do you know why she's so afraid of her dad?"

"He's really strict."

"'Really strict' doesn't explain her panic when I told her I was going to talk to him. She's hiding something."

Michael shrugs, looking down. If he knows, he's not telling, either. Does he think by keeping her secrets he's protecting her somehow?

"Michael?" Jack speaks gently. It gets Michael's attention. "If he's hurting her somehow, it doesn't help her to keep silent."

He shakes his head. "You're crazy, Dad. You think everything is evidence of child abuse." Despite the apparent insult, the anger has left his voice. "He's not *hurting* her."

Either he believes what he's saying, or he's simply not giving anything away.

"Okay, fine, he's not hurting her. But I felt like something was up, so I waited a while before taking her home. We had a good talk until she thought she was okay and could deal with him."

"What did her dad say when you dropped her off?"

"I didn't talk to him." Jack hesitates. "He thinks it was you dropping her off."

"What?" It's difficult to tell if he's angry or just surprised by this, too. "I thought for sure you'd—"

"Look, I hope it wasn't the wrong thing to do, but once I decided to cover for her . . ." Jack shakes his head, wondering all over again if she snookered him. Part of him doesn't think so; her fear was real. But deciding to go along with her story protected Michael, too; Jack is well aware of that. Is that why he so easily agreed to her request? "I don't know. It just seemed worse to talk to the man and have to lie outright to him, you know? Because it was either that, or tell him everything. And if my instincts are right and I *did* tell him everything . . . well, I didn't want to risk it."

Michael nods slightly. "Dad?" His voice is smaller, reminiscent of the little boy he used to be. "I'm sorry. I'm sorry we put you in this position."

The tension in Jack's shoulders melts upon hearing Michael's apology. Despite how young he sounded when he made it, it's the most mature thing he's ever done. Jack stares at him for a long time, even though Michael can't bring himself to meet his eye. It's not just tonight's tension that begins to dissolve, but four years' worth.

"Okay. I appreciate that. I do. But it doesn't let you off the hook."

"I know."

"I can't punish her, and maybe because of what I did she's getting off scot free, but you're my son and I'm still responsible for what you do." Michael doesn't respond, just continues to nod—more with his eyes than his head—and listens. Jack breathes deep, not wanting to ask the next question. "Do you at least use birth control?"

Michael shifts on the couch and pushes hair out of his face.

"Oh, Jesus, Michael." It doesn't occur to Jack that, in his own moment of stupidity, he didn't think about birth control either. And really, the potential consequences were much more devastating. "What are you thinking?"

"She says she can't, you know, because she's Catholic. But we make sure—"

Jack grunts in disbelief. "Yeah?" he interrupts angrily. "Well, then she's *also* not supposed to be" —he almost says *fucking around*— "having sex, either, is she?" Jack can't believe he's having this conversation with his son. He can't believe Michael would let some girl convince him *not* to use birth control. "What about STDs? Did it ever occur to you that if she's sleeping with you, she might have slept with others?"

The sound of creaking floorboards above their heads interrupts the conversation.

"Jack?" Claire's sleepy voice floats down the stairs. "Is that you?"

"Please don't tell her about Celeste, Dad," Michael whispers. "Please." His desperate tone is similar to Celeste's in the car.

"Yeah, it's me and Michael."

"Michael?" She flips on the hall light at the top of the stairs and starts down. "What's Michael doing up?"

"Dad, please. Tell her about the drinking if you have to, but not about the other. *Please.*"

When Claire reaches the bottom, she's still fussing with the tie of her robe. She stops when she sees them. "What's going on? Why are you guys down here so late?"

Michael looks at Jack, wide-eyed and scared. Suddenly, he's eleven again. He'd been playing with a Nerf gun and had accidentally knocked over a porcelain figurine heirloom of Claire's. There'd been some historical significance to it. Had it been snuck out of a European country by her ancestors during some war? Jack can't remember. But he knew how devastated she'd be. Even though Michael didn't fully grasp the importance of the heirloom, he understood it meant a lot to her. He became hysterical at the thought of her knowing what he'd done. Everything he did, every achievement, he did for his mother. He couldn't bear the thought of disappointing her. It broke Jack's heart, seeing his son so upset. He hadn't planned it, but when Claire walked into the room, asking "What's going on?" just as she did tonight, Jack stepped up and took the blame. Before Michael could confess, Jack claimed they'd been roughhousing and he'd been the guilty one. She didn't doubt his explanation; there was no reason to. She simply assumed Michael cried out of sympathy.

Jack became Michael's partner in crime that day, and by extension, his hero. A little over a year later, he'd become Michael's villain.

Jack turns to Claire. And this is when he makes his third mistake. "I heard him come in. He broke curfew," he glares at Michael, "by about three hours."

Claire sinks into a chair. She holds her body close, her shoulders hunched a little, her hands in her lap, as if she's cold. "Where were you?" she asks Michael. For now, she's more confused and disappointed than angry.

Michael hesitates. "I, um—"

"He told me he had trouble with his car," Jack says, "but when I pressed for details, he finally admitted that after he and Celeste left Jason's party, they hung out on the trail with some friends for a few hours before he took her home."

He sees the flicker of a question cross Claire's face as she takes in the fact that Jack is fully dressed.

"Michael, you know you're not supposed to be on the trail at night," she says, apparently deciding that the explanation for Jack's attire can wait until later. "And my God, with Celeste? Who knows what kind of creeps hang out there at night?" When he starts to say something, she cuts him off. "I don't know what bothers me more: that you think you can wander home whenever the mood strikes you, or that you put Celeste at risk like that."

"Mom, it's just other kids like us. There's never—"

She interrupts him again, turning to Jack. "I can't believe her dad didn't call here looking for her."

Jack stares at Michael, letting him know that he's protected him from the big stuff, but the rest is up to him. Michael gets it.

"She texted him and told him my car had trouble and she'd be late," he says.

Claire's mouth falls open. It's not breaking curfew, it's not being in the woods. It's the lying that bothers her most, and Jack suddenly wishes he could do it over, because, like Celeste, he's now exacerbated the situation. *Why am I taking the fall for him?*

"I think we need to talk to Celeste's dad tomorrow."

"Mom, no! Please! Punish me all you want, ground me, take away my car, but please don't get her in trouble."

She stands. "If anyone got her trouble, Michael, it's you." To Jack she says, "Why don't we all get to bed and talk about this in the morning?" He nods slightly, certain by morning she'll soften towards Michael.

She always does.

CHAPTER THREE

ON SUNDAY AFTERNOON, Claire sits at her desk at the law school and stares at a photo of Michael and Jamie standing at the top of Art Hill in Forest Park. The Art Museum in the background frames the boys. Both are bundled in parkas and ski pants, mittens on their hands and snow boots on their feet. Michael holds the sled between them. Their cheeks are bubblegum pink; they've already been down the hill a few times and are anxious to do it again. They stood still for the picture only after she threatened to leave right then if they didn't. Sometimes she looks at the picture and thinks, *Where's Jack?* She knows the answer, of course, but she thinks it nevertheless because it's the question she sees on her sons' faces.

Jack has always loved sledding on Art Hill. When he was a kid, he did it every winter with his own dad. It's one of the few memories of the man he shares with them. He continued the tradition with Michael and Jamie. The year this picture was taken, the winter she forced his four-month exile from their home, is the only winter he missed.

He's never said so, but she knows he doesn't like that she displays the picture on her desk. She's not sure why she does.

She turns her attention back to the student papers in front of her. The assignment had been to write a summary judgment motion along with the argument to support it. Grading the papers of first year law students is difficult enough on a good day—for some reason, even those who'd attended the best universities for undergraduate school have difficulty structuring a coherent argument on paper—but today she finds her task particularly hard. It's the weekend and she'd rather be home.

The incident with Michael the night before has been on her mind. If he simply broke curfew by fifteen minutes or a half hour, she could understand Jack's desire to go easy on him. But three hours, followed by the news that he'd spent those three hours on the trail and then lied to Celeste's dad about it? To brush it off as typical teenager stuff, as Jack convinced her to do this morning, seems a bit too lax, and she's perturbed with herself for letting him convince her. She's also a bit confused, because usually the slightest misbehavior on Michael's part ignites Jack like flint ignites a fire. It's Claire who usually argues for letting things go.

She keeps glancing at the clock on the opposite wall. She thinks, *Where's Jack?* Why hasn't he returned her calls? She wants to talk to him about reconsidering Michael's punishment, or really, the lack thereof. Taking away his car for a few days, in her opinion, isn't much of a consequence.

She knows the answers to these questions, too. The police chief called their house earlier to inform Jack that they'd picked up the suspect in a recent murder case and to ask him if he wanted to be there to watch the interrogation. Claire doesn't know why Chief Matthews bothered to ask the question; for the bigger cases, Jack's answer is always yes, even if he has already assigned one of his assistants to prosecute it. It's one of the reasons he's so good at what he does. It's also one of the reasons his team respects him—he doesn't mind getting down in the trenches and he always makes himself available to do so. His efforts sometimes take a toll on their family life, but she does her best to understand. He gets results, too; his office has one of the highest conviction rates in the state, which is all the more impressive because of the large size of the population it serves.

This latest case mesmerized the city when the crime first occurred two months before. Jack expects it to become a full-blown circus once the arrest is made. On the surface, the case sounded like so many other domestic murder cases, but Jack's instincts told him this one was different. Perhaps it was the fact that the husband was the victim, the wife the presumed perpetrator. Perhaps it was the gruesome way the murderer disposed of the body. It had been wrapped in plastic sheeting and duct tape and buried under ten inches of cement in the couple's basement. Or maybe, even, it was simply the pictures of the couple in their younger, happier days that repeatedly appeared on the front page of the paper when the story first broke. Regardless, Jack's instincts are usually right.

She's already called the DA's office twice, thinking he might have stopped there after the interrogation; she refuses to allow herself a third attempt. She hasn't tried his cell because if he's still at the jail, she doesn't want to disturb him.

Two graded papers later her phone rings and she sees it's him calling from his cell phone.

"Wow. That must have been some interrogation." She smiles and swivels her chair around to look out her window as she talks. Heavy clouds march across the sky, pushed eastward by the cold front. The deserted campus is winter brown, but the air smelled of snow when she arrived several hours ago; it's only a matter of time and her view will be transformed into a white wonderland.

He doesn't respond. She hears the tap of his footsteps on the sidewalk. She guesses he's walking from the jail to his car. Or maybe to his office.

"Oh, you mean Bedford," he says finally, referring to the couple's surname.

"That's the case you went over to the jail on a Sunday for, isn't it?"

"Yeah, yeah. It was fine. I mean, we got a confession from the wife, so you know, that makes it easier."

"So what was her story? Why'd she do it?"

Again, he falls silent. The branches of the leafless oak tree next to the building bend from the wind and scratch against the glass in front of her.

"You there?" she asks.

"Look," he says, "I don't know that I should be discussing the details of the case."

In all the years he's worked at the prosecutor's office, she can't remember him ever saying this to her. Even if there were details he thought he couldn't share—and she knows that's often the case—he'd never couch it as a refusal to answer her questions. He'd simply craft an acceptable answer that neither denied her nor gave away confidential information.

"I'm not asking you to tell me anything that won't be on the news."

"She said he cheated on her."

Claire closes her eyes. Why did she persist? Why didn't she trust his instincts? It might have been naïve of him to think he could protect her, protect them, from the specifics about the case—after all, it *will* be on the news—but still, he tried.

When she doesn't respond—she simply has no idea what she could say now—he speaks up.

"I'm sorry it took me so long. I wouldn't have known you'd called if I hadn't checked my office messages. I wish you'd tried my cell."

Still shaken, she says, "That's okay. It wasn't important enough to disturb you."

"Why are you at the law school today?"

"I dunno. Since you wouldn't be home anyway, I figured I'd catch up here. I made Michael watch Jamie. A little extra punishment, I guess."

"Good idea."

When she doesn't say more, he says, "What were you trying to reach me about?"

"Nothing. It wasn't a big deal. We can talk about it tonight." She swivels back around toward her desk and collects the papers she was grading. Holding the phone between her shoulder and ear, she places them in a manila folder and sets the folder on the corner of her desk for later.

"Are you still there?"

"Yeah. I'm sorry. I'm just gathering my notes." The activity outside her open door has picked up as students pass in the hallway.

"Will you be on campus for a while? I thought I'd head over later this afternoon after I stop by my office."

In the last few years, once a week or so, he's taken to spending evenings at the law library at a study table on the fifth floor. He claims it helps him escape the distractions of the DA's office, but Claire knows the DA's office after hours is just as quiet as the law library. It's a government office; come five o'clock, most of his attorneys and staff are long gone. She suspects his visits to the library began instead as an effort to spend more time with her. Sometimes, after enlisting Michael to watch Jamie, they'd leave campus to have dinner alone before heading back to their house.

But his visits became a habit. Now he often stays late into the night, even after Claire has locked up her office door and left for home. He seems to appreciate the unique solitude he finds at the vacant library, where he sits hidden from sight between the stacks. He's always been a quiet man, preferring the company of his thoughts to the social chatter of others, but after he accepted responsibility for imploding their lives, his preference grew to a need. She doesn't begrudge him the time alone.

"No, Michael wants me to take him to Sports Authority, and I also want to stop by the grocery store." She picks up the folder again, yanks on a file drawer and fingers the files inside until she finds a spot for the folder. "We've got a lot of errands to run, so take your time. No rush. I'll feed them while I'm out."

Two students—a young man and woman—loiter in her doorway. It's obvious they're waiting for her to hang up. She wishes now that she'd closed her door.

"I'm sorry, Jack, but I really need to go. Two students have noticed I'm here and they're waiting to talk to me."

"Okay." He sighs. "Claire? Before you hang up . . ."

She stops her busyness, reclaims the receiver with one hand. Listens.

He hesitates. "I don't know for sure, but the press might, you know, decide to have some fun with me about the Bedford case."

Oddly, the warning calms her. She feels a surge of affection for him, for his desire to protect her, even though he can't.

"Oh, well, we've survived worse, right?" She tries to say it lightly, tries to insert a short laugh after the words, but her efforts fall flat. She hears him take a deep breath.

"Right. I guess we have."

CHAPTER FOUR

HE SMELLS THE scent.

It's happened before. The first time, when he and Claire cut through the cosmetics department at the mall, his heartbeat soared with such trepidation that he clutched at his chest, startling Claire. Another time, alone in line at a coffee shop near their house, it came up behind him like a wind on a blustery day. Both times he experienced the same physical sensation, the fleeting but intense pounding of his heart. It ended as soon as it began, after the mistake in his assumption quickly (and with much relief) became apparent.

Those other times, no touch came on the heels of the scent. Neither the girl at the cosmetics counter nor the woman who stood behind him in line at the coffee shop knew him intimately enough to touch him.

This time is different. It happens so fast. So fast that his brain doesn't even have time to think, "Someone wearing the same cologne must have just walked the same path I'm about to walk." No time to reassure himself, "It's nothing more than a scent."

It's late. Almost midnight. He just left the law library at the university. He approaches the pedestrian tunnel that will take him to the other side of Forsyth Avenue, past the dorms and to the spot where he parked his car. He glances at the blue light above the emergency phone near the tunnel entrance, but other than the simple recognition of the phone's existence, he doesn't think twice about it. His footsteps become louder inside the tunnel. The tunnel isn't lit, as it usually is, but he doesn't think twice about that either. He's not thinking at all, really, and it's nice, the respite from the usual noise in his head.

If a hand unexpectedly reaches out of the dark and touches you at midnight on a deserted college campus, your first emotion is probably fear. Your first instinct is one of two—fight or flight. But not when the hand touching you has already left its mark. Not when, in the split second before you feel the touch and hear the voice, you smell the scent that has the power to weaken your knees and make any protective response impossible.

No, in that case, your response is altogether different. It's still instinctive, but it's not the response that will save your life.

* * *

"Jack, it's me," comes a voice from the past, barely a whisper, its owner unseen, but known.

He's left with only one response. Just one.

He turns to the voice.

The hand slips down his arm and grasps his wrist. It pulls him, and he takes a step, allowing it to happen.

"Jack," she says again.

"Jenny," he says, but maybe he only thinks it. Maybe he remains mute.

He hears her shallow breathing, and he realizes she's as nervous as he is. Everything is happening so fast, and yet he still has enough time to have this thought before the hand moves to the back of his neck and pulls his head closer. Before the lips touch his.

The kiss doesn't last long. Not like the first one so long ago. *Fool me once, shame on you. Fool me twice, shame on me.* And he's no fool.

This time, he resists from the start.

The lies come fast, also.

Later, he climbs into bed, and Claire rolls over to greet him, barely awake.

"Your skin is so cold," she says as she pulls him into her arms.

"It's freezing out." That part is true.

"You're shivering still."

"Yeah," he agrees. But that part is a lie. He turned up the heat in the car on the way home, and the interior grew toasty in minutes. He's not shivering; he's shaking. And there's a difference.

As Claire drifts back to sleep, he lies in the dark and wonders why she didn't smell it, too. Because even now, he still can. It settled on his coat and then, when the hand made its way to the back of his neck, burned its way into his skin.

Morning comes and he's still awake. He still smells it.

Her. He still smells her.

He takes a shower but even afterwards, even after he's toweled off and dressed, he still smells her. In the kitchen, he drops a kiss on Jamie's head as he eats his Cream of Wheat at the table, and he hopes he didn't leave the scent on his son the way she left it on him. He kisses Claire, too, and she looks him in the eye for a long moment, and he looks back. He wants to say, "Please save me." But instead he's silent. She places a palm on his cheek in the same way she's done so many times before and says, "I love you, you know."

He smiles, a genuine smile, and says, "I know." Because he does. He also says, "I love you, too." Because he does. The lies aren't what he says; they're what he doesn't say.

After breakfast, he drives out to St. Charles, to the little motel off Highway 94 where she told him she's rented a room. He told her he'd only be willing to listen away from prying eyes. Yet even this, he knows, has its own dangers.

He stands at her door and pulls his coat collar up around his neck. It's even colder today—26 degrees, with a light snow beginning to fall—but this isn't why he does it.

Her hair is still wet when she answers. She invites him in while she finishes in the bathroom. He says he'll wait in the car. He pretends not to hear her sigh.

When she climbs into the passenger seat, snowflakes sprinkle her black hair. The hair is now dry, and warm from the blow dryer, he imagines. In an instant, the flakes melt and disappear.

He drives. He knows her eyes are on him, but neither of them speaks. He prays for restraint.

He drives north on 61. He considers stopping in Bowling Green, but no, he wants to be even farther away. He remembers a little café in Hannibal, next to the river, and feels sure it will be empty on a day like today.

"Jack," she says, trying to begin, but he cuts her off with a shake of the head. Not yet.

His cell phone rings and as he pulls it from the front breast pocket of his coat, she turns to face the window. Giving him some privacy.

"Hey," he says into the phone. There's no way he won't answer. There's no way he's going to send the message to the woman in the car that the woman on the phone comes second.

"Hey," Claire says back. "Sorry to bother you. I just got off the phone with Mom and she wants to know if we're coming for Christmas. I didn't want to answer without checking with you."

His mother-in-law, like his wife, has forgiven him. His father-in-law never will, but he puts up with his presence nevertheless. He'd have a gun at his head if he knew where he was just then, the bullet already on its way.

"Sure. I think the kids would like that, too." Well, at least Jamie will. Michael, at sixteen, doesn't like anything. Least of all, his father.

"You got a lot going on today?"

"Yeah, a few meetings out of the office." He swallows.

The lies aren't what he says; they're what he doesn't say.

* * *

"Claire?" she asks after he's said his goodbye and hit disconnect.

Without taking his eyes from the road, he nods slightly.

She turns to the window again.

In Hannibal, the snow is sticking. An inch, maybe an inch and a half, has already accumulated. He pulls into the gravel lot of the café. After parking, he walks to her side of the car and opens the door. She knows him so well. She knows he'll do this, despite everything, and so she has waited. She meets his eye as she steps out, and mouths a polite "thank you." Again, he simply nods.

Last night, lying in bed and unable to sleep, he considered whether meeting in public, even so far away, is best. He decided, without much debate, it is.

He glances at the river. A large tree has fallen over and juts into the water from the bank. The exposed roots are white from the snow. The brown water bubbles and swells before finding its way to the other side.

He asks the waitress for a booth near the window in the back. This way he can see who comes, who goes. They both order coffee as they take off their coats and hang them on the chrome coat hook that stands between each booth. He sneaks a look when her back is turned. She's wearing slim jeans, a white knit turtleneck, boots. When the waitress leaves, he lowers himself into the booth. Leaning back, he rests one arm along the back ledge and scans the restaurant, looking at everything except the woman across from him. He knows it's forced nonchalance, so he drops the arm and props both elbows on the table. While the waitress pours the coffee, the two women engage in meaningless banter and he finally allows himself a long look at her face.

She hasn't changed. Not much. Her dark skin is still smooth and flawless; her thick hair still falls to mid-back in a straight, sleek curtain. She's lost a few pounds she didn't need to lose, and when she smiles, the corners of her eyes reveal a few wrinkles he doesn't remember, but these details feel organic and therefore don't diminish her beauty. He wishes they did.

The waitress leaves and he busies himself with fixing his coffee. Hers remains untouched.

"Jack," she tries again, but he cuts her off.

"Am I sitting across from a murderer? Did you kill Maxine Shepard?"

For a long time they stare at each other. He hopes she says yes. For the first time, he wants so badly for her to say yes.

"What do you think?"

He doesn't answer at first. He continues to stare at her. She stares back.

Finally, he says, "I know who Maxine was."

"I'm sure you do."

"She wasn't simply your client. She'd been your father's mistress."

"Yes."

"A very expensive mistress. You thought she was the reason the mob put out a hit on your father. That she was the reason your parents and sister were executed."

Her jaw clenches but she doesn't avert her eyes. "Know. I *know* she was the reason my parents and sister were executed."

When she reaches with her right hand for the small pewter creamer, her sleeve rises up her arm and he startles to see an angry scar on her inside wrist. She notices his reaction but doesn't say anything.

"Where have you been? If you're innocent, why did you run?"

She shakes her head in disgust. "You, of all people, are asking me such a question?" Her eyes become glassy but he's prepped himself for that. "Since when did innocence inoculate a person from being convicted?"

"They dropped the charges against you, remember?" he answers sarcastically.

"Oh, please, spare me, Jack." She stirs cream into her cup too forcefully; the spoon clinks loud against the sides. "Coming after me again wouldn't constitute double jeopardy unless I'd been tried. You know that. Dropping the charges doesn't mean a damn thing. I'm at risk of being charged now as much as I was the day she was murdered. Maybe more."

"Well, taking off in the dark of the night doesn't lend much support to your claim of innocence."

"Easy words from a prosecutor." She glares at him over the top of her cup.

"Where have you been?"

"Chicago. My brother's."

"They looked there."

She scoffs. "Not very well."

She's right, of course. The feeble attempts to find her were all for show. Despite her professed fear of being charged again, they'd gotten one conviction already. Why muddy the waters?

When the waitress reappears he realizes, as they talked, they have leaned closer to each other across the table. Old habits die hard. He sits back. She does the same, swiping underneath each eye with the heel of her palm. A strand of hair clings to her cheek and he resists the desire to touch it, to smooth it back in place. She orders oatmeal and sliced bananas, honey on the side. He orders a grapefruit but doubts he'll get even that down.

Left alone once again, he asks, "So why'd you come back?"

"There's something happening." He waits, and she adds, "I need your help."

He grunts at that unintelligible response.

She suddenly reaches across the table and her scarred hand covers his. "Jack, please." It happens so fast, like the kiss the night before, but somehow this feels more intimate. He starts to pull his hand away but she tightens her grip and he relents. "Please don't be like this."

The words make him angry. "Do you have any idea the position you've put me in, just by being here? Just by showing up?"

"Yes, I do, I—"

"She gave me a second chance. I don't get any more, you know? Just being here, *just being here.* . ."

She releases his hand and leans back, crosses her arms. "Yet knowing that, you're still here."

He lays down the rules. He tells her he won't make any decisions until he knows everything, and if for one minute he thinks she's not being honest or telling him everything—*everything*—his answer will be "no."

"You don't trust me?"

"No, I don't." He answers quickly.

She lowers her eyes, bites her bottom lip.

"You will answer any question I ask you, and you will answer it truthfully. You will tell me everything I need to know, even if I don't ask first. Understand?"

She nods.

"Let's start again. Am I sitting across from a murderer?"

"No."

"Look me in the eye when you answer."

She raises her head and he knows he could easily get lost in those eyes again. She knows it, too. "No."

"Am I sitting across from an accomplice to a murderer?"

This time her answer doesn't come so swiftly. She's still staring at him. She tilts her head; he sees the trace of a grin, evidence of the woman he remembers. "What? Did you bring handcuffs to take me out of here?"

Finally, when he doesn't react, she says, "No."

"You're aware that I have to tell someone you're back in town?"

"I know you might. I'm aware that's the risk I'm taking."

"Did you not understand the question? Do you understand I *will* tell someone you're back?"

She sighs. "You said you wanted me to be completely honest."

He nods.

"Like I said, I know you might. But the truth is, despite what you say, I don't think you will."

She's right. But still he asks, "What makes you so sure?" He's so angry at her. He's so angry that she still has this much power over him, after so much time. After everything.

He expects a sarcastic answer, but she says, "Because of exactly what you said," and then surprises him with an apologetic shrug. She suddenly seems so lost and alone. "Because, just being here . . . I know what I'm asking, and what it could mean to you, if someone finds out."

She reaches up again, but the tear falls this time before she catches it. "I'm sorry." She's apologizing for the tears, and he wants to believe she's acting. It took him almost four years to believe she'd been acting. Almost four years to accept that he'd been duped. He wants to believe that's what she's doing right now.

But she's so damn good.

"Do you know about Alex's conviction?"

She nods, brushes the stray hair away from her cheek, and the motion almost crushes him. She doesn't otherwise react to the mention of her former boyfriend's name, and Jack wonders if she ever had feelings for him. Maybe she was merely biding her time. For what, though? For Jack? *Don't let yourself go there.*

"Is he on death row for a crime he didn't commit?" *Or more accurately, was an innocent man railroaded, and was I, as your alibi, unwittingly at the helm of the train?*

"I don't know."

"Jenny." Saying her name out loud makes his chest tighten. "Did Alex murder Maxine Shepard?"

"*I don't know,*" she insists.

They talk all morning in the café and then, when a small lunch crowd straggles in, they move to a bench overlooking the river. The snow has stopped. At two-thirty, they return to the car. He opens the door for her again and realizes she has marked the car, too, with her scent. By three-thirty he has her back at her motel. He still hasn't given her an answer about whether he'll help her; he tells her he has to think about it.

He drives for hours, thinking about what she's told him. That she's received threats, that she thinks they've come from the same men who murdered three-fifths of her family. He doesn't try to figure out whether it's the truth or not, or what she expects him to do about it. He simply drives. At some point he puts the windows down, but it gets so cold he shivers and puts them back up.

When he asked "Why me?" she simply stared at him. *Who else?* her eyes asked.

He arrives home just before dinnertime. In contrast to the three inches in Hannibal, the snow here has only dusted the yard. Claire stands in front of the center island, the glow from the oven light behind her. When she moves to greet him, he sees a roasting chicken through the oven window. Potatoes in water are just beginning to boil on the stove. In another pot, fresh green beans. The burner underneath the beans hasn't been turned on yet. He knows she's making the chicken for him, for his willingness to spend Christmas with her parents.

"Hi," she says, and kisses his cheek. She takes his overcoat even though he was about to head to the coat closet himself. He wonders if the scent lingers on the coat.

"I can get it," he says, but she waves him off.

"I opened a bottle of wine," she calls from the front hall. Back in the kitchen she adds, "It'll be another 45 minutes or so to dinner. Michael should be home from practice by then."

Jack grabs two wine goblets from the cabinet and pours the wine. It's red, some sort of Australian Syrah. She's never cared about matching wine to the food, and he's always liked that about her. He hands her a glass and sits on a barstool. She slides onto the stool next to him and smiles.

"To an early winter," she says, and raises her glass. She loves winter, especially snow. He lifts his in turn and the small sound when the glasses clink makes him feel better about everything, somehow.

After their first sip, she asks, "So how were your meetings? Did you have to go far?" She sips again and waits for his response.

He remembers the trip to Napa Valley. The first trip together, after. They both spent the summer trying to heal, but in the glare of the media, and even surrounded by those who meant well—family and friends—it wasn't easy. When her mother offered to take the kids for them to get away together, he didn't hesitate. It'd been the right thing to do, too. In the small tram overlooking the golden valley, on the way up to the gleaming white walls of Sterling Vineyards, she reached for his hand and gave him a look. It took his breath away, that look, because for just that moment, she'd let it go. He knew it'd be back, it was only a respite, but he thought the bottom was behind them.

The next day, they took the tour at Robert Mondavi. Unlike Sterling, it was in the valley. What had the guide there said? *You can't judge the wine until the third sip.*

"Not too bad," he says in answer to her questions—both of them. He sniffs his wine before taking the next sip, but he barely picks up anything. His memory of the other scent is too strong.

"Not a good day?" The question is so innocent. She can read him, she always could, yet he knows she doesn't suspect a thing. She's learned to trust him again.

"Just a lot on my mind, I guess."

"Bedford?"

She's asking about the new case, trying to face it head on rather than letting it become a white elephant for them. Unbeknownst to Claire, he answers about that other, long forgotten one.

"Yeah, I've got a bad feeling about it. It's not how I want to spend the holidays."

The lies aren't what he says; they're what he doesn't say.

That night, she's all over him in bed. It's not sexual, not yet. Curled up in the crook of his arm, then almost on top of him with her face inches from his as she tells him a funny story about something silly Jamie did that day. It's the wine, and the snow. She's excited, happy about life in general, and she wants him to be, too. There was a time when it would have been so easy to ignore the noise in his head, to let her cajole him out of his mood. He'd kiss her, or she'd kiss him, and they'd respond to each other. Within minutes, nothing else would matter. After all the years together, she still turns him on.

But he made a vow to her, to himself, really, that he'd break that habit. Ignoring the noise never extinguished it; it merely delayed it and, ironically, fed it.

So instead, he speaks the question as soon as it comes to mind, before he loses his nerve.

"Claire, do you trust me again? I mean, fully, completely. Can I tell you anything and know you'd still trust me, even if what I say won't be easy to hear?"

There's a sudden shift in the room. He hears her breathing in the dark. He thinks he hears her swallow. Even though the bedroom door is closed, he hears footsteps climbing the stairs, Michael finally going to bed. He suddenly wants to take it back, to turn back time just one minute. One minute only.

The wait is interminable. He barely sees her face outlined in the dim light seeping through the blinds. But he knows she's staring at him.

"Do you want the truth?" she whispers, and her voice quivers. She's terrified, and he despises himself for doing this to her. But the alternative is even worse. He knows that now. "Or do you want me to tell you want you want to hear?"

"I want the truth."

She rolls away from him onto her back. She pulls the covers higher, as if protecting herself. Their shoulders are still touching underneath the sheet.

"It depends. Yes, I trust you again. But it's a very fragile trust and I can't promise you that it can withstand anything you might say." She pauses. He knows what she's about to ask. "Have you done something to break that trust?"

"No, I don't think so. But . . ."

The light goes out in the hall, the room grows even darker.

"Don't keep me waiting, Jack. Just spit it out."

Her voice has changed. It's louder, clearer. And stronger. She's braced herself.

Under the covers, he reaches for her hand. She lets him take it.

"Jenny's back."

CHAPTER FIVE

THE WORDS HIT Claire like a sucker-punch. She'd bend over if she weren't already lying down. Fear clutches at her throat, making it impossible to speak. It's worse than the fear she felt four years ago. When he first asked the question, she thought he was about to admit to an attraction to another woman, a *different* woman. Nip it in the bud by telling her. But now she realizes how ridiculous this was. *Of course* it's Jenny. Who else could it be? Although he's always radiated a boyish innocence that charms women—all women—without even trying, he's never been a player. It's why she fell for him.

Jenny is the only other woman capable of harnessing his light for herself.

It's almost as if she's stopped breathing. He can't hear a thing, not a thing. Suddenly she springs up and sits on the edge of the bed, her lovely, naked back facing him. When he reaches over and touches her lightly, she shudders.

"Claire?"

When she speaks, he hears the tears in her voice. "Listen to me," she says. "I'm not going to ask you questions. I don't want to have to guess at what questions to ask, even, to pry it out of you. I just want you to tell me everything." The statement reminds him of what he said to Jenny in the café in Hannibal.

"Okay," he says quietly. He can do this. He can tell her everything without fear because he's done nothing. Nothing, at least, that he can't tell her about. He's already convinced himself of that. The one single thing he won't tell her about—the brief kiss in the tunnel—had nothing to do with him; he's already convinced himself of that, too.

"Last night," he begins, "heading to my car from the law library, I was walking through the underpass, and she was there, waiting for me." It sounds so freaky now that he's said it out loud. It sounds as if she was stalking him. At the time, after the initial shock of seeing her, he didn't find it so odd. It was as if he'd been waiting for that moment for four years. As if he knew, eventually, it would happen. He simply hadn't known when, or where. But the fact of it, the certainty? Yeah. He always knew.

"She didn't say anything, not then . . ." Claire twitches, then fiddles with the covers to disguise it. She doesn't miss a thing. She knows, simply from his words, that he's seen her twice already. Just since last night. "Only that she needed to talk to me. She wouldn't say why." He waits at first, but remembering this isn't a normal back and forth conversation, he goes on. "She wouldn't tell me anything at first. Not where she'd been all this time, nothing. She wanted to go somewhere right then, but I said no. I told her I needed to get home." Claire grunts, an editorial. Jack's not sure if it's directed at him or Jenny. "But . . ." He breathes in deep. The next statement will be the hardest for her to hear, even though she's already expecting it. "I told her I'd meet with her today, and I did." Her shoulders fall.

Everything. He needs to tell her every detail. That's what she asked.

"I picked her up this morning from a motel in St. Charles. That's where she's been staying, I guess, I don't know how long, and we drove up to Hannibal. We sat in a café up there and talked."

She lifts hand to her face. She still has her back to him, but he knows what she's doing. She tugs at the sheet, pulling it up. He reaches over to his nightstand and grabs a tissue, holds it out for her. They were on his side of the bed because he was the last one to have a cold. Claire, it seems, never gets sick. "The mother doesn't have time to be sick," she always says.

She takes the tissue.

He's not sure what to do. He hears the question in her head— "What did you talk about?" —but he's not sure whether to answer, since she hasn't asked it. But she said she wouldn't, didn't she? She said she wouldn't ask any questions. And he *does* trust *her*. Implicitly.

He decides to keep talking until she tells him to stop.

"She said someone's threatening her, that she needed my help."

Claire whips her head around. Her eyes are narrowed. She's so angry that he leans back slightly. He hasn't been slapped, but he might as well have been.

"God!" She's yelling, but it's under the breath so she doesn't wake the boys. Even in her anger, even in her apparent disappointment in him, she thinks of the kids. "Have you learned nothing?"

"Yes," he says quickly. He jumps ahead so she understands he *has*. He really has. "I didn't agree to help her. I told her I'd think about it." Another grunt. "Claire, I told her that because I wasn't about to do anything without telling you, without talking to you first." She's quiet, so he adds, "That's why I'm telling you all this, don't you understand?"

He rises and slips into the boxers he left on the floor earlier when he undressed. He moves to sit beside her. Surprisingly, she lets him take her hand. "Don't you understand?"

She looks him straight in the eye. "Don't *you* understand? Why didn't you tell her to go to hell the minute she pounced on you?" He finds himself thinking: how interesting, Claire's choice of word, because "pounce" is almost exactly what Jenny did last night. It's the perfect description. "Why didn't you tell her to *go fuck herself?*"

"Because—"

"Don't even answer, Jack! I already know the answer, okay?"

"What do you mean?"

"She's like a drug to you. I know that. I *get* that. I thought you got it, too. I thought you understood that the only way you'd stay clean was to stay away from her."

He looks away, shaking his head.

"You know how I know for sure?" she asks.

He turns to her, waiting for the indictment.

"Because otherwise, you wouldn't be telling me this now, after you'd already met with her. You could have told me last night, when you got home. But you didn't, because you were afraid then you wouldn't be able to see her again."

She sounds like a lawyer. She hasn't sounded like one in a long, long time. She was a good lawyer. She hated practicing, but she was good. She was smart, *is* smart, and she also has a psychological grasp of people that gave her an edge. But now he feels as if she's badgering the witness. He feels as if he came as close to telling Jenny to go to hell as was possible.

"Look." He doesn't want to argue. He tries to remember the point of all this, of the decision to tell her. He wanted to do the right thing. He didn't want to give her any reason not to trust him. "I *should* have said something last night. I shouldn't have waited until after I met with her today. But you're wrong about her being a . . ." He can't even say the word *drug*. "It's over."

Claire stares into her lap. All the fight has left her. She wants to believe him.

He drops to one knee in front of her, almost as if he's about to propose again. "Claire?" She raises her eyes. "I swear to you, it's *over*. It has been for a very long time. I wouldn't be telling you all this if it wasn't."

She nods slowly, and the tears let loose. He doesn't question if they're crocodile tears, as he did when Jenny cried. He knows they're not.

"Okay, okay," she whispers through quiet sobs. "Okay, Jack."

He takes her in his arms. He holds tight, eyes closed. He questions his judgment. He tries to think of what he might have done differently. What he could have done to prevent her pain. Because he promised himself he'd never hurt her like this again.

He's angry, but he's not sure why, or at whom. He just feels this boiling anger inside.

Suddenly, he knows. Suddenly it occurs to him: no matter what he did—tell Claire, not tell Claire, help Jenny, not help Jenny—he was fucked.

And Jenny knew it, too.

He holds her late into the night. After a while, she stops crying and simply lies against him in the dark. He thinks she might ask for the rest of the story. He thinks she'll want to know more about why Jenny feels she's being threatened, how she expects him to help. Instead, she clings to him quietly. It's as if they're both wondering what lies ahead.

Finally, she falls asleep, but he doesn't. He can't.

When he thinks she's sleeping deeply enough, he crawls from the bed, pulls on a T-shirt and heads downstairs for a drink of water. He tells himself this, but he could have cupped his hands and drank from the bathroom faucet. It'll be colder downstairs, so he stops near the landing and pulls a fleece blanket from the linen closet. It's one of Jamie's and is festooned with a repeating Spiderman pattern.

The light under Michael's door is still on.

He knocks gently. Michael mutters, "Come in."

Michael is in front of his computer, but nothing's on the screen except the Chuck Norris desktop. Jack knows he minimized whatever was up there upon hearing the knock.

"You still awake?" Stupid question.

"Yeah." With a snap of his head, Michael flips his hair out of his eyes. Jack stopped trying to get him to cut it about the same time he lost his son's respect. Even after what happened on Saturday night, he doesn't think he's earned it back yet; he wonders if he ever will.

Michael notices Jamie's blanket in Jack's arms. "What are you doing up?"

Jack glances down at the blanket as if he's forgotten it. "Oh, couldn't sleep and didn't want to wake Mom." Michael stares, waiting for more. He has doubted everything his father says since the day he learned the truth. Jack nods at the computer. "What's up with you?"

In the same way Jack reacted to Michael noticing the blanket, Michael acts as if he forget the computer in front of him. "Just IMing some friends. I'm getting ready to go to bed."

Jack wishes he looked at the alarm clock, because he has no idea how late it is.

"How is Celeste? Was everything okay when she got home?"

Michael stills. Then, "Uh, yeah, I guess."

"Good." Jack sighs. "Okay, then. See you at breakfast?" Sometimes Michael meets friends for coffee before school. Jack finds it odd that teenagers drink so much coffee nowadays, but as Michael proved on Saturday night, there are worse things they could be drinking.

"Yeah, sure." His leg is shaking now; he's ready to have Jack gone. Someone, Celeste perhaps, waits patiently at the other end of cyberspace for him to return.

After awkward "good nights" Jack softly closes the door.

He tosses the blanket onto the couch on his way to the kitchen, still clinging to the fiction that he came down for a drink.

* * *

Claire waits until Jack leaves the room and then opens her eyes. She hears him talking to Michael. She thinks about what he told her. She thinks about what it means that Jenny has returned.

When she first learned Jenny had run, she was surprised, but relieved. At the time, she hoped it would douse the fire Jenny stoked in him.

And it did. For once, she saw Jack starting to believe that maybe, just maybe, Jenny was guilty of Maxine Shepard's murder. Claire saw it in his face during Alex's trial. Even as he confessed to the world he'd spent the night with a woman who wasn't his wife, causing him to become that woman's alibi, he also admitted under oath that he'd slept for a good part of that night and really couldn't be sure she'd been with him the whole time. He wouldn't have ever admitted his growing doubts to anyone—after all, Claire knows his testimony was intended to prove Jenny's innocence (not, as he'd convinced himself, to prove Alex's guilt)—but she could tell. Claire always found his effort a bit ironic, because it was so contrary to what he usually did in court. *Innocent until proven guilty*, not vice versa.

A few months after the trial, after Alex had been sent to death row to wait for his attorneys to make their appeals, she silently watched Jack's nagging suspicion grow to a reluctant acceptance once he discovered the contents of the case file from Jenny's family's murder. Only then was it discovered that Maxine had been her father's mistress. At the time, some speculated that the mob had ordered a hit on Harold Dodson for his failure to pay his debts—debts he'd allegedly incurred to support that mistress. If Jenny had blamed Maxine for the murders of her parents and sister when she was a child, murders that occurred before her very eyes, then it didn't stretch the imagination to believe she would later murder that same woman in retaliation.

Even after discovering the information about Maxine, Jack posed the issue as "maybe Alex isn't guilty" as opposed to "maybe Jenny is," but Claire knew. He choked up when he told Claire what he'd learned. He hadn't wanted to tell her, he said, because it might be "pouring salt into your wounds." But he also didn't want her to find out through the press. He'd tried to keep his promises by telling her, just as he was trying to do tonight. But still she remembers thinking, "Are you upset about what you're doing to me, or for what you think you've done to Alex?" even though she knew it was both. And neither.

Because she knew, above all, he was upset over what he'd finally accepted about Jenny.

Now, Claire imagines him downstairs in the dark, his dormant desire for Jenny to be innocent given new life. In one stroke, Jenny has managed to re-ignite a fire that Claire thought had been extinguished.

She believes everything he's told her so far. She wonders what else Jenny said to him, and if she should ask for the rest. But she knows herself, too; she knows she interrupted his story for a reason.

She rises and slips the silk camisole at the end of the bed over her head. She also knows what she needs to do.

"Jack?"

The sound of Claire's voice pierces the dark. She's coming down the stairs. How long has he been sitting there, he wonders? He pulls the blanket tighter and whispers, "I'm on the couch."

The blue moonlight shining through the tall Palladium windows illuminates her figure. They both loved those windows when they first bought the house. She's wearing her camisole, the soft pink one that looks so good against her skin. He holds the blanket open to signal her to join him underneath it.

When she's settled in, he takes her left hand and holds it. He plays with the rings on her finger, the one he presented when he asked her to marry him, and the one he slipped on in front of 150 people. It's cold in the room, so they're loose, and he twists them, around and around. She watches silently. He lifts the hand gently, then, and places it against his lips. He breathes in and inhales the scent of her lotion. It smells like rain.

"This is all that matters to me. This. Us. I'll do whatever you want me to."

She's quiet for a long time, as if she didn't hear him. A hoot owl whistles in the backyard; it's taken to hanging out in one of the Maple trees towering over the back deck.

"I believe you," she says finally. The nerves in his stomach relax ever so slightly. "But there's something else that matters to you, too, I know."

He leans back to see her face better, to protest, but she shakes her head.

"No, no, I'm not talking about her, not in the way you're thinking." She brings her legs up, pulling her hand away to tuck her knees under the camisole. "What I mean is, the truth also matters to you. About her, and about Alex." She pauses. When he doesn't respond, she says, "Am I right?"

"I don't know." But he does because what she said is true. It does bother him, not knowing if Alex was wrongly convicted. And more than anything, it bothers him about Jenny. That he simply doesn't know. That he may never know.

"Jack?"

He meets her eye.

"I won't tell you to stay away from her. If you think she's the path to the truth, then you have to follow it."

Jack doesn't quite believe what he hears. She sees the disbelief on his face.

"I don't have any choice, do I? What am I going to do? Tell you she's off limits?" She laughs softly, sarcastically. "You'll do what you have to do, no matter what I say. If you say you're over her, then I have to trust you. I have to believe that you can find out what you need to know without betraying me again. But if you're not, then it doesn't matter what I say, anyway. Because I can't control what you feel."

"What I feel is angry," he whispers. "I've felt angry since the moment I saw her in the tunnel."

"Good. I hope you continue to feel angry. I hope you remember what she did to us, and whether she's innocent or not, I hope you realize what she's doing to us now, by coming back."

"I do."

"I hope you remember what *you* did to us."

They sit in the moonlit dark, listening to the owl. He continues to rub her hand but he's barely aware of the action.

"Let's go to bed," she says finally. She starts to rise; the blanket slips off her shoulder.

"Claire?" Jack holds tight to her hand to stop her. Her face is wet with tears he didn't even hear her cry. "I *do* remember. I'll never forget, and I'll never forgive myself." She nods and bites her lip. She believes him, and he loves her even more for it. He only hopes she believes the next words out of his mouth, too. "You can trust me."

CHAPTER SIX

THE MORNING AFTER Jack's confession, the mood in the house reminds Claire of how it felt when he first moved back in three and a half years before. She'd gained a sense of power she didn't necessarily want, and his attempts at normalcy made everything more awkward. But there's a difference between now and then, she's noticed. The first time, they waited for Jenny's front-and-center presence to go away. This time, she's with them in the house again, but she's lurking in the wings, and both Claire and Jack are left to wonder when she'll step back onstage.

Jack's secretary, Beverly, peeks her head into his office and says, "Chief Matthews is on the phone."

"Hey, Chief," Jack says good-naturedly. Jack and Chief Gunner Matthews aren't the best of friends—their politics are too different—but they both do a pretty good job of convincing the city that they make a good team.

"Jack."

Something in the Chief's voice causes Jack to sit straighter in his chair. Have they discovered that Jenny is back? "What's the matter, Gunner?"

"I'm wondering if you might have time to come over to the station. There's a matter we need to talk to you about in person."

We? "Sure, Gunner. I always have time for you. When are you thinking?"

"Now would be best."

When the receptionist interrupts Claire's lecture, the worry on the young woman's face makes Claire think something must be wrong with one of the kids. Once Claire steps into the hallway, the receptionist advises her that two police officers want to speak with her. Her gut twists and for an instant, she has to consciously resist losing her lunch.

A man and a woman, both in uniform, wait for her outside the Dean's office.

"Are my children—?"

"Your children are fine, Mrs. Hilliard."

She shakes their hands as they introduce themselves. For reasons she can't

—

explain, she immediately dislikes the man. "Please, let's go to my office to talk." As she starts down the hall, she turns back to the receptionist and motions in the direction of her classroom. "You probably should just dismiss them for me."

At five minutes before the last bell rings, Michael's chemistry teacher taps him on the shoulder and whispers that he should stop by the front office before heading to basketball practice. When he asks why, his teacher shrugs.

At the station, the Chief greets Jack and leads him in the direction opposite his office. As they enter the corridor that houses all the interrogation rooms, Jack gives the Chief a look, as if to say *Why are we going this way?* The Chief ignores him and keeps walking. He stops outside one of the rooms and motions Jack in. Three cops are seated inside at a table. The Chief follows Jack in and closes the door.

"Jack, please, take a seat. Would you like something to drink?"

Jack eyes the Chief warily. It's the first line they always give to certain types of suspects.

"No, thank you, I'm fine." He scans the faces of the other officers and tries to read them. To the Chief, he says, "What's going on? What do you need to talk to me about?"

"Please, take a seat." Gunner grabs a chair for himself and lowers himself into it. Jack is the only one standing now, so he finally complies.

"What's this about?" he tries again.

"We need to ask you some questions."

"Okay."

"Something's come up. We're sure it's probably a simple misunderstanding, but we're obligated to follow up, and—"

"What are you talking about?" Jack's voice is slightly louder than it should be, but something about this whole scenario is wrong. It's making him crazy that Gunner won't just get to the point.

The Chief turns to one of the officers. "Tommy?"

Tommy leans forward a bit in his chair. "Mr. Hilliard, can you—"

"Jack."

"Jack." He nods. "Certainly." He breathes in. "Can you tell us where you were on Saturday night?"

"I guess that would depend upon what time on Saturday night you're referring to." He's being smart, and they know it. He stares at the Chief. "What's going on, Gunner? I'm the DA. Are you interrogating me? Because if you are, I think you'd better damn well tell me that's what you're doing, and why."

Claire sits behind her desk and motions for the officers to sit in the chairs on the opposite side.

"Mrs. Hilliard," the female officer starts. Officer Caruthers, she said. She's petite but projects a confidence that probably results from years of having to prove herself. "We're so sorry to disturb you at work like this, but we need to ask you a few questions. Please understand that you're not in any trouble."

"Okay." Claire notes that the woman talks to her the way cops talk to laymen, as if she's forgotten Claire is a lawyer. But she isn't about to remind them.

"It's about Saturday night."

Claire tenses. She thinks of the incident with Michael and wonders if he lied to her and Jack. Did Michael and Celeste do more than just hang out in the woods and come home late? Was he even with Celeste *at all* that night? She really doesn't know for sure, not for a fact.

"We're wondering if you can tell us where Mr. Hilliard was that night." Officer Caruthers speaks softly and her gentle hazel eyes regard Claire with sympathy. And even though Claire knows exactly where Jack was, she's suddenly furious with him. But for him, she'd never have to be in another's presence and maintain the charade that neither remembered what her husband had done four years before. Has she forgiven him? She thinks so, but she'll never be able to forget. Because no one else does.

She glances at the other cop. He eyes her coldly, his notepad in his left hand and a pen poised to write in the other. Claire thinks he looks a little too eager.

"Are you referring to Jack? Or my older son?"

"We're asking about your husband, ma'am," the man says, deadpan. "The DA."

Claire is certain he didn't vote for Jack.

"He was at home with me. Why? What is this about?"

With a mere glance, Caruthers shoots a dagger at her partner. But her voice is still warm when she speaks to Claire. "Was there any point between, say, after dinnertime on Saturday evening and before breakfast on Sunday morning that he might not have been at home with you?"

An image of Jack flashes through her mind, sitting in the chair at the end of the couch in street clothes. In the middle of the night. She thinks of Jenny being back. Did he see her even before the two instances he told her about?

She stands. She feels tears coming, but she's not sure why. She rifles through a folder on her desk, avoiding their eyes, feigning busyness. "I have to ask you to leave unless you tell me what this is about."

The two whisper together. When Claire looks up, she sees they do not enjoy being partners. Caruthers finally raises a curt hand as if to say: *Let me handle this.*

"Mrs. Hilliard, please," she says. "I apologize. If you'll just take your seat again, we'll tell you what we can."

When Michael steps into the lobby of the front office, two cops are waiting for him. Staff and students turn to stare. The cops introduce themselves but their names don't register with Michael.

He follows the men into a small conference room next to the row of guidance counselors' offices. The room is small, barely large enough to accommodate the round table and four chairs. As one of the officers fights with a chair to move it away from the door, Michael eyes the side arm at his waist. When the man finally gets the door closed, his face is flushed.

"Michael, thank you for agreeing to talk to us."

He looks at the other man who's spoken. He's much taller, with thick eyebrows that remind Michael of a caterpillar. He wants to say *I didn't agree to shit*, but doesn't. He doesn't say anything. He knows not to talk, his dad has drilled that into his head for as long as he can remember, but Jack would also expect Michael to be polite.

"First, we want to make it clear that you're not in any trouble. Please don't misunderstand."

Michael simply nods.

"It's about Celestina Del Toro," says the officer who battled the chair.

Suddenly, Michael is incapable of considering what Jack would expect. "What do you mean?" he asks anxiously. "Is she okay? She hasn't been at school." He doesn't add *and hasn't answered her phone or responded to any of my text messages since Sunday afternoon.*

The officer hesitates. "Yes, she's . . . she's fine. We need to ask you a few questions, but unfortunately we can't tell you much at this point. There's an ongoing investigation that—"

"You're investigating Celeste?" His eyes dart from one officer to the other.

"No, no, please." The man with the bushy brows raises his palm. "Celestina's not in trouble with the law. And neither are you."

Relieved, Michael falls back into his chair.

"She told us she was with you at a party on Saturday night, and that the two of you had some whiskey afterwards. Is that true?"

Michael lowers his eyes.

"You're not in trouble, remember? We're not here to bust you for underage drinking, okay?"

"Then why are you asking this?" he mutters.

"She said that you couldn't drive her home, that your father had to. Is that right?"

Michael stares from one officer to the other, trying to understand. "He didn't *let* us drink, if that's what you mean. He didn't even know until we got to my house. He freaked when he found out."

"Of course. Any father would. Did he drive Celestina home because you were impaired?"

Michael nods but looks away from the two men. Through the window he watches students cross the campus toward the bus ramp.

"That's good. You were smart not to drive after you'd been drinking. Do you have any idea how long it took him?"

What are they getting at? Is his dad in trouble for covering for Celeste? For not letting her dad know what happened?

"I don't know." He shrugs. "He was just trying to help her."

"What do you mean?" When he doesn't answer, the tall one presses him. "How was he trying to help her?"

Michael glances at the clock on the wall. "I need to get to basketball practice."

"I think we're about done, anyway, don't you think so, Pete?" To Michael, he says, "Thank you for helping us, Mike." Michael cringes at his use of the familiar name. Only his dad and close friends from school call him Mike. "It'd really help to know how your dad was trying to help Celestina, though. We don't want to point fingers at the wrong person."

"Point fingers about *what?*" he asks as they stand. He has the sense his refusal to give them more information will hurt his dad. When the tall man grabs the doorknob, Michael cries, "Wait!" They turn and he says, "He was just trying to help her. He didn't want her to get in trouble with her dad."

"We still don't understand," Pete says gently.

"She said things that he thought meant her dad would hurt her if he knew she'd been drinking. That's why he waited."

"Waited?"

"You asked how long it took to take her home. It took so long because he waited with her in the car. To let, you know, the whiskey wear off."

"Do you know how long it took?"

"I don't know. He was gone about two hours, I guess."

The officers glance at each other. As Pete pulls out a phone, Bushy Brows smiles at him. "Thank you, Mike. You've been very helpful. I know Celestina will appreciate it." With a wink, he adds, "Now go play some ball."

"So your older son went to a party with his girlfriend, and you and Mr. Hilliard stayed home with your younger son?" Caruthers talks as the other officer writes on his notepad.

"Yes."

"And then Mr. Hilliard heard your older son—it's Michael?"

Claire nods.

"He heard Michael come in past curfew, around three a.m.?"

"Right."

"Did he tell you what excuse Michael gave? Or were you there?"

"I'm sorry, Officer. But as I understand it, you wanted to know if Jack was home. He was. I don't think how we decided to deal with our son is any of your business. In fact, in light of the limited information you've given me, I'm not sure Jack's whereabouts are your business either, but we have nothing to hide, so I was trying to be cooperative." She stands again, intent on getting rid of them. "I think we're done here."

The chime of a cell phone fills the office. Caruthers reaches for the phone at her belt and answers it. Claire stares at the calendar on her desk and is relieved to see no student conferences scheduled for this afternoon. She just wants them out so she can call Jack. Or should she head over to the school and interrogate Michael? What hasn't he told them? She'll reach Jack from her cell phone on the way.

"Mrs. Hilliard?" The officer's voice is quiet. She lowers her phone as she speaks. "That was one of our other officers. He just spoke with your son."

"*What?*" What is going on? And how dare they talk to Michael without permission?

"Michael claims that Mr. Hilliard drove his girlfriend home on Saturday night because he and his girlfriend had been drinking. Are you aware of this?"

When Claire stands, she feels dizzy. She rests her palms on the desk to steady herself. Without looking up, she says, "I want to you leave. Now."

Jack's cell phone rings before the Chief answers the question.

"Excuse me," he says when he sees that it's Claire. "It's my office. I have to take this." Let them think it's a business call. "Yeah?" he says into the phone and hopes from his tone and the impersonal way he answered that she knows he's not alone.

"Jack." Her voice is breathless; she sounds upset.

"What is it?"

"The cops just left my office" —Jack stifles a gasp— "and somehow they've talked to Michael, too—"

"What?" Jack tries desperately to control his voice. The men with him are listening to every word.

"Why would Michael be telling them that you drove Celeste home on Saturday night?" She's about to cry. He hears it right through the phone. "And why would they care?"

"I don't know." He needs to let her know that he's with the cops now. "Can I call you back, Beverly? I'm at the police station right now." She lets out a cry. "Tell me what I need to know now and then I'll call you back as soon as I'm done here."

Jack raises a finger to the Chief as if to say, *Give me a moment.*

"They showed up here at the law school asking if I knew where you were on Saturday night. I told them we were home all night, but then one of the cops got a call, and when she hung up, she said that Michael told some other cop that *you'd* driven Celeste home." When he doesn't answer, she cries, "Jack? What's going on?"

What the hell! *They questioned my son?* Jack glares at the Chief as Claire repeats her question, but the Chief doesn't notice because he's reading the screen of his Blackberry.

Claire gets that Jack can't answer her just then, doesn't she? "Okay, I got it," he says into the phone, his eyes still concentrating on Gunner as the chief squints to read his device. "Thanks for letting me know. I'll call you back in a few minutes, okay?"

The Chief glances up and shakes his head. "It'll be more than a few minutes, Jack."

"Call me on my cell," she says. "I'm going over to the school."

"I'd rather you wait for me." He tries to sound calm.

"Just call me when you can." Before Jack responds, she's gone.

When Jack returns his attention to the men in front of him, the Chief doesn't look so good. Whatever he read on his Blackberry has him upset, too.

"What's going on, Gunner?" Jack asks, his voice level. He can't let Gunner know what he knows, not yet.

The Chief sighs loudly. With a jerk of his head, he motions for the other cops to leave the room.

"Okay, Jack," he begins when they've gone, "this is all off the record for now, okay?"

Jack crosses his arms over his chest. "Our earlier conversation wasn't?"

Gunner shrugs. They both know it doesn't matter; it'd be inadmissible anyway.

"Go on."

"Your son's girlfriend is making an accusation against you."

Jack stares at him, his insides twisting like a tornado. "What kind of accusation?"

"The worst kind."

"The kind where it's my word against hers?"

Gunner nods without taking his eyes from Jack. "She went ballistic when they tried to examine her. She refused."

Jack wants to go ballistic himself, but he can't let the Chief know how riled he is. But when he speaks, his shaky voice betrays him. "And what's that tell you, huh?"

"I know, I know." He speaks to Jack as if Jack is a child he's trying to soothe. "But here's the thing. I just received some information that'll make it difficult for me not to arrest you."

At the word *arrest*, Jack jumps from the chair as if his ass has been stung. "*What?*"

"Sit down," Gunner orders. "You tell me what happened, and I'll tell you what she's saying."

But Jack's not listening. He's too busy pacing the small room as he tries not to hyperventilate. He can't let his family go through this again. He can't let Claire go through this again. It's bad enough that Jenny's back, but now, *this*. If Celeste was in the room, he'd strangle her. He might even strangle Michael.

"Gunner, listen to me. I didn't do anything. My only crime is trying to protect that girl from her asshole of a father."

"Why don't you sit down and tell me what happened? What you're talking about?"

His word against hers. Jack knows what his word will be worth when it gets out what his accuser looks like, and that he lied to his wife about taking her home.

"Jack." Gunner practically whispers his name. It works. Jack stops mid-step and turns. The Chief motions to the chair, and Jack falls into it, his legs splayed. He leans forward and clutches his head in his hands.

"What's she saying?" he asks from the small cocoon he's created. "And what evidence do you have other than her word?"

"Look, you know I can't go into specifics yet. Why don't you tell me what happened. Then I'll bring my boys back in to put it on the record. You and I can talk in private again afterwards and I'll fill you in more. Okay?"

"And then you'll arrest me?"

He regards Jack sadly, but doesn't deny it.

"Gunner, you saw me on Sunday afternoon, remember? The Bedford interrogation? Did I look like someone who'd raped a girl the night before?"

"There's too much circumstantial evidence, and given your position, and your past" —Jack cringes when he says *your past*— "there's no way I can get away without booking you. I'll try to make it easier for you, but . . ." His voice trails off and he shrugs apologetically.

Jack tries to remember why, *why*, he thought it was a good idea not to tell Claire. There was no need to protect Michael from his mother. She'd forgive him anything. It seems ridiculous now, in hindsight.

"Why don't you tell me what happened?" Gunner says again. His tone is resigned, as if Jack has no other choice.

But he does.

"I'm ready to call my lawyer."

CHAPTER SEVEN

EARL'S VOICEMAIL PICKS up and Jack is forced to leave him a cryptic message. He gets the same non-response from his cell phone. Jack prays his former boss hasn't decided to spend his private practice salary on a long overseas trip. When Earl Scanlon was DA, and Jack one of his assistants, reaching him was as simple as walking a few doors down the hall. It occurs to him now that he hasn't seen Earl in over five months.

He considers calling Claire—he knows they'll allow him as many calls as he wishes—but he doesn't think he can deal with her questions just yet. Instead, he calls Beverly and asks her to find Earl. He doesn't tell her why.

When he finishes, the investigator who first tried to question Jack silently leads him to the booking area. He passes him off to a booking officer. The booking officer politely introduces herself before she fingerprints him, collects a swab of saliva, and snaps the mug shot. The photography's not done, though. Digital camera in hand, she asks him to pull up his shirt sleeves, and when Jack looks at his right wrist, he understands why. The faint scratch where Celeste grabbed him is still there. Jack meets the officer's eye, but she's unreadable.

The officer takes his phone, his wallet, his watch, his keys and his belt. She takes everything except the clothes on his back, and he's grateful. If they wanted to, they could make him wear the orange jumpsuit. After he signs the inventory form, she searches him with a cursory pat down. Even though he knows the light treatment is a professional courtesy, the humiliation still stings. Afterwards, the Chief apologizes for putting him through the process, but he insists it'd be political suicide for both of them if he treats Jack differently. "I wouldn't ask you to," Jack assures him, even though he suspects his own political suicide is a *fait accompli*, anyway. In fact, might as well throw in familial suicide, too, while he's at it.

"You want to call a bail bondsman?" Gunner asks.

Jack has considered the option of bonding himself out, but it would be too risky. Any bondsman Jack might reach would have no incentive for keeping his mouth shut. If Earl arranges it, however, and the bondsman fails to exercise discretion, he stands to lose a huge chunk of business. Jack might have to wait longer, but just then, his privacy is more valuable than his time.

So he shakes his head at Gunner's question. Better to let Earl handle everything.

Jack sits in a holding cell for hours until finally they come to tell him Earl has arrived. Without his watch, he's lost track of time but he suspects it's the middle of the night. An officer he hasn't seen before leads him to another interrogation room to wait for Earl; on the way he asks if he can call his wife. He's shocked when the officer tells him Claire called the station hours ago and was informed that Jack was being booked. Jack wonders why she hasn't come.

"You can't afford me, you know."

Earl's voice behind Jack startles him. He realizes he fell asleep sitting up. He didn't even hear the door open. He's certain another half hour or forty-five minutes has passed.

When Jack turns, Earl gives him a devilish grin. For a moment Jack allows himself to think Earl might get this resolved before it becomes public. If it hasn't already.

To his surprise, when Jack rises to greet him, Earl grasps Jack's hand and reels him in like a fish for a fatherly hug. Jack can't remember when he was last hugged like this. Perhaps it's everything that's happened over the past several days, perhaps it's exhaustion from sitting in a cell all night, but his emotions are as sensitive as the tentacles on a jellyfish. He clings to Earl a little longer than he otherwise might have. He doesn't even bother asking him where he's been, what took so long.

"Did you talk to Claire?"

"I did. And I told her I'd call again once I saw you and had an idea how much longer this would take." He sees the question in Jack's eyes. "I won't lie to you, Jack. She's upset. She didn't pull any punches with me. She said that once she talked to Michael and he confirmed that you *had* taken—what's her name, Celeste?—home, and that you'd been gone for several hours—"

"It wasn't *several* hours. It probably wasn't even two full—"

"Jack."

Jack stops mid-sentence and drops back into the hard chair. "Sorry. Go on."

Earl takes a chair on the opposite side of the table. "Like I said, she's upset. She doesn't know what to think."

"She said that? What does that mean, for Christ's sake? She thinks I *did* whatever the hell Celeste's accusing me of?" As soon as he speaks the words, he realizes he still doesn't know what, exactly, Celeste claims he did to her. He knows only that he's been charged with a laundry list of crimes—second degree statutory rape, second degree statutory sodomy, sexual assault and deviate sexual assault—all intended, he also knows, to cover the bases. Just in case. "And what *did* I supposedly do?"

"First, you need to understand that it's not clear if she's claiming you forced yourself on her. But that doesn't really—"

"Wonderful. I'll have to send her a thank you note."

Earl sighs. "But with the statutory charges, it doesn't matter if technically she consented. And even on the others, she admits she'd been drinking, so any consent wouldn't really—"

"Yeah, but it *does* matter if *technically*, I didn't do anything." Jack laughs sarcastically. "I'm a prosecutor, remember? Will you stop talking to me like I don't already know all this?"

"Yeah, I will, if you'll start acting like a prosecutor and stop acting like an accused."

"Fuck off."

With that, Earl pulls his phone out of his shirt pocket and with his thumb, starts scrolling through messages. He might have done it for effect, yet Jack sees he really *is* working. His brow furrows as he reads an email; his jaw tightens with deep thought. Jack could be a spider on the wall as far as Earl's concerned.

Earl hasn't changed since crossing over, not a bit. This reassures Jack and pisses him off all at once. Earl's calm in the face of a storm has always been his biggest strength, and something Jack envied, too. Most who know Jack believe he's followed in Earl's footsteps. For the most part, he has. He plays it cool, too, in the courtroom, with opposing counsel, before the media. The only time he ever cracked in public—truly cracked—was on the witness stand at Alex's trial, when he testified about the night spent with Jenny.

But Earl, like Claire, like Jenny even, knows there's another side to Jack. An impulsive side. Claire accepts it, maybe even loves it as long as it's honest. Jenny, he thinks, used it to manipulate him. (Jack has never quite understood how he could know this and yet still be vulnerable.)

Earl, though, ignores it until it passes.

Jack closes his eyes and tries to gather his thoughts. He'd like to react to the allegations as he might if he were representing a client, but that's difficult when he's the one being threatened with time behind bars.

"It's ironic," Jack mutters, almost to himself. "Why would I mess with Celeste when the real thing is just across town?"

Earl lowers the phone. When his expression transforms before Jack's eyes, Jack remembers that Earl doesn't know. "Claire didn't tell you?" he asks.

"Tell me what, Jack?"

But Earl's tone tells Jack that he knew the minute Jack spoke the words "the real thing."

"You're in contact with Jenny?"

Jack nods and qualifies the answer by adding, "She contacted me. She's back in town."

"And Claire is aware of this?"

"Yes."

"Funny, she didn't mention it to me when we talked."

"Yeah, well, I think we both agree it's best if it stays under the radar."

Earl crosses his thick arms over his chest. He rubs his chin as he thinks about what he's just learned. He knows as well as Jack that the authorities would love to question Jenny anew. Yet he represented her back when she was charged with Maxine Shepard's murder. In fact, she was one of his first clients in his new role as a criminal defense attorney, and he'd been instrumental in getting the charges against her dropped. He'd be the last one to rat her out. "I understand why you and Jenny would feel that way, but Claire? I would think she'd love to see Jenny squirm."

Jack doesn't bother responding. Earl knows Claire wouldn't sacrifice her family to the media merely to avenge the pain Jenny—and Jack—had caused her.

"So why's she back?" he asks. "And why are you in contact with her?"

"She's being threatened, and she thinks the threats are coming from the guys who murdered her family." From the expectant look on Earl's leathery face, he wants more. "She wants me to help her find out what's going on."

"She's being threatened thirty years after the fact? Doesn't that strike you as odd?" Earl asks. When Jack doesn't answer—he doesn't have enough facts yet to argue her cause—Earl adds, "And how, exactly, are you supposed to help her?"

Jack shrugs. It's not that he doesn't know. It's just that he doesn't want to discuss it with Earl. Jack has Earl's old job, and he'll always feel beholden to him for it. He groomed Jack for the position, and he did everything within his power to make sure Jack was elected to succeed him. Jack's relationship with Jenny brought disgrace to the DA's office—and by extension, to Earl—once already, and Jack doesn't want him thinking he'll do it again.

"I'm not sure yet."

"Jack—"

"I don't want to talk about this. I won't do anything stupid. I learned my lesson, okay?" His words sound defensive, but they weren't meant to. Earl wants to talk about Jenny, but she's the least of his problems right now. "Can we just focus on getting me out of here? Where do things stand?"

Earl's hard stare sends Jack a clear message: *Fine, but the conversation is merely postponed, not finished.* "I've got the ball rolling. I'll want you to waive your preliminary hearing. I don't want the state to have a practice run. The paperwork for your bail is being prepared. When it's done, you'll be a free man, for now."

Jack pretends not to notice the *for now*. "Did they tell you what they've got?"

"Her word against a known liar, for starters."

Jack holds his tongue. Earl isn't judging him; he's being honest.

"Her fingerprints in your car. What they think—"

"They've searched my car already?"

"Went for the warrant even as they were booking you."

So much for professional courtesy. "Of course her fingerprints are in my car! I drove her home."

Earl nods. "Obviously. They also found hairs they think belong to her, and—"

"Earl, none of this—"

He puts his hand up. "I know. Let me finish. They found hairs on her coat that they think belong to you. But also," he pauses, "one *under* her coat." Jack waits, silent, but his heart beats so hard that he hears it in his ears. "It was on her bra," he adds quietly. "*In* her bra."

Jack stands and begins to pace the small room. "Listen to me. That night, Michael and Celeste were fooling around on our couch when I interrupted them. I didn't actually see them, I only heard them, so for all I know Celeste could have been stark naked. Do you get my point?"

"I get your point. But you know as well as I do that all they needed to make the arrest was probable cause. When they put everything together—hell, they don't even *need* to put everything together, one or two of the things I've mentioned would be sufficient—they've got probable cause. You *know* that."

Jack does know it. He also knows that even though there's an explanation for every single bit of evidence Earl has mentioned, a jury will get bored real fast listening to Earl offer those explanations. Taken in totality, the evidence is damning.

"Did they give you an idea when they'd have the tests back?"

"They wouldn't commit to anything. My guess is we'll hear immediately if the hair belongs to you, and they'll claim a backlog if it doesn't. But even if we can explain away the hairs, there's a larger problem. One that even if you can explain, you might not be believed." He sighs deeply. "She wouldn't let them do a gynecological exam, but she did let them take scrapings from under her fingernails."

Jack closes his eyes and shakes his head. He simply can't believe this is happening. When the Chief first broke the news, Jack assumed that Celeste had something to hide and decided after the fact to use him as her scapegoat. Now he's reconsidering that assumption. Now he wonders if she hadn't already decided to set him up the minute she climbed into the car. Was she that manipulative? Did she know exactly what she was doing when she grabbed his arm and scratched it? He wishes he could talk to her. He feels certain he could break her, persuade her to come clean. But he knows that he won't have the chance to confront his accuser until trial. By then, his life won't be recognizable.

He pulls up his shirt sleeve and shows Earl the scratch they'd photographed. Earl merely nods, barely looking at it. "I saw the photos," he says. He sighs. "What happened, Jack?"

He starts at the beginning, at the point when he first heard their voices downstairs. Earl listens without expression until Jack gets to the part where he lied to Claire in his effort to protect Michael. Earl's square jaw tightens and his gray eyes darken.

"Why didn't you simply tell Claire you'd driven her home?" he asks, even though Jack has explained it once already.

"I told you. When Michael heard her voice, he panicked. He begged me not to tell her what happened. I know I shouldn't have—"

"But you said he didn't want Claire to know they'd been fooling around. You could have told her about the drinking, though, right? And that would have been reason enough not to let Michael drive her home."

Earl questions Jack with the skepticism he uses when cross-examining a witness, and Jack resents it. He understands why Earl is doing it—he's forcing Jack to think about these things now, before a less friendly interrogator forces him to think about them on a witness stand—but he can't help but resist the mirror Earl wants him to look into.

The two of them regard each other for a long moment. "I guess I wanted my son to like me again," Jack finally says.

"Okay, I can buy that. In fact, knowing you as I do, I *do* buy that. But I think there's more."

The small room feels like a balloon with the air being sucked out. Jack remembers when they first arrested Jenny for the murder of her client, how he had to fight to see her. When they finally let him in, he sat with her in a room very similar to this one. At the time, he thought he understood how she felt, confined behind the impenetrable concrete walls.

He didn't have a clue.

He has one now.

"Have you seen Celeste?" Jack asks.

"No, but Claire described her to me."

Jack shrugs. "Well, then you know why it was easy *not* to tell Claire. I didn't want her to wonder. I've never even *thought* of something like that with Celeste— *she's a kid*, for Christ's sake—but I just didn't want Claire wondering. Always wondering."

"You really thought she might?"

Earl eyes Jack as if he's curious about what the last four years have been like for Jack and Claire. Jack wants to tell him that they've been good. That things were different from how they used to be, that a certain thread between them had been irreparably broken, but still, they were good. Good enough that Jack has to think twice before answering the question.

He'd like to say no. He wishes he could. If everything happening now had happened four years ago, before he'd fallen down Jenny's rabbit hole, he could have. But as much as Claire claims to trust him again, *wants* to trust him again, Jack would be deluding himself to think that she does completely. She still loves him, he's sure of that. She wouldn't stick around if she didn't. But her unconditional trust is gone forever.

"I didn't *think* she'd wonder, Earl. I knew she would."

The Chief agrees to hold off recording the charges in the arrest log until Jack and Earl have left the jail and Jack has time to get home. As they leave, an exhausted Jack thanks Gunner as if Jack were a houseguest and Gunner the host.

The sun seems unusually bright for six thirty in the morning. On the sidewalk, Earl offers to buy Jack breakfast. He declines, as Earl knew he would. Earl reminds Jack to keep quiet with the press. "This will be big enough without us fanning the flames." The two of them agree to meet the next day at Earl's office.

Minutes later, safe in the confines of his car with its newly acquired fingerprint dust, Jack turns on his phone. He expects to see a number of missed calls from Claire. He's not sure if he's relieved or disappointed when he doesn't.

CHAPTER EIGHT

JACK SPENDS THE next couple of hours traveling aimlessly down Interstate 55. He simply drives, letting what has happened sink in and preparing himself for the inevitability of what is to come.

When the Chief first broke the news, Jack didn't fully accept it as the truth. Of course it had to be; the city's Chief of Police wouldn't haul the city's District Attorney into headquarters for a practical joke. Especially a bad practical joke. But it was all so surreal. The way Gunner questioned him as if he was a common criminal, the solemn silence of the officer who booked him, the hours spent alone in the holding cell while he waited for Earl to arrive. The whole experience felt like a nightmare.

But only now, when his brief stint in captivity stands in stark contrast to the open road in front of him, does he fully comprehend the raw reality of what Celeste has done to him: Her one lie, seemingly blurted out under circumstances or pressure he can only guess at, has the power to put him back behind bars for a long, long time.

His eyelids become heavier as he drives. He's tired, so tired. He thinks about what might happen if he never stops, if he just keeps driving. He's already long past the Festus and Farmington exits; ten more miles and he'll reach Cape Girardeau. Another three hours, and he could pull into Memphis and reclaim the anonymity he lost four years ago. Maybe he'd go even farther. New Orleans. He wonders if Claire would join him. He fantasizes about starting over with her. A *real* starting over. Going to a place where no one knows his past, the mistakes he made—no one except the two of them.

And Michael.

And then there's the small detail about his bail.

His fantasies will never be anything more than that. Fantasies.

He turns around at the Cape Girardeau exit and heads toward home.

Claire sees the Caller ID and picks up the phone on the first ring. "Where are you?" she asks. "Or rather, where have you been?"

"I'm in my car on the way home. Is it clear?"

"Not anymore. Cars have been cruising in front of the house all morning."

Her voice breaks. She waits for Jack to answer her second question, and when he doesn't, she says, "I've been worried sick about you. Earl said they released you just after six this morning. That was hours ago."

"Where's Michael?"

"He's here. There's no way I was going to make him go to school today. Jack, where—?"

"I'd rather explain everything to you in person, if that's okay. Can we talk when I get home?"

She's so angry with him. She's furious. On top of everything, how dare he not come straight home after his release? It's a ridiculous thought, but she wonders if he went to Jenny. But no, she has to believe he wouldn't do that. He's being so calm right now, so gentle with his words. It's not what she expected. "Okay." The line falls silent. She hears the noise of fast travel, tires on highway. She starts to ask how long he'll be, when he says, "Claire? She's lying. You know that, don't you?"

She wants to say yes. She wants to tell him she believes every word that comes out of his mouth. She wants to think that he'd never do anything again to hurt her or place their family in jeopardy. But she can't. Is it because he lied to her about driving Celeste home? Or is it because Jenny has insisted on inserting herself back into their lives, and Jack has let her? Yet Claire knows she is partly to blame for that, too.

Perhaps a part of Claire wonders if there is some truth to Celeste's accusations. Celeste may be only sixteen, but there's no denying she could pass for twenty-two, and she looks so much like Jenny. He wouldn't ever force himself on anyone—Claire knows that for certain—but if she's honest with herself, she can envision a situation where Celeste comes on to him and in a moment of weakness, he allows it to happen. She knows now he's not as strong as she once believed him to be.

"Just come home, Jack, okay?" Before he can protest, she hangs up the phone.

He'd thought he'd grasped the irrevocability of what was happening.

He was wrong.

When he pulls into his neighborhood, cars and television vans swarm his car. They emerge from side streets and from the playground parking lot like magnets to metal. They don't block his way, but they cling to him like a security detail. A few have backed into his neighbors' driveways.

As he approaches his own drive, they scatter to claim parking spots closer to his house. Like soldiers storming the beaches of Normandy, reporters and their crews burst from the vehicles and sprint across his yard, wielding cameras, notepads and pens as their weapons. Anticipating this, he presses the remote to the garage much earlier than usual. As he crawls in, some of them pound on the window of the car to get his attention. *As if they didn't already have it.* He vows to run them over if they try to block his entrance.

Once inside, he closes the garage door and dials the Chief's cell.

"Jack?" The Chief must know it's him from the Caller ID, and he's clearly surprised to hear from him so soon.

"The press has surrounded my house. I can't stop them from being on the street, but get your men over here to get them out of my yard."

"You're just now getting home? I gave you—"

He has no intention of explaining to the Chief why he didn't head straight home after they released him. "Damn it, Gunner! Get them out of my friggin' yard! You hear me?"

He presses the button and realizes the thing he hates about cell phones—they can't be slammed. Dragging his weary self out of the car to face the next battle, he makes a mental note to have the windows tinted.

Michael's in the kitchen eating chocolate cake and reading the comics. He looks up from the paper, his fork in midair. He was angry after what happened with Jenny four years ago, but the loathing on his face now makes clear that he believes he's living with the devil. He sets the fork down hard and rises from the table. Jack expects him to rush from the room, but Claire's taught him well; he first takes his plate and glass of milk to the sink. After scraping the food into the disposal, he rinses both dishes and puts them in the dishwasher. Jack waits to speak until he finishes and turns around.

"You don't believe her, do you?"

Michael starts for the stairs but Jack touches his arm as he passes. "Mike—"

"Don't touch me!" he says, jerking away.

"That's it? You're just going to take her word? You're not even going to question it?"

Michael takes the stairs two at a time. When he reaches the top, he stops. Jack moves closer to the stairs to listen. He hopes Michael has reconsidered and is about to come back down. That's when he spots Claire, sitting on the couch in the family room. Watching him.

Michael's voice, getting lower with each passing day, comes to life one last time. "*She's* never lied to me." After a few more steps, he gets the physical satisfaction Jack craved in the garage. He slams his bedroom door.

Jack stares at Claire. For a long moment, she simply stares back.

In an emotionless voice, she asks Jack where he's been since leaving the jail, and he tells her. He explains how he needed time to think and driving out of the city seemed the only way to get it without the army outside tailing him. When she reminds him that the Chief gave him a head start to get home, he doesn't respond. What could he say? *I wasn't prepared to have this discussion with you yet.*

"I can't do this again," she says.

Jack grunts softly with frustration. What is he supposed to say to that? "Do *what*? You make it sound as if I've done something wrong. As if I've done something to *you*. I drove her home, Claire. I drove a girl home because our son was too drunk to do it himself. And because she was drunk, too, and deathly afraid of her father—why, I'm still not sure—I gave her the time to sober up, and then I covered for her, and for our son."

"Are you done with your opening statement?"

He doesn't answer.

"You lied to me. If you had nothing to hide, why'd you lie to me?"

He laughs curtly. "What? You think I lied because I actually *did* something with that kid? You really have that little faith in me? She's a *kid*!" He realizes he's yelling. He reminds himself to stay calm. But *Jesus*, she honestly thinks he is capable of sexually assaulting a sixteen-year-old girl?

He wants to say this. He wants to say a lot of things. He wants to remind her that he's taken full responsibility for his prior screw-up, and he's done nothing in the last four years but try to make it up to her. He wants her to understand that *he's* the victim this time, that he needs her by his side these next few months. He needs her like he's never needed her before. In fact, he wants to ask her why she can't just stand up and come hold him. He spent the entire night in a jail cell and right now what he really needs is someone to hold him. But he doesn't say any of this, because the whole situation has left him speechless.

"Why'd you lie to me?" she asks again. If she feels anything other than cold anger, she's hiding it. She's not the same woman she was the first time he broke her heart.

"Claire . . ." he whispers. He's so tired. He hasn't slept in over twenty-four hours.

"Just answer the question, Jack. Honestly."

He hesitates. He thinks of the first answer he gave Earl, and how Earl knew he was holding something back. Earl knew the answer, the real answer. It's the answer Jack needs to give Claire now. He prays to God she believes him.

"Because of this." He waves his arms, motioning back and forth between the two of them. "Because of this conversation we're having right now. I knew what you'd think if I'd told you it took me two hours to get her home. Even if I'd explained why, you still would have wondered. I couldn't bear to think of you wondering like that." When he sees the expression on her face, his eyes well with tears.

She doesn't believe a word he's saying.

Only later, after she's retreated to the bedroom and left him standing gutted in the kitchen, does he wonder if the question he answered wasn't the one she really asked.

I can't do this again, she said.

Maybe *this* was only a peripheral reference to Celeste's accusations. Maybe *this* had nothing to do with Celeste at all.

CHAPTER NINE

THE NEXT MORNING, Claire and Michael treat Jack as if he's invisible. Neither of them speaks to him, and even the conversation between mother and son is stunted and efficient before Michael retreats to his bedroom. Jack assumes Claire told him he didn't have to go to school again today.

He sits at the kitchen table eating cereal with Jamie, who, if he senses the tension, has no idea that his father is to blame. Or, at least, that his mother and brother *think* his father is to blame.

"Can I get a snake?" he asks. Jack peers down at the cereal box. The back is devoted to educating kids about the common garter snake.

"I guess so." As soon as he speaks the words, Claire turns off the water at the sink and gives him a hard stare. "I don't see why not."

She resumes her activities but makes a point of being loud. When she returns a frying pan to the cabinet, she lets it clang against the others. She slams the drawer after she puts potholders away.

"Hey, how about if I drive you to school this morning?" Jack says to Jamie. Claire clears her throat.

"Can we get a smoothie on the way?"

"Jamie," Claire says, "I thought you wanted to stay home with Mikey today? And I don't think Daddy has time to—"

"Sure, I think so, if we leave soon." Jack pretends he doesn't hear her. "Why don't you go upstairs and get dressed? Don't forget to brush your teeth. I'll get our coats."

Jack and Claire watch Jamie leap up the stairs. When Jack hears the bathroom faucet running, he says, "What is your problem?"

"Where's your brain, Jack? Oh, wait, forget I asked because I already know."

It takes a few seconds for her insinuation to sink in, but when it does, he's furious. *Fuck you,* he wants to say, but he doesn't. He's never said those words to her, and he won't start now.

"Have you looked out the window?" she asks. She stomps around the kitchen as she talks. Tugging the refrigerator open, she slams it shut after she's replaced the milk and the butter. "The sharks are circling, waiting for you to leave. Are you going to subject him to that circus? Haven't you already subjected this family to enough? I mean, my God, Michael was *interrogated* at his school!"

"I didn't do anything. I'm not hiding as if I did."

She scoffs at that. "Oh, please! You're—"

"But you don't believe me, do you?"

She stops and crosses her arms.

"Do you?"

When she still doesn't answer, he shoves his cereal bowl away and rises from the table. "You know what?" He moves closer to her but she stands her ground, her eyes narrowed. "If anyone's lying around here, Claire, it's you."

"Me?"

"Yeah, you. You told me you'd forgiven me. You told me you trusted me again. But you don't. You won't let it go. You take every opportunity to remind me of what I did, of how I hurt you, of how I hurt our family. But I already know that, okay? I *get* it." He's making fun of the phrase she uses, and she knows it. "I'm sorry. I truly am. I've told you how sorry I am, and I've spent every day of my life since then trying to make it up to you. But it's not enough for you, is it? What are you going to do, persecute me the rest of my life?"

"I guess that depends on *your* plans." Her small nostrils flare with sarcasm. "What are *you* going to do?"

"Will you stop talking in code?" he shouts, and she flinches. "What are you talking about? Just say what you mean for once, will you?"

"You're smart. Figure it out."

He closes his eyes and tells himself that he can rein this conversation back in. He can make her see reason if he just approaches it differently, calmly. If they both approach it calmly—without anger, without yelling, and simply talk, like two sane, reasonable adults—they can get past this. When he opens his eyes, she's still staring at him; she's not having similar thoughts.

"Claire," he says softly. He moves to touch her arm, but she jerks away. "Can we please not fight? I need you right now. I need you to believe me. *I didn't do anything.*"

"Nothing?" She spits the word. "Think about it, Jack. Do you really think what's happening with Celeste would be happening if you hadn't fucked around with her?" He knows without asking whom *her* refers to. "He would have never started dating Celeste."

"Really? You're so sure of that?" The fact that she's rejected his plea for peace makes him madder than he was before. His next words slip out so fast he has no time to censor them. "Did you ever think that maybe we just have the same taste in women?"

She gasps. He immediately realizes what he's done. How cruel it was. Before he can recant it, her palm hits his cheek with surprising force. The sting is so severe his eyes water.

"Get out."

When he doesn't move, she yells. "Get out, Jack! Get out now! Before I do something I'll regret."

He thinks of the wife in the interrogation on Sunday, how she shouted at the detective, *He'd been with another woman!* As if that were justifiable cause to smash her husband's skull with a Louisville Slugger.

He remembers Claire's rage after learning what Jack had done.

Is it true? she'd asked. And when he hesitated answering, when he failed to deny it, she knew. *I hate you,* she said. *I hate you.* Screamed it at him, over and over. Struck him, over and over.

If she'd used anything other than her hands . . .

When Jack pulls out of the garage, he can't see sky for the hard rain that pelts the car. He has a vague sense of having heard the storm when he and Claire were arguing inside the house, but at the time it didn't register. He's now glad she didn't let him take Jamie.

The media vans and SUVs wait for him, their station call letters on the sides blurred by the curtain of rain. Wishing for a distraction, he considers calling Earl to confirm their meeting. But Earl won't forget. Jack is now his highest profile client.

He's almost at the last Missouri exit when his cell phone rings. The Caller ID reads Harley Lambert. It's Claire's father, and Jack knows Harley is at his office because when he calls from home, the cell phone simply reads Harley and Ruth. The man makes Jack nervous—he always has—and Jack dreads talking to him. But Jack especially hates talking to him when he calls from his office, which, because he's been retired from the FBI for years now, isn't really an office where he works, but some sort of space he rents in an office park near his home. Jack knows there's a good chance Harley records the call. He's seen the recorder on Harley's desk, the way it's hooked up to the phone, and though Harley claims to record only those who give him permission, Jack knows better.

"Good morning, Harley." Jack keeps his tone as neutral as possible, but he still hears the resignation in it. He knows Harley must hear it, too. The man doesn't miss a thing.

"Don't 'good morning, Harley' me, you little prick! There's not a damn thing good about this morning because of you."

Jack doesn't respond. After all, what could he possibly say to that?

"Listen to me, and listen to me good."

"I'm listening." The media vehicles trail his car, matching each turn through the downtown streets. They follow too close, close enough to be dangerous even without the rain.

"I won't let you hurt my baby again. I stayed out of it last time at her request, but not this time. Say goodbye to your ticket, Jack, because if I have any say in the matter, Jeff City will be pulling it sooner than you can say boo."

"It'll be a bit difficult to support my family without it." He surprises himself with his nonchalant response to the threat of disbarment. Is he growing numb already?

"Don't you dare talk back to me!"

Harley yells so loud Jack holds the phone away from his ear.

He drives under the interstate, where he's granted a brief reprieve from the rain. In the relative silence he glances out the left window and sees Jenny's homeless friend tucked next to a concrete pillar. All these years later, he still haunts these city streets, even without the few dollars and the food she gave him as she walked by each morning on the way to her office. Jack almost wants to buy him a plane ticket south somewhere, where at least he'll be warm.

"Did you call simply to harass me or would you like to hear what actually happened?"

"I called to tell you you're done hurting my daughter. She might insist on sticking by you while this is going on, but don't be fooled. Once your ass is behind bars, she's done with you. My grandchildren are done with you."

What Harley says gives Jack hope. Claire plans to stick by him, at least for a while. Based upon the conversation at the house that morning, he didn't think she would. And if she told her dad this, there's a good chance she believes Jack really is innocent.

"I think I'll wait until I hear that from her to believe it."

Jack can't see him, of course, but he knows every vein in Harley's neck is bulging, and his ears redden as Jack talks. He's not used to Jack fighting back; Jack has never challenged Harley on anything. There'd never been a need to, really. He's Claire's father, and though Jack has never felt close to him, Harley liked his son-in-law until Jack did the unthinkable. He saved his bullying for other targets.

"You're garbage, Hilliard. She's finally starting to realize it. Even her mother believes it now."

Though Jack is skeptical of this, it still stings. Ruth has always loved him like a son—she forgave him even before Claire. She's filled a maternal role since Jack's own mother passed away years ago. Harley knows it.

At a stoplight on Market & 4th, an SUV bearing KMOV call letters pulls up along the right side of the car. Jack knows without looking that their camera is trained on him through the passenger side window. They can't possibly have a clear shot, though, not with the sheet of rain that forms an opaque film on the glass.

"Look," he says to Harley, "I'm about to pull into a parking garage where I'll lose reception. If you'd like to hear both sides before you reach your verdict, I'll call you later from my office, okay? But I've gotta go."

Harley grunts in response.

The reporters are forced to stay behind when Jack uses the keycard Earl gave him to enter the underground parking garage. As usual, Earl anticipated everything.

But he still has to traverse the lobby from the parking garage elevator to the separate banks that take him to Earl's firm on the twenty-eighth floor. If he's not fast, they'll attack him in the lobby. The last thing he needs is to get stuck talking to Harley while they claim their stakeout.

"I gotta go," he says again. The words come out a little too loudly now that he left the battering rain behind.

"Your ticket, Jack. You're gonna lose your ticket this time. Your ticket and your family."

Jack drops the phone onto the passenger seat and searches for Earl's parking spot, all the while trying to convince himself that Harley's threats haven't shaken him.

Four or five reporters ambush him as soon as he steps off the parking garage elevator. But it's Jim Wolfe, the legal reporter for the *Post-Dispatch*, whom Jack sees first. He leans calmly against a marble column in the center of the lobby. As the one who first suspected Jack of being Jenny's alibi, Wolfe worries Jack more than the rabid bunch at his side.

You've done this hundreds of times, he tells himself. *You've crossed this same stream before without drowning. You can do it now.*

"Mr. Hilliard!" the reporter standing directly next to Jack shouts. "Do you have a comment about the charges brought against you?"

Jack keeps walking but says, "I'll have a statement for all of you later this afternoon."

"Are you guilty of the charges?"

"Of course not."

Earl will murder Jack when he finds out he engaged them in any conversation at all, but it's not Jack's style to ignore questions with easy answers.

"How do you intend to effectively represent the city on other matters if you're busy fighting these charges?" says another.

A short blonde in bright red pumps gets more specific: "Will your being a defendant in *this* case affect your handling of the Bedford case?"

He can't help but glare at the woman who asked that question, and yet they've only just begun. The questions get more personal as he approaches the sanctuary of the elevator.

"Is it true your accuser is your son's girlfriend?"

"What is your wife's reaction to these charges?"

But it's Wolfe who's done his research, who knows Jack's true weakness. His matter-of-fact voice reaches Jack's ears above the din of the others.

"Can you tell us, Mr. Hilliard, is it true the victim could be Jennifer Dodson's twin?"

Earl, who waits in the elevator, hears the last question. Once the doors close, sealing them in silence, he drops his game face. "You okay?"

"I'm okay." It's a lie, and Earl knows it, but they both pretend otherwise as the small cage whisks them to the top floor of the building.

The long walk down the corridor to Earl's corner office is only slightly less painful than the interrogation downstairs. Secretaries stare over the tops of their cubicles at Jack, then quickly avert their eyes when he attempts to greet them. Young associates traversing between offices nod and say, simply, "Mr. Hilliard." He returns the gesture, but he hears them congregating after he passes, waiting until he disappears into their boss' office to start their gossip. His suspicions are confirmed when Earl stops at his secretary's desk. "Tell them to get their asses back to work or they'll be writing research memos for the next five years," he orders brusquely.

In Earl's office, the first thing Jack sees is the morning's newspaper resting on the coffee table in front of the leather couch. He reads the large headline as he removes his coat. The bold black letters ask: ST. LOUIS DA: GOLDEN BOY OR SEXUAL PREDATOR? Underneath, a subtitle reads: IS SEXUAL MISBEHAVIOR 'ALL IN A DAY'S WORK' FOR MODERN DAY POLITICIANS?

He knew it would turn into this—the last time taught him that—and he knows it will get worse. Earls waves it off as he takes a seat behind his desk. "Yellow journalism. Ignore it."

That would be easier if it wasn't staring me in the face. Jack turns the paper over. To his relief, national news takes up the bottom half of the front page.

"First things first." Earl opens a small refrigerator behind his chair, pulls out a Michelob, and offers it to Jack. If someone had told him that the man who was his boss at the DA's office all those years now kept a refrigerator full of beer in his office, he wouldn't have believed it. Earl winks, and Jack understands then that he's joking, trying to help Jack relax.

"It's a little early and I didn't get much sleep last night. I think I'd prefer coffee." Jack pulls out the chair in front of the desk and falls into it. "But feel free to have one yourself."

Earl laughs. "I'm working," he says, replacing the beer and retrieving a can of Coke for himself. He picks up his phone and asks his secretary to bring a coffee for Jack.

"So am I," Jack says when Earl hangs up.

"We'll get to that, but there are few other things I want to talk to you about first." Earl swivels around once more to grab a book from the shelf next to the refrigerator. Jack recognizes it: the Missouri Rules of Professional Conduct. Get to *what?* he thinks. His gut tightens as he remembers Harley's threat. *You're gonna lose your ticket this time.*

"I heard you chewed out the Chief," Earl says as he leafs through the pages.

Jack stares at him blankly. "When you got home from the jail."

"Oh. Yeah, I guess I did. The press had camped out on my lawn. I could barely get into my garage."

Earl looks up from the book for a moment and nods slowly, as if he's absorbing Jack's answer. After knocking, Earl's secretary enters with the coffee. Jack thanks her, but she won't look him in the eye, either. *I'm not a rapist*, he wants to shout at her.

Earl asks her to close the door behind her.

"How can that be?" he says. "He claims he gave you plenty of lead time to get home before logging the charges."

"He did. I wasn't ready to go home yet, though. I wasn't ready to deal with Claire." Jack sips the coffee but it's much too hot and burns his lip.

"Where'd you go?" As Earl talks, he continues to flip the pages.

"Nowhere, really. I drove around."

Earl looks up, his finger holding his spot. "Were you with Dodson?"

He wasn't, of course, but that Earl asked the question disturbs Jack. Have Celeste's allegations already destroyed the trust he's spent the last four years rebuilding?

"No. I simply drove around, tried to clear my head before going home." When Earl seems to accept his answer, Jack goes on quietly, "Let's move on. What else do we need to talk about?"

Resigned, Earl tosses the book onto his desk and drags his hand over the top of his stubby gray hair, a habit when he's faced with an unpleasant task. He stares at the discarded book.

"What is it? Just tell me."

"Do you wonder how I knew you chewed out Gunner?"

"You obviously talked to him."

"Right." Earl finally pops the tab on his soda can. "He called me."

"Why?"

"He wants to talk to you, but felt he should run it by me first."

Every nerve warns Jack to be alert. "He wants to talk to me about what? About Celeste? I'm not talking to any of them. Why would you even think I might?"

"Whoa, hold on a second. First, stop jumping to conclusions. It's not like you. Second, remember they're not enjoying this, either, okay? Gunner and his crew are not out to get you, Jack. The only one out to get you is Celeste, and we need to find out why. I suspect it's not personal."

It sure feels personal. "Then what does he want to talk to me about?"

"He thinks your personal issues will impair your decision-making. Especially with the Bedford case. He thinks there's a conflict of interest. That you might identify with the victim a bit too much to prosecute the case fairly."

"I like to think I identify a little bit with all the victims in the cases I prosecute. It's sort of what motivates me, you know?" What do they want him to do, stop working altogether? "He thinks I should take myself off the case?"

"Yes."

"Well, if he wants me off the case, he'll have to ask the judge to order it."

"Jack—"

"It's not open for discussion. I refuse to constantly justify every move I make because of something stupid I did four years ago. Or because some girl now decides to accuse me of something I *didn't* do. If I have to argue my position, I'll argue it to the judge."

A slight grin grows on Earl's face. For the first time since Jack arrived, his former boss relaxes. He sinks into his high-back leather chair that would swallow another man of his height and rests his hands, fingers interlaced, over his belly. "Okay, point taken," he says. Jack is surprised by his sudden acquiescence. He has the sense he was just tested.

"Will you at least tell me how you and Claire are doing, then?"

"About as good as can be expected. I think she believes I'm innocent. I mean, she's hasn't said that outright, she won't give me that, not yet, but I think she knows. If this had happened in a vacuum, and the girl had been any other girl, well . . . it still would have been difficult, but . . . I don't know."

"But it wasn't any other girl. And it's happened right about the time Jenny showed up."

"Right."

"Has it occurred to you there might be a connection?"

"I've considered it, but there's no way. Jenny didn't contact me until the night after I drove Celeste home. Whatever game she's playing, it doesn't involve Celeste. I'm certain of it."

Earl sucks in a deep breath, blows it out. Jack knows he wants to argue. "You have to know how difficult this must be for Claire right now."

"I do."

The phone on his desk buzzes. "Excuse me. I was hoping to hear about the test results while you're here. This could be Gunner now."

Jack rises and goes over to stand at the two walls of glass that meet in the southeast corner. The hard rain falls at an angle and attacks the floor-to-ceiling panes. Yet even through the deluge he sees the Arch and, below that, the Mississippi. The red light at the top of the Arch blinks intermittently to warn errant air traffic; its lazy rhythm captivates him. He closes his eyes and makes a conscious effort to relax the tightness in his shoulders. It's not just his shoulders, though. Every muscle in his body is tense. He's carried the tension with him ever since his trip in the car to Celeste's house. Jenny's reappearance, and now his arrest, have made it exponentially worse.

With some effort he opens his eyes and watches a tugboat pushing a long barge north up the river, against the current. He imagines returning to his office, closing the door, and slipping into the chair behind his desk for a nap. The chair once belonged to Earl and still bears the indentations from years of his use. It's the most comfortable desk chair Jack has ever sat in. It wouldn't be the first time he's napped there.

"Gunner says the tests show the hair in her bra was yours."

Jack surprises himself by laughing. *Of course they do.* "They were fooling around on our couch, where I sit almost every day of my life. This is evidence?"

"You'd use it."

Earl is right. Jack would use it. The presence of his hair supports one side of the story, Celeste's. The State's. He's not sure how he ended up on the opposite side.

Frustrated, he takes his chair again.

"There's another problem, too," Earl says. "They ran tests for other hairs collected in the car. Some they thought belonged to Celeste don't match."

"So?"

"So who do they belong to, Jack?"

"You know who they belong to."

"Is Claire aware that she's been in your car?"

"Yes."

Earl regards Jack skeptically.

"*Yes.* She knows."

"Are you prepared to explain from a witness stand why Jenny's hairs are in your car?"

"Why would I have to do that?"

"Because if Gunner or someone else at the station puts two and two together, they'll suspect who those hairs belong to. When they do, they'll run the results against Dodson's records." He turns to the computer on his side desk and begins tapping at the keyboard. "You know as well as I do that they'd want to question her if they knew she was back."

"To my knowledge, there's no outstanding warrant. I'm not harboring her."

"No one said you were. But have you considered, as DA, you might have a higher ethical duty?"

Since the night Jenny appeared in the tunnel, Jack has asked himself repeatedly whether he needs to report her return to town, as he threatened he would. He hasn't answered the question for himself satisfactorily. He does know, by not doing anything—not even bothering to research the issue—he's done *something.* He made a decision by his failure to act.

Earl sighs. "Look, in any other circumstance, your relationship with another woman might not be anyone's business except yours and Claire's. But—"

"There is no relationship."

"Like hell there isn't."

"I haven't seen her since before my arrest."

"Good. Keep it that way. Stay away from her while all this is going on."

"Or what?"

"Or I won't represent you. I can try to protect you from the state, but I refuse to spend the next several months trying to protect you from yourself."

Jack knows he's bluffing. "Like you said at the jail, I can't afford you anyway."

"God dammit, Jack." Earl slams his fist on the desk. Jack starts from the surprise of it. "Why are you being so stubborn about this? Are you *trying* to get locked up? You heard Wolfe's question downstairs in the lobby. What do you think he'll start asking if he finds out she's in town and you're in contact with her?"

"Frankly, I think it might help my cause."

"And why's that?"

"If you accept their logic, that I simply couldn't help myself because of Celeste's resemblance to Jenny, well, that logic crumbles, doesn't it, if Jenny's readily available? I mean, think about it. If I want to betray Claire again, then isn't it more likely I'll do so in a way that doesn't land me in prison?"

Earl shakes his head in disgust. It's obvious he can't believe he's having this conversation. But Jack thinks that Earl is the one who isn't looking at things with clear eyes. He's worried about Jack and Claire just as much as he's worried about a conviction. Probably more.

"Earl, listen. Claire *knows*, okay? She understands the position Jenny's put me in. She doesn't like it, but she knows why I just can't let it go. If the threats are legitimate, and I ignored them, then—"

"Tell her to call the police."

Jack simply rolls his eyes at that.

"What if they're *not* legitimate? What if she's just playing you?"

"I'm well aware she might be doing that." Jack grabs his coffee and settles back into the chair, a signal to Earl that he wants to drop the topic. "You just need to trust me, okay? I won't agree not to see her, but I'll guarantee that no one will know about it for now. If I learn something that needs to go public, I'll come to you first. Will that satisfy you?"

Earl grunts and closes whatever he'd pulled up online. Jack wonders if he found what he was looking for. He's struck by what he sees on Earl's face, the burden of what he's trying to hide: he's too close to the case; he cares too much what happens.

Jack wants to remind Earl how difficult all of this is for him, too. He wants to confess his profound fear of being convicted, of losing his freedom to a prison cell. He wants to explain to Earl that the only fear greater than his fear of being convicted is his fear of losing his family for good.

But he knows Earl needs to hear something else, so he says none of this.

"Look, I *do* know how hard it is for Claire." Grinning just a bit for Earl's benefit, he thinks of Claire's comment the other day and adds, "We've survived much worse. We'll be okay."

Now, if only he could convince himself.

Once Earl drops the topic of Jenny, they spend another hour planning the next steps of Jack's defense. Earl focuses on Celeste's allegations—a subject upon which Jack is unequivocal. He takes Earl one more time though the events of the night, step-by-step, word-by-word. They agree to meet again once Earl has made his formal discovery requests and the state has responded. Meanwhile, Earl will hire a private investigator to work Jack's case.

Earl escorts him out and offers one more piece of advice.

"Whatever you do, talk to your staff about the charges. You need them to be on your side, and if you handle it right, they will be. Most of them look up to you, Jack. And they're smart enough to see through the rhetoric. But don't wait. The longer you wait to address it with them, the less they'll trust what you tell them."

As they stand in the reception area waiting for the elevator to arrive, he also reminds Jack not to speak to the Chief about his case. "It's business as usual on other cases, but you can't talk to him about—"

"I know that."

"And Celeste. Don't try to speak to her, either, not even indirectly via Michael. You have to be careful. Your communications with him have no privilege, and any prosecutor worth his salt would be able to spin anything you say in the worst direction."

Jack nods and steps into the open elevator. He presses the button for the lobby.

"Don't try to solve this case on your own, you hear me? Let our PI do that."

"We'll talk later," Jack says. As the doors close, Earl inserts his arm to stop them.

"*Jack*, you hear me?"

"I hear you."

The lies aren't what he says; they're what he doesn't say.

CHAPTER TEN

THE RAIN DRENCHES Jack on the way from his own parking garage to the court building. He can't help but notice the difference between the benefits of a job at a silk stocking firm versus the DA's office. Even as the head of that all-important office, the public employee's equivalent to a firm's managing partner, he still parks in an off-site garage. Even a lowly first year associate at Earl's firm gets a spot in the building's garage, not to mention a salary that probably surpasses Jack's. He's never cared about any of this—his two years at Newman, Norton & Levine right out of law school taught him that an attorney pays for those benefits in other ways, many times over—but he knows his life would still be his own right now but for his being DA.

He doesn't mind that he's soaked, not really, because the rain probably forced the media to finally give up the chase—if only for a few hours. He's seen no sign of them since he left them clamoring in the lobby of Earl's building.

He nods at the guards as he passes through security. To his relief, they seem content to pretend it's just another typical Wednesday.

In the empty elevator he anticipates the reception he'll receive in his own office. He spoke briefly with Beverly by phone the day before. She was gentle and sympathetic with him as she always is, but they didn't broach the reactions of everyone else in the office. He thinks about how to implement Earl's advice. *The longer you wait to address it with them,* he said, *the less they'll trust what you tell them.* So Jack decides he'll ask Beverly to gather everyone in the large conference room while he takes a few minutes to comb his wet hair and put on the dry shirt that he thinks is hanging behind his office door.

But the minute he steps off the elevator and turns right toward his office, he knows something's up. He hears the television in the large conference room. The new receptionist, Sharon, bolts from her chair and stutters, "Uh, Mr. Hilliard, I don't know if . . . uh, maybe you should wait . . . " Those words alone tell him *not* to wait—something is happening, something she doesn't want Jack to see—and she's done a lousy job of covering.

He steps to the open double doorway of the conference room. Every attorney on his staff, it seems, either sits around the long table or stands along the perimeter of the room, mesmerized by the large, flat screen television on the far wall. With their backs toward him, they're oblivious to Jack's presence.

Frank Mann's in charge of the remote. He flips from station to station. Fox News. MSNBC. CNN. ABC. CBS. *Five fucking national news stations are talking about Jack's arrest.* Stunned, Jack watches, transfixed not only by the fact of the story making the national news, but also by the restrained revelry that flavors the discussion of it. He watches the dissection of his life: his career, his marriage, his education and any other irrelevant tidbit the hosts dig up. On CNN, Nancy Grace rips him apart as if he's already been convicted of the charges. A former prosecutor, she should know better. Greta Van Susteren on Fox seems willing to give him the benefit of the doubt. She reminds viewers that "Mr. Hilliard is innocent until proven guilty, of course," but she still refers to him as an "admitted adulterer." Even in Jack's shock he's fascinated by how much they get right. He's also fascinated by how much they get wrong.

"I can't believe this!" Frank says, a little too enthusiastically.

What Jack finds most interesting is how little time they spend on Celeste's allegations. Instead, his history with Jenny carries the hour. They rehash all of it: how Jenny was charged with the murder of Maxine Shepard; how Jack was with Jenny on the night Maxine was killed and became her alibi; and how eventually investigators instead decided Jenny's ex-boyfriend, Alex Turner, had committed the murder. That conclusion came much too late for Jack, who had already lost his wife and reputation after his one reckless night with Jenny became public.

"He's gonna shit when he sees it's gone national," Jeff McCarthy adds, sounding only slightly more sympathetic than Frank. Like so many of Jack's relationships, his once close friendship with Jeff also suffered, albeit indirectly, because of Jack's wrongdoing.

Jeff was given the task of prosecuting Jenny' ex-boyfriend, Alex, because Jack, as a witness in the case, couldn't. After a very public trial in which Jack humiliated himself on the stand by reluctantly testifying to his tryst with Jenny, Alex was convicted. Months later, however, after both Claire and the city miraculously, if not grudgingly, accepted Jack's repentance as genuine and forgave him, he stumbled across the information that Maxine had been much more to Jenny than a disagreeable client.

Jack immediately went to Jeff with what he'd found. It was one of the most difficult things he'd ever had to do. He desperately wished for Jenny to be innocent—but he also couldn't live with the knowledge that he might be partly responsible for the conviction of a possibly innocent man. But despite Jack's pleas, Jeff made only a cursory investigation into Jenny's whereabouts. He defended his position by resorting to that typical prosecutor's defense Jack had always hated: *the jury has spoken.* And even though Jack was Jeff's boss on everything else, he had no say, no power at all, in that decision.

Knowing that Jeff didn't pursue it further because he didn't want his celebrated conviction tainted, Jack went public with the information anyway. Jeff continued to resist, objecting successfully to the defense attorney's motion for a new trial. This forced a lengthy appeal before any further investigation would ensue. It caused a rift between Jack and Jeff that still hasn't been fully repaired. Jack's not sure it ever will be; only one of them can be vindicated by the appeal.

"I actually had a reporter from CBS call me," Maria Catalona announces proudly. "He'd done his research, that's for sure. He knew I'd been there back when they first hauled Jenny in."

"What'd you tell him?" Frank asks. He reminds Jack of the tigers at the St. Louis Zoo, panting with eager anticipation as they wait for meat to be tossed into their open air enclosure.

Maria huffs. "Nothing! I wouldn't betray Jack."

Thank you, Maria.

Frank makes a grunting noise. "Why not? He'd betray you."

Jack is about to lay into him, when Frank switches back to CBS and a split screen. On the left half is a television reporter; on the right, via satellite, is none other than Jim Wolfe. Jack breaks out in a sweat. He's acutely aware of the perspiration on his forehead and at his temples. He pumps both hands into fists, opens them. Closes them, opens them. He suddenly wonders if Jenny is watching, too, and realizes he hasn't thought of her this way in a long, long time. It's not that she hasn't entered his consciousness; she has. More than he'd like, especially once Celeste started hanging around their house. But it was always with a sense of guilt and shame, not in the context of *I wonder what she's doing now.*

The reporter glances briefly at her notes as she reads through Wolfe's credentials. Graduate of the University of Missouri at Columbia journalism program. Longtime legal reporter for the *St. Louis Post-Dispatch.* Acclaimed expert on legal matters. Jack scoffs at this last claim. Since when did reporting on legal matters make one a legal expert?

"Mr. Wolfe," the reporter begins, "the story from four years ago surrounding Hilliard's affair with fellow attorney Jennifer Dodson has been widely reported." *It wasn't an affair,* Jack wants to object. *It was one time. One idiotic, life-altering time.* "Now it seems he's gotten himself entangled in another situation that calls into question, among other things, his fitness to hold office. This story, too, has been widely reported and appears to be an entirely new impropriety on his part. But you claim the two incidents are related, is that true?"

Jack clears his throat as he flips off the lights. Every face in the room turns to see him. A few of the newer assistants gasp. Frank turns off the television.

"Thank you," Jack says politely, though his expression sends Frank a different message. Frank looks unconcerned, as if he's done nothing wrong.

Jack turns the lights back on and enters the room, closing the doors behind him. People fill every available seat, so he half sits, half stands against a credenza to the left of the doors. The attorneys against the walls edge back closer to the rear of the room, giving him a wider berth.

"You can all relax. I'm not busting you for being curious." As he speaks, he tries to meet eyes with a few of them, but they lower their gaze. All except Maria, and Monica, the newest assistant prosecutor. They both give him a sympathetic smile.

"I'm going to tell you what happened. It'll be up to each of you to decide for yourselves whether to believe me or not. I can't force you to trust me. You'll have to make up your own mind based upon what you know about me." As he pauses to give everyone a moment to think about what he's said, he notices Frank roll his eyes. He waits to make sure Frank knows Jack noticed. "I'm also asking you to keep what I tell you inside this room so as not to disadvantage my defense, but just like your trust, I know I can't enforce my request of confidentiality. So I'll have to trust *you* to understand that my right to a fair trial takes precedence over your desire to gossip about this matter. It's a very natural desire and I don't fault any of you for having it, but nevertheless, I do hope you'll show the same restraint and discretion you show in all your cases."

They're beginning to relax; some nod at Jack's words.

"On Saturday night I was woken by the sound of my son and his girlfriend in our family room. They'd been drinking. My son was supposed to have taken his girlfriend home, but he was in no condition to drive, so I took her home. On Monday, Chief Matthews informed me that she'd accused me of sexually assaulting her between the time we left my house and arrived at hers. Unfortunately, her statement, together with some circumstantial evidence, didn't leave the Chief much choice about filing charges against me.

"You'll hear that the round-trip took two hours, even though her house is only about twelve miles from mine. That's true, and the reason for the delay is legitimate, one that has nothing to do with any criminal or otherwise inappropriate actions by me. I can't say more, but it will be explained at trial if it goes that far. You'll also hear that my son's girlfriend—" He stops, unsure how to word the next thing he wants to say. *Just say it. It's that simple. Look them in the eye and say it.* "—that she resembles Jennifer Dodson." Two of his senior assistants glance at each other; another tries to hide a smirk. "I think you're all aware who Jennifer Dodson is and what my connection to her was, so I won't rehash that. But yes, this young woman *does* look a lot like Ms. Dodson. I know the media will have a field day with this fact. I'll simply say this: you're all lawyers. You know how to evaluate the relevancy of this information."

Frank snorts, barely audible, but Jack hears it. He considers whether to hammer Frank right there in front of everyone or wait to do it in private. Frank has resented Jack for years, since the day Jack first set foot in the DA's office. Until then, Frank saw himself as the assistant DA most likely to succeed Earl. But Earl favored Jack from the beginning; even more so once he saw how juries favored him, too. So four years ago, when Earl gave up his position and moved to private practice, he persuaded Jack to run for DA. And Frank's never gotten over it.

Jack decides not to give him a stage.

"Obviously, this office won't be prosecuting my case. Still, I can't tell you much more just yet. But each of you should feel comfortable coming to me if you have questions. I'll answer them if I can. Otherwise, business in this office continues as usual. It's important that none of us allow this to distract us from our jobs. There are a million reasons why, but the most important one is that we owe it to the victims of the crimes we prosecute. Understood?"

Jack scans every face around the room. Most look him in the eye now, but, except for Frank, even those who won't nod in agreement. Jack knows it doesn't matter—they'll do what they're going to do—but at least he broached the subject. This is what he should have done a long time ago with respect to what happened with Jenny.

"Any questions?" They continue to stare at him; a few shake their heads. "Okay, then." He opens a door and motions them out with a forgiving grin. "Time to get back to work. You can watch the news—if you want to call it that—at home tonight."

They file out, talking quietly, but Jack hears their topics are innocuous. Almost all of them nod at him on their way out; a few of the men shake his hand and offer words of encouragement. The lone holdout, Frank, slaps the remote into Jack's hand without a word. He knows Jack will be talking to him later.

The women are even more demonstrative. Monica hugs him and says, "I'm really sorry, Jack. We know this is ridiculous." Maria is next to her. "What can we do to help you?" she asks.

"How about if you ask Beverly to bring in the administrative staff in about ten minutes so I can go through the same thing with them?"

"Sure thing." He gets a hug from her, too.

Jeff brings up the rear. He waits until the room empties before speaking.

"Jack—" he begins.

"You know, I expected it from Frank, but not from you."

He lowers his head. "You're right, and I'm sorry. We all let our curiosity come first, instead of taking the high road."

"Understood. You're not the first to get your priorities screwed up." Jack smiles a little and Jeff relaxes. "But maybe you felt it was a little bit of payback, too, huh?"

"No. You and I might disagree about the appeal, but I wouldn't wish this on anyone."

When Jeff leaves, Jack shuts the door. His curiosity gets the better of him, and for now, he's forgotten his intense desire to sleep. Sitting back against the credenza again, he aims the remote and presses the power button. A reporter in a faraway city appears on the large screen as the television comes to life. Jack watches, fascinated, as she still discusses his.

CHAPTER ELEVEN

AT JUST SHY of noon, Rebecca Chambers steps out of the shower. Her loose schedule is one of the things she loves about her job as an assistant to a private investigator. She works a lot of nights, and when she does, her boss doesn't mind if she sleeps in the next day.

Her latest boyfriend lies in her double bed waiting, watching her slip on her panties and bra with lustful eyes. He'll try to remove her clothes as soon as she gets them on, but she's not interested. They've only been dating two months and she already knows it won't last. He's good looking, but not very smart. Rebecca might not have a college education, but she has a brain, and she wants a guy who has one, also.

To avoid a confrontation, she gives him a smile as if she's as anxious to do what he wants. She figures when the time comes she'll claim she has an appointment, or maybe pre-menstrual cramps. Her cell phone rings just as she's about to return to the bathroom across the hall to apply her make-up. She smiles to herself. *Perfect timing.* Her boyfriend is thinking the opposite; he lets out a tortured sigh.

Grabbing her purse from the dresser, she gets to the phone before he does; he'd shut it off if given the chance. On the small display, she sees it's her boss.

"How'd last night go?" he asks when she answers. "Any luck?"

"No, not yet. You just gave me the assignment, Lee." She rolls her eyes for her boyfriend's benefit. "You couldn't have waited until I got to the office to ask me that?"

"Oh, honey, that's not why I called." He chuckles. "Have you seen the news this morning?"

"No."

"Turn on your television."

"What channel?"

"Take your pick, babe. Take your pick."

Rebecca started working for Lee Randolph almost six years ago when she was still in high school. The job began as a summer clerical position in his one-man office. Lee admired her work ethic so much that when fall arrived, he asked her to come in three or four days a week after school. He was an excellent private investigator, but his organizational skills left a lot to be desired. Rebecca solved the problem.

When she graduated two years later, he offered to promote her to his assistant and teach her "the tricks of the trade." She declined his first offer, not because she didn't want the promotion, but because she knew how much he relied upon her and she also knew, by declining, he'd raise his salary offer. He did, and she accepted immediately. College could wait. She was having too much fun.

The first case on which she tagged along at Lee's side was a doozy. They'd been asked to conduct surveillance on the city's newly elected DA. The client wanted to know where the DA went and who he went with. No reason was given for the request, only that discretion was of utmost importance.

Rebecca remembers Lee's loud whistle when he hung up from the first phone call with the client. "Honey," he said to her, "hold on tight. We've snagged a big one for your first lesson. And only a day after the election."

Rebecca's excitement soon diminished, because following the handsome DA proved to be a snooze. The guy led a boring life, as far as she could tell. Each day he left for work somewhere between six and eight in the morning, the only variations being an early morning jog or a stop along the way to drop off one or both of his sons at their respective schools. He spent most of his time at his office. Sometimes he left the courthouse for lunch with colleagues or to attend some function. If he went to court, which, in those early days following the election, was rare, he didn't need to leave the building.

"Just be patient," Lee kept telling her. "The client's instincts are almost always right. Sometimes it just takes a while to get the goods."

Problem was, neither Lee nor Rebecca knew exactly what "goods" they were expected to get. Their only instructions were *follow him and report back.*

As it turned out, Lee was right in one respect, but wrong in the other. The client's instincts *were* right, but it didn't take long—only a week and a day—to get the goods. And once they had them, Rebecca wasn't so sure she enjoyed her job anymore.

They'd followed the DA to the Stadium East garage, where they watched him meet a beautiful woman who, Lee confirmed to Rebecca, wasn't his wife. "She was his treasurer during the campaign," he said. "They worked together years ago at one of those silk stocking firms downtown." Rebecca and Lee observed the pair from their respective hiding spots—she through binoculars, Lee through the lens of his camera.

"He's crazy about her," she'd blurted into her walkie-talkie. "It's written all over his face."

Lee had shushed her. "Don't go soft on me, Becky."

But soft she went. How could she not, after seeing the way the DA looked at this woman? She and Lee followed them from the garage to the woman's house in Lafayette Square. Lee staked out the front, Rebecca the back. The DA stayed the night. According to Lee, another unknown man came to the door shortly after they arrived; Rebecca later learned he was the woman's ex-boyfriend. He was followed minutes later by a carry-out deliveryman. Both left soon after, the deliveryman only a moment before the ex-boyfriend.

At one fifteen in the morning, the woman emerged onto her small, covered rear deck that overlooked the alley, wearing only a man's white dress shirt. She sat on the deck with her back against a post rail, her long legs resting on the steps leading down. Rebecca remembers thinking, how cold she must be! But the woman appeared oblivious to the temperature or the gently pattering rain that made her shins glisten. She cried—powerful, wracking sobs that made Rebecca want to cry, too—and only when she'd collected herself did she go back into the house. The rest of the night passed without obvious incident. In the morning, Lee summoned Rebecca to the front where their target emerged to sit on the stoop. Later, the woman also came out, and Rebecca was surprised when they didn't speak to each other.

"They've had a tiff," Lee said.

Rebecca wasn't so sure. The look exchanged between the two lovers before the woman descended the steps and drove away in her car reflected something other than anger. Maybe Rebecca had formed too many stereotypes in her head based upon all the reports she'd read in her first two years working for Lee. Maybe she'd watched too much bad television and attributed the clichés on TV to the subjects she read about in the reports. Whatever the reason, she expected all male adulterers to be obvious cads, playboy types, and their mistresses to be loose floozies who stole other women's husbands without thought or regret. But that's not what she saw the night before in the garage, or the next morning, when the DA sat on the stoop looking utterly despondent. If she had to label what she'd witnessed, she would have called it unrequited love.

She realized she might never know, though, because once Lee reported this one sleepover, the client stopped the job. Rebecca wasn't sure whether to be upset or relieved. She felt as if a television show to which she'd become addicted had suddenly been cancelled.

Three days later, the woman—whose name Rebecca learned was Jennifer Dodson—was accused of murdering her client on the night she'd spent with the DA.

"But she didn't do it!" Rebecca had cried to Lee.

"It's not our concern."

"Lee, you can't let this go forward without saying something. How could you live with yourself if they convict her?"

"It's not our concern," he repeated. "One, we don't know the basis for the charges. She could still be involved even if she was home the whole time. Two, I promise confidentiality to my clients. I can't breach that. And neither can you, especially if you want to keep your job."

"Can't you at least talk to the client?" she begged. "Convince them to come forward with what we know?"

"It's not my place, Becky."

Rebecca finally, reluctantly, let it go.

Until a few days later, when she got an unexpected call.

At first it was like any other inquiry. A potential client, calling to ask about Lee's services. When Rebecca asked for a name, the caller hesitated.

"It's extremely important that my identity be kept confidential."

"Absolutely," Rebecca said. "Confidentiality is assured not only to those who hire us, but to everyone who inquires about our services. It's in our mission statement and in our contract. We take it very seriously. But until I know your identity, I can't tell you if I can help you. I need to ensure our agency would have no conflicts."

The line fell silent. She heard the caller take a deep breath.

"My name is Jennifer Dodson."

Stunned, Rebecca couldn't respond.

"You recognize my name, don't you?" the woman at the other end asked.

"Yes, I do."

"Then do you understand why I need my privacy?"

"Yes, I think so."

Rebecca glanced over to Lee's empty desk chair. He'd been out since early morning on a job. She didn't even know what this woman wanted, but she already knew Lee's answer. *No. The potential for conflict is too great.* The job following the new DA had ended just one week before.

Rebecca asked, "What would you want our agency to help you with?"

"You may be aware I've hired Earl Scanlon to represent me."

Rebecca murmured her acknowledgment.

"There are things . . . events . . . from my past that I think might help my defense, but I don't want to share them with anyone, even my attorney, until I've done some investigation myself. Or rather, until I've hired someone with the proper skills to investigate for me. I know I'm being somewhat cryptic, but—"

"Ms. Dodson, I'm sorry to interrupt you, but I don't think we'd be able to take this assignment."

"Why not? Isn't that what you guys do?" She spoke the next words with heavy sarcasm. "Work for the accused to counterbalance the unlimited resources of the state?"

"We're hired for many different situations," Rebecca said softly. She wanted so badly to say, *I want to help you. You have no idea how much I'd like to help you.*

"Why wouldn't you take this, then?"

"I really can't say much without breaching another client's confidentiality. Our agency recently had an assignment that is arguably related to what you're asking us to do. Simply stated, it requires us to decline your job. I know, as an attorney, you understand conflicts."

"It doesn't sound simple to me." The voice on the phone went cold. "What kind of assignment?"

"I'm not at liberty to explain that to you."

"Who was your client?"

"I'm sorry, Ms. Dodson, I can't tell you anything. I'm sure you understand."

"No, frankly, I don't. Did this other job have anything to do with the charges against me?"

"I can't—"

"My *life* is at stake here. I'm sure you're aware what punishment the state is seeking."

"Yes, I am." Rebecca closed her eyes. This wasn't right. The woman was entitled to know anything that might help her defense. "I'd be happy to refer you to another investigative agency."

"How kind of you."

"I'm sorry, ma'am. Good luck, and thank you for considering us." Rebecca replaced the handset back onto the receiver before the woman could wear her down.

A car horn sounded on Soulard St. below her window, causing her to check her computer screen for the time. It read five fifteen; rush hour had started and she was supposed to meet some girlfriends for drinks at five thirty. She quickly gathered her coat and purse. As she fumbled with the lock on the door, she stopped and stared at the phone.

She returned to the desk and checked the Caller ID. Pulling a Post-It note from its pad, she jotted down the number and tucked the note into the front pocket of her jeans.

Just in case.

Rebecca spent the next several hours listening to her girlfriends discuss such important topics as whether their earrings matched their outfits and whether they had the time and money for pedicures on Saturday. When she broached the DA, they stared at her with blank expressions. She explained who he was and they finally connected him to the television news about his lawyer friend who'd been accused of murdering her client. Rebecca quickly understood that her girlfriends equated "accused" with "guilty." Nothing she said convinced them otherwise.

By the time she bid her girlfriends goodbye, she'd ingested just enough alcohol to loosen her inhibitions and heighten her conscience.

Inside the privacy of her locked car, she pulled the small piece of paper from her pocket. In the fluorescent light of the parking lot, she read the number and dialed it on her cell phone. When the woman answered, Rebecca said without preface, "Look, we can't take the assignment, but if you meet me at our office in an hour, I'll explain why."

By the time she returned to her office, she'd decided to do more than explain. She photocopied Lee's report and made additional prints of the pictures they'd taken the night they followed the DA. When Jennifer Dodson arrived, Rebecca simply handed over a manila envelope, the contents of which required no explanation.

Not long after that late night meeting, the entire city knew about the DA's tryst with the beautiful lawyer. The charges against her were eventually dropped, and Rebecca always wondered if the information she'd given Dodson had anything to do with it. At the time, she assumed she'd never know.

Now, four years later, she perches on her bed watching the news, her mouth dropped open. Her boyfriend gave up pestering her for sex. He sits at the head of the bed eating a bowl of ice cream.

The sexual assault charges against the DA surprise her, and so does the fact that the national news has picked up the story. But neither requires her to call up long-buried memories. In the four intervening years since Lee promoted her, Rebecca hasn't forgotten that first short assignment, or her brief interaction with Jennifer Dodson a few days later. How could she, with the DA being somewhat of a local celebrity? His boyish face, with its slight dimples when he smiles, regularly shows up on the local television news. His reserved but assured voice is heard on the airwaves whenever a high profile crime hits the city. Not to mention his frequent appearances during the lead-up to his recent re-election. She was a little amazed at how well he recovered from the debacle with Jennifer Dodson, but she understands how it happened. People simply love him, despite his past bad deeds. Men envy him. They want his power, his looks, his easy way with the jurors in the courtroom. Women want to be his smart, pretty wife, or barring that, the woman who causes him to stray again. Rebecca developed a crush on him herself. She can't see his face without remembering the look he gave the Dodson woman in the garage, a look she's yet to get from any man. What woman wouldn't want a man to look at her like that? His appeal lies in the fact that, despite his abundant gifts—physically, legally, and socially—he seems innocently unaware of them. He isn't cocky. If anything, he appears at times to be slightly uncomfortable with the attention the town bestows on him, as if he doesn't deserve it.

She doesn't know if he does or doesn't.

But one thing she does know: he doesn't deserve what he's getting now.

"He's innocent," she says.

She twists to look back at her boyfriend. He's absorbed in his ice cream. "Huh?" he says, and gives her a sheepish shrug.

CHAPTER TWELVE

THE SUN DIPS into the horizon a few minutes earlier each day as the winter solstice grows nearer. By the time Jack arrives home at six, it's been dark for over an hour. The rain stopped a few hours earlier, causing the media vermin to reappear, just as they did that morning. Even though he feels, mentally and physically, it could be midnight, he's grateful for the cover of night. Maybe he should simply become a nocturnal creature for the duration of the case.

As soon as he steps into the laundry room from the garage, he hears footsteps bounding up the stairs. Michael, making his escape before his father appears. Will Claire go into hiding, too? Or will they spend the evening engaged in another exhausting argument? He detects the aroma of her homemade spaghetti sauce, and for the first time since his arrest, has an appetite. He hopes she intends to share.

In the kitchen she faces the stove. Her right hand holds a long wooden spoon and she slowly stirs the contents of the large pot in front of her, but there's no awareness associated with the movement. She had to have heard him come in, but she doesn't turn around. She's lowered every window blind in the kitchen and closed the slats. The family room drapes that frame the large windows, usually mere decoration, are unhooked and pulled shut.

He hangs his coat on a bar stool and comes up behind her. She tenses when he wraps his arms around her waist, but at least she doesn't push him away. His lips are near her left ear, her curls brush his cheek.

"I'm sorry about this morning." The spoon stops stirring. "What I said was cruel. I didn't mean it. I was lashing out because I was so upset." When she doesn't respond, he says, "Claire?"

"Do you know it's gone national?"

He's caught off guard by the question. "Yeah. I know."

When she resumes stirring, he reaches and takes the spoon from her. She sighs. He leans the spoon against the side of the pot and turns her to face him. She doesn't resist, but neither does she meet his eye.

"I don't want each of us to go through this alone. I know it's horrible for you, too."

"The phone has been ringing non-stop. After the first few calls—one of which Jamie answered—I took it off the hook. Now I'm wondering how long it will take them to figure out our cell phone numbers."

"I'm sorry." He tries to keep in mind what her father said this morning. *She might insist on sticking by you.* He hopes this was more than a mere assumption on Harley's part. "I wish I could go back to that night. I wish I'd woken you to ride with us, or called her dad to come for her—"

Claire lets out a short, weary laugh. She doesn't say anything, but he hears her thoughts nevertheless: *Why didn't you?* She's still not sure what to think, whether to believe him.

"—but I didn't, and I'm sorry." He touches her cheek and then lifts her chin so that she has no choice but to look at him. "I'd really like for us to do this together. I *need* you. We've got enough to deal with in the next few months without fighting each other, too, you know?"

She nods. For just a moment, he sees a flicker of the old Claire in her eyes, the Claire who once respected him. But he also sees something else. Regret, maybe?

She turns back to the pot. "Let's just eat, Jack."

Michael refuses to come down for dinner, so it'll be just Jack, Claire and Jamie. Jack wants to try again to talk with him, but Claire insists it would be a waste of time. "You need to give him space. You can't force him to think what you want him to think."

He wonders if she isn't speaking for herself, too.

The reporters give up for the night, so he sits with Jamie on the front porch while Claire finishes preparing the meal. Another cold front followed the rain. The air is now clear and sharp, the sky is littered with stars. Jamie holds a book of constellations on his lap and a small flashlight in his right hand to see the pages. Together they search the heavens of the Northern Hemisphere.

"Can I go to school tomorrow?" He asks the question with his face raised to the sky.

"What did mom say?"

"She said maybe. She wanted to talk to you."

"Oh." Jack has no idea what Claire told him about why he and Michael stayed home from school today, and why so many cars and vans were parked outside the house this morning and then again this evening. "Okay, I'll talk to her. I think it will be all right."

"Are you in trouble?"

Jack tries not to react. Once again, he's grateful for the dark. He keeps his face toward the sky, too, when he answers with a question of his own. "What makes you ask that?"

He shrugs. "When I was at Billy's house, I heard the TV in his family room. The news lady was talking about you."

Jack finally lowers his gaze, but even as he stares at his son, he's blinded with rage at Billy's mother. Marcia has been Claire's best friend in the neighborhood since Jack and Claire moved in more than nine years ago. Jack knows she tried to talk Claire into leaving him after what happened with Jenny. "Mrs. Edmond let you watch the news about me?"

"She didn't really know. We were in Billy's room but the door was open so we heard it."

Like hell she didn't know. Jack has the urge to march into the house and tell Claire what he just learned.

"What exactly did you hear?"

Jamie looks down at the book with the flashlight, but he's not seeing the words or diagrams. He's merely avoiding Jack's stare. And all Jack can think is, *I'm about to lose another son. That bitch across the street will do everything in her power to make sure I lose another son.*

"Never mind. You don't need to tell me if you don't want to. But no, I'm not in trouble. Someone is saying I did something bad, but that person is lying. Once the truth comes out, they won't be talking about me on the news anymore, okay?"

"Does Mom know that?"

"Does Mom know what?"

"That the person is lying? 'Cause she seemed really sad today."

Jack's throat closes. He struggles not to lose his composure. "Yeah, I think so." *I hope so.*

Jamie smiles. All he needed was confirmation from his dad. "Yeah, I think so, too." His arm shoots up. "Look! I think it's Monoceros."

Jack looks at the diagram in the book and then at the sky. He searches, but he simply can't see what Jamie sees.

Several hours later, Jack makes his way down the hall toward the master bedroom. Claire put Jamie to bed an hour ago but never came back downstairs. Jack assumes she went to bed, too. Michael has sequestered himself in the bathroom for a shower. Jack hears the water running and the rumble of the exhaust fan. As he passes Michael's bedroom, he sees his son's cell phone on the desk next to the computer.

He hesitates only a moment before making his decision.

He steps into the room and grabs the phone, presses buttons on the screen until he finds the text message history. The two most recent messages read, **gtg take a shower call u later** from Michael, and then simply, **ok**, from Celeste. Jack scrolls back further to the first messages of the evening.

> Hes home
> Whatre u gonna do?
> Idk
> Does he try to talk to u
> He will if i go downstairs
> Did u tell him u believe me

Michael doesn't answer, and the next message comes from Celeste just ten or so minutes ago.

> U there . . .
> Yea
> Whered u go
> Dinner
> Was he there
> Yea
> Oh . . what happened

Again, Michael doesn't answer the question. His next message is the one about taking a shower.

Jack hears the water shut off, followed by the scrape of the shower curtain rings as Michael pushes the curtain aside. He quickly replaces the phone where he found it.

Michael lied to Celeste. He claimed he went down to dinner, he claimed he saw his father. Even more significantly, he didn't answer her when she asked if he told Jack he believed her story. What game are they playing? What game is *Michael* playing?

Claire watches Jack enter their bedroom from over the top of her book. He stands before the dresser and unfastens his watch, digs his wallet and loose change from his pockets, and deposits all of it into a shallow tray Michael painted for him in an art class many years ago. The actions are habitual and take no thought; his eyes stare trancelike at an empty spot on the dresser as he begins to unbutton his shirt, and she wonders where he's gone to.

When he turns to the bathroom, she sees his bloodshot eyes register her presence, the fact that he's being watched. He gives her a small smile before closing the door behind him.

Claire? She's lying. You know that, don't you?

She never answered him. She never said, *yes, I know she's lying.* She sees something broken in him and she knows Celeste didn't do it.

She did.

For her own sake, she should put it back together.

* * *

He's still thinking about the text messages when he emerges from the bathroom. He's already decided he needs to see more. He also wants to see what Michael's computer might reveal, but he knows Claire will balk at the idea.

When he reaches the bed, she quickly sets her book on the nightstand and switches off her lamp.

He pulls back the covers and the motion releases the clean scent of the sheets as if they hung outside on a line to dry. He knows they didn't; the scent is artificial. He also knows the scent, artificial or not, is nonexistent in prison.

"Is it okay to turn out my light, too?" he asks, just to be sure.

She nods, but as he reaches for the lamp, she says, "Jack, wait." As badly as he needs sleep, he does as she asks. "I'm sorry, too. About this morning, about my reaction to everything. What I said was cruel, too. I just—"

"It's okay."

"I know you feel like you're been sent to a unique form of hell or something—"

He laughs a bit, despite himself.

"—and you don't need me to make it worse."

"It's okay. It's an enormous amount of stress for all of us." He thinks again of Michael avoiding Celeste's questions. "It's okay, really."

She slides deeper into the covers and motions for him to do the same. He turns out the light and they lie in the dark like two chaste nuns.

And then she surprises him, twice.

Since the night he told her about Jenny, she hasn't cuddled with him like she usually does before they go to sleep. Instead, the two of them have lain side by side, staring at the ceiling in the darkness. Sometimes, one or both of them would roll over toward their own edge of the bed. But tonight, she moves close, and he lifts his arm for her to rest her head in the hollow of his shoulder. Lying on her side, she presses the full length of her naked body against him, one leg flung over both of his. It's a nice surprise.

He's about to caress her face, to gently lift it to kiss her. But then she asks, "Have you seen her again?"

The question is the second surprise, but it's not so nice.

"No."

"Are you going to?"

Is he? He might have covered for Michael, but he won't cover for himself, not anymore.

"I don't know. I haven't decided. But if you've changed your mind, if you don't want me to, I won't."

She sighs and shifts, a burrowing-in movement that tells him she's done for the night. Ever consistent, she's asleep within minutes. He lies awake, acutely aware of what she didn't say, of the assurances he needs to hear but that she refused to give.

CHAPTER THIRTEEN

ON MONDAY MORNING, the press follows Jack during his short walk from the parking garage to the courthouse. Their numbers are smaller, but they cling to him like mongrels waiting for scraps. He made a formal statement on Wednesday after talking to his staff, but these lingering reporters must still hope for a spontaneous comment. He ignores them and instead focuses on the screen of his phone to review the day's schedule.

Once he arrives at the DA's office, he stops by the IT department and asks Nick, the office computer whiz, to come see him in fifteen minutes. He then sequesters himself behind closed doors and hits the speed dial to call his younger brother.

"Hey, Jack," Mark says when he hears Jack's voice. "How're you doing? You and Claire holding up okay?"

"We're good." He thinks they are, at least. Like he told Earl, as good as can be expected. After the brief discussion in bed on Wednesday night, Claire's anger has been replaced with resigned sadness. "But I need a big favor from you."

Jack's brother Mark works as an independent sales rep for a toy company and runs his one-man business from a home office in his basement. His house, though modest in size, is located in a residential neighborhood of Clayton, one of the tonier, inner suburbs of St. Louis known for, among other things, the number of young, urban professionals who live there. His particular neighborhood is a moment's drive from the restaurants, shops, galleries and office buildings of Clayton's downtown business district, which makes it a perfect home base for Jack's single brother.

Jack shows up at Mark's house just before lunchtime. They chat on the front porch for a good five minutes, just as they planned, and then Mark waves Jack in. The delay gives Jack's stalkers time to get a look at Mark's casual attire: sweatpants, sweatshirt, sneakers, baseball cap. Inside, Mark changes into a suit and tie similar to Jack's; Jack dons Mark's discarded sweats. The transformation is complete once Jack fits the cap on his head.

"It's scary," Jack says.

"Nah." Mark laughs. "It'd be scary if I had your gray hairs."

Jack whips the cap off and leans closer to the mirror, runs his fingers through his mostly dishwater blond hair. "What gray hairs?"

Mark laughs again, and the sound of it eases Jack's tension. He wonders why he didn't call his brother sooner.

Mark leaves first, driving Jack's car. Jack stands watching at the edge of the front window. Once he's sure the press has taken the bait, he grabs the suit he just shed and carries it with him to Mark's car in the garage. After raising the garage door and backing out enough to confirm that no one has returned, he makes his escape.

The joy of Mark's car, a Porsche 911 Carrera, infects his veins as he maneuvers from the Inner Belt into the curve of the cloverleaf leading to Highway 40. Mark sold his BMW convertible only months ago. He owned the BMW for almost seven years, a new record for Jack's thirty-six-year-old brother, who goes through cars even faster than he goes through women.

Twenty minutes later, Jack glances at his watch as he pulls into his own garage. Lunchtime traffic was light. He made it from Mark's house to home in record time, and he did it without picking up a tail.

He didn't eat much all weekend, so before climbing the stairs to Michael's room, he scarfs down a couple bites of a leftover pork chop he's found in the refrigerator. He has several hours before Claire returns home from the university. He doesn't like doing this behind her back, but she would be steadfast in her opposition to violating Michael's privacy. He has to ask himself if what he saw in Michael's text messages Wednesday night justifies what he's about to do.

He gazes around Michael's room as he waits for the computer to boot up. Dirty laundry spills out of the open closet. One closet door holds the same type of toy basketball hoop that hangs from the back of Jack's office door at work; they bought them together when Michael was eight and first showed an interest in basketball. The full-sized net in the driveway came a few months later.

Michael's bed is unmade, and the sheets look as if they haven't been washed in months. Jack notices that Michael has taken down the pictures of Celeste he had stuck to a corkboard above the bed. Did Claire ask him to? And if so, was it on her behalf, or Jack's?

He also notices that Michael has removed all of the pictures of the two of them—father and son. Most were taken some years back when Jack coached Michael's Little League baseball team. They weren't the typical team photos, with everyone standing stiffly in two rows, facing the camera. They were candids taken by the mom of a player. A professional photographer, she'd stood on the sidelines at games and captured the reckless joy and the spontaneous tears of the pint-size players and their coach. Her photos recorded a moment in Michael's life when he still worshiped his dad with awe.

Jack turns back to the screen. With the mouse in his right hand, he clicks on the icon for Michael's desktop and watches as a box appears, waiting for the user to key in a password. With his free hand, he calls Nick from his cell phone.

"Hey, Jack. You at the computer?" Nick's short greeting makes obvious he's been waiting for the call. In the few years he's worked in the IT department at the DA's office, he's shown himself to be not only a computer prodigy, but more importantly, trustworthy.

"Yeah. I'm staring at the desktop sign-in as we speak."

"Okay, hold on a sec." Jack hears tapping of a keyboard. "Look," Nick says with a sigh when he comes back, "I gotta ask you one more time before we do this, because once we're in, it's too late. Are you sure we won't compromise your ability to use whatever you might find?"

"I own the machine, Nick. It's in my house. I can't violate my own rights. Anyway, I don't represent the State in this case. I'm the defendant, remember?"

"Yeah, yeah, I know, but you lawyers always come up with creative arguments for why the regular rules don't apply. You're sure someone won't argue that your son had some sort of expectation of privacy that required a warrant, even for you?"

Jack can't help but laugh. "You're good. Maybe you should go to law school."

"I spend way too much time with you fuckers."

"Anyone can make any argument he wants. But I don't think it'd fly."

"Okay, you're the boss. Are you at the sign-in screen?"

"Yeah, I clicked on the icon, and now it wants his password."

For a moment, Nick is quiet. Then he says, slowly, "How many other icons are there?"

"Two others. Mine and Claire's. It used to be our computer."

Nick laughs. "Jack, who is the system administrator?"

"Beats me."

Nick sighs, the amused sigh of one frustrated by the ignorance of others who lack his expertise. "Click on your own icon, go into your desktop. Once you're there, click on Control Panel and then find the folder for Account Users."

Jack does as instructed. "Okay."

"Did you click on it?"

"Yeah." He checks the screen. Now he laughs, too. "Oh, I guess I am."

"That means you already have access to his files without the password. You don't need one to get in. Now, if he has his email password-protected, which he probably does, that's another story. And he might have individual files protected, too."

"I'm in."

"Let me know when you get to the email account sign-in."

"Okay, found the email. Just a second, it's slow."

"He's probably got his hard drive packed with videos and music, like most kids. They take up a lot of space and slow everything else down.

"And games," Jack adds. "He plays a lot of video games." He clicks on the email icon and, just as Nick suspected, he's prompted for a password. "I'm there."

Nick walks Jack through the necessary steps to hack into Michael's email account. In a few minutes, the inbox appears. Except for a few emails about homework assignments and others Jack would classify as junk mail, it's empty. A quick check of the "old mail" and "deleted mail" folders reveals the same thing.

"There's nothing here."

"Kids don't use email much anymore. They're into their texting and instant messaging. And Facebook, of course."

Jack gets a kick out of Nick's frequent reference to what "kids" do and don't do. He's all of twenty-three years old.

"So how do I see the instant messages? Can you get me into those? The investigators pull up those records for us all the time."

"Yeah, well, they get them from either the service provider or the company that makes the software, because most of the instant messaging programs don't save the messages. You would need to install software for that purpose."

"So you're saying I could see future messages if I get the right software, but I won't be able to see what's already been done unless I go the regular route of a subpoena to the company that makes the instant message program he's using?"

"Yeah, basically."

Jack makes a mental note to talk to Earl about a subpoena. Yet he's leery of having a subpoena issued for records that could expose not only Celeste but his son, too. "So what do you recommend?"

"Web Watcher is good. Go online and Google it. You can buy it and download it in a few minutes. You'll be able to see everything he does going forward."

Better than nothing, but Jack hoped to get a history of what's happened with Michael and Celeste these past few months. And maybe glean some clues to Celeste's state of mind.

"Don't forget, Jack," Nick says, interrupting his thoughts. "Any messages they exchanged on Facebook might still be there, if he didn't delete them. I can help you hack into that, too, but you may not even need to. He may stay signed in."

As Nick talks, Jack opens a window, types in the URL for Facebook, and sees that Nick is right. "Perfect."

"And unless he's password protected his other files," Nick continues, "you have access to them, too. My guess is, he didn't. He wouldn't see a need since he thinks his desktop is protected."

Of course. Jack exits email and minimizes Facebook to examine the subfolders in Michael's documents folder.

"Jack? You there?"

"Yeah. I'm checking the names of all the folders, trying to see if anything looks promising."

"Anything good?"

"I'm not sure yet. He's got a bunch of subfolders. Hold on." He scans the names of the subfolders. School, iTunes, CDT. "CDT" has to stand for Celeste Del Toro, doesn't it? He clicks and sees even more subfolders. Pix, Poems. *Poems? Is his son a poet?*

"Well?"

"Listen, let me hang up and look at some of these. I'll call you back if I need you, okay?"

"Sure, whatever you want. I'll be here."

Jack sets his phone on the desk without removing his eyes from the screen. He clicks on the Poems folder and finds numerous files. Most are well-known poems and one contains song lyrics to Aerosmith's "Janie's Got a Gun." One file titled "Relief" doesn't ring familiar. He double-clicks on it.

It's not a poem or song lyrics. It's a . . . what? A story? An essay? He's not sure. Yet he doesn't have to read past the first few lines to understand Michael didn't write it.

> I always lock the bathroom door behind me but I don't turn on the exhaust fan. If he comes home unexpectedly, I need to hear him.
>
> I wash my hands, and then I spread the hand towel flat across the counter next to the sink, smoothing it gently with both palms. I open the medicine cabinet and grab the rubbing alcohol and Band-Aids. I carefully set them in their assigned spots—the alcohol in the far left corner of the towel, because I need it first, and the Band-Aids on the far right. They come last. I then open the cabinet underneath the sink. The large box of cotton balls is always near the front next to the nail polish remover and the can of Scrubbing Bubbles. I retrieve a fistful of balls from the box and place them on the counter next to their partner, the rubbing alcohol. The last item on my list is the only one I really have to keep out of sight. I get down on my knees and tug at the strip of molding that connects the bottom of the cabinet to the tile floor. It doesn't really. The molding just covers the gap behind it. It gives easily, just as I've fixed it to.
>
> I stretch my arm toward the back of the space, feeling around for the small Ziploc bag where I keep my most important supply. I hate doing this. I hate to touch the floor behind the molding. The space under the counter feels dirty and I always expect a roach or something to scurry over my hand.
>
> I feel the bag way in the back, exactly where I last left it, just in case, and pull it from its dark hiding spot. In the light, I see the razor blades are still neatly wrapped in toilet tissue. After opening the bag, I set it on the bare counter—I don't want to soil

my towel with any debris from under the cabinet—and then for
the second time I wash my hands with soap and water. I dry
them on the large bath towel hanging over the shower curtain
rod.

Carefully, so I don't touch the outside of the bag, I retrieve
the wrapped blades and move them to the center of the towel.

I lower myself onto the toilet lid, take a deep breath and then
let it out. Only then am I aware how tense I was as I set up my
work space. My hands tremble as they always do, but I know
they will stop once I have the blade between my fingers and am
poised to act. The heady anticipation of the relief waiting for me
just on the other side of the cut has a way of stilling my nerves
and calming my fear.

He sits back and stares at the screen. He tries to comprehend what he's just read, and why it's on Michael's computer. He moves the cursor, clicks "File" on the toolbar, then "Properties." The document was created in October, almost five weeks ago. Celeste is the author. He can't tell when it first showed up on Michael's system, though. He doubts she wrote it while at their house; he assumes she wrote it at home and sent it to him. *Is she a cutter?* Or is this meant to be fiction?

Jack prints the document, closes it, and moves to the folder entitled "Pix." He hesitates, the cursor resting on the folder, blinking. He fears what he'll find. The lawyer in him asks whether pictures might be relevant. If he were in front of a judge, could he reasonably make the argument that he should be entitled to pictures? But the father in him doesn't care. Relevant or not, he wants to know what kind of pictures his son has on his computer.

He clicks on the folder and waits as the photo software loads. He's aware of his racing pulse and the tight nervousness in his stomach. Closing his eyes, he tries to calm himself. Whatever he finds, it can't be that bad, can it?

But nothing prepares him for what he sees when he opens his eyes.

Small photo squares form an array across the screen. Four across, four down. He blinks, he tries to swallow the emotion welling up in his throat. Otherwise he doesn't move. As much as he knows he should, he can't pull his eyes away from the woman in the pictures. In most, she gazes directly at him, smoky-eyed and eager, beckoning him to come closer. *I'm all yours*, she seems to say, her eyelids heavy and her lips slightly parted. In others, she looks away from the camera, but still posing brazenly. Most of the photos show her scantily clad in lacy attire lifted from the pages of a Victoria's Secret catalog, but in a few, she's completely nude.

His body responds even though his brain tries to send it a different message. He closes his eyes, but that only brings more attention to his physical reaction. Finally, his right hand obeys and he moves the mouse. But instead of closing the whole folder, he clicks on the first photo. It quickly expands to fill the screen.

It's Celeste. She appears older than her sixteen years, but there's no doubt the woman in the pictures is Celeste. Yet it's not Celeste that Jack sees.

It's Jenny.

The ring of his cell phone on the desk startles him. He sees that it's Claire calling. He takes a deep breath. Despite his attempt to answer with a simple *hey*, he hears the false note in his voice.

Claire doesn't notice; she gets right to business. "Can you pick up Michael today?" she asks. "The Dean called an impromptu meeting. I won't get away until late this afternoon."

Before Jack's arrest, he and Claire had agreed that part of Michael's punishment for breaking curfew was the loss of his car. Even after the full account of Michael's role that night came to light, his punishment, through mere inertia, remained the same. But Jack has noticed it's not Michael, but Claire, who suffers the punishment. If Michael can't drive, someone else has to. So far, that has been Claire. Jack wonders if she really has a meeting or if she's simply decided it's time for him to bear some of the burden.

"Sure," he agrees readily. "I'll be out and about anyway"—no need to tell her he already is—"so I'll swing by and get him."

Jack can't imagine Michael will be glad when his dad picks him up, but after what he just saw on the computer, he doesn't care. He's anxious to have a talk with his son.

Practice ends at five, but Jack shows up at four fifteen. He parks Mark's car in the lot outside the new gym and walks past the double glass doors at the main entrance. He heads instead to the single metal door at the rear, which he knows is mostly obscured by the bleachers. During the school day the door is locked from the outside, but after school the students who stay for sports prop it open with a brick so they can go in and out with ease.

Sure enough, the brick is in place. He slips into the gym undetected. For a moment he stands hidden behind the bleachers and waits until he thinks he can turn the corner and climb to the top without being seen. His chance comes when the coach hollers for the boys to gather round him for a talk. Climbing the bleachers two steps at a time, Jack quickly reaches the top. It's darker up here; he sits at the end of the highest bench with his back against the gym wall, confident he's invisible.

He watches his son. Unlike the slumped stance Michael affects at home, on the court he stands as tall as a Maasai warrior and moves as gracefully as a gazelle on the plain. He traverses from one end of the court to the other, moving from side to side to evade an opponent. He makes it look so simple that Jack wishes he could join them for a few scrimmages.

Michael's face is always tight with intensity while he plays. Today is no exception, but Jack notices that his sideline countenance is different: his usually quick smile is scant and the good-natured teasing of his teammates is non-existent.

A gaggle of shrieking young females interrupts Jack's worrying. The commotion comes from the direction of the same door Jack used. The volume grows as the girls' volleyball team emerges from the side of the bleachers into the open gym. They must have been practicing in the old gym. They head across the lacquered wood floor to the locker rooms at the south end. Several of the girls stop at the bleachers. Only then does Jack register the jumble of backpacks scattered on the lowest two benches below him. Each girl who stops digs inside her bag and checks the screen of a cell phone. As the last of the group turns the corner and enters the gym, Jack spots Celeste and the volleyball coach at the back of the bunch. He scoots back farther, pressing his back harder against the wall as if he can disappear into it, but his fears about being seen by Celeste are unwarranted. She walks past the backpacks and focuses on the basketball team. Michael's attention to his game lapses, and he waves to her. Jack doesn't hear him, but the coach must chastise Michael, because he quickly turns back to the game.

Jack relaxes only after the last of the volleyball team has disappeared into the locker room. Minutes later, the boys take off in the same direction and vanish into the boys' side. The two coaches chat as they bring up the rear and then part to follow their respective teams. Except for the distant laughing and shouting coming from the locker rooms, the gym falls silent. Jack is left alone with the backpacks. He wastes no time moving to the bottom of the bleachers. He scans the backpacks quickly. If Celeste's bag is here, he'll recognize it.

The emerald green ribbon she ties to a strap helps him locate it easily. Despite his rapid pulse that warns against doing this, he unzips the largest compartment. A clean conscience won't save him from being locked up; what he finds inside might.

He pushes past textbooks to the spiral notebooks. She has several, each a different color, and each titled by subject: Pre-Calc, History, LA, Chem, CW, Spanish, Psych. He figures it's a long shot to find anything helpful with her schoolwork, but he pulls out the LA notebook anyway and flips through a few pages. He sees pages and pages of vocabulary words and literature notes. Nothing, though, that appears to be her own creation.

Next up, the Psych notebook. But he finds more of the same: class notes about Freud, Jung, Adler, Skinner and others Jack has never heard of or forgot as soon as he graduated. He wishes he had the time to peruse the notes closely; he'd love to see what gems she's picked up from her studies. She could probably write her own psychology how-to manual: *How to Play Mind Games with the Men in Your Life.*

He has no idea what CW stands for, but he chooses it next. On the inside, he discovers the answer: CW is the acronym for Creative Writing. He finds page after page of stories, journal entries and poems.

He scans the gym. He's still alone, but he knows someone could walk in at any time. He has three choices: leave and never know what she's written, read the journal now and hope no one sees him, or take the whole thing with him. He doesn't like any of the options, but after he scans the gym one more time, he chooses one anyway.

Unlike the other notebooks in her backpack, the Creative Writing notebook has nothing to do with school. Instead, it appears to be a journal for her eyes only. Much of it reads like the musings of a melancholy amateur poet, but one post, if he assumes memoir instead of fiction, tells him immediately that *someone* has messed with her.

He came at me from behind. He tugged roughly on my hair, like I was a horse and my hair was the reins. It hurt. And afterwards, he wouldn't even look at me. Even when I started crying. He just zipped up his jeans, told me how great I was, and started the engine. He didn't say anything else, not even when he dropped me off in front of my house.

It wasn't like that at first. He started out by just kissing me. His lips were rough, and I could smell whiskey on his breath. I didn't like it, but he looked me right in the eye and told me I was beautiful, so I didn't think he'd hurt me. I thought if I just let him kiss me a minute, he'd feel like he gotten something and would leave me alone. But that's not what happened. Instead, he started to unbutton my shirt, and I tried to scoot away. All of a sudden he changed. It was like he became a different person. All of a sudden his fingers were digging into my arms and he was pushing me against the seat. I turned my head side to side so he couldn't kiss me again, but that's when he grabbed my hair. He twisted it, wrapped it around his hand so I couldn't get away. He yanked it, pulling my head back, and told me to look at him. I wouldn't at first, but he said "We can do this the easy way or the hard way" and that scared me, so I finally did what he said. I looked at him. He smiled and said, "That's better." He finished unbuttoning my shirt, and then he used a pocket knife to cut my bra. He asked me how it felt when he caressed the sides of my breasts, and if I liked it when he touched his tongue to them. I think I whimpered, I was so scared, but he liked that, when I made noise, because he encouraged me to make more. If I didn't answer his questions, or do what he said, he would start to get angry again. He stuck his finger in my mouth and told me to suck on it. It tasted salty. I'd heard that guys liked that sort of thing, and I think he did because he grinned at me, and then he grabbed one of my hands and jammed it between his legs.

> But then he slipped his hands up my skirt and asked me in a strange voice if I was ready for him. Without waiting for an answer, he slipped his finger under my panties to find out for himself, I guess. I told him no, but he wouldn't listen. His actions became faster, and his touch even rougher as he pushed my skirt up and pulled my panties off. He rolled me over and issued instructions for how I should position myself. I told him I didn't want to do it, but he kept on, and threatened me. After that, I gave up. I just gave up and let him do what he wanted.

Jesus. Jack rereads it, searching for some evidence, some assurance, that the piece is nothing more than the overactive imagination of a hormonal teenage girl. But a hormonal teenage girl with an overactive imagination would, he hopes, write about consensual sex, not rape. Because if he's sure of anything, he's sure the words in front of him describe a rape.

He's not sure why, but Jack doesn't think what he just read is about Celeste's dad, the man he originally feared was hurting her. But nothing in the journal suggests who it might be. She neglected to date the entries. Without more information, it's impossible for him to determine whether she wrote it before or after she moved to St. Louis. Even worse, it's impossible to determine whether she wrote it before or after the night he drove her home.

His first instinct, his prosecutor's instinct, is to call the abuse hotline immediately. Self-preservation kicks in, though, and he quickly understands the hotline is not an option, not yet.

Because without proof that the words he just read came first, the journal entry has the power to seal the State's case against him.

Hands trembling and sensing the opportunity is about to expire, he rips the incriminating page from its home, replaces the notebook in Celeste's backpack, and slips out the rear door.

Michael stops short as soon as he comes out of the gym and sees his uncle's car instead of Claire's minivan. To Jack's relief, Celeste isn't with Michael. He wonders why not.

"Hey," Jack says when Michael opens the door and tosses his gym bag and backpack on the floor. He plops into the passenger seat and buckles the seatbelt. "I thought you were Uncle Mark," is all Michael says, reminding Jack he still wears his brother's clothes. Michael took a shower—his hair is wet, his skin is dry and he's dressed now in jeans and a sweatshirt—but the sour odor of male, teenage sweat leaks from the gym bag and fills the Porsche. "How was practice?"

Michael pulls his phone from his back pocket and gives his full attention to the screen.

"You played—" Jack catches himself. He was about to comment on

Michael's performance, but since Jack is confident no one saw him, he thinks it's best not to tell his son he was there. It will be the first thing that comes to his mind if Celeste notices the page missing and shares the discovery with Michael, which Jack is sure she will.

"I played what?" Michael practically grunts the question with looking at Jack. His fingers rapidly work the small touchpad.

Jack can't come up with a cover fast enough, so he lets it die. Instead, he says, "Mom had a late meeting so she couldn't pick you up."

If this information interests Michael, he doesn't show it.

The ride home is short—ten minutes at most—and the closer they get, the nearer the questions Jack wants to ask come to leaving his tongue. He doesn't know when he'll next have Michael as a captive audience.

"Mike, can you put the phone down for a minute?"

Michael gives a teenage sigh, but he complies. He then reaches over, turns the radio up loud and punches at buttons to find a song he likes. Jack turns it off from the controls on the steering wheel. Another grunt from Michael.

"I want to ask you something," Jack says.

Michael simply stares forward. Jack decides he can't do this while the car's in motion, so he pulls into a small playground parking lot near their house. It's vacant; at this time of day, all the stay-at-home moms and their children are home for naps or dinner.

"Is there something you know that you're not telling me? About Celeste?" Even as he questions Michael, he thinks of Earl's warning about how his communications with his son won't be privileged.

Michael lowers his eyes.

"Remember when I asked you whether her dad was hurting her? If you knew something, you'd tell me, wouldn't you?"

"I told you, he's not hurting her." He still won't look at Jack, but at least he answered.

"Is someone else hurting her, then? Or *has* her dad or someone else hurt her?"

Michael crosses his arms.

"At least tell me if she's in any danger. For her sake, at least tell me that."

Finally, he gets a fleeting sideways glance from his son. Jack waits.

"She's *not* in danger."

It's not much; at least it buys Jack some time on the journal entry. But it certainly doesn't explain Michael's reaction to her accusations.

"Look, I know you're mad at me about all this. I know you think somehow I'm to blame. You must, because you continue your relationship with her. But have you thought through the allegations she's made against me? I mean, really thought about them logically?"

Michael sits in sullen silence.

"Let's just assume something happened between us in the car that night. Do you think it would have happened because I forced myself on her?"

Nothing.

"Michael, you don't have to answer any other question I ask you, but I want you to answer this one. Truthfully. Do you really think I'm capable of rape?"

Michael turns his face slightly toward the passenger side window, and to Jack's surprise, his son's eyes are glassy. He's having trouble holding it together. "Do you?" Jack persists. When Michael shakes his head, Jack's entire body lets go of a tension that was so enduring, he'd stopped noticing it as unusual.

"So if anything happened, it would have been consensual, right?"

Michael gives the smallest of nods.

"And if it was consensual, and you *really* believe it happened, you have every right to hate me. And I would deserve anything that happens to me. But I want you to think long and hard about what that means about her, and your relationship with her. Do you understand?"

He's not sure if Michael follows, and he doesn't want to get any more specific. He'd like to list all of Celeste's other inconsistencies, starting with her claim that she can't use birth control because she's Catholic, yet she doesn't have any problem disobeying the mandate against sex before marriage. But he's afraid to push too hard. Better to let what he's said marinate in Michael's brain for a while.

He stares at his son a bit longer, but Michael senses it and he keeps his face to the side window. As the moment stretches, he fidgets under Jack's scrutiny. Finally, in a voice devoid of emotion, he says, "Can we just go home?"

They arrive home early enough to precede the nightly media stakeout, so Jack sends Michael across the street to retrieve Jamie from Billy's house. Jack agreed to let Jamie resume his afterschool playdates at the Edmonds' only after he told Claire what Jamie said on the front porch the other night. Simply having the conversation was an accomplishment. Claire seemed skeptical that Marcia intended for Jamie to hear the television, but she tersely assured Jack that she'd ask her friend to be more careful. He wished he'd been a fly on the wall for that conversation. Or maybe not. Maybe he wouldn't want to hear what her meddling friend has to say about him.

Once Michael leaves, Jack wants to pull the torn notebook paper out of his briefcase and re-read it right then for clues, but it will have to wait. Michael and Jamie will be back before he even gets the briefcase open.

Instead, he decides to make dinner. He finds three large rib eye steaks in the refrigerator and a bag of Idaho potatoes on a shelf in the garage. He's no chef, but steak and potatoes he can manage. Claire, he hopes, will appreciate the gesture.

* * *

Claire enters the kitchen, arms overloaded with her handbag, her satchel and a bag of carryout food she picked up on the way home. She stops when she sees potatoes baking in the oven and seasoned raw meat resting on a platter, ready to be taken out to the grill. The table is set, and an open bottle of wine waits on the island next to two wineglasses and a lit candle. Even the family room looks straightened.

Jack stands on the far side of the island slicing a baguette. The candle bathes his face in warm light. Despite the exhaustion she knows he feels, he looks younger tonight than his forty years.

He gives her a tentative smile. "Hungry?"

"Yeah, I guess, but . . ." She lifts the bag to show him before placing it on the counter. She knows she should thank him for making dinner, but why didn't he call her? Why didn't he let her know he planned to do this? Stopping for food on the way home was the last thing she wanted to do tonight. "Did you get Michael?"

His smile fades. He sets down the knife. "Yeah, I got Michael. Did you think I wouldn't?"

"Where is he?" she asks instead of answering his question. "Was it okay?"

"He's upstairs, as usual. And yes, it was okay. We made it home without killing each other, if that's what you mean."

She sets her satchel and handbag on the kitchen table. "I'm heading up to change. You choose which meal we eat."

Her foot barely touches the first step when he says, "Claire? Are you okay? Did I do something wrong?"

She thinks of the reporter she dodged in the parking lot outside the law school, of the way the Dean avoids her eye in meetings, of her son who can barely stand to be in the same room with his father. She fears what will happen if Jack is convicted. She thinks of the woman who caused all this and wonders when he plans to see her next. She hates that she cares, yet she loves that he tries so hard to convince her that she doesn't need to worry. She loves *him*, and that's the problem. She knows if she loves him, she should forgive him, and she's just not sure she has. Or can.

"I'm peachy, Jack. Just peachy."

CHAPTER FOURTEEN

THE NEXT MORNING, in the acceleration lane for I-70, Jack gives the Porsche gas and the two-seater explodes onto the interstate like a horse out of the gate. He turns on the radio and searches for music, but all he finds are morning talk shows and traffic and weather reports. He flips it off. He doesn't want to discover they're talking about him.

He tries not to think about where he's heading, or why. Last week, when Claire asked if he planned to see Jenny again, his answer was honest. He hadn't made up his mind about what to do, whether to help her. Even whether he'd listen to her anymore. Part of him fears Claire might be right about Jenny being a drug.

He wonders briefly whether to find a pay phone and call Jenny to let her know he might come by. He doesn't remember the name of her motel, but she gave him a cell phone number to reach her. He didn't want anything connecting them, so when he programmed the number into his phone, he identified its owner by naming it, simply, ABC.

Who was he hiding the number from anyway, he wonders, when he did that? Not Claire. Claire knew what he might do. Claire would say that she knew all along what he would do, and as he crosses the Blanchette Bridge into St. Charles, he realizes he is already doing it.

He knocks on the motel room door. It's the metal kind, hard, and cold from the freezing air.

It seems he's stood there a while. His watch reads nine fifteen. He's about to knock again and give up if there's no answer the second time when, at the edge of the drapes, he sees a light turn on. The silence is dense; he doesn't even hear footsteps. He notices the peephole and looks down. And then he hears the chain being unhooked, the deadbolt being unlocked.

The door opens and she stands there in gold Mizzou sweatpants that ride low on her hips and a white T-shirt, sans bra, just short enough to give him a glimpse of her brown belly. She rubs at her face and then combs through tousled hair with her fingers. She's barefoot. When she looks at him with lazy eyes and gives him a crooked smile, he almost collapses on the threshold. Suddenly he knows that Claire is right, because the sight of Jenny this way weakens his knees and sends a wave of heat through his body like an addict's first hit after a long abstinence. Showered and dressed and made up, she's beautiful, striking. But this way, sleepy and vulnerable and warm—he imagines that her naked skin, fresh from bed, is still warm under the clothes—it's all he can do not to scoop her up and carry her back to it. And then climb in beside her.

"I woke—" His voice is a bit hoarse, as if he's been smoking. He clears his throat and swallows, starts again. "I woke you. I'm sorry."

She shrugs, a "no worries" shrug. She stares at him and he stares back. Last week, he felt so in control; *she* needed *him*. Suddenly, it seems, the tables have turned.

"So," she says, tilting her head slightly, rubbing sleep from one eye, "does this mean you decided?"

She immediately sees the desire in his tired eyes. Desire so strong that he appears to be in pain from the effort of resisting it. He's trying to hide it—she sees that, too. She knows she could take a step closer, touch her lips to his, and though he might resist as he did in the tunnel, he'd eventually relent. If she put her mind to it, she could coax him into her bed, even. But she understands the power she has over him, and she has no intention of abusing it. It might satisfy her short-term desires, but it wouldn't serve either of their long-term needs.

"I'd like to see the letters," he says.

She's surprised that he came, given everything that has happened since she last saw him. But she doesn't mention it. She simply nods and motions him in. "It'll only take a second for me to get ready."

"No. I'll wait for you in the car."

"Jack, it's not necessary to keep—"

"I told Claire."

She shifts her weight to the other foot. This news surprises her, too; she didn't think he'd be so upfront with Claire. It also makes things a bit more difficult. "Okay." She crosses her arms, tucks in her hands to ward off the cold coming in through the open door.

"I told her how you stopped me in the underpass, and how I came out here, and that we went up to Hannibal and talked."

"Look, why don't you just come in? You can tell me all of this where it's warm. I'm freezing." She quickly scans the parking lot. "I don't feel too comfortable standing here, anyway." He has to realize, doesn't he, that she's watched the news, that she knows her own name has been pulled into the story about Michael's girlfriend?

"She said for me to do what I have to do, to learn the truth about you. But she asked me to tell her everything, and I promised I would."

She wants to say, *Oh, yeah? Well, good for her.* But she remains quiet, her lips tight.

"I don't want to have to tell her I was in your motel room as you got dressed, okay? So I'll wait in my car."

He starts to turn, but halts when she says, "So that's what this is all about? You asked me to tell you the truth, and I did, but you don't believe me and so now you'll help me only because you want to *learn the truth about me*?" She says the last words with heavy sarcasm.

He doesn't answer. He just stands there, looking at the ground, and then into the room behind her, at the two double beds. Her open suitcase rests on the one that hasn't been slept in. The black coat is next to it, and beyond that, her purse. The jeans, the sweater and the boots she wore to Hannibal are piled on the floor at the end of the bed. He must wonder if she left the room at all since he dropped her off last week. On the nightstand is a half glass of water, a prescription bottle, her watch, a soda cup from Steak 'n Shake. She watches his eyes sweep the room until they return to the nightstand, and she finally realizes what has caught his attention so intently.

"What's in the prescription bottle?" he asks.

"None of your goddamned business."

He almost smiles, and she remembers he always liked this about her, her smart mouth.

"It's part of the deal."

"What is?"

"If you want my help, you have to answer any question I ask you. Truthfully."

She marches over to the nightstand, grabs the bottle and flings it at him. He catches it in mid-air, surprising her with his quick reflexes. He glances at her a moment and then looks at the label on the bottle.

"Happy now, Jack?"

She pretends to be angry, but instead she's embarrassed. Like her smart mouth, she knows he also liked her apparent strength, and she's ashamed to admit to the emotional weakness she believes is evidenced by the pills in the bottle.

He meets her eye and his expression visibly softens. "Jen."

She hasn't heard him say her nickname in a long, long time. The unexpected change in his tone threatens to overwhelm her. She suddenly has an urge to tell him everything right then. But she's imagined the various reactions he might have if he knew, and if she's not careful, she'll just end up hurting him more.

She stands straighter and fights not to look away. "Give me twenty minutes."

He holds her eyes a bit longer, but still, she feels a small victory when he turns away.

He tosses the bottle onto the bed. "I'll be in the car."

* * *

"So whose car is this?" she asks. They've ridden for ten minutes in silence. He hasn't considered where to go today. He's too busy trying to ignore the musky scent that wafted in his direction when she entered the car.

"Mark's. I borrowed it."

Thanks to Claire's early attempts at matchmaking, and long before Jenny became a *persona non grata* in their lives, Jenny briefly dated Mark. Only much later did Jack realize his wife had sensed Jenny's threat early on and tried to dilute it by finding a facsimile for her.

Jenny's gaze lingers on Jack's face after he answers. When he can no longer bear it, he says, "I assume you've seen the news lately."

"Yes."

"I've tried to dodge the press, but it's becoming impossible. Mark and I traded cars yesterday, but it's only a matter of time before they figure it out. I went into work at four thirty this morning to avoid them. I knew if I waited for daylight they'd be lying in wait." He shrugs. "I'm not really sleeping, anyway, and I get more work done when I'm there alone."

"You're not worried they followed you here?"

"I'm being careful. I came while I still can."

Another minute passes before she asks, "What do you think her motivation is?" It doesn't escape his notice that she hasn't asked if it's true. Unlike Claire, Jenny knows for certain it's not. But then, Claire has more reasons to mistrust him, doesn't she?

"I don't know. That's what I keep asking myself, because I just don't get it. That night, the night she claims it happened, I caught her and Michael fooling around in our family room, and they'd been drinking. So I drove her home. I was leery of doing it, but not because I didn't trust *her*. I was afraid of appearances if someone happened to see us. And the thing is, we actually had a really good talk, you know? I never thought. . ." He takes a deep breath and sighs. Should he tell her what he found on the computer and in the notebook? He decides against it.

He feels her continued gaze and finally steals a glance. "I'm sorry," she says softly. He hears her honesty. Is she thinking what Claire thought, that it would have never happened but for what the two of them did?

A few miles later she asks, "Do you enjoy it?"

"What's that?" He keeps his eyes on the road.

"Being DA."

That's right. He'd been on the job less than two weeks when she was arrested for Maxine's murder. It was another four or five months before his life returned to normal, if he could call it that, and by then, she was long gone.

The question reminds him that she was the one who first suggested he run for DA. And she's the one who supported his decision from the beginning, and encouraged him. Unlike Claire, who really only gave him her blessing, finally, on the morning of Election Day.

He shifts in the driver's seat, feeling as if he's betrayed his wife again merely by acknowledging that truth.

"I love it," he says, speaking another truth aloud. "I really love it."

"Good." She nods like a proud mother. "That makes me happy, knowing that."

She turns and looks out the window. When he sneaks a peek at her, she wears a small, contented smile on her face.

"What's it for?" he asks.

"What?" She still faces the window.

"The medicine."

"You don't know what it is?"

He's at a stoplight now, still on 94, heading toward 40. It's been a long time since he's been out this way. He's surprised by the number of stoplights, by the proliferation of strip malls and new neighborhoods. He wonders what happened to the families who used to farm this land.

"I know what it is. Why are you taking it?"

She cuts her eyes in his direction. Raises her right arm and tugs on the sleeve of her coat to display her wrist. And the scar he noticed in Hannibal.

He reaches across and opens his hand, palm up, an invitation to give him her arm, to let him see. She has to turn in her seat, facing him, to do so. She complies, but slowly. Maybe she doesn't trust him anymore, either.

Her wrist is small, like he remembers, and warm. He wraps his hand around it easily and gently rubs the scar with his thumb. It's parallel to the length of her arm. She meant to be successful.

The car on his left moves forward and he realizes the light has changed to green. Reluctantly, he lets go of her arm and directs his attention back to the road.

After he's pulled onto 40, heading northwest, he asks, "When did you do it?"

She doesn't answer at first. Finally, "About a year after I'd been at Brian's."

"How did . . ." He's not sure how to phrase the question. "I mean, what—"

"Why I am still here?"

He nods, and says quietly, "Yeah."

"Brian thought something was up with me that morning. He said I was acting odd. He called home not long after he got to work, and when I didn't answer, he came home on his lunch hour to check on me. My mistake was in not answering the phone. I should have answered the phone.

"I was unconscious when he got there. He was afraid to call 911 because he didn't want them to come to his condo. He thought they might be able to track me that way. He knew I was worried they'd come looking for me there once they found out about Maxine." Jack notices she doesn't say "once they found out about *my connection* to Maxine." She leaves vague what, exactly, they might have found out. Is Jack reading too much into things? "He drove me to the ER."

Jack has trouble focusing on the road as she tells her story. He remembers the other story she told him, the story of her family's massacre. How a nine-year-old Jenny and eleven-year-old Brian hid in a closet while their parents and younger sister were murdered, execution-style, before their very eyes. And even though he knows she told the truth—according to the news articles he found in the old case file, they *had* been murdered just as she described—he also reminds himself how much of the story she left out. As she talks now, he tries to figure out what she's leaving unsaid in this tale. He's afraid that's all it is: a tale. A tale meant to manipulate him the way the other one did. Yet even as he has these thoughts, he's starting to understand that she didn't just leave town. If what she says is true, she almost left the earth for good. The thought scares him. So does his reaction. He's not supposed to care that much.

"He told them I was just some woman he'd found in the park near his condo." She laughs a bit, sadly. "The funny thing is, I was so messed up at that point, I probably did look homeless. When they balked because I had no insurance, he played the good Samaritan and agreed to pay for everything up front. I cursed him when I came to."

He looks over at her. She still gazes outside the window. The whole time she's been gazing out the window. He tries to remember her brother from the pictures she showed him, but all he remembers is her sister. The murdered sister with the light hair. "It was that easy to keep your identity a secret, huh? They didn't see a resemblance between the two of you?"

"We *don't* resemble each other. He takes after our dad." She doesn't need to say who she takes after. Except for her height and the thin nose, which he remembers as features of her fair-haired father, she's her Indian mother's daughter.

"So what name did you give them? Once you regained consciousness?" He feels as if he's taking her deposition.

She shifts in her seat. "You really don't trust me, do you?"

When he doesn't answer, she says, "Ayanna Patel."

"And the name of the hospital?"

She whips her head at him. "Jack, why are you doing this to me?"

"What am I doing to you?"

"Interrogating me."

The anger he felt before returns. He wants to ask her the same question: Why are you doing this to *me?*

"I don't know, Jen. Why don't you tell me? Maybe because the last time I trusted you, I found myself on the witness stand testifying in front of a crowd of people, including my wife, about the night I spent with you. I helped send a man to death row by being your alibi and now I'm not so sure he's guilty." She stares as if she just learned that he testified. But she must have known. She might have left town, but she must have followed what happened. "So forgive me for thinking perhaps I should check out your story before I believe it."

She turns back to the window, and the silence returns.

He leaves 40 at the I-70 interchange and heads due west toward Kansas City.

As he passes the Warrenton exit, she says, "Where are we going?" She sounds nervous. Does she think he'll betray her? That he'll turn her in to someone?

But he has no idea where he's going. He doesn't have a destination in mind. It's almost as if he's driving merely so they can talk, because nowhere else except the car seems private enough. Or safe enough.

"So why'd you do it?"

She gives him a curious look, and he realizes it's unclear what he's asking. Why'd she skip town? Why'd she try to commit suicide? If she thinks he doesn't believe her, he might even be asking: Why'd you murder Maxine Shepard?

"Your wrist," he says softly. "Why'd you cut your wrist?"

"Oh."

He waits, but beyond that word she doesn't speak. When he glances over at her, she's slumped in her seat. It suddenly occurs to him that whatever her reason, it might still exist, and the anti-depressants might be the only thing between her and another attempt.

If he was frightened before, now he's downright panicked.

After a quick glance in the rearview mirror, he brakes and pulls over onto the shoulder. The car comes to an abrupt stop.

"What are you doing?" She must think he's about to dump her on the side of the road, leaving her to fend for herself.

He unbuckles his seat belt and grabs both her hands. "Jen, listen to me. I'll help you any way I can, I'll do anything you want, but you have to promise me you won't try something like this again." He rubs the scar again as he talks. "Okay? Will you promise me that?"

She stares at their hands. His, hers. She watches him touch the scar.

"Jen, look at me." Reluctantly, she raises her damp eyes. "I need you to promise me that."

"Okay." She says it like a child begrudgingly agrees to do a chore. "I'm fine. I'm fine, I promise."

"No. I don't want a promise that you're fine. You might be fine today, but if something happens, or if you stop taking that medicine, you might not be fine tomorrow."

"What do you mean, if something happens?"

If they find out you're back. "Just promise that you won't try to leave this world again. No matter what. Will you promise me that?"

She studies him. He hears the word on her tongue, though she doesn't ask it. It's the same question he asked her: Why?

He can't tell her how it felt back then, when Earl first told him she'd left town. Jack had left town, too, to escape the fallout from all he'd done wrong. He took refuge at Mark's country house in the Ozarks. He'd been there several weeks when Earl showed up to tell him that Jeff needed him back in the city to testify against Alex. When Jack asked about Jenny, Earl said she was "gone," and Jack mistakenly assumed the worst. It passed in a flash—Earl immediately clarified—but however brief it might have been, Jack remembers despair so intense he hurt physically.

"Jenny, please."

"Okay. Okay, I promise." Suddenly she takes back her hands. "Jack!"

He twists to look. "Oh, shit." A police cruiser is pulling up behind them. It's a state patrol. The lights on top are flashing, but the siren is silent.

"Your seatbelt," Jenny says and Jack almost laughs. If the trooper recognizes Jack, which, after the recent media coverage, he most certainly will, the seatbelt is the least of Jack's problems. But he buckles it anyway. If, miraculously, the trooper doesn't recognize him, it'll matter.

"If he asks, you don't have your ID on you, okay?"

She grabs her purse from the floor and digs through it.

"He has no right to search your purse, Jenny."

She narrows her eyes. "I *know* that. I had Constitutional Law, too, remember?" He *does* laugh this time, despite everything, because this is the sassy Jenny he remembers. If she were standing, she'd have her hands on her cocked hips. "I have a fake ID, though. I can give him that."

This admission gives him pause. She really has been using an alias.

In the rearview mirror he sees the patrolman climb from the squad car. Jack doesn't think he ran the plate yet. "What's your name again, then? I should know my passenger's name."

"Ayanna Patel."

He laughs.

"You have a problem with that?"

"It just seems that if you're trying to hide from authorities looking for a woman of part Indian descent, you wouldn't pick such an obvious name."

As the patrolman approaches on the driver's side and Jack accepts the inevitability of whatever's about to happen, Jenny sits taller and quickly ties her hair back with an elastic hairband. With a mischievous glimmer in her eye, she says, "That's exactly why I picked it. Do you know how many Patels there are? It's like the Indian version of Smith."

From the corner of his eye, Jack sees the patrolman on his left. He glances nervously at Jenny one more time and is surprised to see she's wrapped a turquoise dupatta around her head in the traditional style.

From here on out, the two of them will have to wing it.

As soon as Jack lowers the window, he sees recognition on the patrolman's face. *Damn, damn, damn.*

"Mr. Hilliard?"

"Good morning, officer."

"Trooper Smith, sir," he says with a rural twang, "pleased to make your acquaintance."

The trooper, who to Jack looks barely old enough to vote, offers his hand and Jack shakes it. Jenny suppresses a giggle at the man's name.

"Sir, you're a long way from home. Is everything okay?" He leans down and looks into the car at Jenny. "Ma'am," he says with a polite tip of his hat. Jenny smiles shyly from behind the scarf and quickly looks away. Even so, Jack worries that the trooper is staring at her too long. He tells himself he's being paranoid; the guy was probably still in high school when Jenny had her infamous fifteen minutes of fame. Yet, thanks to Celeste, her picture has been all over the news again recently.

"Everything's fine. Thanks for checking on us, though. We're on our way to Columbia to meet some folks at the university." Jack hopes that's enough. From the look of anticipation on the man's face, it's not. "A light came on, on the dash. We stopped to check it out."

The trooper glances at the dash, where nothing is lit. "Oh, okay." *To hell with him,* as Jenny would say; *it's none of his goddamned business.* He adds, "It's a beautiful car."

"Thank you. It's my brother's." Even if the trooper missed seeing Jenny's picture, he must be aware of Celeste's allegations, so Jack decides to act as if he's letting him in on a secret. "You know, trying to maintain a bit of privacy."

Trooper Smith nods respectfully. "Yes, sir, I understand. I . . . well, I'd just like you to know that I think it's crazy, what that girl has accused you of." He looks at Jenny again as he talks, as if he's embarrassed to be discussing such things in front of a woman. From the corner of his eye, Jack sees her try to keep her face out of the trooper's line of sight. She pretends to be busy in her purse. "Well," he continues, "I wouldn't be doing my job if I didn't warn you, it's dangerous to park on the shoulder like this. We've had a number of fatalities where cars parked on the side of the highway were rear-ended by inattentive motorists."

No shit, Jack wants to say. As if he hasn't seen enough traffic fatalities in his job to last him a lifetime. "Of course. We were just about to take off when we saw you."

Suddenly Jenny speaks, but Jack doesn't understand a word she says because she's speaking in a foreign language. He can tell from the lilt at the end that the

unintelligible words were supposed to form a question. Trooper Smith looks
from her to Jack, apparently expecting him to translate.

To Jenny, Jack says, "Yes, in a moment. Everything is fine. He's just
checking to make sure we don't need help." He turns to the trooper and gives
him a wink and a knowing smile. "She needs to use a restroom."

Trooper Smith steps back. "Well, don't let me hold you up any longer, sir."
He leans down once more to see Jenny better. "Nice to meet you, ma'am."
Frowns. "I'm sorry, I don't think I caught your name."

Jack's gut wrenches.

She gives him a demure smile, and to Jack's surprise, she speaks the next
words with a thick Indian accent. "Ayanna Patel. Pleased to meet you, too."

Once the window is sealed, she bends at the waist and howls with laughter,
pushing the scarf back with one hand and covering her mouth with the other.
Jack watches her, his tension easing into relief, a grin growing on his face. He
shakes his head at her antics and pulls away from the shoulder. Clearly, the
trooper is waiting for them to go first. He finally laughs, too.

"Oh, God, Jack, I missed you so much!"

The words comes out so spontaneously that Jack's first thought is to say *I
missed you, too,* but he catches himself in time. She seems to realize she's said
something she shouldn't have and calms down quickly. "I'm sorry, but the look
on your face when I started talking to you, it was priceless," she says, still
grinning.

"I didn't know you could speak . . . what was it?"

"Hindi." She knocks his arm playfully. "Haven't you realized yet? There are a
lot of things you don't know about me."

At those words, all frivolity that blossomed in the car from Trooper Smith's
visit wilts away, leaving in its wake a somber silence. After a while, she resumes
her vigil against the passenger side door and watches the miles go by.

Jack still doesn't know where he's going.

When he finally pulls off the highway in Kingdom City, Jenny sees the eighteen-
wheelers lined up at the truck stop and her stomach growls at the thought of
food. She dismisses the thought because she suspects he wants someplace
farther from the highway. He won't risk the truck stop, which is a frequent lunch
spot for those heading into or out of the capital in Jefferson City.

Sure enough, he drives north on 54 and then takes the business route up to
the town of Mexico, Missouri. He crawls through the streets of the small
downtown until he spots an empty diner.

"How many times are we going to do this?" she asks as he opens the door to
the tiny restaurant on Liberty Street and waves her in first.

"Do what?"

"Drive around until you find a place where we won't be seen. It'd be a lot easier if you'd just get over it and let yourself come into my room." He holds her coat as she wriggles out of it. He closes his eyes briefly, as if steeling himself against something.

"I told you. I don't want to have to tell—"

"Yeah, Claire, I know."

He scans the restaurant, making sure he recognizes no one, scouting for the most inconspicuous spot. After removing his overcoat, he rolls up his shirtsleeves. He sits down at the chosen table, and her eyes are drawn to his exposed forearms, the honey-colored hair on them. When he lifts the menu, she reaches over and slaps it onto the table. Startled, he looks up at her.

"Did you tell her you kissed me?"

"What?"

"You said you told Claire everything." She shrugs as if it's the most basic of questions. In her opinion, it is. "Did you tell her you kissed me in the underpass?"

A muscle twitches in his neck and she wants to touch it. She knows underneath the shirt and the trousers his entire body is tense from her question. She feels a selfish satisfaction at her ability to do this to him, but whatever pain she inflicts on him she suffers, too. She feels a craving so strong it hurts.

Defiantly, he picks up the menu again and stares at the words in front of him. "I didn't kiss you. You kissed me."

She picks up her own menu. "I'll take that as a no."

After they place their orders, Jack asks for the letters. He's worried that during the drive here, he became too soft, too friendly. He wants to remind her of the purpose of their get-together.

She pulls a plastic bag from her purse and hands it over. The letters, envelopes and all, are inside. To avoid leaving prints, he puts on his gloves before taking them out. All three are addressed to "Jennifer Dodson" at her Lafayette Square home; all were forwarded to her brother's condo in Chicago. None have a return address, though he didn't expect them to. All are postmarked "St. Louis" with a 63130 zip code. *The University City area*, he thinks.

"I gave him power of attorney for everything," she says. "He had my mail forwarded."

Jack already knows this. It was why they'd searched for her at Brian's house first. The sender must have assumed Jenny remained in contact with her brother.

"I'd like to get copies made before I drop you back at the motel." He checks the dates of the postmarks and opens the oldest one first.

The message, typed on a plain piece of copy paper, reads, WE HAVEN'T FORGOTTEN YOU.

He looks over the top of the letter at her. She motions to the other envelopes. "Keep reading."

The second message arrived a week later. This time, the message was created from letters cut from a magazine. He almost laughs. The craftsmanship certainly doesn't seem like the work of professionals. But when he reads the message, he feels sick.

FOUR DOWN, TWO MORE TO GO.

Four being her mother, father, sister and . . . *who?* Two being Jenny and Brian?

Without a word, he slips the last letter from its home. His hands tremble as he unfolds it. The waitress interrupts with the food. She sets a salad and bowl of soup in front of Jenny. Jack remembers Jenny as an enthusiastic eater; she never counted calories like so many other women he knew. He loved that about her. The small meal surprises him.

The waitress places his cheeseburger and fries on the table. Unless the third letter is more heartening—and he doubts that—he won't be able to eat.

The last message, to his surprise, is handwritten in pencil. The author has become bold.

WE ASKED HER TO PAY UP TO PROTECT YOU AND YOUR BROTHER. SHE DIDN'T. SHE DIED. WILL YOU BE NEXT? OR SHOULD IT BE YOUR BROTHER?

A fist claws at the inside of his gut. If someone tried to extort Maxine and murdered her when she didn't accede to the demands, then an innocent man has spent the last four years on death row. *Thanks to my testimony.*

He grabs the envelope and looks at the postmark date. It was posted a little over three weeks ago.

"And this is the last one?"

She nods. He wishes he'd listened to her that very first night in the tunnel. Almost a week has passed since then and she's been all alone in an unprotected motel room.

"Can Brian contact you somehow, to let you know if others have arrived?"

Again, she nods.

"Why didn't you show these to me when we drove to Hannibal? Why have you let so much time pass? You're a sitting duck. Who's to say they haven't followed you? Who's to say they aren't watching us right now? What do—?"

"Jack, stop. No one has followed me, okay? If they knew where I was, they would have just sent the letters directly to Brian's place, right?"

Not necessarily. "Why didn't you show me these the other day?"

"You want the truth?"

The question reminds him of the one Claire posed when he asked if she trusted him. Why does everyone think he's afraid of the truth? He's made a career of getting to the truth.

"I wanted your help only if you *wanted* to help me. I didn't want you to help me simply because you were afraid *not* to."

Why *is* he helping her? He wants to know the truth—about Jenny, about Alex—but is it something more?

He thinks back to the last time he was at Jenny's house in Lafayette Square, the last time he saw her before she ran. He remembers how they fought in the kitchen; they'd both begun to crack under the pressure of their secret about to be exposed. How, without him even realizing it, she forced him to make a choice between her and Claire before the choice was forced on him. He thought he'd chosen Claire. He wonders now if somehow he'd already chosen Jenny by deciding to go home with her.

"You knew I'd help you," he says quietly. "No matter what."

"I believed so. But I needed to be sure it was for the right reasons."

"Did I pass your test?"

She smiles sadly. "With flying colors."

After an unsuccessful attempt to convince her to find a safer place to stay, he takes her back to the motel. This time, he doesn't simply drop her off in front. Instead, he accompanies her to the door and makes her wait there while he checks the small space for evidence of intruders. It's silly, but it makes him feel better to do it.

"We dodged a bullet today," he says when they trade places at the threshold. It's as if they pre-choreographed their moves to ensure they won't be in the room at the same time.

She nods; she understands he's referring to the trooper. "Maybe I should go back to Chicago. You have the letters now. There's no need for me to stay, right?" She removes her coat, releasing the scent again. "It won't be good for either of us if someone discovers I'm here."

The panic he felt in the car returns. He should be skeptical. He should ask her why she came in the first place. Why didn't she simply call him? Why didn't she simply mail copies of the letters to him? And the letters themselves are odd, too. Who would threaten someone to collect an almost three-decade old debt? But just then, he doesn't care about the answers to these riddles. He only cares that she might disappear again.

His phone vibrates against his chest. He knows from the ringtone that it's Claire, and he senses Jenny recognizes it, too, from the drive to Hannibal.

"You'd better get that," she says lightly. "We'll talk later."

She begins to close the door, but he stops it with his hand. Her expression turns intense, suddenly expectant. Does she think he might be about to finally come in, to step into the room with her and lock the door behind them? He lowers his eyes. Whether he feels guilt for having misled her, or ashamed to think she might see straight into the darkest corners of his heart, he doesn't know.

"What does it mean?" he asks.

"What does *what* mean?"

"The name. Ayanna. What does it mean?"

She won't answer unless he meets her stare. When he does, it feels like looking into the sun. He needs to look away, but she won't answer if he does. And he needs to know.

"Innocent."

Jenny carefully locks the deadbolt and slips the chain into its slot. She tosses her purse and coat onto the nearest bed and then peeks out the drapes to watch him drive away. Despite what she told him, she lives in fear of being followed, of the writer coming to make good on his threats.

After retrieving a large manila envelope from her suitcase, she sits on the opposite bed. She fingers the envelope, putting off the moment. As many times as she's looked at the contents, it's still hard.

With trembling hands she lifts the flap. The contents are slim: a handwritten note, a typed, three-page report stapled behind it, and several glossy, five by seven, color photos.

She doesn't reread the note or the report. She doesn't need to. She practically has them memorized. But the old pictures draw her back again and again. Always the pictures.

Jack sitting on the hood of her car in the parking garage, alone, waiting for her.

The two of them standing next to the car, facing each other, her hands in his.

The two of them climbing into the car. She drove, he was the passenger. They look as if they're the two unhappiest people in the world. *How ironic.*

The two of them at her front door as she unlocks it.

Her sitting on the steps of her back porch in the middle of the night, her bare legs extended beyond the roof, drenched from the rain.

Jack sitting on her neighbor's front stoop the next morning, looking even more distraught than the night before.

Jack still sitting there as she leaves, as she ignores him. It was so hard, what she did to him that morning. He had fallen asleep holding her, but when he woke, she pretended, in the cruelest move of her life, that it meant nothing. That he meant nothing. She wonders, would everything have ended differently if she hadn't turned on him? She doesn't think so. She was wrong to let him in that night, but she knows she did the right thing when she pushed him away.

She sets everything on the bed and gazes around the room. So why is she back? His life is difficult enough without her interference. She couldn't have predicted Celeste's allegations, but nevertheless, they've been made and the timing couldn't have been worse.

As if to answer her own thought, she grabs her purse and pulls out a small envelope like the others she handed him but with a more recent postmark. She unfolds the fourth letter, the one she didn't show him, the one that brought her back.

WE KNOW THE TRUTH.

When she left town four years ago, she had decided to get out of his way, his life, so he'd have a chance to repair his marriage and keep his family together. She blamed Maxine for what happened to her own family, and she was determined not to follow in her footsteps any more than she already had.

Even when she began receiving the letters, she didn't consider involving Jack. Why would she? They had nothing to do with him. They frightened her, she'd be lying if she claimed they didn't, but she can live with her own fear. She always has.

But this message—this threat, she's certain it's a threat—rises to a whole new level. Like the others, it has to potential to destroy her, but it could also destroy him, too. She can't let that happen.

If he must find out the truth, she must be the one to tell him.

CHAPTER FIFTEEN

"CLOSE THE DOOR behind you," Jack says when Dog Jefferson pokes his head in Jack's office later that afternoon. He waves him in.

In Jack's opinion, Malik "Dog" Jefferson is the best investigator in the DA's office. He's not the oldest or most experienced, but he's the most persistent, and his energy could power the lights at Busch Stadium. He grew up fatherless across the river in East St. Louis, but when a purse-snatcher stabbed and killed his mother, Dog came to Missouri to live with his older sister Lakeisha in Hyde Park. He was only sixteen.

When the police gave up looking for the assailant—Dog insisted they never really tried—he found his mission. Five months later, after skipping too much school to secretly work the case, he marched into the police station and delivered the evidence needed to make the arrest. He never returned to school.

Jack didn't know any of this when Lakeisha, who worked in the DA's office Victim Services unit, asked him to give her little brother a job to keep him off the streets. The murder, and subsequent arrest and conviction, had happened in Illinois several years back and garnered only minimal attention from the media. Only when Dog sauntered into Jack's office with a Cardinals cap on his head and a chip on his shoulder did Jack hear the story. By this time, Lakeisha's little brother wasn't so little. He was twenty years old and at least two inches taller than Jack's six feet. When Jack asked him why he'd dropped out of school, the kid spent the next forty-five minutes intricately explaining about his mother's murder and his discovery of the assailant's identity. Jack was impressed by his resourcefulness. He saw the pride behind the simmering anger and knew the kid was at a crossroads.

"Get your GED and I'll hire you as an apprentice investigator," Jack told him. Sure that Jack was putting him off, Dog uttered an expletive and left the office in a huff.

He came back six months later, diploma in hand and a smart-ass look on his face that dared Jack to keep his promise. Jack put him to work that day under the tutelage of his best investigative team. He's been fiercely loyal to Jack ever since.

Now, Dog drapes his long, slim body in one of the chairs in front of the desk, one leg over the armrest. Three years later, he still wears the same baseball cap. A chewed toothpick dangles from his mouth. His casual, streetwise demeanor belies his meteoric rise to become one of the office's top investigators. Now Dog spends much of his time mentoring others.

"What's up, Boss?"

Jack stares at him, thinking. "I need a favor." His stomach flips in protest.

"Anything."

"It's . . . personal."

Dog's eyebrows speak his confusion.

"By that I mean, it's not official business." He's hesitant. He wants Dog to understand he can turn Jack down without repercussion. "It's just something I'd like you to do for me."

"Does this have to do with that girl?"

"No." Jack takes a deep breath. "Though I might want you to help me with that, too." He rubs his face. He still hasn't had a decent night's sleep since his arrest. If he weren't so exhausted, would he be doing this? He looks Dog in the eye. "Can I trust you?"

Dog's infamous anger flares briefly. "Shit, show me some respect, man."

"If anyone finds out, we'd both lose our jobs."

Dog swings his leg off the armrest and sits properly. Jack now has the level of attention he wanted.

"Boss, you *are* my job. If they toss you out on your ass, they might as well toss me, too."

At that statement, Jack pulls out Jenny's letters.

Later, Dog walks out of Jack's office with copies of the letters in his pocket and the story of Jenny's past in his head. Jack slips his own copies into the large Black's Law Dictionary on the credenza behind his desk, but then reconsiders and moves them to a more obscure tome that hasn't been opened for years. His cell phone chimes. He glances at the lit screen and sees the word "Boss." It's Earl.

"You sitting down?" Earl asks without introduction, and Jack's stomach lurches again.

"Yeah. What now?"

"We've got a trial date."

If Jack had managed to eat his burger earlier, he'd be losing it now. "That was fast."

"I pushed for an early date. We can't let this drag out. It needs to be heard and put to bed before it completely destroys your career."

"When?"

"April 1. We've got a little over fifteen weeks to pull this together. With the holidays, it will seem shorter."

April Fool's Day.

"That's not all, Jack. I have some news you'd have welcomed a few weeks ago, but the timing couldn't be worse now."

Like a kid who plugs his ears to avoid hearing something he doesn't want to hear, Jack closes his eyes and seriously considers simply hanging up the phone. As if by doing so, he can make it all go away. "I'm listening."

"The appeals court just issued a decision on Alex's appeal. They've granted him a new trial."

"Okay." He takes a deep, cleansing breath and tries to consider the implications of this news from all angles. "Okay." His office phone will light up with calls as soon as the media learns of the decision. He'll be expected to have a response, which should, of course, be the response of one who got what he wanted. And that's exactly how he would have responded before Celeste's allegations, before Jenny returned to town. Instead, his reaction to the news is infinitely more complex, because he knows the hunt to find Jenny will resume— this time with sharpened urgency. He also knows his own obligations have become much clearer. Yet, even with this knowledge, all he wants to do is warn her. All he can think of is her answer to his question about her alias. *"Innocent."*

"Jack? Do you know where she is?"

Jack can't help but notice Earl didn't even say her name. He knows he doesn't need to.

"No." Technically, it's true. She said she might go back to Chicago, so for all he knows, she's halfway there. A lawyer's distinction, but that's what lawyers are taught to do, isn't it?

If Earl recognizes the lie of omission, he feigns otherwise. "Good. Try to keep it that way. You shouldn't even be talking to her anymore." He sighs at the other end of the line. "Shall I handle any statements to the press?"

"Yeah, for now. I'd appreciate that. No one will consider it unusual that I don't comment while Celeste's charges are pending."

"I agree. Speaking of Celeste, TC called." Just like that, Earl segues to the next item on the ever-growing list. TC is the private investigator Earl hired to work Jack's case.

"And?"

"He did some digging into the Del Toro family history. You knew her parents are divorced?"

"Yeah, the mom lives in Florida, I think."

"Right. Celeste ever tell you anything about her?"

"Not really. Why?"

"Her parents divorced when she was eight. Her mom got custody, her dad moved back to Puerto Rico. The mom did two short prison stints over the next seven years on drug related charges."

"Jesus."

"Celeste's school records reflect that she lived with her maternal grandmother during the time mom was locked up, but TC's information suggests that the reality was slightly different. Mom's boyfriend, apparently, moved in with them when the grandmother's health deteriorated. On paper, Grandma remained the temporary guardian, but in reality, the boyfriend ruled the roost. Mom's way of making sure Celeste didn't get shipped off to dad in Puerto Rico."

"How old was Celeste when the boyfriend moved in?" Jack asks. After what he read in Celeste's notebook, Earl's report is setting off alarms in his head.

"Thirteen. During Mom's second prison stay."

Thirteen. On the cusp of puberty.

There's so much Jack and Claire didn't know about this girl who attached herself to their son. He thinks of the times Michael had an Away game, and Celeste came to their house anyway and sat in the kitchen while Claire fixed dinner. Sometimes she sat at the center island and did homework; other times she helped Claire by peeling potatoes or setting the table. "It's like she'd rather be at our house than her own," Claire once remarked to Jack. At the time, Jack didn't think much of it, and Claire didn't either. They figured it was her way of loosening her father's grip.

He wonders if her attachment wasn't so much to family as it was to Claire. Did Claire sense it, even if she didn't put a name to it? Is that why she managed to ignore the physical resemblance between Celeste and Jenny? He admires his wife for her ability to bury whatever bitterness she still carried—and he now knows she carried a lot—so she could give a young woman what she needed. Yet if Celeste needed Claire, why go after Jack? As much as her attachment to Claire might make sense, her accusations against *him* are inexplicable.

Jack thinks back to the conversation with Michael after practice, how his answers told Jack only that Celeste wasn't in immediate danger. No more, no less. The son of a lawyer learns just how to answer truthfully without telling the truth, too. Jack wonders how much Michael really knows.

"So did TC find out how she ended up back with dad, and how the two of them came to live in Missouri?" he asks Earl. "Why didn't he take her to Puerto Rico?"

"He doesn't know the answer to your first question. As for Missouri, dad has a sister who lives in Fenton. The sister's husband works at Fabick, same as the dad. We're assuming the job brought him here."

"What about the boyfriend? What did he find out about the boyfriend?"

"He's still working on that. I'll keep you updated when he learns more."

Yet if the boyfriend is the culprit in Celeste's journal, why did she express such fear of her father? Was she simply a teen afraid of a parent's wrath, and Jack blew it out of proportion?

"Do you think Michael can shed more light on Celeste's home life?" Earl asks.

"Probably, if he'd talk to me. But those chances are slim." Jack decides not to tell Earl about Celeste's journal or the files on the computer until after he has a chance to run them by Claire. "Like you said, I'll have to be careful how I approach it so it doesn't come back to bite me at trial. But I'll try." He'll also dig a bit more on the computer. "What do I have to lose?"

CHAPTER SIXTEEN

THE NEWS OF Jack's trial date and Alex's appeal causes renewed but short-lived media attention. A few reporters lingered at the house on and off throughout the week, but they finally packed up their gear and left when none of the Hilliard family appeared on the front lawn for an interview. Their neighbors haven't succumbed to requests for interviews, either. Jack's not sure if they're showing loyalty to him, or to Claire, or maybe they simply don't appreciate the limelight anymore than he does. No matter the reason, he's grateful.

Late afternoon on Sunday, Claire sits in a large easy chair in the corner of the study, skimming the latest Missouri Digest update. Several years ago, over Jack's objection, she painted the room a deep red. He thought it would be too dark and overwhelm the small space. But he grew to love the warm, cozy feel the color gave the room, especially in the winter, and the two of them spent many nights there together, Jack working in front of the computer while she graded papers or, like now, caught up on new case law. But tonight, even standing at the two open French doors, the room feels suffocating.

Indeed, the atmosphere in the whole house is glacial. On Tuesday night, when Claire asked Jack what he planned to do about Jenny now that Alex's request for new trial had been granted, he didn't have an answer. He told her he'd met with Jenny that morning to see the letters and that Jenny had suggested she might return to Chicago. Claire understands that this news doesn't make his decision of whether or not to report Jenny's whereabouts any easier. Yet she didn't insist he take action, as he expected. Indeed, she seemed satisfied that Jenny might disappear again. Instead, her wrath flared Friday after Jack informed her he wouldn't spend Christmas at her parents' house. He's puzzled. He can't understand how she could expect him to go and bear her father's scorn. The two of them have carried on clipped conversations since, but most often their words consist of mere banalities of everyday life. *Do you want more roast beef? Yes, thanks. Can I help you with the dishes? No, Jamie can help me. Marcia is picking up groceries for me, do you need anything? Just some toothpaste.*

Now, the weekend is almost over and Jack still hasn't told her what he found about Celeste. He can't let it go another day.

"Claire?"

She raises her eyes but her expression is unreadable.

"Do you have a minute?" She steels herself. It's so subtle, not more than a slight tightening near her mouth. Only someone married to her as long as Jack would have noticed. In an effort to assure her he's not about to bring up Jenny again, he adds, "It's about Celeste." He doubts that topic is more welcome, though.

She nods slightly and sets the newsletter and her highlighter on the small, round table at her side. Tucking both legs up under her, sets her hands in her lap and waits.

Jack enters the room, closing the doors behind him for privacy. He sits in the desk chair and rolls it closer to her.

"I looked at some files on Michael's computer." Other than a straightening of her posture and a habitual tucking of hair behind her ear, she's still. "I wanted to see if I might find something, some clue, to Celeste's motivation."

"And?"

Her lack of objection is heartening. She doesn't approve, but even she understands some boundaries might need to be crossed, considering what's at stake.

"I've found some things she wrote—"

"On Michael's computer?"

"Yeah. Well, some of it." He reaches into his back pocket, hands her the folded papers. She unfolds them as if they're made of fragile tissue. "I'm assuming she sent the typed one to him in an email or something." When she seems to accept that theory, he continues. "The other is something she handwrote, in a journal." Claire glances up with a question in her eyes. He ignores it for now; she'll ask it outright soon enough. "They're dark. Not typical teenager dark stuff. I mean *really* dark." As she reads, Jack sees her defenses fall. She wants to be skeptical, but the words on the papers won't let her. If there was an invisible wall between them, she might have just come over to his side of it. "I also found pictures."

"Pictures of what?"

"Of Celeste."

"What kind of pictures?" She swallows hard. She doesn't need an answer; she already knows.

"They were quite explicit. More Penthouse than Playboy, if you know what I mean."

She turns back to the papers. She's not reading them again, though. She's simply upset and she doesn't know what to do. "Where did you get this?" She lifts the handwritten piece.

"You don't want to know."

"Jack." He feels the weight of her disappointment in that one word, but instead of being ashamed, he resents her self-righteousness.

"This is my life we're talking about, Claire, in case you forgot. My freedom."

"But—"

"I'll do whatever I have to do. And I refuse to apologize for it."

"Yeah, and you'll keep getting arrested. How will that ensure your freedom?" He grits his teeth and looks away.

"Don't you realize someone reading this will think it's *you* she's writing about?"

"Like you?" *Deny it, Claire. Please just deny it.* But she merely rolls her eyes, and the action disturbingly calls to mind something he once heard a psychologist say on the witness stand: *Eye-rolling in a marriage is a strong predictor of divorce.*

"I do realize that," he says, "which is why I took it. *I* know she wasn't writing about me."

"So now you're adding 'withholding evidence' to your crimes?"

"I didn't realize I'd committed any crimes." When she simply looks away, he adds, "It's not evidence if it doesn't describe what happened between us, is it?"

"So why are you showing me this?"

"Because I want to do something, but not without talking to you first."

"Go on."

"If what she's written is more than fiction, which I think it is, then I need to let someone know about it. But like you said, they'll think I'm the man she wrote about. So before I disclose it, I first want to read the instant messages Michael and Celeste send each other. I think he knows more than he lets on. I think I might find something that proves someone else—"

"You honestly believe your own son would keep things from you, knowing what might happen? Knowing you might be convicted?" She shakes her head. "Jack, you're losing it."

"You're holding the proof! What more do you need?"

"This doesn't prove anything." She holds up the papers as she talks. "What? You think because she wrote these things and posed nude, that somehow gives you a 'Get Out of Jail Free' card? You, of all people, should know better."

"No. But I damn well think it shows there's more to this than we know. That's why I want to find out what they talk about, what she's telling him." She starts to protest but Jack cuts her off. "There's a guy in IT who told me about a software program I can install on Mike's computer, but I thought you should know before I did something like that."

She suddenly flushes. "What kind of software program?"

"It's called Web Watcher."

She hands back the papers and stares at him.

"What is it?" No response. She moves her gaze to the window, but when he turns to look, nothing's there. Just the brown grass on the front lawn and the leafless trees. "What is it, Claire?"

"There's no need to install anything."

What does she mean? Does she already know something and has been withholding it?

"It's already there," she adds.

"What's already there?"

"Web Watcher."

Nothing is making sense. "On Michael's computer?"

She nods. Simply nods. She still won't look at him.

"You've been watching what he does?"

She shakes her head.

"You want to tell me what you're talking about, then?" The irritation in his voice causes her finally to meet his eye.

"It hasn't always been his computer, remember?"

It was Jack's, Claire's. It sat on the desk behind him, in the spot now taken up by the newer one they bought three years ago.

His mind pieces together the information. She knows Web Watcher is on the machine, but she denies that she's been watching Michael's activity. It can mean only one thing.

"You were watching me?"

She looks at him without responding.

"Am I right?"

Nothing, just those translucent eyes staring at him sadly. There's no anger in them. But there's no shame, either.

"Damn it, answer me. Am I right?"

She says quietly, "Yes. You're right."

"Is this computer"—he motions to the desk—"rigged, too?"

She looks down, and he takes that as a *Yes*.

Jack tries to absorb the meaning of this. He feels betrayed, though he has no right to. Not really. Her actions were merely a response to his. And yet, Claire's is a continued deception, revealed only because he stumbled upon it in his efforts to defend himself against Celeste's allegations. The anger he's tried to aim at Jenny redirects itself at Claire. His eyes take in the shrinking room. He suddenly hates the color of the walls, the deep chili pepper inexplicably transformed now, it seems, to the color of coagulated blood. He hates the chair she's sitting in, how it swallows a person. He hates the Missouri Digest on the table, the highlighter next to it. He hates the shirt he's wearing because she bought it for him. He hates the ribs that have braised in the Dutch oven all day, their tantalizing scent wafting through the house. He suddenly hates anything and everything that has her mark on it.

As if to answer his shock, she begins to talk. Her voice is flat, revealing nothing. It's impossible to tell if she's apologizing for her actions or aggressively defending them.

"I installed it when you moved back in. My dad told me about it." *Figures.* "I felt desperate to know if you really had changed. I needed to know whether you remained in contact with her. A part of me didn't believe you could stay away from her. I needed to know. It was the only way I knew to follow what you were doing. I thought if you communicated with her, it would probably be online somehow, but not from your office or on your Blackberry. That would have been too dangerous. And not emails. I knew it wouldn't be anything so easily tracked. But I—"

"I get it, Claire. You can stop. I get it."

"—watched what you did for only a year or so after you returned. He didn't think I should stop, but I realized—"

"I can't listen to this right now." He stands. He needs to go for a run.

"Where are you going?" Her tone still lacks any affect. He almost says "St. Charles" just to be petulant—but it would be more than petulant; it would be cruel. He can't fault her for what she did, especially knowing her dad pushed her into it. He simply needs time to get over it.

Once outside, he takes it slow, but he works up a sweat quickly because their neighborhood is large and quite hilly. He's seen no sign of the press. As he jogs, he listens to his iPod strapped to his arm. The music distracts him enough that he doesn't notice the car turning into the subdivision until it honks and pulls alongside him.

"Hey!" Mark yells as he lowers his passenger window. "What are you doing?"

Jack gives Mark a look that says, *Look at me. What do you think I'm doing?* Out loud, he says, "Is there something else my wife didn't tell me? I didn't know you were coming over today." His breath curls through the bitter air. Wishing he'd worn gloves, he pumps his hands to keep them from getting stiff.

Mark frowns, one eyebrow lowered in thought, not understanding the context of the question. "Surprise visit. But if it's not a good—"

"No, it's fine." At least he'll be a distraction. "Stay for dinner. She's making her famous ribs." Sarcasm creeps into his voice; he tries to check it. She did nothing he didn't deserve.

The rumble of a large SUV pulling in behind Mark causes both men to turn. The call letters KSDK are emblazoned on the side of the vehicle and a small satellite dish sits on top. *Shit.* Jack thought they'd given up on him. He's in no mood for the press. He's bound to spout off something for which, later, Earl will have his head. In seconds they'll recognize him under the black skull cap that covers his head and ears.

Quickly pulling open the passenger door, Jack slides in beside Mark.

"How'd you like to go for a Sunday drive?"

"Where?"

"Head toward the Daniel Boone Bridge. An old friend in St. Charles would love to see you."

* * *

This time Jack calls ahead from Mark's cell phone. The front desk puts him through to Room Five—Jack doesn't specify the name of the guest in the room—and without mentioning Mark, he informs Jenny that he's on his way. She's surprised to hear from him; he's relieved she hasn't skipped town again, as she warned she might.

On the drive Jack brings Mark up to date. Mark already heard on the news about the development in Alex's case, and even with his limited legal knowledge, he understands its significance. After the initial shock of learning that Jack and Jenny have been in touch, he remains wary but reluctantly accepts Jack's insistence that Claire knows everything. Jack suspects his desire to see Jenny overrides his caution.

Funny how Jenny has that effect on both Hilliards.

Standing outside the motel door, waiting for her to answer the knock, Jack feels his brother watching him.

When she opens the door and sees Mark, Jenny flings herself into his arms. Jack thought she might be upset he shared her secret with one more person; this unexpected display of affection is unnerving. She even gives Mark a kiss on the lips.

But it's Jack's hand she takes when she beckons the two of them into the room.

"Did you run here?" she jokes. Only then does Jack remember what he's wearing. To his surprise, she places her warm palm on his cheek as if touching him is the most natural thing in the world, as if Mark isn't watching. The heat surging through him feels as if she's left a burn mark. "Your cheeks are still red."

The room is neater than before. Both beds are made, the nightstand and dresser are clear save for one book next to the bed. He sees some things on the bathroom sink at the rear of the small room—makeup bottles, deodorant, toothpaste, a small cup with a toothbrush standing inside it—but they're organized and tidy. A few clothes hang neatly from the chrome rack near the sink; towels are folded on the shelf above. Her closed suitcase still rests on the unused bed.

But what he notices the most is her scent. The same scent he caught in the tunnel, the scent that marked his car and followed him home the next day. It hangs lightly in the air, just enough that it can't be ignored. Does Mark notice it, too?

"What's going on?" she asks. "Why are you two here?" She directs the questions at Jack, and in her anxious eyes he sees one more: *how much does he know?*

Jack sits next to the suitcase, while Mark sits on the other bed. She chooses a spot next to Mark, and Jack would like to think it's because she wants to maintain eye contact without Mark noticing or intercepting their signals.

Mark lifts his brow at Jack as if to second her questions.

"It occurred to me Mark could help us."

Mark smirks—he knows Jack is winging it—and Jenny simply waits for more.

"It's becoming impossible for me to go anywhere without a reporter on my tail. Driving Mark's car isn't going to cut it anymore. And now that Alex gets another bite at the apple, you've become quite the prize. If the wrong person learns you're back . . ." Jack lets the sentence drop off. He should be encouraging her to come forward, not helping her hide. But he has a better chance of learning the truth, doesn't he, if he stays close? "Mark can be our middleman. No one follows him."

She smiles at Mark. "I like that idea." And suddenly Jack wishes he hadn't suggested it. But really, if he intends to stay in contact with her, what other choice is there? It *is* a good idea. But will Mark go along?

"It's a great idea," Mark says and winks at her.

And that's when Jack knows for sure Mark smelled it, too.

Jack and Jenny explain the threats Jenny has received, and like everyone else, Mark asks why she didn't go to the police. Jenny answers the question with one of her own: "If you were me, would you contact the police?" Jack isn't surprised when Mark lets it go at that; like Jack, his desire to spend time with her trumps his skepticism. He doesn't even ask the follow-up question that Jack, Claire, and Earl asked: *Why Jack?* Jack wonders if the answer is that obvious, even to Mark.

After Jack tells Jenny about his conversation with Dog, Mark asks her innocuous questions about how she's spent the last four years. She leans against the headboard, her legs crossed like a pretzel in front of her. They act as if Jack's not in the room. He watches her, takes in every detail. She wears the same gold Mizzou sweatpants she wore the day his knock on the door woke her.

"Why don't you simply come stay at my house?" Mark asks.

"Hmm, I don't know." She pulls her knees close to her chest and hugs them. The scar on her right wrist peeks at Jack from beneath the long sleeve of her jersey.

"I second her reluctance," Jack says. "It's too risky. Someone will recognize her if she's hanging around Clayton. Too many lawyers."

"You're the only lawyer I let in my house, bro." Mark smiles a Cheshire grin. "I'm not saying she should start lunching at Napoli's. But she'll be more comfortable at my place than here."

"I just don't think it's a good idea, that's all." He glances at Jenny, but she's focused on picking at an invisible thread from her sweatpants. He has the inexplicable urge to reach over and pull her hand away. "She'll be a prisoner."

The instant he says it, he wishes he hadn't. It hits a bit too close to home for both of them.

"Better trapped at my house than in this hole."

"She gets out of 'this hole' every once in a while. She couldn't do that if she were closer to the city. And it would be even more difficult for me to meet up with her."

"Really? That's odd, because I doubt the press would think it unusual for you to visit your brother." Even though Mark's voice has its usual friendly, teasing tone, Jack hears the sarcasm. "I thought you wanted me to be the 'middleman?'"

Jenny sighs loudly. "Will you two stop it, already?" She moves to the sink, leaving a wisp of the unidentifiable scent in her wake. He can't name it. Jenny. When he smells it, the only word that comes to mind is *Jenny*.

At the counter, she lifts the various bottles until she finds the one she wants. She taps a few pills into her palm, tosses them into her mouth, and then chases them with water. When she tilts her head, her hair dips lower down her back, and the slight ripple that follows conjures unwelcome memories of his hands gripping her head, his greedy fingers clawing through her hair. With those memories come others, even more unwelcome. He rubs his face as if trying to wipe them away, but when he drops his hand, he's met by Mark's piercing scrutiny.

Jenny saves him.

"Jack, can I talk to you a minute in private?"

She moves into the small bathroom and he follows even as he sneaks a glance at the pill bottle. Only aspirin, he thinks. She motions him in, closes the door, and flips on the light switch. The exhaust fan grinds noisily.

Mark's words comparing Jenny's room to a "hole" gain power as Jack takes in the stained tub, the moldy grout in the corners of the shower, and the mildew growing at the hem of the plastic curtain. Permanent rust stains line the toilet; the seat is cracked and marred by cigarette burns. The lone towel hanging from the bar is small and threadbare.

She casually touches his arm. Even through his sweatshirt, he feels it.

"Why did you bring him here?"

He steps to the side slightly, into the towel bar, and her hand falls away.

"The real reason," she adds.

"I told you, I—"

"You said you wanted his help. He's trying, but you're fighting it. It doesn't make sense. If you don't trust him, you shouldn't have brought him here. It's one more person who—"

"You *want* to move to his house?"

"You don't want me to? You said last time you were worried about my safety here."

She's still too close to him, but he has nowhere to go. As if she senses his discomfort, she sits on the edge of the tub to put distance between them.

"I really don't care what you do, Jenny. I keep asking myself why I'm risking this at all. I should be calling Gunner."

She gives him a sad, Mona Lisa smile. "If you have to call Gunner, call Gunner. Do what you have to do."

He looks away, behind her, at the Aveda bottles tucked into the corner of the tub ledge. Despite the grunginess of her surroundings, she still spends money on expensive shampoo and conditioner. He sees a pink razor, too, and the unwelcome thoughts return again. Her smooth legs, her brown skin. The feel of her strong calf muscle under his palm. He touched ever inch of her and spent the next four years trying to forget the experience. Convinced himself that he'd succeeded.

They both know he has no intention of calling Gunner.

He reaches for the door handle.

"I won't accept his invite if that makes you feel better," she says quickly.

Why would it make me feel better? he wants to ask. *Why do you think I care one way or another?* But it's not a discussion he wants to have, especially with Mark in the next room.

"We need to get back," he says to Mark when he emerges.

Mark begins to protest, "What—"

"I need to get home for dinner."

His brother shrugs as if to say *I have no idea*, but he's looking behind Jack, and the gesture tells Jack that Jenny is behind him. He flings open the door to outside, not bothering with goodbyes.

In the car Mark gives him a long look before starting the engine.

"You brought me here for a reason," he says as he pulls onto Highway 94.

Jesus, did the two of them plan these things in advance?

"You don't think it's a good idea, to be the go-between?" Jack keeps his voice level and his eyes trained forward.

"Sure. But you didn't have the idea when you first climbed into the car. You didn't even come up with the idea until she pressed us for why we'd come. And then, once it was on the table, you rejected it. You're not making sense."

"I didn't reject the whole idea. Only the part about her moving in with you. Anyway, I knew you'd like to see her."

"That's generous of you, big brother. Just what I wanted to be—what's it called—an accessory after the fact?" He waits, but when Jack doesn't take the bait, he continues. "What'd she say to you in the bathroom?"

"She asked me why I had such an asshole for a brother."

Mark laughs. "Yeah, I'll bet she did." He shifts, and the engine revs as the sports car picks up speed. Jack wishes he were behind the wheel. "I'll tell you why you brought me." *I'm sure you will.* "You recognize you need a buffer. You know you're playing with fire, and the fact that your own wife gave you the matches makes it even harder to resist."

Staring at the lines in the road makes Jack cross-eyed, but he won't react. He refuses to react.

"She's testing you, you know."

Jack looks over. "Who, Mark? Tell me, who's testing me?"

"Claire. But now that you ask, I'd say you're being tested by Jenny, too."

"Fuck you." He turns back to the lines. A light snow falls. The flakes melt as they hit the glass.

Instead of turning onto the ramp at the point where 94 hits Highway 40, Mark drives to the commuter parking lot on the west side of the interstate. On a Sunday, the lot is empty.

"I'm about to be lectured," Jack says wearily.

Mark stops the car, cuts the ignition. He turns to face Jack, his left hand draping the steering wheel. "No. It might feel like that, but really, I just want to be completely honest with you about something."

"I thought you were always honest with me, *little brother.*"

Mark sighs. The sound softens Jack. Despite Mark's "accessory after the fact" comment, Jack knows his brother doesn't mind that he's been pulled into this mess. Rather, Mark is worried for Jack, for Claire, but there's no need. Jack won't make the same mistakes he made four years ago.

"You know how I feel about Claire," Mark begins. "She may not be a blood sister, but she's family. I'd put my life on the line for her just like I would for you."

Jack nods. He watches the cars fly by on the interstate.

"And I know you don't take lightly what you did to her. I know how hard you've tried to make everything right again, for her, for your sons. You don't talk about it, but I see it. And I admire you for that. I really do. But . . ." He takes a deep breath. Whatever he's about to say is difficult for him. "I also see that whatever existed between you and Jenny is still there."

"You don't—"

"Hey, Mr. Lawyer, let me finish, okay? Then you can argue with me." He waits until he's sure he has the floor again. "What I mean to say is . . . I know you're trying hard not to let that mistake define you. But you're so hung up on trying to be a good husband, a good father, to do what you think is the right thing . . . I don't know . . . just that maybe. . ." He lets out another, longer sigh, "maybe the right thing is to stop trying to force something that maybe shouldn't be forced anymore."

"I love my wife, Mark."

"I know you do. And I know she loves you. She wouldn't have stayed with you, otherwise. But haven't you ever asked yourself, after everything that's happened, whether it's enough? Haven't you ever wondered if both of you might be happier if—"

"No, I haven't. Because I don't have your doubts. Okay? You wouldn't know, but every marriage has its ups and downs—" Mark grunts. "But we love each other. It's enough."

"Fine. But I'll make one more point, and then I'll leave you alone." He acts as if he's doing Jack a favor, but Jack doesn't want to listen to this crap anymore. If the road leading to his house wasn't almost all interstate, he'd bolt from the car and jog home. It can't be more than ten miles. "There's something about you and Jenny. Something *between* you. It was there four years ago, and it's still there. I don't know what to call it. I don't know if it's love. I don't think it's simply lust, or desire. I believed once that's all it was, that you were thinking with your dick instead of your brain. But I don't think so anymore. She's a beauty, there's no denying that, any guy in his right mind would be attracted to her, but it's something else. A person can't be in the same room with the two of you and not notice it. It's invisible yet somehow the air is thick with it." Mark stops and Jack wonders if he's done. He's not about to ask. He's not even sure he could if he wanted to. It's an immense effort simply to keep his eyes focused on the snowflakes outside the window. "And don't kid yourself. Claire knows. She loves you too much to accept it, but she knows. As long as you continue to deny it, she will, too."

When Jack speaks, his voice is hoarse. "You've spun quite a tale, haven't you?"

"Call it whatever you want, but it's true. I love Claire like a sister. If I thought denying your feelings for Jenny was best for you two, I'd keep my mouth shut." He laughs a little. "You know, I almost envy you. If you had any balls, I *would* envy you. Some people never have that connection with another."

The last comment compels Jack to look at his brother. Is Mark, the self-professed lifetime bachelor, talking about himself?

"Just remember, Jack, both Charles *and* Diana were happier once they divorced. He stopped caring what everyone else thought and followed his heart to marry Camilla, and Diana blossomed into a new woman."

"Yeah, and then died in a tunnel." Jack scoffs. "At the risk of sounding like I agree to your version of my life—which I don't—I have to ask: I wonder how Claire would feel about what you're saying, even as you profess to love her 'like a sister.'"

Mark chuckles. "Ever the lawyer. You can't even ask a simple question without reserving your rights, can you?"

"Fuck you," Jack says again. "Just take me home."

The two men remain silent on the ride back to Jack's house. Jack's thoughts bounce around in his head like a pinball, but just like that little silver ball, they all end up in the same hole. He tries to still his mind by closing his eyes, but this only makes it worse. He finally inserts the earplugs to his iPod and pretends to concentrate on the music.

Only when Mark pulls into the driveway and Jack opens the door does Mark speak again.

"Don't tell Claire I went with you to the motel, okay? I don't want her to feel I've let her down, too."

His tone suggests that the conversation in the commuter lot never took place. Jack wonders if this is how things will be going forward. Mark has said his piece and now he'll never bring it up again. Jack hopes so.

"Look . . ." Jack sighs. "I promised to tell her everything. I mean, I didn't jog all the way there. I can't tell her I went without telling her how I got there." His earlier anger at Claire has subsided. After Mark's lecture, he's more determined than ever not to break his vow.

"Believe me, Jack, unless you went for the express purpose of solving The Case of the Mysterious Letters"—Mark makes quote marks in the air—"she won't want to know about it, anyway." *To the contrary, Mark. Purposeless visits would probably interest her the most.* "Just tell her we ran into each other as I drove in the neighborhood, and we decided to go for a beer."

"And yet you didn't bother to come in and say hello?"

He shrugs. "Time got away from me. I have to be somewhere."

Jack wonders if he's being set up. Has Mark known all along about Jenny being back? Did Claire already tell him everything?"

Christ, Claire was right. Jack *is* losing it. He mistrusts his son, a boy who's simply caught in the middle. Now he's questioning his brother's motives. No doubt paranoia has set in, but then, after Claire's admission earlier and Mark's speech, maybe it's warranted. Either way, Jack has no plans to cover for anyone again.

"Sorry. I'm not withholding information from her. So don't ask me to."

He climbs from the car and slams the door. Mark lowers the window and calls out: "So that means you'll be telling her about our conversation?" He grins, a "gotcha" grin.

"What conversation? Oh, you mean your heartfelt monologue? Yeah, if I can figure out how to explain it to her without throwing up."

Jack thinks he's finally rid of his brother. He uses the keypad to open the garage door, watching from the corner of his eye for Mark to leave. The Porsche idles, going nowhere. When the overhead door reaches the halfway mark and Jack's about to duck under it, Mark yells one last time.

"Hey, by the way, after you flew out of the room, Jenny said she'd be happy to stay at my place. I think I'll head back over to the motel now and see if I can't talk her into checking out tonight. I can already picture her in my bed." He waits a beat; the dashboard lights illuminate his smirk. "My *guest* bed, of course."

Jack imagines walking over to the car, opening the door and dragging Mark out by his hair. He wants to pummel his brother's pretty face until his nose comes out the other side of his head. He wants to decorate Mark's little blue sports car with so much blood that after he's blurry-eyed and stumbling for escape, he'll think he bought a red model.

The door from the house to the garage opens and even though Jack gives Claire a small smile—a silent *Don't worry about what happened earlier, I understand why you did what you did, we're okay*—the words for Mark are already leaving his tongue before he really registers her presence. "Go for it. Maybe you'll even get laid. But remember, if she dumped you once, she had her reasons. Which means she'll dump you again." He moves for the door and with the base of his palm, smacks the button to close the garage.

Claire looks at him, confused. He grips her head from behind and pulls her in for a kiss. At first she resists, unsure of his mood, but relents and tentatively returns the affection when he goes deeper.

When he releases her, he sees the questions in her eyes: *What's going on? And who were you talking to?* By way of explanation, he motions in the direction of the driveway and says, "Mark. Girl trouble."

She frowns, still not understanding.

"I ran into him coming into the neighborhood," he says. "We went for a beer."

Later, in bed, after Jack apologizes for his reaction to the Web Watcher, Claire promises to show him how to use the software. There's so much more they could talk about, should talk about, but she says nothing else and neither does he. With his eyes closed, he lies on his back, willing himself to sleep. Next to him, propped up against two pillows, she reads a novel.

He rolls onto his side then, facing her. He watches her—the way she twirls her hair around her finger as she reads, the way her chest rises and falls, the way she reaches for the glass of water on her nightstand without taking her eyes from the book—and tries not to think about Mark's lecture. They made it through so much worse, didn't they? There's no reason they can't make it through this.

Minutes pass. He hears a car door slam several houses down, voices. He has the urge to scoot against her, to rest his left arm across her belly, his head in the crook of her shoulder, like he used to. Her fingers would mindlessly play with his hair and caress his scalp, and his eyelids would grow heavy. If he could muster the courage to move the few inches closer, would she still do that tonight? Maybe that's all he needs, and then he could get the good night's rest he hasn't had in so long. He fixes his stare on her eyes, looking for some sign. It's been only two weeks since the night he discovered Michael and Celeste on the couch. It seems like months. The space between him and his wife has grown so wide that he hardly remembers how it was before that night, how the two of them had grown close again.

Only then does he realize she's not reading, she hasn't turned a page for some time. Her eyes are directed at the page, but she's not registering the words. With one finger he barely brushes her arm, just above the elbow, to break the trance. Her skin is cold.

"Are you okay?" he asks.

She blinks, gives the slightest nod. "I guess I'd better stop reading. It's going to be a long week." She carefully folds a corner of the page to mark her spot and sets the book aside. When she stretches to turn off the lamp, he reaches over and touches her back. She tenses but otherwise doesn't react, doesn't respond. And then it's dark.

All he wants is for her to let him press the full length of his body against hers, skin to skin. He needs something, anything, to reassure him that Mark is wrong.

"Claire?" he whispers. "Did you . . . back then, with the Web Watcher . . . did you find out what you needed to know?"

He hears her breathing. He thinks he almost hears her thinking.

"I thought so. I thought I found out my husband had come back." She inhales deeply, as if buying time while she decides whether to say more. "Now I'm wondering if he really did."

Even in the dark, she must sense his surprise. He props himself up on one elbow. "I'm right here." He brings his hand to her face and gently turns it toward him. "Hey," he says more insistently. "I'm right here." She sniffs, and he realizes she wasn't buying time. She was trying not to cry. Suddenly, unexpectedly, she's next to him, burrowing herself in close, and his hands are in her curls, gripping her head, his lips first on her forehead and, then, on her hungry mouth. Their legs twist together seamlessly, thoughtlessly, the beneficiaries of years of practice. Small, pleading sounds come from her throat and her need feeds his own appetite until he's on top of her, sliding one knee between her legs, and then another.

"Dad!"

Jack freezes at Michael's voice outside the bedroom door. Claire quickly pushes Jack away.

An impatient knock. "Some girl from your office is on the phone."

Monica, who had on-call duty for the weekend. Jack heaves a sigh. *What now?*

He slips into his robe. When he opens the door, Michael stands there, holding the phone. "Sorry," he says without meeting Jack's eye. He seems to know what he interrupted.

Jack swipes the phone from his son's hand. He knows the interruption isn't Michael's fault, yet he's still annoyed.

"Hey, Monica, what's up?" He closes the bedroom door and moves into the hall.

"Uh, Boss, I think we've got a problem."

CHAPTER SEVENTEEN

JACK PULLS UP to the curb in front of the courthouse. If they tow him tonight, he'll know for sure that someone's out to get him.

He's not alone. Several empty police cruisers also line the curb, cherry lights still flashing. At the side he sees vans from four different television stations. He wonders if the police presence outside the courthouse brought the media or if they received a tip.

It's just after eleven p.m. Except for this spectacle, the downtown streets are mostly empty, and stoplights at each intersection blink yellow. But the office buildings that tower over the Gateway Mall and Keiner Plaza glitter against the cold, night sky, alive and humming productively even approaching midnight on a Sunday. He imagines young, ambitious attorneys standing at their office windows, watching with voyeuristic pleasure. Anything's better than the tedious drafting of another contract or researching some archaic point of law.

As he steps from his car, the news crews rush toward him, shouting. He spots Earl standing safely just inside the doors and tries to jog up the courthouse steps to meet him, but the reporters and their cameramen block his passage. His eyes can't adjust fast enough to the blinding lights and flashing cameras, so he raises his hand against the glare and pushes through, relying on his other senses to reach the top. "Let him through," Earl demands. Jack moves like a mole in the direction of the voice. Earl holds open the door, and as soon as Jack's inside, he pulls it shut. Only then does Jack see the guards stationed just outside the doors to keep the media out.

"Well, at least they gave me the courtesy of doing this after hours," Jack says. The calm quip disguises his anxiety over the distinct possibility that not only are Jenny's letters about to be discovered, but so too the fact that he asked Dog to investigate them. Did the state trooper recognize her after all?

"Fuck'em," Earl says. "This is uncalled for and unprecedented." With his head down and his eyes on his phone, he starts for the elevators. Jack follows. "What the hell do they think they'll find in the DA's office?"

Jack knows the last question was rhetorical, so he answers with one of his own. "Which judge signed the warrant?" He presses the Up button since Earl is still absorbed in his device.

"Judge Lehman. I've put in my call. Everything's on hold until he hears us."

"Don't we usually argue you can't quash a search warrant in Missouri? That the remedy is a retrospective one via a motion to suppress, not prospective?"

Earl finally glances up from the screen. His look says, *Whose side are you on?* "Yes, *you* usually make that argument. I used to. But now we're on the other side. If I have any say in the matter, we'll make new law."

Making new law might help Jack's cause, but it certainly won't help the state prosecute criminals. "I'm not sure I want to—"

The sudden change in Earl's expression stops Jack. His gray eyes narrow suspiciously as if he's seeing Jack for the first time. "Are you sick?"

"No." Jack self-consciously runs his hand through his hair. "Just exhausted. I'm not sleeping."

"You look like hell."

The elevator comes to a rough stop. When the heavy doors lumber open to the foyer of the DA's office, the first person they see is Elias Walker, the special prosecutor. He's made himself comfortable in the chair behind the receptionist's desk. Like a naughty child caught red-handed, he sits up straight and adjusts his cowboy hat as Jack and Earl step out of the elevator. Three cops hover in the corner, chatting with Monica while waiting for their instructions. Chief Matthews is nowhere to be seen. Jack's not surprised. The Chief will make sure to stay as far away from this as possible.

Jack and Walker eye each other like boxers in a ring. Jack has known the identity of the attorney prosecuting his case since the day of the appointment, but this is the first time they've come face to face in sixteen years. Walker attended the same law school as Jack and Claire, in the class above them. In most instances, this would mean minimal interaction, and it wouldn't be unusual if Jack didn't remember him.

But he remembers. He never spoke to the man, but because of Claire, they know of each other well.

During the fall of Jack and Claire's first year of law school, Walker invited Claire to a Halloween party. At the time, Jack and Claire hadn't even been on their first date, though not from Jack's lack of trying. Unbeknownst to him, Walker's invitation came only days before Jack convinced Claire to picnic with him in Forest Park. They had their picnic, but Claire, feeling guilty about cancelling on Walker, still accompanied him to the Halloween party the following week. It was Walker's first and last date with Claire; the picnic was the first of many dates for Jack, who by Easter had asked her to marry him.

Except for a few dirty looks from Walker when they passed in the halls of the law school, the two men never interacted. Walker soon ceased to be on either Jack or Claire's radar. Jack didn't even know his former rival—if he could call him that—had become a DA of a rural county in upstate Missouri until he heard Walker's name announced as the special prosecutor. Even then, it didn't concern him. Certainly the man wouldn't hold Jack responsible for Claire spurning his interest all those years ago.

But now, as Walker nods slightly and regards Jack sardonically from under the rim of his ridiculous hat, Jack's not so sure.

"Elias," Earl says, and leans across the desk to shake Walker's hand. Walker's smirk fades for the exchange with Earl. Jack has the urge to remind Walker that this isn't his office and suggest that he come out from behind the desk. Instead, he quietly returns the nod and moves to the corner to greet the three cops, whom he recognizes. He hopes their loyalty to him will trump any sense of obligation to Walker.

"What's this about?" Earl asks as he reads the copy of the warrant Walker hands him. Jack, Monica and the cops listen carefully. Searching the DA's office is highly unusual. Earl isn't the only one who wants to hear the answer.

"We had a tip. I'm merely following through on it." Walker speaks out of the side of his mouth. The words are muffled by what appears to be a big wad of chewing gum.

Earl glances up at Jack; Jack shrugs and shakes his head.

"And what exactly did that tip suggest you'd find here?" Earl asks.

Walker rises, but to Jack's frustration, he segues to a half-standing, half-sitting position and plants his behind firmly on the desk. "Read the warrant. Evidence. What else?"

Jack is surprised by the speed at which Earl gets in the man's face. "Look, cowboy," he says, leaning across the desk, his voice low but menacing, "maybe you country lawyers follow a different law, but around here the Constitution still reigns, and you'd damn well better have something specific in mind when we get on the phone with the judge. This is the DA's office."

"I know exactly where I am, Mr. Scanlon." Walker's sudden formality makes clear he didn't appreciate the "cowboy" comment.

Jack can't control himself. He returns to Earl's side. "Then maybe you should show a little respect and get off the desk," he says. "Our receptionist won't appreciate having your ass all over her stuff."

Earl flashes Jack a look—*you, shut up!* But Jack's not having any. Maybe it's the fact he hasn't had a decent night's sleep since the night he took Celeste home. Maybe it's because Walker interrupted the first intimate moment Jack's had with his wife since Jenny showed up and he has no idea when he might have another. But his pent-up frustration refuses to stay contained.

"I may be the defendant in this case, Walker," he continues, purposely leaving off the honorific, "but unless and until you convict me, I'm still the DA in this jurisdiction, and this is still *my* office. *You*, on the other hand, are a mere guest. So get the hell off the desk and take a seat in the waiting area"—he motions toward the cops—"until the judge calls and gives you permission to go anywhere else."

In the weighted silence, Walker's jaw works furiously. Now that he's closer, Jack realizes it's not gum he's chewing; it's tobacco. *I dare you to spit.*

Walker stands, but he insists on the last word. "I already have permission. It's called a signed search warrant. The fact that I'm holding off on executing it is my small contribution to professionalism in the practice of law." As if he read Jack's mind, he leans over the wastebasket next to the desk and spits into it.

Earl sees that Jack is about to explode. He speaks Jack's name under his breath as if commanding a dog to stay. "Why don't you wait in your office and let me handle this?" he says.

Without taking his eyes off Elias, Jack says, "I want to be in on the call with the judge."

"I'll come get you."

"He is *not* to go to his office unaccompanied," Walker says. "You think I'm a fool?"

Jack lunges, and Earl grabs his upper arm to stop him. But Earl can't stop Jack's mouth. "What the hell are you insinuating?"

"I'm not insinuating anything. I think my meaning is clear. I don't trust you. If given the chance, you'll do anything to save your butt—including the destruction of evidence."

Jack's arm strains against Earl's grip. Earl squeezes tighter. "Don't play into it!" he whispers harshly at Jack's ear. "That's exactly what he wants."

The ringing phone startles them all. During the day, when assorted attorneys, secretaries, cops, investigators, victims and witnesses wander in and out of the lobby, the chime of the phone is simply another noise among the myriad sounds of the office. But now, in the still of the night, the volume of the ringer seems set too high.

Earl grabs the receiver. "DA's office. Earl Scanlon here." He laughs then, and Jack is certain the judge made some comment about the irony of Earl's greeting.

"We're all here, Your Honor. Mr. Walker, Mr. Hilliard, Ms. Foley, and the officers who would conduct the search. May I put you on speakerphone?"

He presses a button and replaces the receiver.

"Good evening, gentlemen, Ms. Foley." Judge Lehman's voice booms from the speaker. "Or perhaps I should say good morning? What is it, almost midnight?"

Jack can't tell if the judge's annoyance is directed at Walker for his decision to execute the warrant at this hour, or at Earl and Jack for resisting it.

"Your Honor, I apologize for the late hour," Earl says, apparently deciding to take the blame. Jack knows every move he makes is strategic. "This search warrant took us by surprise and we couldn't convince Mr. Walker to hold off until morning. We—"

"What *is* the point of this, Mr. Walker?" the judge interrupts. "I signed this warrant earlier today. Why did you wait until tonight to execute it?"

Jack resists a smile. As usual, Earl called it right.

Walker comes closer to the phone, but neither Earl nor Jack move aside to make extra room for him. He has to raise his voice to be heard, and doing so makes him sound as if he's yelling. "I'm sorry, Your Honor, but I thought it would be better to execute it after hours so as not to cause the DA's office any additional embarrassment."

Like hell, Jack thinks.

Judge Lehman must think the same thing. "Seven or eight p.m. would have achieved that," he says in a droll voice. "There was no need to wait till all parties were in bed."

Jack and Earl exchange a glance. They haven't even begun to discuss the issue at hand, and they've scored a few points with the judge.

"The officers did arrive before ten, Your Honor," Walker says, assuring him he followed the law, "but they were delayed because Mr. Hilliard's assistant wouldn't allow them to enter his private office until she'd called him. That's why I showed up, too." He adds, his voice falsely contrite, "I'm very sorry, Your Honor."

"Is that true, Ms. Foley?"

Monica starts as if she's surprised to be consulted. "Yes, Judge, that's correct."

"So what's this about?" asks the judge.

"Judge, this warrant is highly inappropriate. To search the DA's office on a tip, without anything else to suggest the tip is valid, is uncalled for. Moreover, I see nothing on the warrant that meets the threshold of specificity required by law. It's quite vague."

"Your Honor, Mr. Scanlon is being disingenuous." Walker plants his palms on the edge of the desk and leans closer to the phone. "The search isn't of the whole office, of course. Only Mr. Hilliard's private office will be searched. And the 'something else' he argues is required is obvious: Mr. Hilliard has already been charged with a crime. It's quite logical to believe his private office might contain the evidence the tip suggested."

"And what evidence does the tip—" Earl begins.

"Excuse me, I wasn't finished." Walker's fierce stare contrasts sharply with the politeness oozing from his voice. "As you know from when I appeared to obtain the warrant," he again directs his words at the judge, "Ms. Del Toro told officers she believes Mr. Hilliard took—"

Like a dog hearing a high-pitched noise, Jack's attention is suddenly heightened, but the chime of his cell phone—Claire's ringtone—distracts him. He moves away quickly so the ring won't disturb the other call and whispers "What?" a little too harshly when he answers.

"Jack, the cops are here," Claire says breathlessly. She's on the verge of tears.

"What?" he asks again, but he needs no answer. He suddenly understands the trick they played on him. They executed the warrant for the DA's office first, knowing Jack would, if not outright fight it, at least insist upon being present during the search. But Jack knows they didn't expect to find anything useful. Not here. This search was a decoy to get him out of his house. Once they lured him to the courthouse, they swooped in to execute a second warrant at his home, where they suspected the evidence they wanted would be found.

"What should I do?" she cries.

Jack tries to listen to the other phone conversation as he tries to formulate a strategy for Claire. "Hold on," he says and presses Mute in the middle of her "Wait!"

"Don't fight it," he whispers to Earl. "They're at my house, too. Buy time on that instead." He's no longer worried they'll discover Jenny's letters. The search of his office will be all for show, and therefore superficial.

The only outward sign of Earl's surprise at this news is a sidewise turn of his eyes in Jack's direction. Without missing a beat, his argument to the judge transitions to the house warrant. Jack returns to Claire. "Tell them we're on the phone with the judge and they need to wait until it's resolved," he says to her.

As she repeats this to the cops, she struggles not to cry. "Are they giving you trouble?" he asks when she comes back on the line.

"No, they're waiting, but they won't let me out of their sight."

"Did they wake the boys?"

"Yes, but I told Michael to keep Jamie in his room. They're scared."

"What time did the cops get there?" he asks. They might have showed up at the courthouse before ten, but Jack knows the ones at his house didn't arrive until later. Technically, he could force them to come back tomorrow.

"Just a few minutes ago. Right before I called you."

"Can they hear you?"

"No." Despite her answer, she lowers her voice even more. "Jack, where did you put it?"

"Don't ask me that. We don't need two disbarred attorneys in the family."

"We don't need one convicted of sexual assault, either."

It's the closest she's come to telling him she believes him.

"You couldn't do anything, anyway. Not with them watching you."

"Only because I'm letting them. They have no right to be in our house until the judge gives them the okay. I could make them stay outside."

Jack smiles. She's finally put on her attorney hat. "Hold on," he says when he sees Earl motioning him back over to the phone.

"What time did they show up at your house?" Earl asks Jack loudly so everyone, including Judge Lehman, hears.

"Claire says it was just a few minutes ago."

"Your Honor," Earl says, "there's no valid reason for a late night search. If

Your Honor signed these warrants this afternoon, they should have executed them then, or they should have waited until tomorrow. Mr. Hilliard has two children, one of whom is quite young. There's no excuse for knocking on his door late at night like this."

Elias is about to speak, but the judge beats him to it. "I tend to agree, Mr. Walker."

"But Judge—"

"Here's what I'm going to do. Despite Mr. Scanlon's arguments, I believe that both warrants meet the requirements of the law with respect to specificity. Mr. Walker has made it clear he's looking for a particular item, and the warrants state that."

"In a vague way, Your Honor," Earl inserts, and Jack just shakes his head. It's unlike Earl to persist when it's obvious the judge is issuing his decision.

Not surprisingly, the judge ignores him. "And since they arrived at Mr. Hilliard's office before ten, and Ms. Foley confirms that, I'll let them go forward with that search. But I can't abide having officers show up after hours at the home of the city's District Attorney, I don't care what he's been charged with. Not without a valid reason for a late night search. And at no time, Mr. Walker, did you mention to me today that you intended or needed this to be a late night search. Had you done so, I would have required some evidence in support of that. Do you understand what I'm saying, sir?"

"Yes, Your Honor." Walker glares at Jack, but as always, his tone to the judge doesn't reflect it.

"So I'm leaving this up to Mr. Hilliard."

Jack and Earl exchange a glance. Neither expected this.

"Mr. Hilliard? If you'd rather, you can let the officers at your house finish their job now. However, if you prefer your family to be left in peace tonight, I will order Mr. Walker to have his men come back tomorrow, during the *day*." The emphasis on "day" is for Walker. "Whatever is most convenient for you, sir."

"Thank you, Judge. I'd like to speak to my attorney before I decide, and Mrs. Hilliard, if Your Honor will indulge me a few minutes."

"Of course."

Jack and Earl move into the same conference room where Jack happened upon his entire legal staff watching the news. They leave the doors open so they see Walker and he sees them, but they're out of earshot.

"Sit tight, I'll call you back," he says to Claire, disconnecting before she argues.

"What's going on?" Earl asks.

"They're looking for something Celeste wrote. It's a description of . . ." He sighs. "It's a description of a sexual encounter. A less than loving sexual encounter by any standard, but in my opinion, a rape. It doesn't identify the man or his age, but it reads like the guy is older. I guess she's telling them she wrote it about what I supposedly did to her."

"You wanna tell me why you might have this, Jack?" His nostrils flare.

"What did they say when I was on the phone with Claire? Why do they think I have it?"

"She claimed you ripped it out of her notebook. She guessed you took it when you picked up Michael at school. She says her book bag was in the gym on the same day you were there. They confirmed with Mike's coach that you were, indeed, in the gym the day she claims."

The coach. So he did see Jack up on the bleachers. He wonders if Celeste suggested the investigators question the coach. He can't help but think she'll make a good lawyer, if indeed she was serious about her future aspirations.

"She's right. I was there, and I did rip it out of her notebook."

"Christ Almighty!" Earl scolds under his breath. "What the *hell* were you thinking?"

Jack pulls out a conference table chair and sinks into it. He hunches over, rests his forehead in one hand while he rubs his tired eyes with the other. "I don't know. I never thought she'd say anything to anyone. There was a lot of fucked up stuff in that notebook. I thought she'd be afraid of it all being exposed. It's obvious from what she wrote that someone has messed with her, but I knew if investigators got a hold of it, they'd automatically assume it was me she was writing about. It's not dated."

"I can't believe what I'm hearing. So now you're destroying evidence?"

"I didn't destroy it, nor did I plan to. I almost called the hotline when I first found it, but I knew it would be the last nail in my coffin if I didn't have some proof that it wasn't me she'd written about. Mike wouldn't answer me when I asked him if someone had hurt her. He did assure me she wasn't in any immediate danger, so I planned to turn it over after I'd searched Mike's computer."

"Mike knew about this?"

"No, I didn't tell him what I'd found. I just questioned him to see if he knew anything. I know he must, but he won't talk." He sighs. "Look, if it wasn't written about me, it's not evidence, right?"

"That's usually left to the judge or jury to decide, don't you think?"

"*She was assaulted.* Someone messed with her. A girl doesn't just write stuff like that."

"Why didn't you come to me first?"

"I didn't expect to find it. I was simply getting Michael from practice. I had to make a decision. Take it and risk her talking, or leave it and risk her showing it to someone." He shrugs. "I chose door number one and lost. She talked."

Earl finally takes a chair, too, and blows out a long stream of air while he thinks. "What do you want to do?"

Jack knows what Earl is asking. Neither will ever say it out loud, but the unspoken is understood. The judge has offered Jack an unusual gift—if he did it intentionally, Jack would rather not know—but nevertheless, he's left it up to Jack to decide whether to accept it or not.

Can the ends justify the means? Is there any outcome that justifies him destroying Celeste's writing before the cops find it? Because once that piece of paper is made public, he might as well plead guilty. It's the best evidence that someone molested her, but unless he proves she wrote it before the night he took her home, Elias will argue it's the best evidence against Jack. He will be convicted in the press if not in the courtroom.

Can the ends justify the means? He thought a lot about that question the first time he ran for office. He knew no city would elect a prosecutor who didn't support capital punishment, so he bowed to pressure from the political party bigwigs and let the voters believe he did. He allowed himself to be convinced that the good achieved in office would outweigh the lie—because if he's honest with himself, failure to put a voice to his position on the issue *was* a lie. He let himself believe the ends *could* justify the means, only to learn the harsh lesson that, despite best intentions, lies will always come back to bite you in the ass.

But what if the means contribute to the conviction of an innocent man, a clearly unjust end? What then?

"I need to talk to Claire."

"You shouldn't have to think about this," she says when he calls back. Her voice is stronger now. She evidently took the few minutes to compose herself.

He knows what he wants to do, what he *should* do. He called Claire because he was certain she'd provide the courage to do it. He thought he knew where she'd stand, because this is Claire. Claire, who always knows right from wrong. Claire, who just a few hours ago tried to make him feel like a criminal for even taking the page out of the notebook.

He must misunderstand.

"Are you there?" she demands.

"Yeah, I just . . . I'm not sure what you're saying."

"You need to do what you need to do. For yourself. For us."

Like the judge, like Earl, she won't say it out loud. But he now gets it. A fist forms in his stomach, and he feels like any minute the fist will punch its way up his throat. This isn't the same woman he's known since their first year of law school, when he spotted her across the Pit and fell hopelessly in love. Has he done this to her?

"Do you hear me?" she asks.

"Yeah, I hear you." He stares at the blank, flat screen television on the far wall, thinks about what they'll say tomorrow, all those cogs in the media machine who think they know him. Who think they know what's in his mind, his heart.

"Can you let me talk to one of the cops?"

Earl, who until this point kept his back to Jack and pretended not to eavesdrop on the conversation, turns to him. *What are you doing?* he mouths.

"Why?" Claire asks.

"Claire, please just put one of them on the phone, okay?"

She sighs a little too loudly and then calls one over. The small speaker at his ear transmits the fumblings of the phone being passed unexpectedly to another person.

"Mr. Hilliard?" an officer says tentatively.

Jack takes a deep breath. "It's in my briefcase, in our study. Mrs. Hilliard can show you."

"Uh, I . . . " he stutters. He didn't anticipate this.

"Just don't scare my kids anymore, okay? Whatever you do, please don't traumatize my kids."

He wakes the next morning fully dressed on the family room sofa. He squints to read the clock in the kitchen, winces when he sees that it's half past eight. He's already missed the meeting he likes to have with his staff every Monday morning. By the time he showers, dresses, and drives into the city, he'll also have missed a nine o'clock call with an investigator.

Last night, he arrived home just after one thirty to Claire's stubborn silence, a clear indicator he'd done the opposite of what she thought he should. Rather than spend another night lying next to her, immersed in the tension that had taken up permanent residence in their bed, he collapsed in a sleepless stupor on the couch. He has a vague memory of her calling down to him from the top of the stairs, but maybe, in a bout of hopefulness, he only imagined it.

Michael, he knows, left for his bus much earlier, but he hears the bedroom floor creak upstairs from Claire's quick footsteps. Water runs in the bathroom at the top of the steps and he hears Jamie brushing his teeth. Jack forces his aching body up from the sofa. He sees Claire left him two gifts: a full pot of freshly brewed coffee and the *Post-Dispatch*. She propped the newspaper up against an empty coffee cup placed in his usual spot on the table.

Once again, Jack has made the front page.

In an ironic twist, late last night police searched the office of St. Louis DA Jack Hilliard for evidence relating to the pending sexual assault charges against him. Police searched the Hilliard residence as well. Sources close to the case, who asked to remain anonymous, say police found a document created by Hilliard's teenage accuser that they believe may be a written account of the alleged rape of the victim by the District Attorney. Hilliard's accuser informed authorities that she believed he had stolen the document from her backpack when she left it unattended on school grounds. The special prosecutor, Elias Walker, plans to appear in court this morning to seek a restraining order against Hilliard to prohibit any further contact between the DA and the alleged victim.

No mention that Jack willingly handed the document over. Or that the police showed up at his home well after the time allowed by law. Or that the document failed to identify the male written about. Or that the document wasn't dated. Or that Jack consented to the restraining order.

He glimpses the street from a front window. A few media types lie in wait.

He thinks about what might happen if he invited them in, offered himself up for an in-depth interview, instead of waiting until trial to tell his side of the story. Or maybe he'd choose only one of them. Call Jim Wolfe and grant an exclusive. He imagines Wolfe's startled reaction to the invitation, his wide eyes made to look even larger behind the Radar O'Reilly glasses he wears. He then imagines Earl's reaction and turns for the stairs to fight his next battle.

A small suitcase rests on Claire's side of the bed, open flat like two butterfly wings. She comes out of the bathroom fully-dressed and carrying various items—a blow dryer, her hairbrush, and a make-up bag, which he knows doesn't have much make-up in it, but instead most likely holds toothpaste, a toothbrush and miniature bottles of shampoo, conditioner, and body lotion. She places everything in the suitcase, tucking the items around the clothes which have already been packed inside.

"Going somewhere?" he asks from the doorway.

"I need a few days away from this." She answers without looking at him. "Mom and I are flying to Arizona for a few days. We both want to see Sedona."

She makes her announcement as if she and her mother take off on vacation together all the time. Jack can't remember Claire ever traveling alone with Ruth except to visit relatives in Kansas City. And yet now she's leaving only days before Christmas? He wants to ask her how long they've had this in the works; she couldn't have spoken to her mom since just last night. And aren't her students in the middle of exams? Wouldn't she have had to arrange for someone to cover for her? It also doesn't escape his notice that their chosen destination is a place he and Claire always talked about visiting together. He wonders how much it will cost and then feels ashamed. He should probably be concerned that this is the first step in his wife leaving him. Instead, he agrees with her: they both need a few days away from everything. From each other.

She zips the suitcase shut and yanks it upright onto the floor. "I'll take Jamie to the bus stop on my way out, and Marcia will meet his afternoon bus and drop him with my dad for the rest of the time."

"Is there a reason he's not staying home with me?" Jack asks the question without emotion even though he's outraged by the insult.

"I think you have enough to contend with."

Jack crosses his arms over his chest, holds his tongue.

"I'll call to let you know we arrived," she says, and without another word, not even goodbye, she starts for the bedroom door, the suitcase rolling behind her.

And despite all the questions in his head, the things he wants to say, he moves aside and lets her go.

He stays home for the rest of the morning rather than battle the small crowd outside. He knows they'll abandon their posts soon enough; the story, even with fresh developments, is old enough to die quickly if they don't get a newsworthy reaction from him. Avoiding the press is a perfect excuse to hibernate and explore Michael's computer. He can't access Web Watcher without Claire, but he can read Michael's Facebook messages.

"Jesus Christ, Michael, do you ever sleep?" he mutters when he sees the many messages. Most of them reflect exchanges with Celeste, but plenty are communications with others, too.

He opens the message with the oldest date and begins reading.

His weary-eyed patience bears fruit an hour later in an early October message from Celeste to Michael, but Jack is surprised by the subject matter.

> Celeste: who's jenny?
> Michael: why?
> Celeste: people at school keep making comments about how i look like her. who is she? an old gf?
> Michael: no . . . definitely not
> Celeste: ?
> Michael: my dad cheated on my mom with her, long story --__--
> Celeste: ur dad? no way!!
> Michael: u dont even want to know
> Celeste: what happened?
> Michael: long story, cee. it happned after he was first elected. he got caught cus she got arrested 4 murdering some lady and my dad was her alibi
> Celeste: u got to b shitting me!
> Michael: i wish . . it was all over the news, google youll see
> Michael: u there . .?
> Celeste: OMG . .
> Michael: told ya
> Celeste: she does look like me O.o
> Michael: yea i guess a little, she was hot, i'll give her that ;)
> Celeste: cant believe ur parents stayed together
> Michael: yea me either
> Celeste: ur lucky
> Michael: not quite

Celeste: i mean, that they stayed together. my rents got a divorce cus
my mom fucked around a lot
Michael: ur MOM?! #usuallytheguy
Celeste: ha! they all do it . . adults are fucked up . . my moms still with
one of the douchebags!
Celeste: i hate him hes a total asshole, what kinda guy screws around
with someone whos married?
Michael: i sorta liked jenny, believe it r not, least til he fucked her. after
that, i hated her
Celeste: you knew her . . ?
Michael: yea she was friends with my rents, she even babysat me and
jamie a couple times when we were little
Celeste: damn . . . that sucks
Michael: tell me bout it
Celeste: so did she actually do it . . kill the lady?
Michael: no one knows 4 sure, its all online
Celeste: is that why u like me, mike? cus i look like her? cmon, tell the
truth ;)
Michael: lol . . trust me that would be a reason for me not to like u

Jack has always known how angry Michael was about what happened with
Jenny. Even at just shy of twelve, he understood the gravity of the betrayal. After
Claire kicked Jack out of the house, Michael assumed the role of her protector—
he insisted on accompanying her everywhere, he screened every phone call—and
in doing so, he grew up that year faster than he should have. His anger at Jack
only intensified when his parents reunited, because Jack's return to the family
knocked Michael back down in the family pecking order.

Yet seeing him discuss it with a friend gives Jack a new understanding of his
son's feelings. Michael had always liked Jenny. Even after he learned what Jack
had done, he never spoke badly of her. He heaped all his vengeance on Jack, so
it never occurred to Jack that Michael might hate Jenny, too. Yet four years have
passed and Jack feels the hot resentment buried in his messages with Celeste.

Jack watches for more discussion of Jenny, but the one conversation seems
to be it. The next messages to catch Jack's attention are ones that make clear
their relationship had become physical.

Celeste: hey babe :) what u doin?
Michael: hey :) nm just got home
Celeste: can i come over, its been a while ;) . . oh and i have good news!
Michael: nah not tonite. oh yea? whats the news
Celeste: . . . why not
Michael: hw
Celeste: i could help u :)
Michael: lol . . u hate chem. what news??

> Celeste: true, lets just say ive dropped the bait ;)
> Michael: ?
> Celeste: r plan?
> Michael: what plan
> Celeste: juris doctr lol
> Michael: what r u talking about
> Celeste: dont u remember? im just gonna call u

Jack remembers how she sat in his car so doe-eyed, insisting what she and Michael were doing on the couch was a first. He knew she was lying. Now, the *its been a while* followed by the winky face confirms it. They met at the start of the school year, and this message is from late October. *A first, my ass*, Jack thinks.

He wonders what she meant by "juris doctr." Did it have something to do with her wanting to be a lawyer? He can't imagine them talking about that, yet he didn't think he'd find a file named "Poems" on his son's computer, either. And why had she wanted to call Michael to answer his questions? What didn't she want in writing?

He opens the next message, dated the very next day.

> Celeste: heyy
> Michael: hey.
> Celeste: u still mad?
> Michael: i guess not.
> Celeste: it was just 4 fun, i thought u'd be happy
> Michael: i know
> Celeste: call me when ur in bed tonite . . i'll make it up 2 u ;)
> Michael: yea? hows that ☺
> Celeste: using my seductive voice and talents of persuasion, obvi
> Michael: :-)

What the hell, she's offering him phone sex. Jack wonders what Michael was mad about. Was it something that had occurred that day at school? Or did it have to do with the messages from the night before? Or the phone conversation that followed those messages?

The messages over the next few days are seemingly innocuous, but then Jack reads one that he thinks references Celeste's dad.

> Celeste: i fuckin hate him
> Michael: what happened?
> Celeste: don't wanna talk about it

Jack can't quite believe how skillfully she manipulates his son. She's a master. Jack wants Michael to ask, "Then why'd you bring it up?" No such luck.

Michael: aw cmon whats wrong cee
Celeste: he wont let me wear the dress i bought for homecoming
Michael: why?
Celeste: "too revealing"
Michael: i find "revealing" sexy
Celeste: lol u would
Michael: ehh, idk, i dont want other guys looking at u ;)
Celeste: ur sweet, i dont think hes worried about that, he says i'll look like a slut
Michael: he said that . .?
Celeste: yep
Michael: want me 2 beat him up? :)
Celeste: lol yea please do
Michael: wear something he likes out the door and you can change latr
Celeste: alright :)

Jack remembers the dress she wore to Homecoming, and he's not surprised by her father's reaction. Claire wanted pictures of them, so she insisted that Michael come back by the house after he picked up Celeste. Celeste walked into their house already wearing the dress, and Jack now wonders where she accomplished her quick-change act. The dress was a liquid, pale orange number that clung to her like quicksilver and plunged so far down her back they couldn't help but see the butterfly tattoo at the base of her spine. He remembers, too, being surprised by the tattoo and her lack of fear about him seeing it. He doubted her highly conservative dad was aware of it, which, given her age, would mean she'd obtained it illegally. Celeste called it right, though. Jack and Claire conferred about it later as parents, but as DA, he let it go.

The next messages of any interest come just after the dance.

Michael: u there?
Celeste: yea
Michael: how'd it go?
Celeste: not good
Michael: ?
Celeste: he's crazy
Michael: what u mean?
Celeste: he's just crazy
Michael: tell me
Celeste: its good i left my dress n stuff in ur car
Michael: why
Celeste: he went psycho
Michael: how
Celeste: he made me show him my panties
Michael: ?
Celeste: proof
Michael: ?

Celeste: u know, that were not doing it
Michael: jesus

Jack's thoughts exactly.

Celeste: told ya, he's crazy
Michael: what did u do?
Celeste: i'm smarter
Michael: ?
Celeste: I carry an extra pair :)

Jack's been a prosecutor too long not to recognize the difference between the natural disappointment, even anger, of a parent who learns his child is sexually active and one whose reaction is more akin to that of a betrayed lover. The hard part is figuring out whether the latter reacts like a betrayed lover because he *is* one. As strange as Del Toro's behavior is, Jack still doesn't think her father is the man described in the journal. Yet that doesn't mean he's not sexually abusing her, too.

He glances at the corner of the screen and is alarmed to see how long he's been reading messages. It's almost two. If he doesn't get to his office soon, he'll miss his rescheduled staff meeting. He's certain he's only scratched the surface of the chatter between Michael and Celeste, but the rest will have to wait. The trail will be there tomorrow, but there's no guarantee he can say the same for his job.

CHAPTER EIGHTEEN

CLAIRE COMES HOME from Sedona four days later with a healthy glow to her skin, but darker shadows under her eyes, suggesting to Jack she spent a good portion of her time crying. Yet she avoids mentioning the events that preceded her leaving. Jack follows her lead and doesn't share with her the messages he found on the computer.

Instead, they engage in an uneasy détente as if, by some unspoken agreement, they have decided not to talk about anything remotely related to the allegations against Jack—not Celeste, not even Jenny.

And even though Jack prefers Claire's overt anger to her Stepford-wife acceptance of their plight, he does nothing to break the spell. Instead, he spends the few remaining days before Christmas holed up in the DA's office, where his staff does a better job of pretending to believe in his innocence.

The call is reminiscent of the call Rebecca received four years before, except, because of the holiday, this one has been forwarded to her cell phone. She's in the passenger seat of her boyfriend's pick-up truck on her way to his parents' house in Affton. She'd planned to break up with him by now, but her own parents have gone south for the winter, and she thought spending the holidays with him would be better than spending them alone. It's not even nine a.m. on Christmas Eve and she already regrets the decision.

She recognizes the voice immediately. It's warmer, but it's unmistakably the same voice.

"Rebecca, I don't know if you'll remember me, but—"

"I remember you." How could she forget?

The line falls silent; the slight static is the only evidence of someone at the other end. Is she surprised Rebecca remembered?

Then, "This is confidential, but I'm in St. Louis for a few days, and I'd like to meet with you."

Rebecca's pulse quickens. Four years have passed, but a conflict is a conflict, isn't it?

"Can I ask what the purpose of this meeting would be?"

Her boyfriend grunts and she glances over at him. He's got one arm
propped at the top of the steering wheel; a cigarette dangles from his lips. He's
losing patience with Rebecca's job as quickly as she's losing patience with him.

"I don't want to say much over the phone. I'd rather meet in person to talk
about this."

"I don't think that would be—"

"Please. I have no one else to call."

Does Rebecca imagine it, or does she hear the tightness a voice acquires
when its owner tries not to cry? It can't be a coincidence that this call comes on
the heel of that teenager's accusations against the DA. She'd have to go behind
Lee's back to do it. She did that once for this woman; she can't risk doing it
again. It's simply out of the question.

Yet she finds herself asking, "When would you like to meet?" Before she
knows it, she has a date to meet Ayanna Patel at the Ritz-Carlton in Clayton on
the first Tuesday of the new year. When she suggests that the Ritz might be a bit
conspicuous for a confidential meeting, the other woman laughs sadly. "I assure
you, no one will ever know it's me."

After another in a long run of restless, sleep-deprived nights, Jack trudges into
his office on Christmas Eve morning already wishing it was time for bed. Even
before he gets his coat off, Dog knocks on the door frame and enters without
invitation, but Jack is too tired to care about his lack of manners.

"Got news for you, Boss," Dog says. He hands Jack a cup of steaming black
coffee before he plops into a chair. He exchanged his baseball cap for a lime
green skullcap, and his jeans sit so low on his hips that Jack sees his boxers. He's
about to tell Dog to pull up his pants, but decides he doesn't care about his
clothes just then, either. Especially after the gift of coffee.

"As long as it's good."

"The hell I know. It's just news."

Dog chomps loudly on his gum and stares at Jack as if waiting for
permission to continue. Except Dog never waits for permission to do anything.

"Am I supposed to read your mind or something?" Jack asks.

"Nah. Just thinking." He squints. "You don't look so hot. A little . . . what's
the word? Sallow."

"In case you missed the news, I've had a few rough weeks."

"Yeah, they really chasin' your ass, aren't they? You growin' a beard?"

"No, I'm not growing a beard. I simply didn't feel like shaving this
morning." He didn't feel like showering, either, but Dog doesn't need to know
this. "So what's your news?"

"It was a chick."

"*What* was a chick?"

"Your Unabomber. The dude who mailed the letters to your girlfriend."

Jack's exhaustion evaporates, if only for a moment. He leans across his desk, eyes narrowed at Dog, finger pointed. "Malik?"

Dog raises his hands in surrender. Like a child, he knows he crossed a line if Jack uses his real name, even if he doesn't know which line he crossed. That Jack raised his voice, too—something he rarely does—erases all doubts.

"She's *not* my girlfriend. You got it? Don't *ever* refer to her that way again. Not to me, not to anyone else. I'll fire your ass so fast you'll—"

"Okay! Jesus! I didn't mean nothin' by it. I'm sorry, man."

Jack leans back, but his glare lingers. "Start over."

Dog eyes him cautiously.

"Did you hear me? Start over."

"I gotta friend who works at the post office. He took a look at the security tapes from the branch where the letters were mailed. It was a girl. Your letters were mailed by a chick."

"A girl?"

Dog nods. "He says he can only see the back of her, but it's a she."

"That's it? Did he give you a description? And by girl, do you mean a *woman*? Or you really mean a girl, as in *child*?"

"Well, he remarked on her fine ass, so I hope that means she's legal, eh, Boss?" He realizes his mistake even before Jack registers it. "Fuck. Sorry. I didn't mean it like that."

In that instant, Jack decides his life will never be normal again, even if he's acquitted. Unless he leaves town and assumes a new identity, he will forever be surrounded by people who worry about what they say in his presence, who remember what he did, and who remember what he didn't do but was accused of doing. He decides to ignore both Dog's comment and apology.

"Can he get copies of the tapes for me? I'd like to take a look myself."

"Not a chance, man. Already broke the rules doin' this favor for me. He said no more without a subpoena."

A subpoena is out of the question. Anything Jack does must stay under the radar. "Would he talk to me? You know, answer a few questions about what he saw?" He could relay the information to Jenny and see if the woman sounds familiar to her.

"You think you might know her?"

Dog's question abruptly scrambles Jack's thoughts. When they reassemble, his brain sends him a whole new message. Is it possible Jenny mailed the letters to herself? She had to know the post office cameras would be watching.

"Your friend said she never faced the camera?"

"Never saw her face."

Is she playing him all over again? If so, why? *Why?*

"I need to talk to him. Can you set that up?"

"I'll ask him, but he'll ask what's in it for him, risking his ass for a cop."

"I'm a prosecutor, not a cop."

Dog shrugs and inspects his fingernails. "Same difference to him."

"It's just a conversation. Five minutes."

Dog sighs and rises to leave. "I'll try." At the door, he turns and asks again, "Do you think you know her?"

"I sure as hell hope not."

Earl shows up unexpectedly after lunch. From the commotion in the hallway, Jack is aware of his presence long before he reaches the door to his former office. Most of the attorneys and administrative staff from Earl's tenure still work there, and they clamor to greet him. No one seems to care much that he now represents the other side.

In any other circumstance, Jack would join them. But the minute they saw him, they'd remember why Earl was there and the gaiety would evaporate. So instead he waits for Earl to come to him.

"To what do I owe the pleasure of this unscheduled visit?" he asks when Earl finally enters Jack's office and closes the door behind him.

"I don't like to deliver bad news over the phone on Christmas Eve."

"Ah, I see." Jack's thoughts churn. Are they revoking his bail? Forcing him into an administrative leave? Do they know about Jenny? Has Celeste manufactured more evidence against him? "Might as well cut to the chase."

"Someone over at the police station has leaked all their evidence to the press. Everything. They've got the pictures of your arm. They know about the hairs, what she told the cops. It should hit the airwaves at the top of the hour. Even a copy of her journal entry got released. Merry Christmas. If you thought you were being tried by the press, you're about to feel convicted and hung, too."

"What happened to 'Gunner and his crew are not out to get you'?"

"He had nothing to do with it. He's furious. A witch hunt is taking place over at headquarters as I speak."

"Yeah, that's what he said."

"I've known Gunner for over twenty-five years. I know when he tries to pull one over me. He's as mad about this as I am."

"How do they know the leak comes from the station? Maybe it was Walker."

Earl simply grunts. He doesn't care who did it; he only cares about the ramifications to his client. "How much does Claire know?" he asks.

"What do you mean?"

"How much does she know about the evidence they've collected against you? Like the hairs. Does she know the tests showed the one in Celeste's bra belonged to you?"

How to explain that he and Claire haven't really talked about the specifics of Celeste's allegations? Even before she went to Sedona, they were in a holding pattern, avoiding any in-depth discussion of Celeste's allegations or what will happen if he's convicted. Jack wants unconditional assurance from Claire that she knows he didn't do it. Claire just wants the whole thing to go away. This news won't put them closer to either goal.

"Am I to assume from your silence the answer is *no*?"

"What about the other hairs?" Jack asks. "Jenny's?" He ignores another grunt from Earl that follows Jenny's name.

"I didn't ask. I didn't want to draw attention to them. He'd wonder why I cared."

Jack nods.

"There's something else," Earl says. "Walker called. He's willing to bargain."

"Tell him to go fuck himself."

"You don't want to hear it?"

"Sure, but only because I need a good laugh about now."

"Two years in exchange for a plea on the statutory charges, and he'll drop the rest."

"Like I said, tell him to go fuck himself." When Earl remains quiet, Jack adds, "Oh, come on. You really don't expect me to consider a plea, do you?" Jack *will* fire him if he says yes.

"Absolutely not." Earl grins. "I was simply imagining the pleasure I'll get from telling him to fuck himself."

"Wish I could do it myself," Jack mutters.

"Look, I think you should do yourself a favor and take off early for the holiday. Call Claire and go home. You need the rest, and I have a feeling this thing will be bigger than anything you've dealt with so far. In the eyes of a reporter, it's no longer an unfounded allegation. Now there's some hard evidence to back it up."

"How much bigger can it be? It went national."

"It went national for a day." He pauses. "It can get a lot bigger, trust me."

After Earl leaves, Jack forces himself to call Claire. As much as he dreads it, he doesn't want her to find out about the leak from the news. She's learned of too many other things that way.

He's relieved when he gets her voicemail. He leaves a message with the basics, and then he calls Beverly into his office to explain what's happened and why he's taking off for home.

"Jack," she asks, "have you looked outside? You might want to let everyone leave now."

He spins his chair to face the window; snow falls from the sky with the blinding force of a rainstorm. "When did this start?" In his mind's eye he suddenly sees himself as an inmate in a windowless cell, reliant on the security guards to tell him the weather, and his chest tightens.

"About an hour ago. They're calling for a foot, at least. Looks like we'll have a white Christmas this year."

An hour ago? How could he not have noticed?

"Jack? What do you want me to do?"

He should take Jamie sledding. Michael, too, if he'll come. He should take them both sledding while he still can. Why has his desk been situated with his back to the window all these years? Why has he looked at a wall and a door when he could have looked at the sky? If he's convicted, who will take them sledding? He needs to talk to Mark about these things. Time is running out.

"Jack?"

He swivels back and looks into the kind face of the sixty-one-year-old woman who has mothered him since the day he started at the DA's office. And like a mother, she always refuses to believe the ugly accusations tossed his way. Even when he admitted to being Jenny's alibi, she forgave unconditionally. Has he ever thanked her? He thinks so, but not enough. It's never enough. "Yeah. Sure. Tell everyone to take off before the roads get bad. I'm going to stay a moment more, watch the snow."

"Are you—"

"I'm fine. Thanks." She turns reluctantly to go, but he calls her name to stop her. "I mean that. Thank you, for everything, okay?"

"Try to get some rest."

He shrugs, waves her out. "Merry Christmas, Bev."

"Merry Christmas, Jack."

Once his staff clears out, he takes the elevator to the top floor of the courthouse and slips into an empty, unlit courtroom. The tall windows afford him a magnificent view of the Mall below. Through the prism of the blizzard, the multi-colored Christmas lights strung through the tree branches resemble glowing gumballs. Traffic on the city streets is light and the television crews he anticipated on the sidewalk haven't materialized. Has everyone evacuated the city already, eager to start the holiday early?

He sits in the gallery, at the end of a row closest to the windows, and stares at the front of the courtroom. He's not sure what drew him upstairs, to sit here like this. Maybe he's simply too weary to face what waits for him at home. He knows his sledding fantasy is just that—a fantasy.

He thinks about the second case he ever tried, when he first understood his special rapport with juries. He was still at Newman at the time, and the case was a pro bono civil rights case. He represented a prisoner suing the government for abuse he'd allegedly suffered at the hands of prison guards. It was the type of appointed case every lawyer had to take in order to practice before the Federal District Court. Neither the firm nor Jack received compensation, and the partners made it clear in their subtle way that associates were to spend as little time on such cases as ethically possible. Almost without exception, the cases were losers.

Jack had already won his first trial, a straightforward wrongful termination suit in which he'd represented the employer being sued. All of the evidence supported the employer's position; only an idiot could have left the courthouse without a verdict.

But the prisoner case was different. The odds of winning were slim to none. But whether too naïve at the time or simply too stubborn, he refused to accept that the case was the loser all the partners told him it was. He believed his client's claims of abuse and was convinced he could make the jury see the facts the way he saw them.

On the first morning of trial, as he left Newman's offices on foot for the courthouse, file boxes in tow on a rolling caddy, he received pats on the back and pep talks that focused not on winning, but on not letting the impending loss bother him too much. He knew then that a career at Newman wasn't in his future.

Three and a half days later, he left the courthouse with a verdict so rare it made the front page of the next day's paper. He knew then that a career as a trial lawyer was.

On the way home, Jack picks up Jamie from his friend Christopher's house. Ironically, Jamie was at this same friend's house four years earlier when the news broke about Jack being Jenny's alibi. Now, Christopher's mother eyes Jack with a look somewhere between sympathy and skepticism, and this tells him the story has hit the news. As Jamie ducks under his arm and heads for the car, she wishes them Merry Christmas with forced cheeriness and quickly shuts her door before Jack can return the sentiment.

By the time they enter their neighborhood, the snow completely blankets the ground. He turns onto their street and sees the news trucks and vans waiting. The flap on their mailbox hangs open.

"Why are they back?" Jamie asks.

"Just keep your door locked and your window up, okay?" Jack pulls alongside the curb and sees mail inside the box, the top envelope swollen and moist from the snow. Now they're rifling through his mail? He considers whether to remind them it's a federal offense. Instead, he lowers his window and quickly retrieves the mail as he tries to ignore the crush of bodies shouting questions at him and the microphones shoved in his face.

"Daddy!" Jamie shrieks at seeing the rising window about to close on a hand gripping a microphone.

"It's okay," Jack assures him. The hand slips out before getting trapped, as Jack knew it would. He grabs a pen and yellow legal pad from his briefcase, quickly scribbles a message and holds it up for the crowd to read.

IF YOU USE VISUAL AND/OR AUDIO FOOTAGE OF MY
SON, I WILL PURSUE ALL LEGAL REMEDIES AGAINST
YOU.

When he pulls into the garage, Claire's side is empty. He lowers the door, shuts off the ignition, and closes his eyes. For a moment he understands Jenny's desire to give up. Fighting, even when innocent—especially when innocent—is exhausting. *Have I decided Jenny is innocent?* He feels Jamie's worried gaze. "It's okay, buddy," he says again. "Everything will be okay."

"Are they the reason we didn't put up lights this year?" Jamie asks, startling Jack with the direction of the question. This is the first year they didn't string outside lights. Even the Christmas Jack missed, after Claire kicked him out, the house had lights. She didn't decorate as much as he usually did, but it was something. This year, both Jack and Claire were unwilling to brave the cameras they knew would be pointed at them if they tried to adorn the house with holiday cheer.

"Yeah," Jack sighs, "they're the reason." Jack now thinks, for Jamie's sake, they should have at least hired someone to do it.

His phone rings and he sees Harley and Ruth on the screen. Knowing it's probably Harley, he debates whether to answer or ignore it. But maybe Claire went to her parents' house and is trying to reach him. Maybe her cell phone battery died.

But Jack's luck still hasn't turned. "Jack," Harley says with mock kindness. "Harley."

"Enjoying the little Christmas gift from my friends at the SLPD?"

The question stuns Jack into silence—at first, because he's trying to process its meaning, and then, because of his rage. *Harley. The leak was Harley's doing.*

He feels Jamie's gaze, waiting to see what Grandpa wants. Jack somehow stills his shaking hand enough to hit the End Call button. "The call dropped," he says. A lame explanation, but one Jamie accepts. Or else the look on his father's face has made him afraid not to.

He fingers through the mail then, barely registering its contents. But when he sees a letter addressed to John W. Hilliard from the "Office of Chief Disciplinary Counsel, Missouri Supreme Court," his throat closes and he has trouble breathing.

Harley has also made good on his original threat.

His attempt to have Jack disbarred has officially begun.

Jack hears the television as soon as he and Jamie enter the house. Realizing it's tuned to the news and the news is about him, he makes a racket so Jamie won't hear. He slams the garage door; he jangles his keys and swings his briefcase so it lands with a thud on the dryer. By the time they round the corner to the kitchen and family room, Michael has taken the hint and switched stations. He lies on the couch, one hand behind his head, the other gripping the television remote.

He pretends not to notice Jack and Jamie. Jack is about to say hello—he's not looking for a fight—when he notices the bags of groceries on the counter. Jamie sees them, too; he hurries over to peek into each one to see what surprises await him.

"Has Mom been home?" Jack asks. No response. "Michael? Has Mom been home?" Still, nothing. "*Michael.*"

"What?" Michael mutters the word so quietly that Jack has trouble interpreting the tone.

"Has Mom been home?"

"No."

"Did *you* go to the grocery store?"

"No."

He obviously plans to make Jack work for every bit of information. Jack sets the mail on the middle island, walks over to the couch, removes the remote from Michael's hand, and shuts off the television.

"Where did the groceries come from?"

"Mrs. Edmond dropped them off."

Jack pieces together what happened. Claire must have heard his message and understood immediately that the media would descend upon them again, so she asked Marcia to pick up groceries for her. Jack wonders if Marcia met up with the crowd outside, too, or if she dropped them off earlier.

"Did you already put away the cold stuff?"

Michael shakes his head.

"*Was* there cold stuff?"

Jamie yanks open the refrigerator just as Jack asks the question. "Yup, there's the ham!" He seems to have already dismissed the spectacle outside.

"Yeah," Michael says as if Jamie hasn't already answered. "She put it away."

The door from the garage is suddenly flung open. It bangs loudly against the wall in the laundry room. The violence of the entrance tells Jack that Claire is home and that she plans to get right to the heart of the matter. The post-Sedona calm is officially over.

She drops her purse and satchel on the kitchen table. Her keychain follows, clanging as she lets it fall from her grip.

"Michael, Jamie, get started on your homework. Jack, can I see you upstairs?" The chill in her voice rivals the air outside.

"But we're on Christmas break!" Michael protests.

"You still have homework, don't you?"

"Yeah, but—"

"Then get started on it."

She climbs the stairs without a further glance at any of them. Despite her command, Jack plans to wait a few minutes before he follows.

"You want me to fix you a snack, Jamester?" he asks Jamie, who managed a minute ago to get excited about Christmas. Now he's slouched over the kitchen table digging books and papers out of his Iron Man back pack. It breaks Jack's heart, seeing him so confused. Michael's feigned apathy upsets Jack, of course, but it doesn't surprise him. Jamie, though, has always been oblivious to the cruelties of the world.

"I'm not hungry. I ate lunch at Christopher's." He answers without looking at Jack.

The whoosh of water behind the family room wall draws Jack's attention back to Claire. The sound that comes from the poorly insulated pipe whenever anyone flushes a toilet upstairs has irritated him since the day they moved in. For months he dogged the builder about it, but eventually gave up when more important things demanded his attention. Now what he wants is to take a baseball bat to both the wall and the pipe.

He swipes the only piece of mail he cares about off the counter and heads up after his wife.

Claire sits on the bed, staring out the window at the snow. He tucks the envelope into his back pocket. Quietly he closes and locks the door in case Jamie decides to act as peacemaker and tries to join them. Jack reminds himself not to take his anger at Harley out on Claire.

"Sorry I interrupted whatever you had going on at the university. Earl was afraid—"

She stops him with a look. "Tell me exactly what happened that night."

For a moment he simply stands by the door; they stare at each other. "With Celeste?"

"Yes, with Celeste. Unless there's a different night I should know about."

He crosses the room. Instead of taking a spot next to her, he sits on the sill of the window just across from her. The glass is cold against his back, but he ignores it. He needs to be facing her. "I've told you everything."

"No, you didn't tell me about hairs. You didn't tell me she scratched you."

"When have we taken a moment alone to talk about this in any detail?" When she doesn't respond, he says, "You know how it works, Claire. You know as well as I do where the hair in her bra came from."

Her gaze remains unyielding even as her eyes tear up. "Do I?"

"Don't you?" His frustration builds. The one person who should have his back still doubts him. "You know they were on the couch. I didn't see Michael or Celeste until *after* I told them to get dressed, but you know she was probably—"

"I don't know anything, Jack! I don't know anything except the little you've told me. So it's all hearsay as far as I'm concerned!" She spits the word 'hearsay' at him. "*Unreliable* hearsay."

He lets out a disgusted laugh. Shakes his head. "Thanks for that."

"What do you want me to say? That I believe every word that comes out of your mouth even though you continue to keep things from me?"

"I haven't kept anything from—"

"You didn't tell me about any of this evidence. Why do I have to find out everything from the press?"

"Maybe because every time we start talking about the case, it disintegrates into this!"

She purses her lips, but he sees she's weary and might be willing to listen.

He lowers his voice, tries to say the next words gently. "Tell me what you want to know. I'm not hiding anything from you."

"I just want to know what happened that night, okay? Everything, good or bad. I don't want to be the last to find out. Can't you understand that?"

"I do understand. I've told you what happened. Maybe I haven't been specific enough, but it's not because I have anything to hide."

"Explain the hair in her bra."

He told this to Earl several times, but Claire's right; he never explained it to her, not in any detail. "I woke to hear voices. I looked at the clock. It was past time for Celeste to be home. I was about to go down to see what was happening, but when I got to the top of the stairs, I could tell from their voices they were drunk and fooling around on the couch."

Claire listens with her head tilted. Her lips are pressed tight, her arms crossed. He realizes she doesn't absorb the meaning of what he just said. "Your son was screwing his girlfriend, Claire." She's about to protest, but he cuts her off. "I heard her say, 'I think someone's coming.' And do you know how he responded?"

"He's *your* son, too," Claire mumbles, but Jack catches the spite in the remark. Is she even listening to him? Or does she simply want to fight? He won't take her detour this time.

"He said, 'I hope so.' That was his response to 'I think someone's coming.' I'm willing to bet he didn't mean he hoped one of us was about to show up."

The phone on the nightstand rings. Claire glances at it as if debating whether to answer. *Don't you dare*, Jack thinks. *You're the one who wanted to have this conversation.*

After three rings it stops. After so many harassing calls, Jack instructed both Michael and Jamie to let them go to voicemail if they don't recognize the number.

"I made my presence known, but I gave them time to get dressed. I can't swear her bra was off, but I think it's likely. That had to be when she picked up the hair."

"Why didn't you tell me this?" Her tone hasn't changed. He can't decide whether she believes him and is angry that she didn't know, or whether she's still skeptical. He doesn't answer because anything he might say will sound as if he's blaming her for his silence. He shrugs and raises his hands in a *what can I say* gesture.

She scoffs at his vague response. "Is it true you parked for a couple hours with her in Rockwoods?"

There it is. There's the question that, when answered, will cause her to distrust him more. Somehow, he and Claire have never even talked about where he and Celeste were while Celeste sobered up. He may be able to explain away the physical evidence, but Jack and Celeste are the only two who will ever know with certainty what happened in the car that night. He can't prove or disprove any of it. Whatever Claire ultimately decides, it will have to be a decision based on nothing more than faith, or lack of.

"Yes." At the word, Claire's face tightens. It's slight—she tried to remain impassive—but he sees it. "She'd asked me to pull over. She said she was going to be sick. She was just stalling. When I started to leave, she begged me to wait. She didn't want her dad to know she'd been drinking."

Claire reaches over and grabs his right wrist. She roughly yanks his arm toward her, forcing him off the windowsill. His shirtsleeves are already rolled up; she searches his arm. When she doesn't find what she's looking for—the scratch was superficial and didn't leave a scar—she pushes him away. He feels like a specimen.

"They're saying they have pictures of your arm that prove the two of you struggled. And that your skin was under her fingernails. What are they talking about?"

"She started to panic when I said I had to tell her dad everything. She seemed terrified of him, what he might do. She went a bit crazy on me. I reached down to put the car in gear and she grabbed my arm."

"She grabbed your arm so hard that she scratched it?" The way she speaks the question, he knows what she left unsaid. *Yeah, right.*

"Yes. She didn't just grab me. She *clawed* at me."

Claire won't meet his eye. She looks past him outside the window and shakes her head. She doesn't believe him.

"Claire."

"What?" She whispers the one word, still staring at whatever has her attention in the yard.

"Are you honestly telling me there's a part of you that wonders, truly wonders, if I did something with her? Or are you just angry about the situation, and about . . ." When he pauses, she sneaks a look at him but quickly looks away again. ". . . Jenny."

Nothing.

"Claire, please look at me." She finally does, but reluctantly. "Look me in the eye and tell me if you believe me, no doubts. None whatsoever." She blinks slowly, as if it's an effort to keep her eyes open. "I need to know."

Her response comes slowly, and when it finally does, she's so quiet he strains to hear her. "I can't give you an answer."

His stomach churns. He swallows to quell the bile rising in his throat. He stands, causing her to lean back slightly, nervous about what he'll do. He starts for the door, but suddenly stops and pulls the folded envelope from his pocket. He tosses it onto the bed next to her. She glances at it and then looks up at him as if waiting for explanation.

He breathes in, ready to tell her what her father has done, but then changes his mind—let her read it herself—and says something else entirely.

"I think you just did."

CHAPTER NINETEEN

WHEN JENNY OPENS the door, a different Jack Hilliard stands before her. In the glare of the parking lot floodlights, his face is pale. Despite the blowing snow and the frigid temperature, his cheeks lack the usual hint of pink that gives him a perpetual look of having just come out of the cold. The beginning of a beard shadows the lower half of his face. He hasn't been sleeping well, she sees that. His normally bright eyes are bloodshot; the periwinkle blue of his irises has darkened to steel. If he's combed his hair at all recently, it's been with his fingers. Under his coat the collar of his starched white shirt is open, the necktie loosened and hanging limply.

Except for his obvious exhaustion, she decides she prefers this scruffier look. She thinks it better suits the side of him he usually keeps hidden. She only wishes something else had caused it.

It's eight thirty on Christmas Eve.

"I'll get my coat," she says.

He grabs her wrist, and his hand is so cold she winces. Their eyes meet and the despair on his face makes her want to embrace him. She doesn't. She knows what he's about to say and she hears the voice inside her head screaming, *No, no, no.*

"I'll come in this time."

She backs up and he steps into the warm motel room. He glances at the unused bed where her suitcase is open as if waiting for inspection.

"You want to take off your coat?"

He wriggles out of it. While she hangs it from the chrome rack near the sink, he sits next to the suitcase. The bed creaks from his weight.

"Sorry," she says when she returns, quickly zipping the lid shut and placing it against the wall. She sits on the bed opposite him, an expectant look on her face.

"It wasn't in my way."

"Why are you here, Jack?" she asks, ignoring his comment about the suitcase. "It's Christmas Eve."

"I know."

"Perhaps I'm asking the obvious, but don't you think you should be home?"

"Yeah, you'd think so, huh?" The bitterness in his voice surprises him. "Did you turn on your TV today?"

"You're talking about the release of the evidence?"

He nods. He waits for the same questions Claire asked, about the scratch on his arm, his hair in Celeste's bra, but instead she asks, "Who do you think leaked everything?"

"I don't *think*. I know. Claire's father was behind it."

She gasps. "Wow," she whispers.

Wow is right, Jack thinks.

"Did Claire know?"

The question takes an instant to register because it never even entered his mind. "No." He has to believe no. "She'd strangle him before she'd let him do that." *Wouldn't she?*

Suddenly restless, he stands and goes to the window. He pulls the drapes aside to look outside and make sure he wasn't followed.

"Jack?"

He turns.

"Claire doesn't know you're here, does she?"

Jenny states the question as a conclusion, gently, and without the sarcasm she's probably entitled to, given his smug insistence the other day that he promised to tell Claire everything.

"No." He returns to the bed. "But I didn't mention I was going to Mark's house, either. I didn't know *where* I was going when I first left home."

"I don't understand."

Neither do I, he wants to say. Although that's not entirely true. On one level he understands; he simply doesn't want to put words to it. He doesn't want to be that cliché Claire accused him of being, when she first learned what he'd done and he tried to make excuses for it. He knows what she thought, what everyone thought: *just another middle aged man who feared the better part of his life was behind him and sought to forestall the inevitable in the arms of a mistress.* He didn't believe it then, he doesn't believe it now. But by making these denials, does he make it so?

"We fought. She didn't know about some of the evidence. Not specifically. We were going back and forth, what I'd told her and what I hadn't, and it dawned on me . . . She really thinks I could have done it. I asked her point blank if she believed me, and she wouldn't answer me. She said she *couldn't* answer me. I was angry, so I left the house and ended up at Mark's."

"And then you came here."

"Yes. And then I came here."

Jenny looks away, and he realizes he shouldn't have shared all this with her. It wasn't the point of his visit. He *has* become that cliché, sharing his marital problems with another woman.

"I'm sorry, I didn't come here to—"

"It must really hurt," she says, meeting his eye, "not being believed by the one person you desperately need to believe you."

He opens his mouth but no words come. She holds his gaze, waiting, forcing a response. Softly, he says, "You're right. It does."

Suddenly, Jenny stands as if she has an urgent task across the room. "Did you have dinner?" she asks, apropos of nothing.

"Mark fed me." He grabs her wrist. "Jenny, don't walk away."

"I need to go outside a minute. I need some air." She tugs, but when he doesn't let go, she reluctantly turns to him again. In the dim light, her eyes shine like black onyx and the look she gives him is just as hard.

"I believe you," he says. When she only blinks, he adds, "I would have led them straight to your door if I didn't believe you. Don't you realize that? I've risked everything because I believe you."

Despite his protests that it's too cold, she steps outside onto the small walkway without a coat or shoes. She sucks in the fresh air. The wind has died down and the snowfall has settled into a silent shower. It can't be much past nine, but it feels like midnight. She can't see the road. The only sign of life is a snowplow she hears in the distance. The small banker's lamp in the motel office is on, but no one sits at the desk. The three cars in the parking lot wear a blanket of snow and any tire or foot tracks from earlier have disappeared. None of the cars belong to Jack. Or his brother, for that matter. Did he park far away and walk? Is that why his hand was so cold?

She leans against the doorjamb and closes her eyes. It's so cold on her back, it almost burns, but she doesn't move away. She tries to gather her thoughts. If she's ever going to tell him the full truth, now would be the time. He's vulnerable, feeling alone, and therefore more likely to understand the actions she took when she found herself in a similar situation. Yet how can she? Her confession might be the burden that finally breaks him.

She hears him switch on the television. He's torturing himself, she knows, watching the media recast his life until it becomes unrecognizable. She did the same thing, back then. She wishes she could tell him what it took her a few years to learn: if he's not careful, he'll start to believe he's the man they say he is.

When she can no longer bear the cold, she steps back into the room. He's lying on top of the bedspread with his right hand on his stomach, the remote under his hand. He propped two pillows behind his shoulders. The television is still on, but his head is tilted slightly to the side and his eyes are closed. He's not snoring, but his breathing is so deep and regular that she knows he's sound asleep.

His phone rings several times while he sleeps. The first time, she retrieves it from the breast pocket of his overcoat and turns down the volume. She sees that it's Claire trying to reach him. She wants so badly to answer and say, "He's with me." But of course she doesn't. She doesn't hate Claire, although sometimes she thinks she should.

She studies his face in the blue glow of television light. She wonders if Claire still watches him sleep, if she's still fascinated with the shape of his eyebrows, the curve of his upper lip, or the scar on his chin. Or is that something a couple stops doing after they've been together as long as Jack and Claire?

He rolls onto his right side and rests his left hand on the edge of the bed closest to her. His wedding ring, a simple gold band, circles his ring finger. Her eyes well. She remembers how it felt when he touched her with that hand, how her resistance dissolved when he first slipped it under her blouse and placed his palm against her spine. And then later, when both hands traveled her body as if they owned it. Does he realize they do? They're strong hands, with the veins and tendons visible on the back, and she craves their touch on her bare skin again.

She returns her gaze to his face. His eyes move slightly under his lids as if he's dreaming. She suspects the only time he ever fully relaxes is during deep sleep.

She stared at his face like this only once before. Then, he forced her to look at him. Even when her body began to respond without any conscious direction from her brain, he held her head and insisted she keep her eyes open, insisted she meet his stare.

But that time was different. His expression had been all man, and the intensity of it scared her. Now, during his brief respite from the world, it's all boy.

It still scares her, but this time she intends to fight the fear.

Around eleven she tries to wake him. She speaks his name, and when he fails to respond, she says it louder, sharper. Nothing. If she didn't see the slow rise and fall of his chest, she'd think he'd died. She decides it would be cruel to force him awake. Instead, she gently pulls off his shoes and then covers him with the spare blanket. Before she climbs into her own bed, she flips on the bathroom light and leaves the door slightly ajar so he'll be able to see if he wakes later.

In the middle of the night she wakes, startled by another presence in the room with her. And then she remembers. Jack. Jack showed up at her door last night. She closes her eyes and falls back asleep to the even rhythm of his breathing.

She emerges from her own dreams near nine the next morning. The bright light of a snowy day peeks through the slit in the drapes. His phone rings again, but he's still sleeping. She's not sure what to do. Should she wake him? She crosses to his bed, gently sits on the edge. She whispers his name at his ear but he doesn't respond. She yearns to touch his face. She settles for his arm.

"Jack," she says, trying again. He stirs, then nothing. She dares more than a touch this time and rubs the smooth underside of his forearm. "Jack," she whispers louder.

He opens his eyes and looks at her, but she's not sure he sees her or knows where he is. He gives her a tiny smile, then, and slips his hand behind her head, through her hair, and pulls her closer. A short whimper escapes her throat—she told herself she wouldn't let this happen—but he surprises her when his lips touch her forehead instead of her mouth. He holds her briefly and then releases her. When she leans away, his eyes are closed again. The rhythmic breathing resumes.

Like a bear in hibernation, he continues to sleep. His phone continues to ring. Sometimes it's Claire, sometimes it's Mark. Once it's Earl. As the sun reaches its zenith, she decides when Mark calls next, she'll risk answering. She hopes it's really him and not Claire using Mark's phone.

Only a few moments pass before it chimes again. In the bathroom, she answers but doesn't speak. At the silence, Mark says, "Jack?"

"Mark, it's me. Jenny."

He sighs, as if his worst fears were just confirmed.

"He's sleeping. He showed up around eight thirty last night. We were just talking. I stepped outside for a moment for some fresh air. When I came back in, he was sleeping. He's been sleeping ever since. It's going on sixteen, seventeen hours."

"You're joking."

"What do you want me to do? I've tried to wake him, but unless I set off a bomb, it's not happening."

"Claire's looking for him. He came to my house yesterday afternoon. I didn't realize he'd left until she called for him late last night and I found the guest room empty. He must have taken a cab because his car is still in my garage."

"What do you want me to do?"

The line is silent. Finally, he says, "Let him sleep. He needs that more than anything right now."

Later, she notices his tie twisted and is straining against his neck. Sitting at the edge of the bed again, she loosens the knot and slowly slips it off. Sensing movement, he rolls over. His hand brushes her back, and whether by habit or instinct, he tries to pull her closer. For an instant she hesitates, poised in a space between her selfish need to lie next to him and the knowledge that he thinks she's Claire.

She swallows a sob and carefully pulls away before he discovers his mistake.

* * *

When Jack opens his eyes, it takes a minute to get his bearings, to remember where he is and why he's here. He's lying on his side, facing Jenny's bed. He watches her. She's propped up against her headboard reading a book with a small book light. She wears long pajama bottoms and a white tank top. He assumes this is what she sleeps in, or at least what she sleeps in with him in the room. Her long legs are bent and the book rests on her thighs. Something she reads makes her sigh, and she sets the book face down on her chest and turns to look at him. She smiles slightly when she sees he's awake.

"I'd say 'good morning' but noon has come and gone. I guess I can still say Merry Christmas."

Merry Christmas? He throws the cover off and springs to a sitting position on the edge of the bed. "Fuck," he says when the date on his watch comes into focus. He's in his stocking feet but otherwise still fully dressed.

"You've been asleep about nineteen hours. I tried to wake you."

How can that be? Nineteen hours? *How can that be?*

"Wonderful. I've made it worse for myself now."

He makes an urgent trip to the john. He's starting to smell ripe, but he's not about to ask to use her shower, too. When he comes out, he goes to the window and peeks outside. He squints from the brightness. It's Christmas, a white one, just like Beverly predicted. He's holed up in the motel room of the last woman on Earth he should be with today. He should have stayed home, or at least at his brother's house. No matter how badly things have deteriorated with Claire, this will only make it worse. He thought he would come out for a few hours, talk to Jenny, maybe question her more about the letters—anything to take his mind off things—and then catch a cab back to Mark's for the night and drive home in the morning before anyone woke. Instead, he slept right through most of Christmas, and in Jenny's motel room, of all places. He thinks of Jamie, who won't understand why his dad missed the biggest holiday of the year.

"Claire's probably got an APB out on me." He's not sure why he said it. Claire wouldn't need an APB; she probably knows exactly where he is, at least in theory. He's never given her the exact location of the motel, or its name. Oddly, she's never asked. "I'm sorry I showed up here last night. I couldn't sleep at Mark's. I didn't mean to crash here, though."

But I did anyway. I slept like a baby. He suddenly understands how much of a refuge his visits with her have become, how much of a refuge *she* has become. He swallows, but his throat feels permanently closed.

"I talked to him." She must read the confusion on his face. "Claire, and then Mark, kept calling your phone. I finally answered one of Mark's calls" —she shrugs— "so at least they'd know you were alive. He said to let you sleep."

Jack wonders if Mark finally admitted to Claire that he knew about Jenny's return.

Jenny surprises him by laughing a little.

"What is it?"

"Maybe you need to go back to Newman. You slept there easily enough, too." Her tone is teasing.

"What do you—?"

"You don't remember? The first time we met?"

Almost fourteen years ago now. *The second worst night of my life*, she called it the night they slept together. When he asked her to explain, she refused. Instead she deflected his attention by telling him about the first worst night of her life: the night of her family's murders.

"I remember. What about it?"

"I was new to Newman, remember? I'd just come back to St. Louis after my year practicing in Manhattan. You were just starting your second year. When I passed your office door one rainy evening, I peeked in and saw you sleeping. Your feet were propped on the desk and your arms were crossed over your chest. You might have even been snoring a little."

"I don't snore."

"You're right. I made that part up." She laughs again. "But you were sleeping, no doubt about it. I woke you up. Do you remember how?"

He stares at her, unable to answer. Not wanting to think about it. He remembers everything. Sometimes he wishes he could forget. Other times, against his better judgment, he's glad he doesn't.

He finds his voice and says quietly, "You said 'Hypnotic, isn't it?' You were referring to the rain, the way it sounded against the window."

"Yeah." She shrugs. "I never told you so, but I did it as a favor."

"Really?" He sprouts a smile. "And what favor might that have been?"

"I knew no partner wanted to walk by an associate's office to find him sleeping, even if the clock did read half past seven."

"You could have simply pulled my door shut."

The grin fades from her face. "I guess." He watches as she traces a seam in the bedspread with her finger. She seems to be considering whether to say more.

"But?"

She lifts her head and looks at him in doubt.

"It's part of the deal, remember?" he reminds her.

She starts to protest but instead nods in resignation. Why does he persist in this game with her? Honesty, in this case, isn't necessarily the best policy.

"If I'd closed your door," she says, her voice halting, "I wouldn't have met you. And I wanted to meet you."

He doesn't respond. He stares at her numbly. He tells himself nothing would have been different, even if she had closed his door. They would have eventually crossed paths. News of her arrival to Newman had already traveled the firm grapevine. By the time she stood in his doorway, he'd already heard about her beauty and her spirited personality. All that remained was to meet her.

Yet he can't help but wonder if there's some alternative reality, some other plane of existence where, had they met at a different time, on a different day, their relationship would have taken a different road. She would have been just another pretty woman to admire and then forget. They'd have never become such close friends and, for one night, lovers. *Keep telling yourself that, Jack.*

At his silence, she claps her hands and abruptly stands. "You need to get home." He nods. He slips on his shoes and grabs his suit coat from the chair and his overcoat from the rear of the room. She meets him at the door.

"Listen, I'm gonna head back to Brian's soon, okay?"

"Why?" It's a ridiculous question, in light of the appellate court decision. But she threatened to leave once already and she's still here.

"I think you've got enough problems without me making your life more difficult. It'll only get worse for both of us if someone finds out I'm in town."

"Don't go," he blurts. Is this the panic the addict feels when his supply is about to dry up? He quickly adds, "I mean, not yet," and then remembers what Dog told him. "I told you I'd help you and I meant it. I'm making progress. We'll get together in a few days somehow, after this blows over, and I'll tell you about it. I have some questions for you, too."

She narrows her eyes but her interest is clearly piqued. "What kind of progress?"

He wonders again if her skepticism is merely a disguise for knowledge she possesses but he doesn't. The memory of what he said last night comes back to him. *I believe you.* Does he, or was it just exhaustion speaking?

"A lead, maybe."

"What kind of lead?"

"Is it Claire you're worried about? She won't mention to anyone that you're in town. I'm telling her everything, that's all she wants."

"Actually, you're not. She doesn't know you're here. You said it yourself. What kind of lead, Jack?" she persists.

"She probably suspects it, if Mark didn't already tell her. If not, I'll fill her in when I get home."

"I'm sure she'll appreciate that."

"Look, she won't interfere. She's said as much to me. It wouldn't benefit her, either."

"No, it wouldn't, would it?" she mutters, looking away.

"Jen, don't go yet. I feel like you just got back."

"There's no point using up all my savings just to sit in a motel room, you know?"

Is that why she was ready to accept Mark's offer? "So stay at Mark's then."

She shakes her head, and at first he thinks it's because of his flip flop on the issue. But then he remembers the night he begged her to take him home and into her bed, and he realizes that then, as now, her instinct for self-preservation kicked in long before his did. She hasn't forgotten that every day she stays in Missouri is another day she might be hauled in for questioning. Or worse.

"I'll be here a few more days," she says, "and then we'll see, okay?"

She unchains and opens the door, signaling the discussion is over. The cold air blows in.

Jenny pulls back the curtains just enough to watch him walk away. He crosses the freshly plowed asphalt, navigating around ice patches as he heads in the direction of the motel office. Where is he going? She watches until he disappears around the back of the building.

If I'd closed your door, I wouldn't have met you. And I wanted to meet you. Despite their "deal," as he likes to call it, she left out a few small details about the night they met. She didn't tell him how she didn't see his wedding band until after she spoke her first words to him, and how, if she had, she *would* have closed the door. Nor did she tell him how many times since that night she's wished it had happened that way.

After a quick shower, she sits on her bed and stares at the vacant spot he left on the other one. He slept so soundly that it appears almost undisturbed. Until last night, she'd barely noticed the extra bed. Now, the emptiness makes his absence all the more pronounced.

The discarded tie rests on the nightstand; he didn't notice she'd taken it off. She picks it up, drapes it over the palm of her hand. It smells vaguely of him, like she remembers his skin smelling.

She calls Brian. When he answers, she warms from hearing his voice.

"Hey, Merry Christmas," she says.

"Same to you. I wondered why I hadn't heard from you. You sound sad."

"I'm fine," she lies. At his silence, she says, "I had a surprise visitor. He stopped by unexpectedly last night and didn't leave until a few minutes ago." Silence still, and she realizes he misunderstood. "He slept, Brian. He slept. Get your mind out of the gutter."

He laughs. "Yeah, okay. Whatever. I won't even ask you to explain that one."

"Listen," she says, her voice turning serious. "I'm heading home soon, I think."

"To your house? Is that wise?"

"No, not Lafayette Square. I mean, to Chicago."

"Did you tell him?"

She wishes. "No. He doesn't know anything, and I've decided that's how it should be. I—"

"Jenny, we talked about this."

"I know, but I've changed my mind. I can't do it."

"You can. You need to. He deserves to know."

"No, you don't understand. He's dealing with so much right now. He's—"

"I do understand. We get the national news here, too, you know."

"Then—"

"What about the letters? What if he finds out from whoever is sending the letters? You wanted to be the one to tell him. You didn't want him to find out from anyone else. You need to get it over with and get back up here, especially now that Alex gets his new trial."

"I know! But I can't. I can't do that to Jack right now."

"You don't have much of a choice. He either finds out from you, or he finds out from someone else."

"Or he doesn't find out at all. We don't even know what those letters are about. We don't know for sure."

"What else would they be?"

"I don't know. Someone's simply trying to scare me."

"Someone's trying to scare you, all right. You need to find out who's behind it."

"I'm trying. I'm meeting with that PI in a few days, and then I'm coming home."

"Jen—"

"And even Jack said he might have a lead, but he wouldn't tell me more. I promise I won't leave until I find out what that is, too, okay?"

"I think you'll regret this, if you don't see it to the end."

"Brian, listen to me. He's at the end of his rope. You haven't seen him. Last night, when he showed up here . . ." She swallows, suppressing the tears about to fall. "I just don't think he can take one more thing. He's about to lose it." *And so am I.*

Her brother sighs. She thinks she got through to him.

"I see my former self in him right now, okay? He's close to the edge, and I don't want to be the one who pushes him over."

Jack's fear over what awaits him at home eases slightly when he spots Mark's car in the driveway. No matter how mad Claire might be, her anger will be tempered by his brother's presence. He ignores the news vans parked at the curb and slips past Mark's car into the garage. Let them fabricate a story about where he's been; anything they report will be better than the truth.

Just as he's about to enter the house, he hears laughter inside. It stops abruptly when he swings open the door. The aroma of baking ham washes over him. He comes into the kitchen to find Claire, his sons, and his brother sitting at the table playing Scrabble. He sees the ham in the oven. In the dining room, he glimpses the china Claire inherited from his mother set out on the long table. The Christmas tree glows proudly, their gifts still wrapped below it. A fire blazes in the fireplace. A perfect Norman Rockwell holiday, if only Mark was Jack.

"Dad's home!" Jamie bolts from the table to the tree. "Can we open presents now?"

Claire stands. "In a minute, Jamie."

"Hey, Jack," Mark says, his voice tentative as he takes in the sight of Jack, unshaved and disheveled. He sees something in Mark's expression—he's trying to send some sort of message—but Jack can't read it.

He glances at Claire. She wears black, brushed cotton pants and a red cashmere sweater that buttons up the front. The pants are snug like a favorite pair of jeans and the sweater is unbuttoned just enough to show a slight cleavage of her perfect, cream-colored breasts. He's always thought they were perfect—not too large, not too small—and neither their shape nor his opinion of them has diminished in the last nineteen years. For the first time since his arrest, she's let her hair down. He didn't realize it had been pulled back in one style or another every day since until he sees the blonde curls loose today.

"How'd everything go?" she asks. The words are neutral, but the cold tone is barely disguised. She fixes her large, green eyes on him, as if willing him to understand the sub-context of the question. He does. What he hears is, *I told the kids you were gone because of work, and please don't ruin Christmas any more than you already have.*

"Fine. It was fine," he manages to say as he pulls off his coat. His body odor is even stronger now. He needs a shower, badly.

Claire makes no moves to take the coat from him as she usually does, but when he heads to the front hall to hang it up, she follows.

"Where have you been?" she demands in a quiet, but fierce, voice.

He doesn't answer. The way her mouth drops open tells him she's read more into his silence than he intended. In his helplessness, she reads a lie.

"I should kick you out on your ass right now," she hisses under her breath.

He notices how different her reaction is this time to what she perceives is the same offense. Something breaks open in him with this knowledge. He doesn't know what it means, but he's acutely aware of it.

"I'm sorry. I went there only to talk to her, but I accidentally fell asleep. That's it." His voice is preternaturally calm.

"You *fell asleep?*"

"Yes, I fell asleep. I didn't mean to."

"Really?"

"Really. I told you that you can trust me, and you can. I didn't do anything, Claire. I went there, we spoke maybe twenty words to each other, and I fell asleep. I woke almost nineteen hours later and came home. I slept for almost nineteen hours. That's how badly I needed sleep."

"Am I supposed to applaud you now?"

"No. But you're supposed to believe me."

"And you're supposed to find out who threatened her, not sleep with her."

"I didn't sleep with her."

Claire plants her hands on her hips, and his eyes are drawn again—inappropriately, he thinks, given everything else happening—to how shapely she is. The slim waist giving way to the curve of her hips. He wants to place his palms on either side of that waist and pull her close, make her believe him. He wants her back. He wants what they had back.

But then he remembers what she said—"I can't give you an answer"—and wonders for the first time if what he wants might not be possible.

He doesn't touch her, but he says, quietly, "You look beautiful today."

She shakes her head, her lips tight with fury. A tear slips down her cheek, surprising both of them, and she swipes at it quickly. He doesn't think it was something she wanted him to see.

"It's Christmas, Jack. *Christmas.*"

"I know that."

"You went to her on Christmas."

"I went to her motel last night after I couldn't sleep at Mark's. I needed some air, something to take my mind off everything—"

Claire mutters something unintelligible.

"—so I figured I'd go out there for a few hours to talk to her, see if I could learn any more about the letters. I accidentally fell asleep. She'd gone outside for a moment and I closed my eyes to rest them, and when—"

Exasperated, she tosses her hands up. "I can't believe we're having this conversation. What, you figured if you can't sleep with her, you can still sleep near her? Is that it? Did you draw a line down the middle of the bed?"

"There are two beds. I—"

"Shut up! I don't care!" She still whispers, but Mark rounds the corner just as she says the words.

Mark takes in the sight of them—Claire with her hands back on her hips, Jack's in his pockets. He must have heard Claire's last few words. "Uh, Claire, there's a buzzer going off."

Her face transforms for Mark. When she speaks, her voice is almost demure. "Thank you." If Jack didn't know better, he'd swear something was going on between them.

She walks away from Jack then, as if their conversation was just another chore she had to accomplish to get dinner on the table, but stops at the corner. "Jack, you stink, and you look like hell." Mark's eyes widen. He's never heard her talk like that to Jack. She never has. "Please think about someone else for once and clean up before you sit down at the dinner table."

Once she's out of sight, Mark whispers, "Just so you're aware, she doesn't know."

"She doesn't know *what*, Mark?" Jack's patience is shot. He thinks about bed again, how he'd rather go upstairs and pull the covers over his head than endure the next several hours pretending for the kids' sake that everything is fine. What's the point? They know better, anyway.

Think about everyone else for once. Is he really that selfish? He didn't think so. Except for the luxurious nineteen hours he spent sleeping at the motel, he's felt everything he's done since the moment he stumbled across Michael and Celeste was done for others or to keep himself from going to prison—a reasonable goal in his opinion. But her words have their intended effect. He'll take his shower, and in about fifteen minutes, he'll be back downstairs at his assigned place at the head of the table.

"That I knew Jenny was in town," Mark says. Jack has to concentrate to remember the context of the words. "Claire thinks I know because she told me. She called me last night when you didn't answer your phone, and when I discovered you weren't in the guest room and told her that, she spilled the whole story. She figured you were with Jenny."

"Okay. And?"

Both men keep their voices low.

"That's all. I just thought you'd want to know."

"Why? If you recall, I was prepared to tell her. You're the one who didn't want her to know you'd seen Jenny. That was your secret, not mine. I don't keep secrets from her anymore."

Mark's jaw tightens. "No, you just keep them from yourself."

"What the fuck's that supposed to mean?"

"You know what it means."

Jack turns for the stairs. *To hell with him.* When Mark starts to say more, Jack cuts him off.

"Can it wait for later, Mark? Apparently I have a shower to take before I'm allowed to eat my ham ration."

CHAPTER TWENTY

ON THE MONDAY following Christmas weekend, Jack loads a bundled-up Jamie in the front seat of his car and a Flexible Flyer in the back and takes off for the courthouse. Jamie will spend the morning with Jack in his office. Then, after lunch in the courthouse cafeteria, the two of them will head to Forest Park for sledding on Art Hill. He warns Jamie that cameras might be pointed at them the whole time, but Jamie simply shrugs. Jack isn't sure whether he's grateful or disturbed by his eight-year-old's increasing comfort with the reporters.

He invited Michael, and even Claire, to join them. Both, not surprisingly, declined.

A rare calm settles on the DA's office during the week between Christmas and New Year's. This year is no exception. Most of the attorneys and staff take the week off, but Beverly is there. She keeps Jamie busy with small copy jobs and easy filing.

Jack calls Dog. "Are you in the office this week?"

"Yes and no. I'm working, but I'm on the road this afternoon."

"Have you made any more progress on the letters?"

"Oh, yeah. Didn't I tell you? I worked my magic. Demetri will talk to you."

"Demetri?"

"My friend at the post office. He's not in 'til next week, though, and you'll have to buy him lunch. We'll meet you at O'Connell's. Around one next Tuesday?"

The thought of a dark pub appeals to Jack. "We? I guess I'm buying for both of you."

"You guessed right, Boss."

When Jack arrives at O'Connell's the following Tuesday, he takes a corner booth. The pub's décor, with its dim lighting and the dark woodwork preserved from the original location in Gaslight Square, grants a level of privacy not found at the brightly lit chains that litter the metro area. The food is as authentic as the pub, although Jack's appetite is almost non-existent.

It's nearing one, and the lunch crowd has thinned. Other than a large table in the middle of the room crowded with co-workers, and a couple in the far opposite corner, Jack is the only customer in the dining room. He spots Dog and his friend coming through the large opening from the bar side.

Dog greets Jack and then introduces Demetri Griffin, who, to Jack's surprise, is closer to his age than Dog's. He's tall, with a brawny build, and when the two of them slide onto the bench across from Jack, the wood groans from the weight. The waitress arrives with Jack's earlier drink order—a Coke—and asks Dog and Demetri for theirs. When she returns quickly with two dark microbrews, Jack eyes the tall glasses with desire. He's not much of a beer drinker, but the knowledge that he can't get any booze in prison suddenly makes it more appealing.

Once she takes their food orders and steps away, Dog leans back and says, "Demetri is a busy guy, Boss, so shoot. What do you want to know?"

"Malik exaggerates, Mr. Hilliard," the man says. His voice has a deep, clear timbre that reminds Jack of Barry White. "You have me as long as you wish."

Jack decides he likes the man.

He explains how he needs to learn the identity of the woman who mailed the letters, and that if he gets a better description—crimes are often solved by the minor details—he might find out what he needs to know.

Demetri stretches an arm across the back of the booth. "May I ask what the crime is?"

"In my opinion, the letters constitute criminal threats."

"Why didn't you subpoena the tapes? I would think in your position that wouldn't be a problem."

The man is smart. Jack wonders what, exactly, his role is at the post office. He glances at Dog in hopes that somehow he'll signal Jack how much he can trust this guy. But Dog isn't paying attention. Instead, he's watching a cute, young waitress flirt with guys at a nearby table.

"At this point, until I know more, it's simply a favor for a friend."

Demetri lifts his beer and takes a long, slow drink. He sets it down carefully and wipes the foam from his lip with his napkin.

"It was a woman," he says. "I couldn't see her face. I don't know for sure, but I suspect she was aware of the camera location and made a point of hiding her face."

Jack reminds himself that anyone would do the same before mailing letters of a threatening nature. Why not use a box on the street, though, away from cameras?

"What makes you say that?"

"Nothing I can put my finger on. Body language."

"How do you know this woman mailed the letters? No time stamp is on the postmarks."

"True, but she's the only one who was in the post office on all three dates. And each visit took place at about the same time."

"Which was?"

"Saturday morning, a little after eleven."

Jack knew the dates all fell on a Saturday, but the time is new information. "Can you describe her? I mean, from what you *did* see of her?"

"Dark hair. Long. Thick."

"Dark, as in brown? Black?"

"From the tapes it looks black. Could be dark brown."

"Could you see the side of her face?"

"No. Her hair was always in the way. That's what I mean. Like she was purposely trying not to be seen."

"Curly? Straight?"

"Straight. So straight it was like she'd used an iron, you know?"

The waitress places a plate in front of each man, burgers for Dog and Demetri, a roast beef sandwich for Jack. Jack looks at the sandwich and knows, because of what he's learned so far, he won't be able to eat it.

"What race was she?" he asks when they're alone again.

Demetri shrugs. "She wasn't a sister, if that's what you mean."

"Was she dark, fair?"

Demetri presses his lips together, looks to the ceiling in thought. "Like I said, I couldn't see her face, but her arms were probably what I'd call dark. Darker than the typical white girl."

"Like a tan? Or naturally dark?"

"I don't know. Hard to tell from a tape. Just dark."

"What was she wearing?"

"Well, in the first one, she had on one of those shirts the girls wear in the summer. You know, like a man's undershirt, the sleeves up here." He motions at his shoulders. "And jeans."

"You mean, like a tank top?"

"Yeah, that's right."

"What color?"

"White."

Jack sees Jenny on the bed when he woke up, pajamas on her bent legs, white tank bright against her brown skin.

"Boss? You okay?" Dog asks gently, so out of character for him.

"I don't know," Jack says. "Let me ask you one more thing," he says to Demetri, "and then you can eat in peace."

"Sure."

"You keep saying 'girl.' Was she really a girl? Or a woman? You know, an adult? How old would you put her? How tall?"

Demetri's eyebrows rise, and he shrugs again. "Can't say for sure how tall, because the camera angle makes it hard to judge. But she wasn't a child. She was built, at least from the rear. Nice ass, you know? I mean, maybe a bit skinny for my tastes" —he laughs— "but nice and tight, especially in her jeans."

He bites into his burger then. When he moans with pleasure, Jack's not sure if the food or his memory of the mysterious woman's ass is to blame.

By the time he leaves O'Connell's, Jack is convinced Jenny mailed the letters to herself. He questioned Demetri about the other tapes, and except for changes in attire, the description of the woman on each tape remained the same.

He takes a detour on his way back to the courthouse to find a payphone—a difficult task since they've become a scarce commodity. He first calls the motel, but when he asks to be connected to Room Five, the desk clerk tells him the guest checked out. Even though he trusts Jenny less and less, he still feels a pang from her departure.

He then calls her cell phone. It rings four times before he gets a recording telling him "the cellular customer you are trying to reach has chosen not to have voice mail service on this account." He knows he'll hear that message until he calls from a number she recognizes. He calls her then from his own phone, his desire to talk to her trumping his fear.

"Did you just try to call from a different number?" she asks, not bothering with hello.

"Yeah, we need to talk. Where are you? The motel says you checked out."

"I did."

"Yeah, and?"

She's quiet for a moment. Then, "I told you I planned to go back."

"You also told me you'd talk to me first."

"I said I'd be here a few more days, and then I'd decide. I never said I'd run it by you."

He can't remember the specifics of their last conversation, but he left the motel on Christmas assuming that before she left, she'd let him know.

"What do we need to talk about?" she asks.

"I have a lead on the letters, remember? I don't want to talk on the phone, though." *I want to see the look on your face when I spring the news.*

"We don't have much of a choice."

"I would love to see where you've been living," he says quickly, calling her bluff. "I can head up to Chicago today."

She laughs—to make him think she takes it as a joke, he guesses—but he hears nervousness in her voice. Despite the restrictions of his bail, he's tempted to attempt a brief trip up and back to see what has her spooked about the suggestion. A flight is out of the question, but he might be able to manage a drive without anyone knowing.

"I don't think the court or your bail bondsman would appreciate you leaving," she says, reading his mind.

"I wasn't aware we now have patrols at our state borders."

"You'd risk that? You'd really risk getting caught and having your bail revoked?"

Would he? He thinks again of Claire's words: *She's like a drug to you*. And like a drug, the hard-earned knowledge of how much harm she can do is weak armor against her pull.

"So what's your lead?" she says, apparently deciding the answer is no.

He considers his strategy. He didn't anticipate the problem of being in two different places. Should he toss her a few bones to see how she reacts or keep what he knows close so he doesn't spook her?

He chooses the latter. "Not on a cell phone, Jen. No way."

"How about if I call you at a landline, from a pay phone?"

He doesn't trust that the government phones at the DA's office aren't bugged, and given Harley's efforts to go after Jack's law license, he's not really sure his home phone isn't either.

"Let me think about where that could be." He also needs more time to decide how much he'll tell her. Maybe, even, he'll convince Demetri to let him see the tapes for himself, possibly rendering all of this moot. "I'll get back to you, but do a favor for me, next time I call?"

"What's that?"

"Answer."

Jack sits in his car and thinks about their conversation. He didn't imagine her nervousness, yet if she had something to hide, why ask him to help in the first place?

Once again, he calls Dog.

"Miss me already?" Dog asks without greeting.

"You know it." It gets a laugh from Dog. "I have a question for you."

"Shoot."

"What do you know about how cell phones works?"

"Depends. What do you need to know?"

"Let's say I don't want to go through the legal hoops required to ask the phone company to locate a cell phone. Is there still a way, if I place a call from my phone, to find out the general location of the other party to the call?"

"Sure, roughly."

"Like maybe which state they're in?"

"Oh, yeah, no problem. It would depend on the phone's capabilities. But if all you want is the state, or even the city, you only need to know where the call was routed."

"Go on."

"You know, like which towers were used? Just call your phone company and they'll tell you which towers the call routed through."

When Jack doesn't say anything, Dog mutters and continues slowly, as if talking to a child. "Okay, for example, a few months back my cell bill showed a roaming charge for calls from Texas. I ain't ever been to Texas, so how could I have made a call from there, you know? When I called the phone company, they checked and saw that none of my calls were routed through Texas. Mistake in the billing. Got it?"

"Got it." In fact, Jack got it even before Dog launched into his example. He was already thinking several steps ahead of Dog. If Jack's hunch is right, finding out whether Jenny lied to him will be easier than he thought.

Ten minutes later, after speaking to an AT&T representative, he learns that his last call to Jenny was routed through a tower in Clayton. It never left the state.

CHAPTER TWENTY-ONE

ON THE WAY into Clayton, Jack calls Mark. When he gets voicemail, he leaves a short message: "We need to talk. I'm coming over." Unless his brother is traveling for work, he should be home.

Jack rings the doorbell, following it with a hard knock. When no one answers, he flips through his keychain until he finds the key.

He unlocks the door, cracks it open, and calls out. Mark doesn't respond, but Jack hears water running through pipes. At first he thinks the sound comes from an appliance—the clothes washer or the dishwasher—but as he moves into the house, closing the door behind him, he realizes it's the shower. His watch reads almost three fifteen. An odd time for a shower, unless Mark has a date later.

While he waits, he circles through the family room around to the kitchen, casually taking in the scant evidence of his brother's life. With no children to mess it up, the house is immaculate. Mark dated an interior designer back when he bought the house, and the décor is all hers. The black granite kitchen counters are empty save a cell phone, coffee maker and toaster. The door of the large stainless steel refrigerator is a blank slate. No magnetic letters for impromptu poems or messages, no school pictures, no basketball schedules. A bowl with a colorful mixture of Granny Smith and Red Delicious apples rests on the middle island. The apples look so perfect that Jack touches them to see if they're real; he's surprised to find that they are.

He swings back into the family room, where the furnishings are European modern, all clean lines with a Danish influence. He notices that even the newspapers and magazines, still unread from the looks of it, are stacked in a neat pile on the coffee table. He settles onto the stiff leather sofa with a GQ magazine he finds on the top of the pile. Quickly bored, he tosses it back onto the table and pulls out his phone to listen to voicemail. He's on the fourth message when he hears the shower shut off. He saves the message and moves on to the next one, from Claire, tersely reminding him she'll be home late. He doesn't remember why, but from her tone he knows she already told him and therefore assumes he'll know what she's talking about.

He's about to press the "call back" button and confess to his faulty memory when the cell phone on the kitchen counter plays a tinny version of Green Day's "Wake Me Up When September Ends." He finds this odd, too; Mark has always been more a fan of jazz. He debates whether to answer it, but before he finishes the thought he hears the bathroom door swing open, so hard it slams into the doorstop. In the moment before the bather appears around the hall corner, he knows it isn't Mark who will emerge. The footsteps are too light. And even though logically it could be any woman—Mark's house is like a hotel in that department—Jack is certain it's not. He knows who it will be and he can't escape fast enough.

He sits frozen as Jenny, wet hair clinging to scalp and shoulders, towel hastily twisted across the chest, comes into his line of sight.

But she doesn't even see him as she darts to the kitchen to reach the phone before Billie Joe Armstrong stops singing. It's evident she hasn't yet used the towel for anything but a wrap. Her skin glistens and water trails behind her, leaving dark, wet footprints in the thick beige carpet. On the way, she hastily readjusts the towel. With arms stretched wide, she holds the towel out straight and layers first one end and then the other over the front of her body. She seals it by tucking the second layer into the first. The whole motion takes less than five seconds, but it exposes her breasts and stomach to Jack, and like a tiny drop of viper's venom, the glimpse paralyzes him.

She gets to the phone on the third go-around of the song. "Hey." Her tone when she answers is casual, intimate. Even as he fights his body's instinctive response to what he just saw, he listens carefully. "No, I'm at his brother's house," she says, and now Jack's curiosity is piqued almost as much as his libido.

He rises from the sofa and make his way quietly to a spot just behind the open doorway to the kitchen. He stands with his head against the wall, his ears tuned to every breath she takes.

"He doesn't know. I'm sure of it." *Is she talking about him? Mark? And what doesn't 'he' know?* "He doesn't, Brian. I can read him. And she's not stupid." *Who is 'she'?*

He steals a glance around the wall. Strategically, it does him no harm. She's turned away from him. "I don't know," she says.

But emotionally, the sight of her leaning on the island cripples him further. She's bent over, her elbows on the granite, her left hand holding the phone and her right hand mindlessly playing with one green apple. The angle causes the towel to hike farther up the back of her leg. A millimeter more and the soft flesh of her bottom will be exposed. One foot is propped up on the footrest; her calf muscle is flexed.

"I told you, I don't know. I've only talked to her on the phone. I'll find out for sure once I meet with her."

Who is she talking about?

"Yeah. Today."

He twists back to his spot against the wall and tries to steady his breathing. If he's going to confront her, he needs to be calm.

"I just think it's better this way. The letters were the only reason she put up with him seeing me, but—"

Claire. She's talking about Claire. Calming down is no longer an option.

"Yeah, exactly. I'll call you as soon as I have something to tell you. I promise." Her voice softened with the last two words, but with the next ones, it quavers. "Trust me. He will." She lets out an exasperated sigh. She sounds on the verge of tears. "He *will*, Brian. If there's one thing I know for certain, it's how he feels about me, okay?"

He fights the urge to let her see him. He needs to wait until she ends the call.

"It'll be okay. . . Yeah. Okay. . . .I'll call you soon. . . I love you, too. Bye."

As soon as he hears her set down the phone, he steps into the doorway. She shrieks and steps backward, grabbing at the top of the towel.

"Goddamn you, Jack!" she shouts. "You scared the living shit out of me!"

"I guess so. You weren't expecting me, huh?"

At his flat tone, she regards him warily but says nothing. Her hands on the towel tremble.

"Do you walk around like that when Mark's home, too?"

She glares at him, but it's clear his unexpected appearance has shaken her.

"What are you doing here?" she asks. "What do you want?"

"I could ask the same questions."

"He invited me, remember?"

"And you declined. In fact, you're supposed to be in Chicago."

"I changed my mind."

"Funny you didn't mention that earlier. In fact, you said you were already there."

"No, I didn't. You just assumed it, and I didn't bother to correct you." She moves in his direction for the doorway, lowering her head like a ram planning to plow right through him. He steps to the side and blocks her exit. "Stop it, Jack. I'm cold. I want to get dressed."

"I think you should stay just as you are. It might give you an advantage, don't you think?"

He moves forward, causing her to move backwards. They engage in a strange dance, but she runs out of dance floor when, without even touching her, he has backed her up against the island. She still clutches the towel with both hands.

"Who were you talking to?" he asks, even though he knows.

"Brian." She whispers the answer.

"Who were you talking about? Who are you so sure 'doesn't know'? And who is the 'she' you're meeting?"

"It doesn't concern you. It has nothing to do with you, or us."

"No?"

"No."

"What if I said I don't believe you?"

She shrugs, but won't meet his eye.

"Have you been talking to Claire? Are you both going behind my back now?"

"You're out of your mind. I'd be the last person Claire would talk to."

His phone rings with Mark's ringtone. He ignores it.

"We had a deal," he says. At her silence, he asks, "Whose feelings are you so sure of? Who are you manipulating now?"

He knows the answers to the last two questions. Still, they're the ones that get a real reaction. She whips her head up. In her dark eyes he finally sees the aggression he expects. "I'm not manipulating anyone. You think you know everything, but you have no idea what you're talking about."

"Maybe you should tell me, then. Maybe you should honor your agreement."

She grunts and shakes her head.

"Tell me something." He reaches up and slicks her wet hair behind one ear, letting his thumb brush her cheek. She closes her eyes as if enduring something painful. Slowly then, he peels her hands—first one, then the other—away from the towel. She watches but doesn't fight as he substitutes his hands for hers. Her fingers are icy and her skin has the faint scent of Dial soap. "Have you fucked my brother yet?"

She doesn't answer, but he knows she hasn't. Except for the rise and fall of her chest, she doesn't move. Except for her nervous breathing, she makes no sound. Goose bumps develop on her bare skin.

His breathing is labored. His heart is beating so hard his whole body throbs. He knows intellectually what he wants, why he's doing this to himself, to her— he needs to prove to both of them that he can resist her—but his body refuses to cooperate with his brain. It wants something else entirely. It wants to rip off the towel and devour her.

She sneers. "It's interesting. I'm the one who's cold and wet, yet you're the one who's shivering."

"Why'd you lie to me?"

"I didn't lie to you." She tries to pull his hands away but he holds tight. *Let her be the vulnerable one, for once.* She doesn't try again.

"I think you did. You mailed those letters to yourself. Why?"

"What are you talking about? Where are you coming up with these things? I didn't."

"I saw the tapes," he lies.

"*What* tapes?"

"I guess you didn't cover your tracks as well as you did with Maxine."

"You're so wrong. I didn't kill her."

"You're a liar, and you're a murderer."

"I'm not, Jack." Her voice breaks.

The rumble of Mark's automatic garage door interrupts them. She grabs at his hands again, but she's no match for his strength. "Quickly, tell me why you sent the letters," he demands. "Convince me I'm wrong."

For a moment she looks as if she might answer, but at the slamming sound of a car door she tugs one last time and he lets go. She hurries to leave the kitchen. This time he doesn't try to stop her. He feels her hesitate in the doorway behind him.

"Sometimes the culprit is right in front of you, Jack."

He wheels around. "What are—?"

The door connecting the kitchen to the garage opens. Mark stops at the sight of them. Jenny races for the back of the house, Jack for the front door.

"Jack, wait," Mark yells. Jack stops with his hand on the doorknob. "What's going on?"

Jack turns to study the expression on his brother's face, searching for any evidence of duplicity.

"I don't know, Mark. You tell me." After a quick glance in the direction Jenny headed, he mutters "You tell me" again. He slams the door behind him and leaves without an answer.

His hands shake so much he has trouble inserting the key into the ignition. No sooner has he pulled out of the driveway, his phone rings again. He pulls it from his coat, confirms the caller is Mark, and tosses it on the passenger seat. He doesn't know what to think. He doesn't know where to go. He only knows he needs to get himself away from here.

So many thoughts and competing emotions bombard his mind. He can't hold one still long enough to make sense of it. He tries to recall the things Jenny said to Brian on the phone, but he only grows more frustrated. None of it means anything to him, not without more information, information that only she can provide. He considers whether she might have talked to Claire. If so, why would Claire keep this information from him? He doesn't think she would. Despite Claire's simmering disgust with him that erupts at the slightest provocation, he trusts her.

He wonders what his brother knows, and why he's providing shelter for Jenny behind Jack's back. What did she mean, *the culprit is right in front of you*? Is Jack overlooking another reason she accepted Mark's invitation, other than the obvious ones of money and preferring the luxuries of his Clayton home to the dirty bathroom and thin mattress of the motel? Is there any reason she'd want to keep an eye on Mark? Jack can't even fathom a connection.

Mixed in with all of these thoughts is the image, vivid in his mind's eye, of her trapped against the counter, so exposed and yet so defiant. And so beautiful.

Despite his anger at her lies, the memory causes his body to betray him all over again. The raging hunger returns. It's so strong even in her absence that he wonders whether, but for his brother's arrival, he would have withstood the desire to satiate it.

Like an alcoholic who recognizes when his attendance at an AA meeting is long overdue, Jack suddenly knows, simply from having asked himself the question, where he must go and whom he must see.

Even though Jack knows Claire's class schedule and office hours, he still tries the handle on her fourth floor office door. It's locked, as he expected. He reads the various scribbles on the dry erase board beside the door. After determining all the messages are outdated, he rubs clean a large enough spot to leave her a conspicuous one of his own: I'M ON THE 5TH FLOOR. COME ON UP. He doesn't need to sign his name or specify his exact location. She'll know who wrote it.

He finds his usual spot in the largest seating area on the fifth floor. The rest of the floor is made up of faculty offices that line the perimeter, a few study rooms, a few stacks of federal materials, and many stacks of periodicals. Three students are scattered among the two tables at the center of the space, but the chairs and couch at the edge are empty. The students watch him as he takes a seat on the couch, but their attention returns to their open books when they don't recognize him. Or maybe they do and they simply don't care.

He sends Dog a quick text message: Surveillance job for u. 77## davis dr. If tall indian woman leaves, follow, call me & report

Dog texts back: U mean dodson boss?

Jack sighs and texts: yes, I mean dodson

He spends the next half hour trying to read and respond to the emails he's let accumulate over the past few weeks. He can't concentrate because his phone, now set to silent, vibrates every time Mark tries to reach him. He shoves it in his back pocket and switches to his laptop, using Claire's pass code to access the university wireless. Yet even this solution fails; another half hour passes and he's done nothing but stare at the computer screen and replay in his mind what happened at his brother's house. Her last words—*sometimes the culprit is right in front of you*—gnaw at him.

There's not a window in sight, but as time passes, he feels the sun ease toward the horizon. One by one the students gather their backpacks and leave.

When he is alone in the immediate area, he finally answers one of Mark's calls. "I'm not somewhere I can easily talk," he says, keeping his voice down.

"Then listen, at least, will you?" At Jack's silence, Mark launches into his defense. "She called me right after Christmas and asked if my offer was still open. She felt like you already had too much to contend with to deal with her problems, so she wanted you to think she returned to Chicago. She asked me not to tell you. I agreed because I think she's right. If you meant what you said in my car that night, then you need to stay away from each other." Jack understands the last comment to be a reference to what Jack said about his marriage. "She has a meeting today with someone she says will help her investigate the letters—she wouldn't tell me who—and then she plans to go home. She—"

"Her home is St. Louis."

"Jack." Mark sighs. "That would be her call, wouldn't it?"

"She ran for a reason."

"You still believe she did it? Even in light of the letters?"

"The letters are a red herring. She's lying. She lied to me, and now she's lying to you. She sent those letters to herself."

"What are you talking about?"

"Just what I said. She sent the letters to herself. I don't know why, or why she came back. I'm still trying to figure that out."

"You're not making sense."

"That's true. None of this makes sense. Let me ask you, where is she now?"

"I don't know. Whatever happened between you two before I walked in, it upset her. She apologized to me—"

"For what?"

"Everything. She was rambling. For coming back, for causing problems between us, for being at my house. You name it, she apologized for it. She packed up and left after you ran out."

Damn. Does that mean Dog missed her? "Did she apologize for murder?"

Mark grunts with disgust. "Look, I really don't think she's lying, to either of us. You didn't think so, either, the night we drove out to the motel."

"I guess I was thinking with my dick instead of my brain" —Jack laughs bitterly— "like you said."

"Is that what you were doing on Christmas, too?"

The question startles Jack, and rankles him. "Not by a long shot. Why, is that what *you* were doing?" he shoots back, remembering the holiday card he interrupted at his own home.

"*What?*"

"Forget it. Look, I gotta go."

"What are you suggesting, Jack?"

"Nothing. Just forget it. I have to go." He glances at his watch; Claire's class should be long over. "I have to meet Claire."

"Really? That's interesting, since Claire is at a law school bash."

Her message earlier, which Jack just remembers, now makes sense. She'd mentioned the event—a reception for a visiting Supreme Court justice—several weeks back, before Christmas. At first, Jack thought she wanted him to accompany her as he always did to such events, but she quickly corrected his assumption. "I just think it will be less awkward for everyone if I go alone," she'd said. He also understands why the library emptied out so quickly tonight. How did Mark know, though?

"*I* pay attention when she talks," Mark says, as if to answer Jack's unspoken question.

"Fuck you. You don't have a clue what happens between me and my wife. You'd better hang up and think about what your house guest said to you. Just don't forget to read between the lines."

"Yeah, right," Mark snarls. "Spoken by a man who learned the hard way."

When Jack hangs up, he sees he missed an earlier text from Dog—Target left house, following—then another just a moment ago: Just entered Ritz. Think checking in.

Jack has no idea when Claire might return and the Ritz is just down the road. Thx. I'll take it from here, he texts back. He's decided to do a bit of surveillance of his own.

He nods briefly to the doorman who holds the door for him as he enters the warm foyer of the hotel. The howling wind and the noises of rush hour traffic are replaced by soft classical piano music and the murmurs of guests and staff. Two extravagantly-decorated Christmas trees still cast their glow over the small foyer, and the elegant sofas and stately chairs in the wood-paneled lobby lounge to his left are lit by subdued table lamps. A long, marble bar at the far end of the room completes the tableau. It's a welcome refuge from the cold.

He makes his way through the wide entranceway leading into the lounge. A flash of color—so out of place among the subdued blacks and grays—catches his eye. He stops and quickly moves behind a post. The hostess says, "Sir, would you like me to show you to a table?" She doesn't recognize him.

What kind of bar requires a hostess to show the clientele to a table? he wonders, even though he knows. This kind, where tea and petit fours trump the cocktails.

Realizing she's waiting for an answer, he says quickly, "No. No thank you."

The color comes from the rear of the room, near the bar and grand staircase, where a woman in a turquoise blue sari and headscarf perches on a sofa across from a young woman who can't be more than twenty-four or twenty-five years of age. The younger woman is dressed in jeans and a short black leather coat. Her legs are crossed, one swinging as she talks, and her black boots sport unusually high heels. Her highlighted auburn hair is pulled back into a stylish ponytail, giving him a clear shot of her face. She's attractive in a tough, urban sort of way. The face of the woman wearing the sari is hidden; the head scarf blocks his view. But he sees her hand when she picks up a cup of tea from the table between them. He knows that hand.

He finds it odd that she'd wear such a bright color when she doesn't want to be noticed, but then, maybe the ones who look as if they're trying to hide are the ones who stand out.

"Sir?" the hostess tries again. She can't discern what, exactly, Jack wants.

"You wouldn't happen to know the name of the woman in the sari, would you? Did she have a reservation for high tea, maybe?"

The hostess hesitates. Jack sees it's a privacy concern, so he pulls out his credentials and flashes them so fast that she gets the point without reading his name.

"No reservation, sir. But the other woman arrived first and said that if an Indian woman came in looking for her, I should direct her over." She motions to the woman in the sari as if to say *And there she is.*

"And the young lady's name? Do you know it?"

"Rebecca Chambers, I believe she said."

The name means nothing to Jack, but thanks to the internet, it soon will. He stares, waiting for Jenny to turn even just a bit so that he can confirm it's her. Although the scarf covers most of her face, he's certain he'll recognize her eyes.

"Are you sure I can't seat you, sir?" the hostess asks again. He hears voices approaching; the question is her way of telling him she has others to attend to.

He pulls out a twenty and hands it to her. "No, thank you. You've already helped me more than you'll ever know."

While he waits them out, he uses his phone to search Rebecca Chamber's name on the internet and discovers she works for a private investigator named Lee Randolph. Does this mean Jenny told Mark the truth, that she really did hire someone to help her investigate the letters? But then, why involve Jack in the first place? And why did she lie to him? Why did she want him to think she'd returned to Chicago?

He thinks of the comment Earl made when Jack told him about the threats: *Thirty years after the fact? Doesn't that strike you as odd?* It *does* strike Jack as odd. He's certain Jenny is the woman Demetri described from the tapes, but if she sent the letters to herself, why would she hire a PI? It has to be for some other reason.

If Jenny won't tell him, he'll have to find out another way.

After the Dodson woman leaves for her room upstairs, Rebecca takes off on foot for her car, which she parked several blocks away. As she turns the corner at Bemiston, she senses she's being followed. The tentative tapping of her boot heels on the slippery sidewalk is matched by a more solid footstep. She tests her theory by ducking into the lit alcove at the entrance to The Fatted Calf. No one passes, and when she reemerges, the masculine tread resumes behind her. She digs in her purse for a compact, slowing to open it and then pretending to check her hair in the mirror. She stifles a gasp when she sees who's on her tail.

He waves at her reflection and says, "I don't mean to scare you. Can we talk a minute?"

She stops and lets him catch up. Despite the cold, her face grows hot as the blood rushes to her cheeks. Whether her blush comes from her assumption that he saw her with Jennifer Dodson, or from the girlish thrill she feels in his presence, she can't say. She only hopes the dark hides it.

"There's a Starbucks a block over," he says. His voice has the same smooth quality as when he speaks to reporters. "Can I buy you a coffee?"

"I don't really like Starbucks," she says, managing, she thinks, to speak the words breezily, "but okay, sure."

He laughs, and a small dimple appears in his right cheek. "You do look a little anti-establishment."

He holds open the door and helps her shrug off her coat. She can't remember the last time a guy did either for her. *Get a grip, Rebecca. This guy cheated on his wife. The chivalry is skin deep.*

"What's your pleasure?" he says as he carefully hangs the coat over a deep leather chair. It's apparent he believes introductions are unnecessary. He's right, of course.

"A regular coffee with cream. Thanks." In the land of grande lattes and vente cappuccinos and assorted chais, she sees he appreciates her simple request.

He returns with one cup and hands it to her. "I have enough trouble sleeping at night," he explains, answering a question she hasn't even asked.

"'There's no pillow so soft as a clean conscience.'"

With an amused grin, he watches her take her first sip. "Is that so?"

Rebecca shrugs. "It's a French proverb."

He laughs again. "Where'd she find you?"

"Who, Mr. Hilliard?"

"I'd rather you call me Jack. 'Mr. Hilliard' makes me feel like I'm your dad."

"Okay. Where did *who* find me, Jack?" It sounds so unnatural coming out of her mouth. He's always been "the DA" to her.

"Ayanna Patel. Who else?"

The use of the alias reminds Rebecca that she's playing a game with someone much more experienced at it than she is. She suspects it was his way of telling her he knows more about Jennifer Dodson than she ever will.

"My communications with Ms. Patel are confidential."

"You're aware that's not her real name?"

"Yes. And I also know why she chooses to use an alias."

"Well, not exactly. You know the reason *she* gave you."

He holds her gaze until she relents and looks down at her coffee. She has no idea where things stand between him and his ex-mistress. The two women never discussed the DA. For all she knows, *ex-mistress* is the wrong term. She doesn't even know if he's aware of the previous surveillance.

His phone rings. Muttering "Excuse me," he pulls it from the inside pocket of his coat. Anyone else and she would have walked away right then, but she figures the DA has no choice but to be perpetually on-call. She's impressed when he doesn't answer. "Sorry about that," he says, replacing the phone. She nods to let him know she took no offense.

"Mr. Hilliard, why did you want to talk to me?" *And why did I agree?*

He frowns, she assumes, from her reversion back to his surname.

"I'd like to know why she hired you."

"What makes you think she did?"

"Well, I saw you together in the bar, and you're a little young to be an old friend. Why else would she be hanging out with you?"

She notices how others in the coffee shop recognize him and then glance at her. He seems not to care. If she hadn't seen him in the garage that night four years ago, and then sitting on the stoop outside Dodson's house the next morning, she would think he's always as cool as he appears to be now. "*If* she hired me, you know I couldn't answer that question. It would be an egregious breach of duty. But I will tell you this: she didn't."

One eyebrow goes up. "Really? Why?"

"I have a conflict."

He leans back and rests one arm along the back of his chair. He still has on his overcoat, and he wears it well. Perhaps it's simply an expensive brand, but on a prosecutor's salary, she doubts it. She suspects anything looks good on him. She really wishes she'd stop idolizing him. *He's just another man.*

"What kind of conflict?" he asks.

She shakes her head. "You're used to having your questions answered, aren't you?"

"It's what I do."

"Well, I'm not on the witness stand and I have no obligation to answer. In fact, my obligation is to her, to *not* answer. I would think you'd respect that."

"I do. She chose wisely."

Her curiosity gets the better of her. "Maybe you should ask *her*."

"I don't trust her."

The blunt, obviously honest remark stuns Rebecca, and confirms that he knows nothing of Lee's report. "Why not?"

He tilts his head as if to say, *Oh, come on.*

She sets her cup on the table next to her and leans forward. "But they dropped the charges against her. They convicted her boyfriend. You testified for her!"

His expression softens as he looks away. She sees in his eyes the same thing she saw in the garage. He's still wild about Jennifer Dodson. Even if he did forsake her, he's a married man smitten by a woman he thinks is a murderer and it's killing him.

"I testified *against* him. Some people like to interpret that as testifying for her. But she wasn't on trial." As he talks, he avoids her eyes. He watches the other patrons in the coffee shop, he stares at the floor. It's almost as if he's talking to himself. "And as I'm sure you know, subsequent to that trial, information came to light that calls into question whether the charges against her should have ever been dismissed. And now that her boyfriend gets a new trial—"

"What do you mean?"

"You haven't heard? The appeals court granted Alex Turner a new trial."

She hesitates, lets out a helpless sigh. How could she have missed that news? And why didn't Jennifer Dodson mention it? Probably because she feared that if Rebecca knew, she wouldn't have agreed to meet. "I know you're the DA and you probably know things that are never made public, but you don't really think she had something to do with that woman's murder, do you?"

Finally he looks at her, his startling blue eyes narrowed in accusation. "I don't know. Did she?"

As strongly as she wants him to know what he so desperately wants to hear, she can't tell him. Not without betraying the confidence of several people. Even if she could get beyond the ethical implications, she senses Dodson had her own reasons for not showing him Lee's report. Who knows what consequences Rebecca might wreak if she opens her mouth?

No, the information is not hers to disclose. Sharing the report with Dodson back then to help her defense was bad enough, even if Rebecca meant well, but telling the DA now what she knows merely because she has some silly idea about the two of them being star-crossed lovers and she wishes, just once, star-crossed lovers could have a happy ending . . . well, that's something else entirely.

"I'm sorry, Mr. Hilliard, but I can't help you." She rises and reaches for her coat. To her dismay, he rises, too, and holds it while she slips her arms in. She doesn't want him to be nice to her. "If you think I know something that will help the State bring her to justice, by all means, subpoena me. If a judge orders me to speak, I guess I'll have to decide then what to do. But—"

She stops talking when she realizes he's not listening. His eyes are focused intently on the screen of a laptop at the next table. She turns to look, too, but catches only the words BREAKING NEWS before the laptop owner closes the lid and rises to throw away his cup. When the DA returns his attention to her, his face is flushed and he's clearly agitated. "I'm sorry."

"It's okay. Is there something wrong? Is something happening?"

He stares at her as if he'll find the answers on her face. "Can I ask you one more thing? Did anyone, anyone at all, know about your meeting with Ms. Patel?"

"No. Why?"

He shakes his head. "It's nothing." An awkward silence follows; whatever he saw has him extremely distracted. "Listen, about what you said . . . If you get subpoenaed, it won't be my doing. I have no say what happens in that case."

She nods and he offers his hand. She shakes it and thanks him for the coffee.

"My pleasure. Thank you for your time, Rebecca."

He says it pleasantly, but her ears hear something else entirely. *Thanks for nothing.*

Jack hangs back in the coffee shop for a few minutes to give the young woman a good head start. Once he's confident she's gone, he steps outside onto the sidewalk where he won't be overheard and returns Earl's call.

"Are you anywhere near my office?" Earl asks before Jack speaks. Jack knows he means *We need to talk* and he'd rather not do it over the phone.

"No, I'm in Clayton. What the hell's going on? I just saw something on the internet about Jenny." He scans the intersection for familiar faces as he talks.

"I got a call from Gunner a while ago. I tried to call and warn you but it went to voicemail. They've received a tip that she's back in town and they want to talk to you."

Jesus. Fearing his legs will give out under him, Jack collapses on a nearby bench.

"He says if you cooperate, he's willing to do it all off the record. But if you don't come in voluntarily, all bets are off."

Jack tries to make his brain fast-forward through all the possible scenarios of how they know whatever they know, but he can't concentrate.

"Jack?"

"Sounds like I'm being blackmailed by the police chief."

"I think he'd say *persuaded*. If I were you, I'd consider myself lucky they didn't just pick you up without advance notice. He's trusting you won't try to warn her."

"Does his tip include information that I've seen her? Or is it limited to the fact of her being around?"

"He wouldn't get that specific."

"Even if I 'cooperate' as he says—though I'm not sure exactly what that means to him—my name will still get drawn into it. If it hasn't already."

"Most likely. And there's another problem, too, one we both knew could arise. I can't represent you during the questioning. Dodson was my client first. There's no way to get around the conflict."

"Earl . . ." Jack sighs. Earl's right; they did both know this could happen. Jack simply hoped it wouldn't. "I don't trust anyone else."

"I can give you some names."

Jack gives a bitter laugh. "Oh, believe me, I know the names."

"You need to have someone with you when he questions you."

"Yeah, yeah, I know. A man who represents himself has a fool for a client, right?" He bends over and rubs his forehead. *Fuck.* "I'm screwed."

"Can you convince her to come in for questioning on her own? That's the only way I see to spin this in your favor."

Can he? And more importantly, if he thinks he can, will he, knowing what he now knows about the letters?

"I'd try myself," Earl adds, "but I don't think she'd listen to me. More importantly, I don't want to do anything to jeopardize my ability to represent you on Celeste's charges."

"Call him back and tell him I'm in a meeting or something. Tell him I'll talk to him, but you have to buy me some time. I'll see what I can do."

"Do you know where she is?"

"Maybe." He glances in the direction of the Ritz. "Just buy me some time, Earl. I'll call you back soon."

He ends the call before Earl argues or questions him more.

As he walks back to the hotel, he calls Information for the number of the front desk.

"I'm trying to reach a guest there, Ayanna Patel?" he says once connected, using his best *I'm just a clueless caller* voice. "She told me her room number, but I seem to have misplaced it."

"One moment, sir." After a pause, the operator adds, "That's Room 312. I'll connect you."

He hangs up before the connection is completed.

Jack stands outside Jenny's room. He wonders if she's seen the news, and whether she'll open the door once she knows it's him. He wonders if she's even in there.

He covers the peephole and is reminded of when she did the same to his hotel room door at a Bench and Bar conference the summer he first ran for DA. Her gesture then was a playful one; his now is far from playful.

He knocks with his other hand. Nothing.

He knocks again. When she still doesn't answer, he calls the hotel a second time and asks to be connected to Room 312. She picks up but doesn't say anything.

"Let me in."

"I don't know what you mean."

She thinks I brought the cops. "I'm alone. You have my word."

She laughs bitterly.

"Je—Ayanna, look, you either trust me, or you sit in there and hope I don't guard the door while I call Gunner. I'd say only one of those two options is good for you right now."

After a moment of silence, she says, "Remove your hand so I see it's you."

He does as asked. He hears the deadbolt turn and then the door opens. She no longer wears the sari. Instead, she's back in her gold sweatpants and a gray sweatshirt so oversized that the sleeves cover all but the tips of her fingers. Her hair is loose but uncombed. He sees a spent tissue clutched in one hand. When he meets her angry red eyes and sees the dried tears on her cheeks, his heart feels as if it's ripping apart. He fights it, tells himself it's all an act.

She yanks him in and slams the door closed. Before he speaks, she pushes the flaps of his coat open and frantically begins to frisk him.

"What are you doing?"

Ignoring his question, she roughly pats his chest and stomach and then slips her hands under the coat to the sides of his waist and his back. He pushes her away when she goes for the crotch of his trousers. "Stop it! *What are you doing?*"

"Are you wearing a wire?" she demands, and moves in again to check his pants legs.

He steps back. "No, of course not!"

She doesn't follow, but she screams, "How could you? You told me you believed me!"

"It wasn't me. I just heard from Earl that they received a tip. I don't know how but it wasn't me."

"You're a liar! You left your brother's house and went straight to Gunner, didn't you?"

"No, I—"

"You think because you heard one half of a conversation that you've got it all figured out!" With open palms, she pushes against his chest. "You have no idea how wrong you are! You have no idea what it would mean if they lock me up again! You think the system—"

"Jenny, calm down." He grabs her shoulders. "You're hysterical."

"Let go of me!" She wriggles out of his grip. "You told me you believed me!" she says again, but at least she's not hitting him.

"I had *nothing* to do with it."

"Then why are you here, Jack? Huh? Tell me. If you're not *leading them straight to my door*" —He simply shakes his head at her mocking his words— "then what are you doing here? Tell the truth for once. Did you cut a deal? Me in exchange for your charges being dropped?"

Go to hell, he wants to say. The truth, he wants to say, is that he can trace the reason for every lie he's ever told back to her, one way or another.

Yet even as they exchange glares, each assessing the other, each trying to read meaning into what the other has left unsaid, another truth is dawning on him: He won't do what he came here to do. No matter what she might have done—even if she's been lying to him, even if everything has been an act, *even if she murdered Maxine Shepard*—he won't try to talk her into turning herself in. And he *won't* lead them to her door. He simply isn't capable of handing her over to the system and hoping justice is served.

He lowers his voice and says, "They want to question me about you and they're threatening to take it all public if I don't come in willingly." Instinctively, he almost reaches for her hands but stops himself. "You need to leave. Right away."

The anger on her face is replaced by shock as she understands what he's saying.

"But—"

He covers her lips with the tips of his fingers. "Don't say anything. Just listen." She nods, but her eyes fill with tears. "I have to tell them the truth, so when I tell them I don't know where you are, I need for *you* to make sure it *is* the truth. Do you understand?"

"Yes. Okay, okay." She quickly surveys the room as if calculating how long it will take to gather her belongings. "I don't know where to go. They're bound to look for me at Brian's again, and this time they'll look harder."

"How much time do you need?"

"I don't know." She swipes at her eyes with the sleeve of her sweatshirt. "Twenty minutes?"

If his heart ripped at seeing the evidence of past tears on her cheeks, seeing them fall fresh is breaking it wide open. He looks away, forcing himself to ignore it all, and reaches for the doorknob. She grabs his arm, but her actions are gentler now.

"Jack, please don't tell them about the letters." Did she just confirm his suspicion that she sent them to herself? "I can't tell you why, not now, there's no time, but please promise me that."

"*Now* is all we have, Jenny. If there's something you want me to know, you need to tell me. If I contact you again, it will be at their request." He hopes she understands the unspoken warning. "And you can't contact me, either," he adds. "If you show up in a tunnel again, they'll be watching."

"The letters," she says quietly. "Please, just promise me you won't mention the letters."

Open the door. Open the door and leave.

"Good luck, Jen."

And somehow, he opens the door and leaves.

CHAPTER TWENTY-TWO

ON HIS DRIVE BACK downtown, Jack calls Earl from the car.

"Let Gunner know I'm ready to talk, but it has to be at my office. If I walk into the police station right now, all hell will break loose."

In typical Earl Scanlon fashion, the response is a brief "I'll meet you there" and the conversation is over.

Jack expects the press to be waiting on the courthouse steps. Sure enough, the cameras have already been set up and the reporters are poised with microphones in hand. As he pushes through, they bombard him with questions.

"Mr. Hilliard, were you aware Jennifer Dodson had returned to St. Louis?"

"Do you know whether she returned to town because of the recent appellate court decision in the Shepard murder case?"

"Has she contacted you?"

"Have you seen her?"

"Does she plan to defend herself against Alex Turner's insistence that she is responsible for Maxine Shepard's murder?"

"Does her return have anything to do with the rape charges against you?"

"Do you think Jennifer Dodson is guilty of Maxine Shepard's murder?"

"Do you agree with those who say your personal issues have become too much of a distraction for you to do your job?"

"Will you be resigning?"

He remains stone-faced through it all, even the last question. He knows a segment of the city's population thinks he should have been thrown out of office long ago, both for his relationship with Jenny, and because he wasn't upfront about his views on capital punishment. He always found it sad—and ironic—that between those two transgressions, his relationship with Jenny caused the more rabid uproar.

He remembers his first day back at work after he'd testified at Alex's trial, how hard it was to walk through the crowd on the courthouse steps to reach the podium at the top, where he addressed the city. Like walking through a gauntlet. Some had come to show their support, but most were there to castigate him for all he'd done. They screamed at him and he absorbed it all. He knew he deserved every bit of their rancor.

He took his second chance seriously. He began the arduous climb back by publicly expressing his contrition. His words bounced like rubber off most of the people in the audience, but a few applauded, providing the little fuel he needed to keep going. A few days later, some of his previous detractors publicly recanted their condemnation of him and agreed to wait and see if his future actions would match his words. He made sure they did. He fought to restore his reputation in the community as hard as he fought to restore his marriage. For the most part, he succeeded. He knows Claire is responsible for a large part of that success, for refusing to leave him, even though she faced her own criticism for her decision. Her grace under pressure was not only a model, but a constant source of strength for him.

He accepted as the price of his sins that some would never trust him again. The renewed call for him to step down doesn't surprise him, not with Celeste's allegations and now Jenny's return. What *does* surprise him is that, for the first time, he wonders if perhaps he should.

Even though five o'clock has long since come and gone, Jack steps off the elevator to find Earl in the reception area surrounded by several of the assistant DA's who once worked under him. They scatter like partiers at a drug bust when they see Jack.

"Gunner will be here shortly," Earl says on the way to Jack's office. "He doesn't want to arouse interest, so he'll slip in through the back when he gets a chance. The delay will give us a few minutes to talk privately."

Jack motions at the chair behind his desk. "Why don't you take the position of honor? I don't really feel deserving of it just now."

Earl sighs but doesn't argue. "Did you have any luck with Dodson?"

"I learned only today that she was staying at the Ritz," Jack begins as he hangs his overcoat on the back of his office door. Earl's eyebrows rise at Jack's mention of the Ritz. "But she's no longer there, and I have no idea where she was headed."

All true.

"Did you try to call her?"

"Since she left the Ritz? No, but I will if you want me to." Also all true.

Earl studies him—he obviously suspects he's not getting the full story—but he declines the offer. "Wait and see what Gunner wants. In the meantime, you need to think about what you'll do if you're asked to step down. I have no doubt the request is coming."

"Do you think I should?"

"Well, let me ask you." Earl picks up a pen and twirls it like a miniature baton. "If you consider everything that's happened since the night you drove Celeste home, or rather, everything you've done, do *you* think you should? If every step you've taken was somehow made public, do you believe your constituents would agree they were the right steps to take?"

"If I answer no, does that mean ipso facto I should resign? Is that the litmus test you applied to your decisions when you had this job?"

Earl's nostrils flare. He lets the pen fall to the desk and leans forward. He doesn't welcome Jack's sarcasm. "Tell me, where were you on Christmas Eve, Jack?"

The question catches Jack off guard. "Excuse me?"

"I tried to call you that night. When I didn't get an answer, I called your house. Claire said you'd gone out but that she'd give you the message. *On Christmas Eve, she claimed you'd gone out.* I didn't have the heart to ask her where. I never heard back, so I tried you again the next morning. Still no answer." Earl crosses his arms. "So what happened?"

"Claire wasn't too pleased with the evidence being leaked. That's what happened. We argued and I left."

Earl rises. He's not a tall man, but he carries a muscular heftiness that has always made him appear much larger than his five feet, six inches. He half-stands, half-sits on the wide sill and looks down on the city below. His silence is unnerving. Jack braces himself for the subtle psychological interrogation he knows is coming, the same type his former boss once used so successfully as a prosecutor.

"Did she give you my message?" Earl asks.

She would have had to talk to me to do that. He shrugs in a noncommittal way, neither yes nor no.

"Why didn't you call me back? I've never known you not to return my calls."

"I wasn't somewhere I could talk."

"On Wednesday *and* Thursday? Where might that have been?"

"Earl, lay off me already, will you? I wasn't anywhere Claire doesn't know about."

"So reassure me." Earl's aging eyes haven't lost their power to penetrate.

Jack looks away and rubs at an imperfection at the front edge of the desk. He told Claire where he was, and as far as he's concerned, she's the only one who's entitled to know.

"You went to Dodson, didn't you?"

"Claire and I fought, so I left and went to my brother's house. But I couldn't fall asleep, so I went out to Jenny's motel, just to talk to her a while. But I accidentally fell asleep and—"

"What?" Earl's composure slips. "Are you telling me you spent the night with her? Jesus Christ! Not again. What the *hell* is wrong with you?"

Something inside Jack flares at Earl's question. "What the hell is wrong with me? Everything!" He's shouting but he barely notices. "I haven't done a damn thing and everyone is treating me like a fucking criminal. I can't sleep, I can't eat.

My wife looks at me like I'm a feral animal she can't trust, but one she allows inside anyway because if she doesn't feed it, no one will. My father-in-law would just as soon shoot me than have me spend one more minute in his daughter's presence, not to mention his grandchildren's, but he can't legally do *that*, so instead he's trying to have my law license revoked. A girl I trusted and welcomed into my home has decided to make me the fall guy for whatever crap she's got herself wrapped up in, and because of that, I'm facing a lengthy prison term for a crime *I didn't commit.* Isn't that enough?"

"Jack, calm down—"

"For the last month, while trying to defend myself against charges that I *raped a child,* I've been trying to juggle the needs of a very public job, a bitter wife who can't even tell me she believes I'm innocent, a conflicted son who knows I am but for some reason won't discuss it or tell me what I need to know to end this, another son who's confused as all hell, and a woman who might be guilty for a crime for which another man is facing execution. But wait, maybe she's not, and yet somehow I'm expected to be the one to throw her to the lions. And I've been trying to do all this on a few hours sleep each night. So forgive me if I'd reached the end of my rope." His anger depleted now, he leans back wearily. "I was about to collapse from exhaustion, okay? I hadn't been sleeping. I even tried at my brother's house. It didn't matter. I couldn't sleep anywhere."

"But you were able to sleep at Dodson's?" Earl asks. The question is no longer an accusation, but an attempt to understand.

"Yes, but *it was an accident,*" he says. "And that's all I did. I slept. For nineteen hours." They hold each other's gaze. "You know, everyone is so quick to judge my actions, but until you've walked in another's shoes—"

Earl raises his hand. "Fair enough."

"And your question about my constituents? Frankly, I think the better question is, do *I* think my actions were right, given the circumstances."

"Fine, I'll bite. Do you?"

Does he? He tries to analyze everything objectively. He thought he'd done the right thing when he drove Celeste home. She'd never given him any reason not to trust her. Even Claire wouldn't have had a problem with the decision if the assault allegations hadn't been made. She would have been grateful he let her sleep. He'd been dishonest with her afterwards, but at the moment of decision, all he'd wanted was to regain his son's love and not give Claire another reason to mistrust him. Had he not been arrested, his claim that Michael drove Celeste home would have been just one more of the many innocuous white lies that long term couples tell each other to keep peace.

Even his decision to steal the page from the notebook was an impulse he doesn't regret. Anyone who claims he would make a contrary decision in the same position would be lying.

But what about how he'd handled Jenny's return to town? He tried to be upfront with Claire, and she'd told him she understood his need to know the truth. He can't deny that he mistook mere dormant feelings for dead, but once he realized it, he tamped them down at every turn. Yet, if it had been anyone other than Jenny, would he have done things differently? He knows he did the right thing four years ago when he came forward as soon as he discovered Jenny's full relationship to her murdered client. Even though he kept her recent reappearance secret, the decision gave him an unusual opportunity to discover the truth once and for all. If he'd refused her plea for help, he's confident she would have gone underground again before trusting anyone else, and any advantage he had would have slipped from his grasp.

Of course, the warning he gave her a few moments ago served the same purpose, didn't it? Even the knowledge that she'd probably played him again didn't stop him from effectively handing her the keys to her own jail cell. It's the one decision he can't justify. How can the DA, of all people, admit that he doesn't trust the system?

"I believe most of the decisions I've made since the night I took Celeste home have been the right ones. And even the ones I might not be proud of . . ." He hesitates. "I'd make them again."

This admission surprises Earl. "Care to tell me which decisions those might be?"

As if Beverly were waiting for the cue to save Jack, the phone on the desk beeps and her sympathetic voice fills the room. "Jack, Gunner's here. Should I show him to your office?"

Jack and Earl stare at each other. Earl understands Jack won't answer his last question. And they both know there's not much Earl can do for Jack at this point.

"Please do."

Let the party begin.

Gunner enters Jack's office looking pale and tired. He's always been slightly overweight, but tonight his jowls hang a little lower and the bags under his watery eyes are more pronounced. Seems Celeste and Jenny are taking their toll on the Chief, too.

Gunner is accompanied by a detective Jack recognizes but whose name he can't remember. The detective has been in the murder division for about as long as Jack has been at the prosecutor's office, and before that he worked in sex crimes. He's one of the best.

"Jack," he says with a small nod. He sees that Jack doesn't remember his name. "Bill Sumner," he adds and offers his hand. "We worked on the Soulard case together."

"That's right, I remember." Jack also remembers that he liked Sumner. The man worked as hard on that case—where a cop solicited a prostitute and then murdered her when she wanted more money for keeping her mouth shut—as he would have on any other case. He didn't investigate any differently when he learned the perp was one of his own, and he didn't assign less worth to the victim as some on the force might have. In his eyes, a prostitute's life was just as valuable as a nun's. Unfortunately, his stellar ethics will probably work against Jack.

Earl explains to Gunner that he won't stay. Jack gives up his chair so Gunner and Sumner have a place to sit, but instead of taking the chair behind his desk, he props on the windowsill that Earl vacated.

"I'll be in the conference room," Earl mouths to Jack before he slips into the hall and closes the door behind him.

To Jack's surprise, Gunner stares at him with genuine concern. "If you'd rather wait until you bring in another attorney, I—"

Jack cuts him off with a shake of the head. "Let's just get started. This is all off the record, right?"

Sumner breathes deeply and shifts in his chair, an obvious signal to Gunner that he disagrees.

"Gunner," Jack says before Sumner speaks, "if it's not, I might as well take the Fifth. What's your goal? Do you want to find her to question her? Or do you want to take me down?"

"We simply want to question her."

"Then it has to be off the record."

Gunner glances at Sumner and nods. Jack waits until Sumner gives him a similar assurance.

"What do you want to know?"

"Everything," Sumner says. "Have you seen her? Do you know where she is? Can you contact her?"

"I'll answer all your questions, but first answer one of mine." Even though the detective had asked the questions, Jack directs his to Gunner. "Where'd you get your tip?"

"A state trooper." Gunner studies Jack for a reaction. Jack merely nods. "It was a bit serendipitous. He was in court on another matter and overheard some local cops talking about you. Not surprisingly, Dodson's name came up, too."

Jack finds it ironic that his decision to stop on the shoulder, a decision made because he was worried about Jenny's well-being, is the decision that gave her away. That gave both of them away.

"He did see us," Jack confesses. "He didn't recognize her, though. I'm pretty sure of that."

"He didn't, you're right. He had only vague knowledge of what had happened a few years back. But when one of the cops brought up what she looked like, that she was part Indian, he began to put two and two together. That's when he called me."

"Are you the only one he spoke to? Or do those local cops know, too?"

"Just me, Jack. You're lucky. He liked you."

Jack's not feeling too lucky just now.

"So why were you with her? And how long have you been in contact with her?"

Jack turns to the window and looks down at the street below. He blows out a puff of air and it briefly fogs up the cold glass. "Where to begin?" he mutters to himself.

Gunner answers for him. "I suggest you start at the beginning."

He tells them how she surprised him in the tunnel. He tells them how he met with her, first in Hannibal, then in Mexico, and about the other visits to her motel room in St. Charles. He gives them the name of the motel, and the room number. He tells them about the letters, how Jenny claimed she was being threatened, but that he only just came to the conclusion, earlier today, in fact, that she'd sent the letters to herself. He explains that he thought he had a better chance of finding out the truth if he kept her return to St. Louis to himself—at least until he knew more. He insists that Claire is aware of his meetings with Jenny. He tells them Jenny had been living at her brother's condo. He even gives them her alias.

He tells them everything they want to know until Sumner asks why Jack believes she sent the letters to herself.

"I can't answer that question without jeopardizing those who helped me with my investigation. I won't do that."

Jack's refusal frustrates Gunner, but he accepts it for now, which forces his detective to accept it, too. They all know a special prosecutor could haul Jack before a grand jury and force the answers out of him.

"Do you know where she is now?" Gunner asks.

"No."

"Do you have a phone number for her?"

"Yes." He pulls up the number on his phone and holds out the screen for Sumner to write it down.

"Are you willing to let us see your phone records to verify what you've told us about your communications with her is true?"

"That's not a problem."

Gunner leans over and whispers to Sumner. The detective immediately pulls out his phone and begins texting.

"I'd like you to contact her now," Gunner says to Jack, "and make arrangements to meet with her again."

Jack swallows. The chief plans to do exactly what Jack feared. He plans to use Jack to bait Jenny.

"I don't think she'll be willing. When we spoke at my brother's house, I accused her of murdering Maxine Shepard."

Gunner smiles slightly. "Why don't you try?"

Jack takes his time pulling up her number and placing the call. "She's not answering."

"Leave her a message to call you."

"She doesn't have voicemail." He wishes she did, because then he'd know whether her phone is on or off by how quickly the system prompts a caller to leave a message. If the phone is off, Gunner's team can't locate her. "But maybe she'll see that I tried to call and she'll call back."

"See if they can triangulate her phone right now, will you?" Gunner says to the detective. "Let's see if we can find her and bring her in."

After Sumner steps out to the hallway, Gunner says to Jack, "So you accused her of murdering Maxine Shepard? You now believe she did it?"

"Honestly, Chief? I don't know. I was simply trying to get a reaction out of her. I thought maybe I could judge whether she was lying to me."

"And?"

"I don't know what to think. If she did commit murder, I don't understand why she'd come back. It makes no sense. Why would she send herself threatening letters and then ask me to help find the sender? And yet, I still get the sense she knows something she's not saying."

Gunner laces his fingers together behind his head, his elbows wide like wings, and regards Jack. "You know, Jack, I believe you're being honest with me. I wish you had come forward as soon as you knew she was back. It would have helped your credibility in your own case. In fact, I think some would have even seen you as a hero if you'd been the one to turn her in."

"Turn her in? You talk as if there's an outstanding warrant for her arrest. There's not, Gunner. At least not that I'm aware of."

"That's true." He shrugs. "But will the public care about that distinction? You have my word that nothing ever goes outside this room, but I can't speak for the trooper." He shakes his head regretfully. "I just don't know if you'll survive this. And I find that sad, because I think you're an incredible prosecutor."

The unexpected compliment moves Jack. Unable to speak, he shows his appreciation with a slight nod. He turns back to the window, thinks of Jenny's question. *Do you enjoy it?* And his response. *I love it. I really love it.*

Gunner's right. If even one member of the press realizes the story is bigger than Jenny being back, Jack's career as DA is over, rape charges or no rape charges. He can't imagine the city will forgive him a second time, even if he could somehow explain his actions. He wonders how long he has left. Days? Hours? Minutes?

The detective returns and hands Gunner his cell phone.

"She appeared to be on the Poplar Street Bridge," he says as Gunner reads the screen. "They immediately called it in to a nearby squad car, but by the time they got there . . ."

Gunner looks up at Sumner; Jack still faces the window but watches Gunner in the reflection. His stomach tightens like a clenched fist.

"The signal was gone."

SPRING

CHAPTER TWENTY-THREE

ODDLY, THE FIRST thing Jack thinks when he wakes up on April Fool's Day is *I'm in my own bed.*

The last time—the only time—he went to court as a witness, for Alex's trial, he woke in the guest bedroom of his brother's house. Then, he wanted so badly to be where he is now. He wanted so badly to wake up next to Claire.

Now, he rolls over and looks at her as she sleeps. He's done this more often the past few months. It's the only chance he has to see the face of the woman he married. He wonders if he'll ever touch her again, really touch her. The way a man is supposed to touch his wife. He tries to remember the last time they made love, and he can't. It's been that long. He's not sure which came first, his lack of desire for her or her not so subtle clues that he shouldn't even try.

He's no longer sure their marriage will survive as he insisted to Mark it would. In the three months since Christmas, when Jack asked for but didn't get Claire's assurance that she believed in his innocence, he's watched for a sign she might have reached that conclusion. He doesn't need or even expect an apology for her lack of faith in him; he simply needs her to believe in him again. Either she truly thinks he's guilty, or she doesn't but has decided to let him believe she does. He's not sure which is worse.

He hasn't seen or talked to Jenny since the day at the Ritz. Claire knows this. He didn't tell her exactly what happened in Mark's kitchen, but he did tell her he thought Jenny had sent the letters to herself and that he was done helping her. He explained he'd met with Gunner about seeing Jenny, but Claire didn't ask for many details, and Jack didn't provide more.

Gunner and Sumner kept their promises to Jack, and Trooper Smith, apparently, never leaked what he knew to the press. Even so, Jack holds his breath, waiting for the day the young trooper sends a blackmail note. He didn't seem like the type, but Jack can't think of any reason the kid would keep what he knows to himself. Perhaps he wants to see if Jack is acquitted. If so, the value of the information would rise considerably, since Jack will then have more to lose.

Jack suspects Jenny eventually returned to Chicago to be near her brother, but he really doesn't know. Even after his conversation with Rebecca Chambers, he's still convinced Jenny sent the letters to herself—why, he can't fathom—and that her meeting with the PI had more to do with mounting a defense to a possible murder charge than investigating the letters. No matter. He resolved to put her out of his mind, or at least back to that dormant place in his brain she inhabited before she surprised him in the tunnel.

But his efforts have had no visible effect on Claire. They settled into the same type of standstill that followed her escape to Sedona. He doesn't know if she's angry with him, or simply numb, but his marriage is disintegrating before his eyes and he has no idea how to put it back together. He does know he's guilty of no longer trying.

He also knows he's on the verge of no longer caring.

Claire's eyes roam beneath her lids; she's dreaming. Like Jack, she had difficulty falling asleep the night before. He heard her restless repositioning, her frustrated sighs, her quiet sobs he wasn't supposed to hear. Several times during the night she rose from the bed to go into the bathroom. He never heard the toilet flush, so he's pretty sure she wasn't using it for its intended purpose. Each time, for a split second after she opened the door to come out but before she flipped the switch, he saw her silhouette against the light. He felt nothing.

He rises from the bed, taking care not to wake her. In the bathroom, he sees the evidence of her nighttime activities. Spent tissues fill the small trash basket next to her sink. He knows she didn't flush them because she was afraid the noise would wake him. Despite everything, she still extended this kindness. As he stands just outside the shower and waits for the water to get hot, he thinks they should have talked about what will happen if he's convicted. Though he's certain his bail won't be revoked during the appeals and they'll have plenty of time to talk about logistics, he worries that her fragile cooperation might shatter if a jury finds him guilty.

She's still asleep when he emerges from the steamy bathroom, or at least she pretends to be. He dresses quietly in his nicest suit, but when it's time to tie his tie, he fumbles with it. It's a skill he learned from his father years before, but for almost eighteen years now, Claire has done it for him. His trembling hands don't help.

As he's about to leave the bedroom, she calls softly, "Good luck."

He stills. *Good luck?* If he responds with even just a fraction of what he'd like to say to that, he'll be late to court.

The silence stretches as he stands in the doorway, his back to her, his emotions seesawing between tears and tirade. In the end, he resists both. He simply says thanks and takes his leave.

The case is assigned to Judge Simmons, but the trial will be held in the Chief Judge's courtroom on the 10th floor, the largest in the courthouse. The hour is still early when Jack and Earl arrive, but already spectators fill most of the right side of the gallery. More will pack the remaining rows well before the trial begins at nine. By the number of guards milling about, Jack knows the judge expects the room to fill to capacity.

Jack knows all eyes are on him, that the courtroom artists note his every expression and the news cameras film his every move. He walks with Earl toward the bar with the same purpose and determination he'd display in any other case. As a prosecutor, he won't take a case to trial unless he's certain of the defendant's guilt. In this case, he's just as certain of his own innocence and he wants everyone to know it. He gives a solemn nod to those he recognizes, and he stops to shake hands and chat with those to whom he has closer ties, mainly fellow members of the bar who've come to support him. He spots Mark on the front bench, next to the center aisle, and excuses himself to greet him. Mark looks up from his magazine and, seeing Jack, rises with a wide smile.

"Thanks for coming," Jack says, his voice suddenly hoarse with emotion as he imagines saying the same thing if Mark has to visit him in prison. When Mark envelops him in a hug, holding tighter and longer than usual, Jack struggles to maintain his composure.

As he passes through the swinging gate, habit causes him to turn toward the prosecution table. Earl subtly touches his arm and guides him the other way before anyone notices the mistake.

Walker subpoenaed both Michael and Claire as witnesses, but since today will consist of pretrial motions and jury selection, neither of them must be here. Claire will come anyway, Jack knows, but because Earl has filed a motion to sequester the witnesses, she'll probably spend her time in the witness room or wandering the hallways of the courthouse. Michael will stay away until the day of his testimony.

The motions take up most of the morning. Earl prevails in his request to sequester the witnesses, but he loses in his bid to exclude testimony about Jack's past with Jenny. Jack isn't surprised. If he was Walker, he'd have argued its relevancy, too, and expected to win.

After a short lunch break, the judge pushes forward with voir dire, which progresses faster than anyone expected. By five o'clock on Tuesday, a jury of eight women and four men has been selected. The judge announces they'll reconvene on Wednesday morning to hear opening arguments.

Not one juror looks Jack in the eye as the twelve of them file out of the courtroom.

On Wednesday, the case begins in earnest. Walker's impassioned opening argument portrays Celeste as a naïve, inexperienced teen with a crush on her boyfriend's father. He paints Jack as an admitted adulterer who looked at Celeste and saw his former mistress, and then used the teen's adoration of him along with his talents of persuasion to take advantage of her. Walker is a strong orator. His presentation impresses even Jack, causing him to question every decision he made the night he took Celeste home. Afterwards, the jurors finally look at him, but their faces reflect only disgust or morbid curiosity.

Earl informs the judge that he'll reserve his opening for the start of the defense case, so Walker calls his first witness to the stand, Ramon Del Toro.

Celeste's father enters the courtroom with the bailiff. As he's led to the witness stand, he crosses in front of the defense table but shows no awareness of Jack's presence. He dressed for court in dark khakis, a white oxford without a necktie, and a navy blue sport coat. A gold chain hangs from his neck, its pendant barely visible at the point of his open collar. Jack knows from the court papers he's thirty-seven years old, but his attire and his hesitant demeanor suggest a younger man. He's handsome, with warm, dark eyes and a strong jaw. Jack already knows from years of questioning witnesses that unless Del Toro does something that comes off as arrogant, the women jurors will believe everything he says. No wonder Walker chose him to go first.

Del Toro answers the oath in a quiet, respectful voice, his Puerto Rican accent still thick. Although he's a slight man, he sits carefully, as though the chair might break from his weight. He cautiously takes in the crowd, and only then does he seem to realize Jack is in the courtroom, too. To Jack's surprise, Del Toro regards him not with anger, but with profound disappointment, as if he, too, is a victim of Jack's betrayal. Jack begins to doubt his instincts. Should he have approached the man privately about Celeste's accusations?

"Sir, can you state your name for the record?"

"Ramon Del Toro."

"And you are the father of Celestina Del Toro, the victim in this case?"

"Yes, sir."

"Your daughter is sixteen years old, correct?"

"Yes, sir."

"Do you have any other children?"

"No, sir, it's just me and Celeste."

"Does Celeste's mother live with you?"

"No, she lives in Florida. We're divorced."

"How long have you been divorced?"

"About eight years."

"When did you move to Missouri?"

"Just this past summer, when I took a job at the Fabick Company, in Fenton."

"Where do you live now?"

"In far West County, off Melrose. Not far from Rockwoods Reservation."

"Sir, as you know, the defendant in this case has been charged with sexually assaulting your daughter. Can you explain how you first came to be aware that he assaulted her?"

I guess I don't have a name, Jack writes on a legal pad. Earl writes back, *Get used to it. You know the game.*

"Well, she had gone out the night before with Michael—"

"Are you referring to Michael Hilliard, the defendant's son?"

"Yes. Michael is her boyfriend. She got home very late, around two thirty or three a.m. She told me that they'd had car trouble. When she got home, I asked her where Michael was, because usually he walks her to the door. She said he didn't that night because it was so late and he needed to get home. I found that strange, because he is usually such a well-mannered boy."

"Then what happened?"

"Nothing, then. We went to bed. Like I said, it was very late. But the next day, I was straightening around the house, and while I was emptying the trash in her bathroom, I found something that disturbed me."

"What did you find?"

"I found bits of torn up instructions from a pregnancy test."

Jack and Earl look at each other from the corner of their eyes, but otherwise remain impassive. Walker pauses, suggesting the testimony surprised him, too.

"What time was this, approximately?"

"It was in the afternoon on Sunday, three thirty? Four?"

"What did you do when you found the pregnancy test instructions?"

"I went to Celeste. I asked her what this means. I was very upset, as you can imagine."

"Did she have an explanation?"

"Not at first. She was just angry. She screamed at me, told me I had no business going through her things, as if I had been snooping or something, not simply emptying the trash. But I insisted that she tell me why this was there. She began to cry, and then she told me what really happened the night before."

"What *really* happened?"

"Yes. That Mr. Hilliard—Michael's father—had driven her home, and that he'd raped—"

"Objection, Your Honor," Earl says quickly. "Anything Mr. Del Toro might say about what Celeste told him happened in the car would be hearsay."

"Your Honor," Walker begins, his tone suggesting that any idiot knows Earl's objection isn't valid. "Mr. Del Toro isn't testifying to what his daughter told him for the purpose of proving the truth of it. Rather, we offer this testimony to show the motivation for the actions her father subsequently took. The testimony fits squarely within the exceptions to the hearsay rule."

The judge's gaze volleys between Walker and Jack. He doesn't want to overrule the objection, but they all know he will.

"Overruled. But Mr. Walker, please keep this type of testimony to a minimum. Any specifics about what happened in the car is best offered by the victim. Continue."

Walker directs his attention back to Del Toro. "Briefly, sir, what did Celeste tell you happened in the car?"

"Like I started to say, she told me he raped her."

"And based upon that, what did you do?"

"I insisted we go to the police."

"Did she agree?"

"She did not want to do this, she was so embarrassed and upset, but I insisted, and she agreed."

"Did you call the police?"

"No, sir. We drove to the station."

"When did you do this?"

"By the time I convinced her she needed to report the rape, it was about dinnertime. I think we arrived around seven."

Walker takes his witness through everything that occurred during their visit to the station. Just when Jack starts to think Walker will leave it to Earl to ask about Celeste's refusal to be examined, he broaches the topic.

"Do you know whether your daughter was asked to submit to a rape exam?"

"Yes, she was, but she said no."

"Did you encourage her to say no?"

"No, at first I tried to convince her that she should let them to do it. But she became hysterical, and finally I thought, okay, this is making matters worse. She already had her virginity violently taken—"

"Objection." This time Earl stands for emphasis. "Judge, there has been no evidence about whether Ms. Del Toro was a virgin on the night in question, and moreover, there has yet to be admissible evidence about what happened in the car."

"Sustained." The judge leans over to Del Toro and says politely, "Sir, please try to testify only about those things of which you have direct knowledge."

Del Toro looks slightly confused by the judge's instruction, but he nods to indicate he'll do as he's told. Jack has no doubt the man believes his daughter *was* a virgin. What father wouldn't want to think so about his sixteen-year-old daughter, regardless of the evidence? Even Jack was in denial about Michael before that night.

"So you didn't insist your daughter be examined?"

"No, I did not. I didn't want to upset her more."

Once Walker exhausts the details of Celeste's accusations, he turns to Jack's actions after the arrest.

"Sir, to your knowledge, has the defendant been in contact with your daughter since the night in question?"

"Well, not directly, no. But he stole some personal writing from a notebook he found in her backpack."

Earl doesn't object. He already fought this fight in pretrial motions and lost. Both Jack and Earl know the jury will see the journal entry, but they'd hoped it would first be discussed with a different witness. Earl argued that to let Del Toro testify about it would constitute hearsay; Walker countered that he would be using it for the limited purpose of showing Jack's state of mind. Namely, a sense of guilt. The judge ruled in Walker's favor.

"What type of writing?" Walker asks Del Toro.

"It was a page from Celeste's notebook. Like her diary. It described what Mr. Hilliard did to her in the car. I guess he didn't want anyone to see it."

Jack grunts quietly, Earl shushes him. "It would just bring attention to it if I object," he whispers. "I'll deal with it on cross."

Walker spends a few more minutes questioning Del Toro about how hard it is for a single dad to raise a teenage girl, "especially in this age where technology allows them to keep so much hidden from their parents." Del Toro waxes poetic about how beautiful Celeste is, and how he's had to protect her from the boys since she hit puberty. He talks about how much he likes Michael, and that although he'd only met Jack a few times, he once liked and respected him. He thought his daughter was safe dating the son of the DA.

"So you weren't aware that Mr. Hilliard committed adultery a few years back?"

"No, not until after his arrest, when the news started talking about it."

On that last point, Walker turns his witness over to Earl.

Earl stands, and for just a moment, he remains behind the table. His face wears concern as he makes his way closer to the witness box. He nods politely to Del Toro, who returns the gesture.

"Mr. Del Toro, isn't it true that everything you know about what happened during the night Celeste spent with Michael, and then Mr. Hilliard, you know because Celeste told you?"

"Yes, I suppose that's true."

"You weren't present at any time, were you?"

"I was there when she arrived home."

"But you weren't with her during the time she spent with either Michael or Mr. Hilliard?"

"No, I wasn't."

"So your knowledge about what happened between Celeste and Mr. Hilliard is based solely on what your daughter told you?"

"Yes."

"You testified that your daughter's diary entry described what happened between her and Mr. Hilliard in the car." Del Toro nods. "Was that entry dated?"

"No."

"Did it identify Mr. Hilliard by name or in any other way?"

"No."

"So it's possible that it had nothing to do with Mr. Hilliard, isn't that so?"

"I guess, but—"

"Now, about the torn-up instructions from an at-home pregnancy test, are you aware that over-the-counter pregnancy tests can't determine pregnancy the day after intercourse?"

"Yes, I know that."

"Didn't you find it odd that your daughter took such a test within twelve hours or so of the time she claims Mr. Hilliard assaulted her?"

"I discussed that with her. She did not understand the limitations of those tests."

"Really?"

"My daughter would have no reason to know about such things, sir. She is not so sophisticated, I am glad to say."

Jack has to restrain himself from rolling his eyes.

"But she is honest," Del Toro adds. "And I believe what she tells me."

"Is that why you check her underwear when she comes home after dates?"

A smattering of gasps and giggles rises from the gallery. Jack sneaks a look at the jury; a few seem to share the surprise of the audience, while others merely wait for clarification from either Earl or the witness. Del Toro looks horrified, not from the accusation, Jack thinks, but from his actions being so blatantly exposed.

"I don't know what you refer to," Del Toro says defensively, and Jack knows then that Celeste's messages told the truth.

Earl pulls out a transcript of the messages between Celeste and Michael. When he hands it to Del Toro, Walker starts to object, but Earl interrupts. "I'm merely using it to refresh his recollection, Your Honor." The judge waves at him to proceed. "Mr. Del Toro, have you read the document I've just handed you?"

"Yes."

"Can you explain what it is, briefly?"

"It appears to be messages between my daughter and Mr. Hilliard's son. But I have never seen this—"

"That's okay." Earl takes the document back. "Does it help to refresh your memory about what I'm referring to? Have you ever asked your daughter to show you her underwear when she returned home from a date with Michael for the purpose of determining whether she had sexual relations with him?"

"No, I have not."

"But you saw in those messages that she told Michael you had, correct?"

"Yes."

"So she's lying to *one* of you, right?"

Del Toro doesn't answer.

"Sir?"

"She does not lie to me."

Earl lets it drop at that. It's enough that he asked the questions.

"You mentioned that you and Celeste's mother divorced about eight years ago. So Celeste would have been about eight years old?"

"Yes."

"And you moved to Missouri this past summer?"

"Yes."

"Where did you and Celeste live before that?" Earl asks the question with the innocence of someone who doesn't know the answer, but, of course, he does.

"I lived in Puerto Rico following the divorce."

"And Celeste?"

"She lived with her mother."

"You didn't have custody?"

"We shared custody. She lived with me in the summers. She wanted to stay in Florida during the school year so she didn't have to leave her friends."

Earl returns to the defense table and pulls a paper from a file. Del Toro repositions himself, sits taller.

"Isn't it true that subsequent to your divorce and move to Puerto Rico, your ex-wife was in prison on two different occasions for drug charges?"

A flurry of whispers sweeps the courtroom. Jack glances at Walker. He sits motionless at the prosecution table, intent on maintaining an expression devoid of emotion.

"Yes, that's correct."

"With whom did Celeste live while her mother was in prison?"

"Her abuela came to live at Celeste's mother's house so Celeste could remain in her same school." His voice has lost its earlier assurance.

Earl looks down at his paper, back up again. "Are you referring to Celeste's maternal grandmother? The one with Alzheimer's?"

Del Toro looks to Walker for help, but Walker maintains a stone face. Jack suspects the DA from Harrison County didn't do his research.

"Sir?" Earl prods.

"Yes, but it was early stage."

"Did anyone else stay at the house with Celeste and her grandmother?"

Del Toro takes such a deep breath that his torso visibly rises and falls. "Yes, my ex-wife's boyfriend. A man named Torrence Nash."

"Do you happen to know Mr. Nash's nickname?"

"No."

"The nickname Torpedo doesn't ring a bell?"

"No," Del Toro says, adamant. Jack believes him.

"Sir, you mentioned you came to Missouri for a job. But how did it come about that Celeste came with you instead of remaining in Florida?"

"She asked to."

"Did her mother object?"

"Not really." His tone is bitter and sarcastic now, and Jack suspects the divorce wasn't amicable. "I think she was glad to have her freedom."

"Just a few more questions, Mr. Del Toro." Earl pauses. Jack waits for the one-eighty he knows Earl is about to do. He wants to catch Del Toro off guard. "On that Sunday following the night in question, before you collected the trash, did Celeste leave the house?"

The tactic works. Del Toro narrows his eyes as he tries to get his bearings. "No," he says, "not that I know of."

"Did any friends come over?"

"No."

"Then can you explain, if she didn't leave the house and no one came to her, how she might have come into possession of a pregnancy test?"

Del Toro stares at Earl. He's obviously just considered this incongruence for the first time.

"Sir?" Earl says. "Can you answer, please?"

"I . . ." Del Toro shrugs helplessly, and Jack feels empathy for the man. "I don't know."

The judge calls a recess, but Jack and Earl remain at the table after the courtroom empties so they can talk in relative peace. Except for the judge's clerk, the court reporter, and a bailiff by the doors, they're alone. Earl scoots his chair to face Jack. Like a quarterback calling his team into a huddle, he hunches over and motions for Jack to do the same.

"So Celeste took a pregnancy test, and when her dad found it, she knew the wrath she'd endure if she didn't come up with an excuse for having it. Without thinking it through, she fingered you instead of Mike. Problem is, all we have so far to support this theory is her father's inability to explain why she already had a pregnancy test in her possession. But it will at least raise some doubt in the jury's mind."

"It doesn't make sense, though," Jack counters. "I mean, maybe it did to her at the time, but for her to go through all this just to prevent her dad from finding out she and Michael are having sex? Because once Mike takes the stand, it'll all be out in the open, right? He won't lie about that, I know he won't, because he already admitted it to me. There's gotta be a larger motivation for her to endure all this. Question is, how do we find out what it is?"

Earl sits back and scans the courtroom. "Oh, I can crack her, no problem, once she takes the stand. The real question is, how do I do it without the jury thinking we're ogres?"

Walker calls his next witness, Officer Thornton. Officer Thornton explains how he took the initial report when Celeste and her father came into the station on

Sunday night. Walker takes him through the timeline (the alleged assault occurred around 2:00 a.m., she came into the station at 7:12 p.m.), Celeste's demeanor (upset, numb, scared), and the procedures followed (collected hair samples, and skin particles from under her fingernails, asked her to submit to the rape exam, which she declined). Even though his testimony is important to the State's case, Thornton is a minor witness, and Walker keeps the direct short.

Jack knows Earl will follow Walker's lead and ask a minimal number of questions on cross. Juries generally respect the police force, so unless a good reason exists to challenge an officer's testimony, they appreciate a defense lawyer who respects it, too.

"Officer Thornton, Ms. Del Toro waited almost eighteen hours to report the alleged assault, is that right?"

"Yes, sir."

"Do you know why?" Earl asks, even though he already knows the supposed answer from the police reports.

"My understanding is that she was afraid, you know, given Mr. Hilliard's position as DA. She apparently didn't tell her father what had happened until around four that evening. She said he's the one who insisted she report it."

"And yet she still had some of Mr. Hilliard's skin under her nails, you said?"

"Yes, sir."

Earl nods as if in deep thought.

"You've investigated many rape cases. In your experience, do victims often bathe extensively after being assaulted?"

"Yes, sir."

"Why?"

"They usually say they felt unclean. It's like they're trying to wash off the assault."

"Does that make it difficult to collect evidence?"

"It can, yes."

"So if a victim were to wash her hands, would you have difficulty collecting evidence from under her fingernails, such as the assailant's skin particles, because it was washed away?"

"Like I said, it can make it difficult."

"Did you have any difficulty finding Mr. Hilliard's skin under Ms. Del Toro's nails?"

"No, sir."

"Did you ask her if she bathed after the alleged assault but before coming to the station?"

"Yes, I did, sir. She stated she did not bathe."

"Did she even wash her hands?"

"She stated she did not."

"You testified that Ms. Del Toro refused the rape exam. Did she tell you why?"

"No, sir. We don't ask that question."

Earl, of course, knows that, too.

"So you have no evidence of Mr. Hilliard's semen being inside her vagina, correct?"

As many times as Jack has asked this question of a witness, he still cringes now. He's glad Claire isn't here to hear it.

"That's correct, sir."

"Thank you, Officer." Earl nods again. The officer returns a tight-lipped but warm smile. Most of the force know Earl well and respect him regardless of which clients he represents.

Walker rises for redirect.

"Officer, with respect to victims of rape washing themselves, in your experience, do victims of statutory rape respond the same way?"

"No, sir, not usually."

"And why's that?"

"Well, with statutory rape, there's an element of consent. It's not valid, of course, but the victim generally has a different mindset about it."

"Thank you, Officer. That's all." Walker's nod is akin to a bow. When he pivots to return to his table, he doesn't try to hide his satisfied smirk from Jack and Earl.

Throughout the day and into Thursday, Walker questions the investigators who talked to Claire and Michael and the forensic expert who searched Jack's car. He questions the child abuse investigator who interviewed Celeste, and the officer who spoke to Michael's basketball coach regarding Jack's access to Celeste's backpack. He questions the coach himself. He questions the officer who booked Jack and photographed his arm. He questions the lab technicians who handled the forensic evidence and determined that the hair inside Celeste's bra belonged to Jack and the hairs in Jack's car and on his coat belonged to Celeste. He establishes the chain of custody for each piece of physical evidence. And even though Jack understands more than anyone how Elias selected which bits of evidence to highlight and which to skim over or not even mention, he still finds it unbearable to remain impassive as he watches the case being built against him. The sum of the parts could easily be a conviction in the hands of the right—or from Jack's point of view, wrong—jury, especially if Celeste performs well on the stand.

Shortly before the lunch break on Thursday, Walker informs the judge that he expects to call only four more witnesses before resting his case. The judge releases the jury but asks the parties to wait "for housekeeping matters."

"Mr. Walker, who are your remaining witnesses?" he asks.

"Janie Cramer, Michael Hilliard, Claire Hilliard, and the victim, Celeste Del

Toro."

"And who is Janie Cramer?" The judge reads the witness list from over the top of his glasses.

"A friend of Ms. Del Toro's. She'll testify about the victim's infatuation with Mr. Hilliard."

"What the—?" Jack starts to mutter, but Earl places his hand on Jack's arm.

"Your Honor," Earl says, "perhaps I should wait until I hear the questions, but I don't see how anything Miss Cramer might say wouldn't be hearsay."

"I assure the Court that Miss Cramer's testimony won't be hearsay, Judge."

"Very well. Do you anticipate finishing with all four witnesses by the end of the week?"

"I do, but, of course, much will depend upon the length of Mr. Scanlon's cross."

"Of course. I'll see you gentlemen after lunch, then. Court is at recess."

Janie Cramer's testimony proves to be so ridiculous and clearly beyond what Walker expected that Earl practically turns her into a witness for the defense during his cross. The "evidence" of Celeste's supposed crush on Jack consists of Janie's assertion that all the girls in Michael and Celeste's group of friends thought Jack was "smokin'" and Celeste made no secret of how much time she spent at the Hilliard's house, and by extension, with Jack. "Everyone" knew what Jack had done "with that attorney who looks like Celeste" and Janie claimed Celeste had a bet going with some of the other girls that she could "bed" him by the end of the year. Although Jack knows Celeste isn't nearly as innocent as her father believes, he also believes Janie's testimony must be a gross exaggeration. He wishes for eyes in the back of his head so he can see the reaction of Celeste's father to this new picture of his daughter. Earl needs only to ask a few questions to capitalize on it.

"Janie, do you have reason to believe Celeste was sexually active?"

"Objection." Walker stands and glares at Earl. "How is this relevant? I'm sensing a *blame the victim* approach here."

Earl's nostrils flare. His thirty-plus years as a prosecutor shape everything he does; he considers blaming the victim in rape cases verboten, no matter which side he represents.

"Not even close, Your Honor." Earl keeps his voice calm. "Mr. Walker first raised this issue in his direct of Mr. Del Toro and in his opening argument. He argued that my client took advantage of a naïve, inexperienced girl. Yet now he puts a witness on the stand who claims that same girl made it a goal to have intercourse with Mr. Hilliard. I think it's appropriate for me to explore the level of sexual sophistication of Ms. Del Toro in order to rebut the claims of naivety made earlier."

"But whether she's sexually experienced is irrelevant," Walker argues.

"What's relevant here is whether the defendant took advantage of her. Even if she *were* sexually experienced and consented to intercourse with him, it's still rape because the consent isn't valid under our laws. Our statutes make clear that sex between an adult man and a sixteen-year-old girl, however *consensual*" —he says the word "consensual" with disdain— "constitutes rape because of her age and the imbalance of power between them."

"Of course we don't dispute Mr. Walker's interpretation of the law, and it's disingenuous of him to suggest we do. But he just put on testimony that Ms. Del Toro boasted of being able to lure Mr. Hilliard into a sexual situation. Whether or not he presented that testimony on purpose" —Earl's tone is even, but any lawyer in the room understands he just suggested that Walker lost control of Janie on direct, to the defense's benefit— "the fact is, he presented it and thus made her sexual experience relevant. The higher charge here is forcible rape, and Ms. Del Toro's state of mind prior to the night in question is certainly relevant to whether any interactions between her and Mr. Hilliard were forced, if indeed, they occurred at all."

Walker tries to argue more, but the judge raises his hand. "I have to agree with Mr. Scanlon. Objection overruled. Let's move on." To Janie, "Ms. Cramer, you may answer."

"Was she a virgin, you mean?" Janie asks Earl before he has the chance to repeat the question. "Oh, *no way*. She and Michael were *always* all over each other at parties."

Jack silently thanks God for the sequestering of witnesses. Janie has no idea that the day before, Celeste's father testified his daughter *was* a virgin.

As if Janie just realized Jack is in the courtroom, she looks over at the defense table and finishes as if she's talking only to him. "I'm sorry, I don't mean they actually *did it* in front of us. But it was no secret, ya know?"

Jack takes a deep breath and keeps doodling on his pad.

CHAPTER TWENTY-FOUR

ON FRIDAY MORNING, the rising sun shines much too brightly. The early spring air smells much too fresh. Too many daffodils have opened their yellow petals in the bed just below their front porch where Jack sits in a rocking chair, drinking coffee that tastes much too good.

After the first two days of trial, the reporters moved their morning vigil from Jack's house to the courthouse. Taking advantage of the rare chance to be outside in peace, he came out to read the newspaper before making the drive into the city. Each morning he reads Wolfe's trial recap and notes what part of each witness' testimony the reporter deemed newsworthy, while Earl reads the daily trial transcript and looks for things they might have overlooked in the moment. This morning, however, Jack's mind wanders as he takes in the natural world outside his home.

He hears the sucking sound of the front door open and then the squeak of the screen door as Claire comes out. He closes his eyes. He doesn't like himself for having the thought, but he resents her intrusion. Her presence only amplifies his sense of being alone in this.

She sits in the other rocker. "How are you holding up?"

"I'm fine."

"I understand Mike and I are the only witnesses left in the state's case except Celeste."

Jack nods, but keeps his gaze on the yard.

"How do you feel it's going?"

He sighs. "Claire, please."

"No one has to know we talked about it, if that's what you're worried about."

She really thinks his main concern is that with her as a witness, the two of them shouldn't be talking about the case? "No, I'd rather just enjoy the morning."

"Your son is testifying today, Jack."

And I'm facing jail time, Claire. "I know that."

"You're really going to do that to him? You're going to put him through that?"

He finally turns to her. "*I'm* doing it to him?"

"You have the power to prevent it. You could revoke your consent for him to testify."

"And if I do that, I look like I'm trying to hide something."

"You could take the plea offer."

He stares at her, stunned. They'll never get beyond this. The chasm between them is too wide. He can't even digest that she would ask him to accept a plea offer, to admit to a crime he didn't commit, to willingly step into prison for two years. He'd lose his freedom, he'd lose his job, he'd most likely lose his law license. Most of all, he'd lose two years with his sons, and the effect of that particular loss would ripple well beyond the 730 days behind bars. It would last a lifetime.

He rises, anxious to get away from her. "If he doesn't want to take the stand, maybe he needs to tell Celeste. Because I'm innocent, Claire. *I'm innocent.* You might not know it, but she does."

He leaves her on the porch and climbs the stairs to Michael's room. When he knocks, Michael yells, "Come in," but his wide, wary eyes reveal surprise when Jack enters the room instead of Claire. Michael wears his boxers and a white dress shirt with the front still unbuttoned, his smooth, bare chest exposed. Jack considers telling him he'll be more comfortable with a T-shirt underneath, but decides to let it go.

"You got a second?" Jack asks.

Michael nods without meeting Jack's eye. His son sits on his unmade bed as if settling in for a long conversation, but he surreptitiously grabs for his cell phone and flips it over so the screen is face down. Jack pretends he didn't notice.

"I wondered if you had any questions about today, you know, like what to expect, the procedure, anything?"

Michael shakes his head. When Jack doesn't continue, Michael says, "Mom already explained it to me."

Jack wonders just what that explanation included. "Okay. Good. Like saying *yes* instead of *yeah*, right?" He asks to lighten the mood, but Michael takes it seriously.

"I will."

Jack motions to the navy suit hanging on the closet door. "Is that what you're wearing?"

"Yeah."

So much for practicing *yes*.

"Do you have a tie?"

"Mom said she'd give me one of yours."

Jack cracks a smile. "She'll probably do a better job than I would of picking one out."

The phone vibrates. Michael glances at it.

"Do you want to answer it?"

"No, it's just a text."

Jack knows what he wants to say but he can't figure out how to begin. Michael's discomfort isn't making it easy. He still hasn't looked at Jack. Jack suddenly realizes he's standing over his son like a predator hovers over its prey, so he crosses the room and takes a seat in the desk chair.

"Mike, look, I know you don't want to do this today, but I want you to understand that I gave parental consent for you to testify because if I hadn't, the jury would think I was trying to hide something. Do you understand?"

Michael nods slightly, his eyes trained on the floor. Jack wants so badly to ask him about the pregnancy test, but Walker will likely ask Michael on the stand if he and Jack talked in advance about his testimony.

"Can you look at me a second?" Jack asks. Reluctantly, Michael looks up. This is when Jack sees the tears pooling in his eyes. He wonders what has Michael so scared that he can't just let it out. "There's only one thing I'll ask of you. I don't care what you say on the stand today, as long as it's the truth. Okay? Say whatever you need to—don't worry about whether it will hurt or help me, or whether it will hurt or help Celeste, or Mom, or whomever—but be honest. The most important thing is to tell the truth. Okay?"

He waits, but Michael doesn't answer. The phone vibrates again, and Michael picks it up and holds it on his lap. When Jack doesn't react to the hint, Michael shrugs and says, "Whatever."

And if that's the best Michael can do, Jack has no choice but to accept it.

"Your Honor, I'd like to call Michael Hilliard to the stand."

After making his announcement, Walker glances at Jack. Then all eyes turn to watch the bailiff bring in Michael. All except Jack's. He hears a woman behind him whisper to her seatmate, "He looks just like his father."

Michael makes his way to the witness stand. As he raises his hand for the oath, he hazards a quick look at Jack, and Jack feels as if his son just offered him an olive branch. Even from the defense table, which is at least twenty feet from the witness stand, he sees Michael's hand tremble.

To Jack's relief, Walker's direct of Michael is short. He questions Michael about the amount of time that elapsed from when Jack left to take Celeste home, to when he returned. He also questions him briefly about the days following the alleged assault, when Celeste didn't show up at school and he couldn't reach her. Walker's point seems to be that Celeste couldn't face Michael after what Jack had done. Michael's testimony is so innocuous that Jack asks Earl if perhaps they'd be better off without a cross.

"And call him back as a defense witness?" Earl answers with a question of his own. "We need him, and I'd rather not make him take the stand twice."

"But don't you think Walker limited the direct so he can limit your cross?"

"Probably, but let's see what we get in. Walker has been frugal with his objections, probably to give us fewer grounds for appeal. He may not even fuss."

Before Jack argues more, Earl rises and approaches the witness stand.

"Mike, do you understand that because you're a minor, one of your parents had to give consent for you to testify today?"

"Yes."

"And your dad, who has been charged in this case, gave his consent, is that correct?"

"Yes."

"Did you want to testify?"

"No."

"Why not?"

Michael's gaze darts around the courtroom before he lets it settle briefly on Jack, then Earl.

"It makes me nervous to be up here in front of all these people, answering questions."

"Are you nervous because your answers may affect people you love?"

"Yes."

"And some of those people are on opposite sides of this case?"

Michael looks down at his hands. Jack can't see behind the box, but he knows his son is picking at a hangnail.

"Yes."

"Well, I know it's hard, but I want you to focus on answering the questions as best, as honestly, as you can, and let the jury decide how those answers affect the outcome of the case, okay?"

"Okay."

Jack hides a smile; of course Earl would extract what Jack couldn't.

"First, let's talk about the night your dad took Celeste home. You were in the family room with her, is that right?"

"Yes."

"And your dad heard you from upstairs?"

"I guess so. I guess he heard us."

"Were you and Celeste being loud?"

"I guess. Like I told Mr. Walker, we'd been drinking. I guess we were loud and didn't realize it."

"Did you look up and all of a sudden your dad was there?"

"No, we heard him at the top of the stairs. He made some noise."

"What kind of noise?"

"He stomped on the steps so we'd know he was up there."

"Why would he do that, Mike?"

Walker rises. "Objection, Your Honor. I don't think Mr. Hilliard's son can testify to what Mr. Hilliard was thinking."

"I'll rephrase it, Judge," Earl says. To Michael, he says, "Why do you think your dad wanted you to know he was there?"

"He asked if we were decent. I think he didn't want to embarrass us, you know?"

"Could you explain?"

Michael's face blushes. "I think he guessed we might not have all our clothes on, and he was giving us time to get dressed before coming down."

"Did you have all your clothes on?"

"No." He whispers the answer. Earl glances at the court reporter to make sure she got it.

"Did Celeste have her shirt off?"

"Yes."

"Did she have her bra off?"

Michael hesitates. "Yes."

"Am I right to assume you and Celeste were engaged in some sort of sexual activity?"

Michael nods.

"I'm sorry, son," Judge Simmons says gently, "but you need to state your answer aloud."

Michaels nods again, this time at the Judge, and then looks back at Earl. "Yes."

"I know it's hard to talk about this publicly, so I won't ask you for details, but it's important for the jury to know whether you and Celeste were having sexual intercourse."

"Yes, we were," he whispers.

"Before that night, did your dad know you and Celeste were sexually active?"

"No, I don't think so."

"Then why would he think you wouldn't be dressed?"

"Because of some things we were saying. I think he overheard us."

Earl nods—his way, Jack knows, of telling Michael he won't make him give the specifics about that either.

"Mike, were you aware Celeste thought she might be pregnant?"

Michael stiffens, sneaks a glance at Jack. "No."

This wasn't the answer Earl expected. Michael might be a reluctant witness, but up to now, he was an honest one. Jack can't believe he didn't know Celeste took the pregnancy test.

"This might be a difficult question for you to have to think about, and I'm sorry I have to ask it." Michael tilts his head warily; his long body sinks lower into the witness chair. "But was there any time that night, before your dad took Celeste home, that you felt like he tried to catch a glimpse of Celeste without her clothes on?"

"No." He wears a look of pure disgust at the question.

"Or was sexually attracted to her in any way?"

"No!"

"What about any other time before that night?"

"No! If anything, he seemed nervous around her when he first met her."

Earl pauses, and Jack sees his mind churning. He didn't expect anything other than a simple *No.* "May I have a moment to confer with my client, Your Honor?"

Earl comes near Jack and writes on the legal pad: *You care if I bring up JD with him?* Jack stares at it, not understanding. All he thinks about, seeing the letters JD, are the words "juris doctr" he saw referenced in Celeste's and Michael's messages. *Dodson,* Earl writes to clarify. Jack still doesn't answer. His mind is too busy trying to piece together older thoughts with new.

"Jack?" Earl whispers.

Jack nods hurriedly and Earl leaves his side to resume his questions.

"Mike, you said your dad seemed *nervous* when he first met Celeste?"

"Yes."

"Was that because of her resemblance to Jennifer Dodson?"

"Yeah, I think. I mean, it sort of freaked out both my mom and my dad the first time they saw her. I think she sort of reminded them of a bad time, you know?"

Earl presses his lips together in sympathy. "Yeah, I do know." He blows out a stream of air. He's not enjoying his job just then. "You explained what happened once your father returned home from dropping off Celeste. Was there anything in his demeanor, or even any physical evidence, that led you to believe he'd had inappropriate contact with Celeste?"

"No. He was gone a long time, but he said—"

"Objection. Anything his father said would be hearsay." Walker doesn't bother to look up from his legal pad.

"Mr. Walker, perhaps we should hear the testimony first," the judge says.

"I don't want the jury to be prejudiced by what they might hear," Walker argues.

The judge sighs and turns to Earl. "Mr. Scanlon, will you be using the witness' testimony to prove the truth of the matter asserted?"

The question is the judge's way of hinting to Earl that he's ready to overrule the objection as long as Earl gives him a legal reason to do so.

"No, Your Honor. We want to show Mr. Hilliard's state of mind during the time he spent with Ms. Del Toro, which will be consistent with and support the explanation Mr. Hilliard later gives on the stand for why the trip took so long."

"I'll allow it, then. Proceed."

Jack glances at Walker, who's shaking his head at being home-towned.

Earl asks the court reporter to read back the question and the start of

Michael's answer. She pulls the tape from her machine until she sees her marks. In a robotic voice, she says, "Was there anything in his demeanor, or even any physical evidence, that led you to believe he'd had an inappropriate interaction with Celeste?" and then "No. He was gone a long time, but he said—" She drops the tape and her hands quickly return to the keys.

"Go on," Earl says, prodding Michael gently. "Please finish your answer."

The truth, Michael. Tell the truth. Don't hold anything back.

"He said she asked him to give her time to sober up, so her dad wouldn't know she'd been drinking. She was afraid of getting in trouble."

"Did your father mention that she seemed extremely afraid of her father?"

"Yes," Michael says.

"Did he say why he thought that?"

Michael shrugs. "He just said he thought she was acting afraid. He said she panicked when he told her he planned to talk to her dad. He asked me why she would be so afraid."

"And what did you tell him?"

"Just that her dad was strict."

"In your opinion, is her father strict?"

"Yeah, really strict."

"What did your dad say to that?"

"He thought she was hiding something. He thought maybe her dad was hurting her."

"Did he say how?"

"No. He asked me if I knew anything."

"What did you say?"

Michael lowers his eyes but sneaks a peek at Jack. Jack subtly nods to let him know it's okay.

"I told him I thought he was crazy."

"Why did you think he was crazy?"

"I don't know. He's always suspicious of little things. I guess doing what he does, you know, he sees a lot of kids being abused, and so sometimes he thinks someone is being abused when maybe they're not."

"Do you think that's the case here? That your dad saw something that wasn't there?"

"I don't know."

"Mike, do you have *any* reason whatsoever to suspect that maybe your dad's concerns were warranted in this case? That maybe Celeste has been abused?"

"Objection." Walker stands and glares at Earl. "Unless Mr. Scanlon has some sort of substantive evidence, these questions call for speculation, which will only prejudice the jury."

Before Earl argues, the judge calls the attorneys to approach the bench.

Earl and Jack discussed ahead of time whether Earl should ask Michael if he thought Celeste had been abused. From the beginning, Jack sensed that Michael knows more than he lets on. The instant messages and Celeste's journal confirmed that hunch. But both lawyers agreed that without knowing how Michael will answer, the question is risky. It forces Michael to choose between honesty and perjury, if perjury is the only way he can cover for Celeste. Jack doesn't like doing it this way, but he believes, if pressed, his son will tell the truth. He hopes he's right, because if Michael lies, Jack refuses to allow Earl to impeach him.

When Earl leaves the bench to resume his questioning, he winks at Jack to indicate victory. Jack's gut clenches in anticipation of Michael's answer.

This time, Earl doesn't ask the court reporter to repeat the question. He wants to ensure emotion accompanies the delivery.

"I know this is hard, Mike." His voice is quieter. "I'll repeat the question for you. Do you have any reason, any reason whatsoever, to suspect that maybe your dad's concerns were warranted in this case? That maybe Celeste has been abused?"

Michael appears to grow younger before their eyes. Jack sees a boy on the edge, reaching out his hand and asking someone to take it and lead him across the abyss. That someone should be his father, but instead Jack feels as if he's the one who pushed him out there.

"I . . . . I don't really know."

"Is there something preventing you from answering my question with a simple *No?*" Earl asks the question with the tenderness of a father who raised four girls.

Michael shrugs again; Jack sees him swallow. "Just . . . I don't know . . . I mean, her dad is just strict, you know? Like I said."

"Can you give me an example?"

Another shrug. "Like, for Homecoming this year, he wouldn't let her wear the dress she wanted to wear. And he doesn't let her do normal things, like wear nail polish, or get her driver's permit, even though she's old enough."

"Do you think those things are abusive?"

Jack admires Earl for playing it smart. He asked the question in a tone suggesting the things Michael listed are pretty typical for a parent who falls on the far side of strict.

"No, but . . . I don't know. He's weird about them."

"In what way?"

Michael avoids Earl's gaze. He must know that even if he doesn't out Celeste, anything he says at this point will probably anger her father enough to ban future contact with his daughter.

"Mike?"

"He's just really mean about it. Like with the dress, he didn't just say 'that dress is inappropriate.' That's what my mom and dad would say. She said he called her a slut for wanting to wear it."

"Objection, hearsay," Walker says with weariness.

"Sustained." Judge Simmons is growing weary, too. "Michael, you'll have to stick to your own impressions, or things you saw or heard yourself, okay?"

"Yes, sir."

"Do you consider it abusive for a parent to call their children bad names?" Earl asks, carefully avoiding a direct reference to the stricken testimony. It's enough that the jury heard it.

"I don't know. My dad might. He might say it's emotionally abusive."

Walker shakes his head—he certainly recognizes Michael's answer as speculation—but he apparently decides it's wiser not to object again.

"What about you?"

"It makes Celeste cry, so yeah, I guess I do, in a way."

Earl glances at Jack, seeking his silent input. *How far do you want me to go?* he wants to know. Michael is obviously trying to help Jack without hurting Celeste, but nothing he's said so far rises to anything Earl can really use. Jack nods, giving his reluctant assent.

"She cries?"

"Yes. She gets really upset."

"Don't you get really upset sometimes when your parents discipline you?"

"Yes . . . but it's different. I can't explain it."

"I want you to try. I want you think carefully. Is there any way—that you know of personally, that is—that Celeste expresses her distress, other than crying?"

Jack sees the realization dawn on Michael's face that Earl somehow already knows the answer. He has the look of a puppy that innocently trusted its master and then got smacked. He squirms in his seat and Jack blinks back tears welling in his eyes. He hates himself for letting Earl do this, but he hates Celeste, too, for putting Michael in the middle.

"Mike, you're under oath," Earl gently reminds him.

"Yes," he says quietly. Earl waits for more, and Michael looks down at his lap before he adds, "She cuts herself."

The gallery emits a collective gasp.

Walker sighs dramatically. "Your Honor, I have to object to this line of questioning. I don't see the relevance."

Earl remains calm but the muscles in his jaw tighten. "It's relevant because it evidences Ms. Del Toro's emotional state, and that emotional state may very well have caused her to make a false accusation."

"I'll allow it. But briefly, counselor. And stay on track."

Earl turns back to Michael. "How do you know she cuts herself?"

"She told me, but she's also shown me the scars on her legs."

"Do you know why she cuts herself?"

"I don't really understand why, but I guess it makes her feel better."

Jack sees Earl's mind working, trying to think of a way to formulate the next question so he doesn't get an objection. "Does Celeste seem depressed to you?"

"Objection," Walker says without looking up from his notepad. "I don't believe Mr. Scanlon has laid a proper foundation to establish this boy as an expert on psychiatry who can diagnose depression."

"I'll withdraw the question," Earl says quickly. "Mike, you said she cries a lot and cuts herself. Does she seem sad to you?"

Someone in the audience snickers. Once again, Earl has made Walker look foolish for his objection.

"Yes."

"Do you know why?"

"I don't know. I mean, she has sort of a weird family."

A few uneasy chuckles come from the gallery and Michael looks in the direction of the sound. Suddenly, he seems more conscious of the crowd dissecting his every word.

"What do you mean?"

"Her parents are divorced, and I get the feeling that they argue a lot. I know a lot of kids have divorced parents, but it's not just that. I think she had a rough time in Florida, when she lived with her mom."

Earl, of course, knows Michael can't testify about anything that Celeste told him happened in Florida. Jack is surprised when he tries, anyway. "How so?"

"Objection. Calls for—"

"Sustained." The judge frowns at Earl. *You should know better*, his look says.

"Do you think her cutting has to do with having a rough time in Florida?"

"Yes." Michael answers so quickly, so insistently, that Jack is certain he knows more.

"Why do you think that?"

Michael shrugs shyly. "Well, some of her scars are old, you know? I mean, it's obvious she was cutting before she ever came to Missouri." Jack wonders if Michael thinks this testimony might get him back in the good graces of Celeste's dad. Jack wishes his son cared as much about getting back into his own dad's good graces.

Earl returns to the defense table and pulls a paper from his file. He shows Walker. Walker frowns, but nods, knowing the judge already gave his approval during pretrial motions for Earl to use it.

Earl hands it to Michael, who pales.

"Have you seen this document before?"

"Not this exact piece of paper, but yes, I've seen what's written on it."

"Where?"

"On my computer." He looks at Jack, aghast. He must now realize, too, that Jack saw the pictures.

"Can you tell us what this document is?"

"It's just something Celeste wrote." He chokes out the words.

"How did it come to be on your computer?"

"I asked her once what it was like, you know, to cut herself. What it felt like, if it hurt? She said she did it because it made her feel better. That didn't make sense to me. A few days later, she emailed this to me." He uses the heel of his palm to wipe his face. "She likes to write," —he shrugs, a gesture of pure wretchedness— "so I guess it was easier to tell me this way."

"Can you explain as best as you can what this document describes?"

"It just sort of explains what she does when she cuts herself." His tone pleads for Earl to let it drop.

"The first two lines read 'I always lock the bathroom door behind me but I don't turn on the exhaust fan. If he comes home unexpectedly, I need to hear him.' Who do you think she means, when she refers to 'he' and 'him'?"

"She means her dad."

"Do you remember what she named this document, when she sent you the file?"

"I don't know."

Michael's cheeks are pink from fighting back tears, and Earl lowers his head as if considering whether to just let it go. Jack wills Earl to look over so Jack can insist he does.

No such luck.

"The second to last line reads 'The anticipation of the relief waiting for me just on the other side of the cut has a way of stilling my nerves and calming my fear.' Does that help you remember the name of the document she sent you?"

Michael nods and tries to collect himself. He takes a rattling breath. "Yes." His voice is hoarse. Finally, the weight of all he's been carrying comes crashing down, and he sobs, "She called it *Relief*."

Earl asks for a brief recess to let Michael compose himself.

"What do you want me to do?" Earl asks Jack quietly. "Should I ask him if he knows anything about the journal entry?"

"I want you to get him off the stand. *Now*."

"Jack—"

"Get him off the fuckin' stand!"

Earl's eyes flash with anger, but he otherwise maintains his trademark composure.

"Fine, but Walker will want redirect. You know that."

"Just end it."

After the break, Earl does as Jack insisted, but just as Earl predicted, Walker saunters to the witness stand for redirect. He positions himself closer than necessary. An attorney usually has one of two goals in mind when he moves in so close to the witness—intimacy, or intimidation. Walker, Jack is sure, intends the latter, but he's in for a surprise. Walker doesn't know Judge Simmons like Jack does. The judge will hammer Walker if he so much as snarls at a minor, especially one who just broke up on the stand.

"Mike . . ."

Michael bristles at Walker's use of his nickname, but Walker pretends not to notice. Earl got away with it because he's known Michael for so long.

"You said your dad thought Celeste's father might be hurting her, yet he didn't bother to talk to the man when he dropped her off, did he?"

"I don't know."

"You don't know whether or not he talked to her father?"

"No. I mean, he told me he didn't. I don't know why, though. Other than he thought it was better if her dad thought I dropped her off."

"Really?" Walker rubs his chin. "I can tell you're a smart young man. Can you think of any reason he would want her father to think you dropped her off? Any reason he wouldn't want to talk to Mr. Del Toro?"

"I told you. He didn't want her to get in trouble. And he probably didn't want to wake up her dad. It was really late."

"That was courteous of him."

Judge Simmons looks up from his notes. "Mr. Walker, if you have more questions, please ask them, but please keep commentary to yourself."

Walker nods but otherwise acts as if he did nothing wrong. "Isn't it possible he didn't want to face the father of a girl he had just sexually assaulted?"

Michael simply stares at him.

"Mike, I'm not asking if you believe he assaulted her. I'm simply asking, *if* he did, couldn't that be why he wouldn't want her father to know he brought her home?"

"Yes, but—"

"You've answered my question. Thank you."

Earl glances at Jack, but Jack shakes his head. He's certain the jury will see this for what it is. He'd rather Walker just finish.

"When you were answering Mr. Scanlon's questions, you said your dad seemed nervous around Celeste when he first met her."

"Yes."

"You said you thought it was because her resemblance to Jennifer Dodson reminded him and your mom of a—" he looks down at his notes "—*bad time* in their lives. Is that correct?"

"Yes."

"What 'bad time' are you referring to?"

This time Earl doesn't bother checking with Jack. He slams his palm on the table and springs from his seat. "Objection! Every person sitting in this courtroom knows what this boy refers to. Mr. Walker should be ashamed of himself for asking him to testify about it!"

Jack can't remember the last time he saw Earl show such emotion in a courtroom. He's not sure he ever has.

"Counsel, approach."

As Earl and Elias argue in front of the judge, Jack waits for his son to look at him, but Michael's eyes are firmly focused on his lap.

Was Claire right again? By allowing Michael to testify, did Jack sacrifice his own son to avoid going to prison? He doubts Michael's testimony is the testimony that will keep Jack from being convicted, so really, what did he gain from today's spectacle? More importantly, what might he have lost? Possibly a son.

"I'm sustaining the objection," the judge announces, interrupting Jack's thoughts. He leans toward Michael. "You can ignore that question, son."

Next to Jack, Earl writes on the legal pad, *He is NOT happy with Elias.*

Walker steps even closer to Michael. Jack glances at the judge to see if he noticed. He's writing something and didn't.

"You don't really know for certain, do you, that your father's discomfort when he first met Celeste was because of her resemblance to Ms. Dodson? Isn't it possible he was aware of his attraction to Celeste, and knew, of course, that such an attraction was unacceptable?"

"I don't know for certain, I guess." Michael shrugs helplessly.

Walker makes a satisfied, smacking sound with his lips as if Michael's answer was some great coup for his case.

"Mike, do you trust Celeste?"

Michael frowns. His expression asks *What type of question is that?* "Yes, I trust her."

Walker nods, savoring the moment before he continues. Jack closes his eyes and braces himself for what he knows Walker is about to do. Earl scratches on his legal pad with his pen, ready to rise.

"You believe that she doesn't lie to you?"

"Yes." Michael drags out the word. He, too, is starting to sense a trap.

"Thank you, son. Let me ask you this, then."

One of Jack's pet peeves is a lawyer who thanks the witness after an answer. Walker's fake gratitude, together with his use of *son* when addressing Jack's own son, is more than Jack can stomach just then. He works to not let the jury see how riled he is.

"Do you think your dad raped Celeste?"

The incredibly risky question comes as a surprise to everyone in the courtroom except the lawyers. Before Earl objects, Jack whispers, "Let him answer." Walker must think that, based upon the last two answers, Michael has no choice but to say yes. Jack thinks otherwise and is willing to take his chances.

In his opinion, Walker left out a key question: he never asked Michael if Celeste *told* him Jack raped her.

Michael stares at Walker.

"Mike, please answer the question."

"It's Michael."

"Excuse me?"

"My name is Michael."

Walker raises his eyebrows. "I'm sorry. *Michael.* Do you think—"

"I heard the question."

Jack and Earl exchange a glance. The jury won't appreciate a smart mouth, even from a teen. Especially from a teen. Any sympathy he garnered earlier will dissipate if he doesn't check his sudden attitude.

"And your answer?"

Michael looks over at Jack with eyes still puffy and red-rimmed from his crying. Jack can't tell if Michael's mad and is about to punish his father, or simply upset.

"You're under oath, Michael." Walker's tone is smug; Michael picks up on it. He turns back to Walker and nods before he answers, an action Jack is sure was meant to show everyone in the room that he fully understands his obligation to tell the truth.

"No, sir. I am one hundred percent certain my dad didn't rape Celeste."

Walker must decide he will damage his case further if he tries to question Michael about the apparent inconsistencies in his testimony, so he releases him. As soon as Michael exits with the bailiff at his side, the judge recesses for lunch. Jack texts Claire and asks her to bring Michael to the law library on the eleventh floor. Only lawyers and judges are allowed into the law library, so he knows they'll have privacy.

He finds them near an east window overlooking the Mall and the Arch. To his surprise, heavy clouds hang low in the sky; they cast a dark, grayish-green glow over the city. The street lamps flicker with uncertainty. His time in the sun that morning feels like days ago.

Michael sits with his head down, his hands in his lap. Claire squats in front of him, talking softly. Mark stands to the side like a sentry, waiting for the order to take Michael home.

Claire rises when she sees Jack. "What happened in there?" she demands.

With barely a glance at her, he turns to Michael.

"Mike." His voice is quiet but firm.

Michael raises his head. His eyes are swollen and red, but Jack persists.

"What's the juris doctor plan?"

"What?" Michael asks, feigning ignorance, but he waited a beat too long to answer.

"Don't fuck with me, Michael."

"Jack!" Claire cries.

"Answer the question. What is the juris doctor plan?"

"*What* are you talking about?" Claire asks.

Michael remains quiet, waiting to see if his mother will succeed in rescuing him.

"Answer me. Don't make me regret that we didn't ask you on the stand."

When Claire touches Jack's arm, he shakes her off. Michael glances at her, and Jack gets it. He doesn't want to answer in front of his mom.

"Leave us alone a minute," he says, his gaze never leaving his son. "Both of you," he adds, so Mark knows Jack wants him gone, too.

"No." Claire is just as adamant. "Not until you tell me what's going on."

"Look, you can leave on your own or I'll call a guard."

Her mouth falls open but she recovers quickly. Her jaw clenches with anger. "What has gotten into you?"

The two of them, father and son, continue to stare at each other. Claire must finally accept that she's the outsider in their cryptic communication and that Jack has no plans to answer her. She tells Michael she'll be in the witness room and to call if he needs her.

"No, wait for him in the cafeteria," Jack insists. The basement café is another spot off-limits to all but courthouse personnel, parties, and witnesses. Without another word, Claire marches off toward the elevator, Mark on her tail.

"Well?" he says to Michael when they're left alone.

"It was just a joke."

"*What* was just a joke?"

"The juris doctor thing."

"Does it involve Jenny?"

Michael nods bashfully, like a kid copping to a kid-sized crime. But Jack knows this offense is full grown. "Tell me."

"I didn't know she would really do it. It was just supposed to be a joke."

"*What* was?"

"Dad . . ."

"*What was*, Mike? Answer me!"

"She sent letters."

"Who sent letters?" he asks, and all the answers fall into place. "Celeste?" Another nod from Michael. "To Jenny?"

"Yeah."

"Why? What kind of letters?"

"I don't know. It was just a joke."

"I'm getting sick of repeating myself. *Why* did she send Jenny letters? In fact, why don't you tell me everything without me having to drag it out of you?"

Michael looks as if he's about to cry again, but at that moment, Jack feels no compassion for him. "A long time ago I told her what happened. I guess I sounded mad at you . . ." He won't meet Jack's eye.

"Go on."

"I guess she looked up everything online, you know, the whole story, more than what I told her, and Jenny's address. She thought it'd be funny to scare her. You know, like to punish her for what she did."

"To punish Jenny?"

"Yeah. But I thought it was just talk. I never thought she'd really do it."

"Tell me, did you think it would be funny, too?"

He shrugs, and Jack takes the gesture as a *Yes.*

"She actually did it?"

"Yeah, but like I said, I didn't know it, not at first. I thought she was just joking. That's all it was supposed to be. A joke. Just talk."

"So how do you know she sent them?"

"She told me. She sent them from the post office by her dance classes."

"Where are her dance classes?"

"In U. City."

That explains the postmark.

"On Saturdays?"

Michael nods suspiciously, as if he wonders how Jack knows that.

"How many?"

"I think four."

This surprises Jack. "Four?"

"Yeah. She didn't even tell me she'd sent any until after the third one. I asked her to stop. I thought she did. She told me later she mailed a fourth one. As far as I know, that was it."

"Do you know what they said?"

"They were just dumb things, meant to scare her."

"Like what?"

He shrugs again. "I don't know exactly."

"Think."

"I don't know the exact words! Like they came from the guy who killed her parents."

"Don't forget her little sister, Mike. She watched her sister take a bullet to the head, too."

About to cry again, Michael's face twists in shame at Jack's sarcasm.

"You didn't see a problem with this?"

"Yeah! That's why I told her to stop!"

"Why didn't you tell me?"

"Why? Why would I?"

Jack really doesn't have a reason, not one that he could admit to his son.

"I need you to try to remember what they said." *The fourth one, in particular.*

Why didn't Jenny show him the fourth one?

"I could tell you if I had my phone. She told me in some texts. But they took my phone downstairs."

"Come on." Jack stands and a touch to Michael's shoulder causes him to do the same. "We'll get it, and then Mark will take you home. But we're having a little talk tonight, got it?"

Jack's phone vibrates in his back pocket.

"Where are you?" Earl asks when Jack answers.

"Upstairs in the library, talking to Mike."

"How is he?"

Jack watches Michael pick at a hangnail. The skin around it has been scratched to an angry pink. "That remains to be seen."

"One of the jurors is complaining of a stomach ache, so Judge Simmons extended the break to three. I'd like us to talk before Claire takes the stand, though."

"I need to drop him off with Claire and Mark, and then I'll meet you in my office." He can't wait to tell Earl what he's learned.

"The press is waiting for you in the lobby like rabid dogs."

"I'll deal with it."

When they hang up, Jack leans close to his son and says, "You are not to breathe a word to Celeste that you told me this, do you understand?"

Michael tilts back, cowering.

"*Do you understand?*"

"Yes. But why?"

Jack ignores the question. They're alone when they step onto the elevator. He hopes most of the media is still on the tenth floor in the hall outside the courtroom so he can retrieve Michael's phone from the guards downstairs undisturbed.

"I have one more question for you," Jack says after the doors seal shut. His voice has lost none of its indignation. "Were her accusations against me meant to be a joke, too? A way to punish me, like the letters were meant to punish Jenny? Because if they were, she's taken it a bit too far, wouldn't you say?"

Michael doesn't answer. His eyes fill again and his bottom lip quivers. He sniffles and uses his hand to wipe under his nose.

"Mike?"

"The letters had nothing to do with all of this!"

"What does 'all of this' have to do with, then? I'd really like to know."

The crying jag on the witness stand is starting all over again. He won't look at Jack.

Jack slams the red emergency stop button, and the elevator screeches to a halt. Michael has to put a hand against the wall to keep his balance.

"Mike, do you think I'm guilty?"

He sobs, shakes his head. "No."

"I don't get it, then. Do you have any idea how serious this is? I could go to prison. Do you really hate me that much?"

Another shake of the head, eyes still down.

"Then *what the hell* is going on? Why is she so afraid for her dad to know that you two were having sex? What could happen that's worse than what she's putting all of us through?"

Nothing but a wretched shrug.

"You sat there on the witness stand and admitted she cuts herself. Do you not see a problem with that? Do you not see she needs help? Accusing me of something I didn't do won't help her, you know?"

Michael tries to wipe away his tears with his sleeve, but Jack thinks he saw a small nod somewhere in the motion.

"What happened in Florida? Did her mom's boyfriend hurt her?"

Michael suddenly stills. Jack knows he's wondering how Jack found out about the Florida boyfriend. He's amazed at how easily his son forgets the resources at Jack's disposal.

"Is that it? Does her fear have something to do with him?" At the continued silence, Jack resorts to pleading. "What do you know that you won't tell me? Why are you so willing to cover for her at all costs?"

Michael finally lifts his gaze. Jack sees some of the contrition he hoped for, but he sees something else, too. Reflected in Michael's sixteen-year-old eyes is the last question being thrown back at Jack, and a wisdom that no boy his age should ever learn from his father.

CHAPTER TWENTY-FIVE

AFTER THEY COLLECT Michael's phone, Jack reads the text messages from Celeste that detail the letters she sent Jenny. Although only the last one—WE KNOW THE TRUTH—is new to Jack, he pretends otherwise in front of Michael. Jack then drops off Michael with Mark and a very irate Claire before fighting his way back up to the DA's office on the second floor. Despite the reporters and other onlookers who crowd him, he goes slowly to give Mark time to escape with Michael unseen.

His staff members who aren't at lunch congregate around him when he comes off the elevator. As they have every day since the trial started, they pepper him with questions about its progress and offer words of encouragement. He gives them a brief update and then escapes to the seclusion of his office by claiming a phone appointment. Fifteen minutes later, when Earl still hasn't arrived, he breaks his self-imposed embargo and calls Jenny with the news.

Jack expects the 411 operator to tell him the number is unlisted and is surprised when she connects him without delay. The phone rings three times before it's answered by a voice that sounds younger than the forty-two years of its male owner.

"Brian?"

"Yes?"

"This is Jack Hilliard."

He receives static in response. He thinks the man is about to hang up on him.

Finally, "Jack." He says it intimately, as if they've already met and he knows Jack well. "Is my sister okay?"

Damn. She's not with Brian, and Brian is apparently unaware that Jack and Jenny haven't been in touch. He has to make a quick decision. Let Brian know why he needs to talk to Jenny and risk having her tipped off, or pretend he saw her just yesterday and use the call to get some other information. He chooses the latter.

"She's fine. I mean . . ." He sighs. "Yeah, she's fine."

"What's wrong?"

"Nothing's wrong." *Everything's wrong.* "I'd like to ask you a question, although I realize you may not want to answer. I'll understand if you don't."

"I'm listening."

"The scar. Can you tell me what happened?"

More static. The impending storm is playing havoc with the reception. Is Brian debating whether to answer? Or is he reliving an event in his mind?

"Did you ask her?"

"Yes. She wouldn't tell me. I get the feeling she thinks she's protecting me from something."

"She's protecting you from a lot of things, Jack." He speaks the words quickly, without the hesitation that preceded his other responses. Jack feels a touch of vertigo at hearing them.

"What do you mean?"

Brian blows out a long stream of air. "She slit her wrist."

An answer to Jack's first question, not his last.

"I know that. I'm wondering why, when, what happened."

"She did it about a year after she arrived in Chicago. She was a mess. She'd been a mess since the day she showed up on my doorstep, and she only got worse. I kept trying to get her to talk to someone, but she worried about being found out. She lived in fear of the day they showed up at the door to extradite her to Missouri. She—"

"They'd dropped the charges. Why was she so afraid?"

"You know as well as I do why she was afraid. She knew what everyone would think once they figured out who Maxine was."

"I'm sure she followed the news, Brian. She's smart. I'm sure she knew their attempts to find her were lukewarm at best. She had to know they had no plans to charge her again."

"Sure she knew. And she also knew Alex appealed his conviction and therefore those plans could easily change."

"That's true, but—"

"She also knew who sold her down the river."

The comment angers Jack. "Like hell. She's the one who set *me* up."

"You honestly think she murdered Maxine?" Brian's question reminds Jack of his own to Claire about Celeste. *Are you honestly telling me there's a part of you that wonders, truly wonders, if I did something with her?* And like Claire, he has only two choices: have faith, or not, because it's unlikely he will ever have proof.

He did have faith in Jenny Dodson's innocence at one time. He's not sure when he first began to lose it, but once he learned who Maxine was, he gave it up completely, if regretfully. He forced himself to accept that everything Jenny had done from the moment she agreed to sleep with him had nothing to do with her feelings for him and everything to do with creating the perfect alibi.

"She manipulated me. She should have told me about Maxine from the start.

What was I supposed to do when I found out? I'm an officer of the court." Brian snorts at that, but Jack ignores it. "She's still trying to manipulate me, as far as I'm concerned. She's got you telling me—"

"You called *me*, Jack."

"She should have told me! If she trusted me enough to tell me about your parents and sister, she should have trusted me enough to tell me about Maxine." He scoffs. "But that would have made it difficult to set me up as her alibi, wouldn't it?

"She didn't know!" Brian shouts, and Jack jerks back in his chair as if the man is standing right in front of him. "She didn't know," Brian says again, softer now.

"She didn't know what?"

"She didn't know Maxine had been our father's mistress."

"I don't understand."

"Maxine was simply another client to Jenny. It wasn't until just before her arraignment that she found out she was more."

Jack, shocked into silence, waits for Brian to continue.

"She called to ask if I could help with her bail, if she were lucky enough to get it. Until that phone call, I didn't even know she'd been arrested. I about shit my pants when I heard the name of the victim." He pauses. "And that's when I told her."

Jack's mind reels with a plethora of memories. He remembers how Jenny would barely look at him when she entered the courtroom for her arraignment. How afterwards she instructed Earl to tell Jack it was best for him to keep his distance. She refused to let him visit her. Earl said she was angry at Jack for revealing their secret to Earl, but now Jack wonders if that was simply the excuse she gave Earl. Brian's earlier comment plays in Jack's mind like a scratched record. *She's protecting you from a lot of things.* Is that why, even after Jack admitted to being with her the night of Maxine's murder, she claimed publicly that he was lying, that he would admit to anything to keep her off death row? Had she been trying to protect him?

Unless, of course, Brian is now trying to protect *her.*

Jack can't wrap his head around this new information. He simply doesn't know what to think, whom to believe. "*You* told her that Maxine was your dad's mistress," he says. "She didn't know until after her arrest." He speaks the words as conclusions he's trying to understand.

"She didn't believe me at first. She thought it was ridiculous. She thought it was impossible."

So she tried to get a hold of the case file.

Although Jack and Jenny had been close friends for nine years, it wasn't until their long night together that she first told Jack about witnessing her family's murders when she was a child. Despite what everyone liked to believe, the two lovers spent just as much time in conversation as they did in bed. But the retelling had upset her, and he was left with too many unanswered questions. Days later, after she was arrested, Jack requested the decades-old case file from storage in hopes of filling in the holes. It was offsite and not immediately available, but a few days after Jenny had been released on bail, the file room called to advise Jack that someone else had asked for it, too. That someone else was Jenny.

He remembers how furious Jenny became when he told her he knew she'd tried to get at the file. When he finally saw the contents of it, long after Jenny had left town, he thought he understood the reason for her anger: she had requested the file to keep him and everyone else from learning the secret hidden inside.

Now, it seems, she wanted the file simply to substantiate what Brian had told her.

"So you're saying, in all these years, she never asked about the woman who destroyed your family?"

"Jenny was nine at the time. She knew nothing of the gossip. As a teenager, she did eventually start asking questions. For the most part, I answered them honestly. But I never identified the other woman, and she never asked for a name. I think she preferred to leave our father on his pedestal." He pauses. "After all, 'the heart wants what it wants or else it does not care.' Right, Jack?" When Jack remains quiet at the sarcasm, Brian sighs. "I suspect she did some digging of her own. But if memory serves, Maxine's name was mentioned only once in the papers because the court issued an injunction preventing them from printing it."

Jack remembers finding only one article in the case file that mentioned Maxine. But he doesn't remember seeing an injunction order.

He decides to confess to Brian he hasn't seen Jenny in months; to Jack's surprise, Brian confesses he already knows that.

"I tried to call her cell a few minutes ago, but she didn't answer. I need to find her."

"Why?"

With that one question Jack senses how close Brian and Jenny are, how loved she is. Even in middle age, her big brother looks out for her.

"I'd like to ask her some of these questions myself, and hear the answers."

"Forgive me, Jack, but I'm skeptical. Aren't you in the middle of your trial?"

"Yes." He sighs, decides to take a chance. "I found out who sent the letters to Jenny. I need to talk to her about it. It could help my defense."

"But will it help *her*?"

"Why wouldn't it?" Jack shoots back. "She's the one who asked me to help her, God damn it, and I risked my job to do it. Now that I have the information she wants, she's going to hide from me? What's she so afraid of?"

"From what she says, the last time you two talked, you gave her plenty to be afraid of. You were convinced she's a murderer."

"She has nothing to fear from me." He suddenly wonders what would happen if he never saw her again. What if he were convicted, and the time between the trial and his last appeal was all he had? He remains suspicious of her, but the desperation he feels to see her has nothing to do with thinking Maxine Shepard's murderer might go free. "Brian, please. Please just tell me where she is."

Brian takes a resigned breath. Did he hear the alarm in Jack's voice? "I don't know. She's in St. Louis, but that's all I know. Since she left your brother's, she's made a point of not telling me her whereabouts. Perhaps she knew how persuasive you could be." He loads the last sentence with implications that Jack resents. At Jack's silence, he asks, "Have you checked her house?"

"Not yet."

"I'd start there. I told her it's risky, but she doesn't listen to me much. If she's not there, I don't know what to tell you."

"Will you be talking to her? Can you ask her to call me?"

"I will, but I don't know that it will make a difference."

Jack tries to remember the original point of his call. He hasn't found Jenny, and he still doesn't understand why she tried to commit suicide. If she's innocent, as she and Brian claim, what had been going through her head?

"I still don't get it. You said she slit her wrist because she was afraid of being arrested again, but I don't buy it."

"That's not what I said. I said she wouldn't go *talk* to someone because she was worried about being found out. I guess she didn't trust the therapist-patient privilege." Again, that disdain of the law. "Her reasons for trying to end her life ran much deeper."

"I'm all ears."

Brian softens his tone. "I think she's the only one who can explain those to you, Jack. And I promise you, although she might pretend otherwise, there's nothing she wants more than to be able to tell you, and for you to be strong enough to listen."

Jack slowly sets the phone on his desk. He hears thunder and he swivels to look out the window behind him. The clouds have finally relinquished their hold on the rain.

Despite Jenny's lies, a small part of Jack held out hope for her innocence and thought the proof to exonerate her would eventually surface, one way or another. Does this news about Maxine qualify? Brian said Jenny didn't know Maxine was the same woman who had been their father's mistress, but even if that were true, does it follow that Jenny wasn't involved in her murder? He can't really conclude it does.

On top of everything, he now knows she also lied about the fourth letter.
He's determined to learn the truth. As much as he hates to admit it, he still fears
if anything surfaces, it will be the evidence that finally forces him to accept her
culpability.

He stands and looks down at the street below. The sidewalks teem with men
and women caught in the rain and rushing to find shelter. They give only passing
attention to the numerous news trucks at the curb; anyone interested in the case
is inside waiting for the recess to end. If he's going to find Jenny, he'll need to
leave the courthouse unseen. The biggest hurdle will be avoiding the press and
the crowd of spectators roaming the halls and lobby, but he knows the bowels of
the building well enough to manage that. The rain will provide cover, too.

Five minutes later, with only a cryptic note to Earl letting him know he'll be
back soon, he escapes out a rear door next to a loading dock and makes haste for
the parking garage before anyone discovers his absence. He greedily sucks in the
fresh smell of the spring storm. For a brief instant, his fears—about going to
prison, about his marriage, about Jenny—are replaced with an unusual sense of
freedom that he hasn't felt in a long, long time.

When Jenny's cell phone rings, she's relieved to see it's Brian.

"Guess who I just got a call from?" he asks.

"He called *you*?"

"Yup. It took him a while to admit it, but he's looking for you."

"What do you mean by *it took him a while to admit it*?"

"At first he asked only about the scar on your wrist. It wasn't until later that
he told me he needed to find you."

"What'd you tell him?"

"About the scar? Or about where you are?"

"Both."

"I told him if he wanted to know why you did it, he'd have to ask you. As
for where you are, I told him only that you're in St. Louis, but that I didn't know
where. To buy you some time, I suggested he try your house. He asked me to let
you know he needs to talk to you. He claims to know who sent the letters."

Jenny sits up straighter at this news. "He said that?" When they talked at
Mark's house, Jack was convinced she'd sent them to herself.

"Yeah, but I'd be wary. There's something he wasn't saying."

If Jack knows who sent the letters, does that also mean he knows about the
fourth one, the one she didn't show him? Is that why he asked Brian about the
scar on her wrist?

"Do you think he knows?" she asks.

"No. He thinks he's getting warm, but based on everything he said, he's
not." Brian sighs. "Look, Jen, just be careful. As much as I think he deserves to
know everything, I also think he's got another agenda, and until you know what

it is, I don't think you should trust him."

"He won't do anything to hurt me."

"If it means saving his own butt, he might."

"No."

"Jenny, you're in denial. When he found out about Maxine, he went public with the information, remember?"

"That had nothing to do with saving his butt. He's always been about right and wrong. He was just doing what he thought was right. He was afraid Alex might have been wrongly convicted. Don't forget, he gave me my alibi even though he knew the consequences. And only a couple months ago he gave me a head start out of town before he turned *himself* in for questioning."

Brian scoffs. "You're thinking with your heart instead of your brain again, sis."

"So what if I am? Maybe we all should be so brave."

Her brother laughs at that. "Then tell him. Take your chances and tell him."

CHAPTER TWENTY-SIX

THE BLACK SHUTTERS around the tall, narrow windows of the rehabbed Victorian duplex need a new coat of paint, and no colorful bulbs pop from the beds like they did every spring when she lived here. Otherwise, the exterior looks the same as the last time Jack was here, more than four years ago. Someone has minimally maintained the small front yard. A bit of shrubbery frames each side of the two sets of steps—one leads to Jenny's door, the other to her neighbor's—and two patches of brown Zoysia grass line the short walkway from the street. The landscape is simple, but neat and tidy.

The house faces Lafayette Square. He parallel parks in front, on the street side closest to the park, and looks up at the house. The pounding rain coats his car windows with a thick veneer of water, blurring the picture. In all this time, he never came back. Not even to look. He never even drove by on his way to somewhere else. Indeed, he went out of his way to avoid it. He always told himself he did it for Claire, but now, looking across the street at the red door, he knows he did it for himself. Out of sight, out of mind, perhaps. Except it didn't quite work out that way.

She's not inside. He knew as soon as he pulled up. It's not that he expected to see lights or other evidence of life. If she were there, she'd make every effort to hide her presence. But somehow, still, he knows. Brian knew, too.

He's going in anyway.

He slams the car door shut and quickly crosses the empty street, stepping around potholes and puddles. It takes only a few minutes to find the faux stone in which she used to hide a key, but already the rain has soaked his head and found its way under his coat. Why is it always raining when he's here? The small stone is tucked under the steps in the same spot as always, mixed in among many real ones. The key, too, is still inside.

He knocks first, but only as a formality. He slips the key into the keyhole. Once inside, a stale smell greets him. The air is slightly frigid, as if the house held winter inside even as outside the season gave way to spring. He locks the door and then stands for a moment, steeling himself.

He tries each of the three switches near the door to see if any lamps come on. The electricity is off, as he suspected.

Everything is in its place. But for dust on every surface, the room is just as he remembers, only more sterile. Impersonal knickknacks line the fireplace mantel; she must have taken any that had meaning. Throw pillows are propped perfectly in each corner of the couch, and draped over the back is the familiar blue and gray afghan he covered her with that night. He remembers her affection for it and wonders why she didn't take it. A stack of magazines rests neatly on the end table. The top one, a Newsweek, is dated a mere two weeks after the last time he was here. She must have skipped town not long after the lie detector tests ostensibly cleared her.

He starts for the kitchen in the back. As he passes the bottom of the stairs, he hears a noise and halts. Silent and holding his breath, he waits for the sound to repeat. Only after he hears muffled laughter through the shared wall of the duplex does he relax and resume his tour.

After a quick glance in the kitchen, he moves upstairs. The stairwell grows darker after the 180° turn at the landing. He heads first to her study at the back of the second floor, a room he's never been in. But like the others, it reveals little about the woman who once lived here.

He finally turns toward the bedroom at the front. His earlier decision to break in can only be blamed on the existence of this one room, on his desire to return to it one more time. *She's like a drug to you.* If Claire is right, then this room is his opium den.

He stops in the doorway. It's been four years, yet here he thinks he finally detects her scent. He closes his eyes and inhales, letting himself be intoxicated by a memory.

He thinks of the morning he woke next to her in her large four-poster bed. In the moment he first opened his eyes, he was prepared to give up everything for the privilege of doing it again and again. She quickly set him straight. Even though he'd fallen asleep holding a woman he thought had finally opened herself to him, he woke next to a cold stranger who belittled the feelings he confessed for her and left him riddled with guilt and despair. He didn't—*couldn't*—understand the transformation, and he tormented himself trying.

Not for a minute, though, did he think her behavior that morning had to do with anything but him. Even after he learned she'd been arrested for her client's murder, he rejected the thought she might be guilty. Despite the mounting evidence against her, he dismissed it all as circumstantial. It wasn't until after she ran away and he found out about Maxine that he finally decided he'd been duped. He felt like a fool, but it made it easier to let her go, and with her, his absurd fantasies of a life at her side.

And then she came back.

He stares at the bed. *Turn around and leave. Nothing good can come from entering this room.*

He steps in slowly. Despite his memories and the lingering scent, or maybe because of them, her absence up here is more pronounced than downstairs. The picture of her murdered little sister is gone from the dresser; so is the jewelry box and cologne bottle he remembers. A few books and a piggy bank remain, but otherwise the top of the dresser, like the furniture downstairs, supports nothing but dust. He lifts the piggy bank and is surprised to find it heavy with coins.

The stereo on top of the tall chest of drawers in the corner is still there, but there are no CDs in sight. She probably has an iPod now, he thinks. He opens each drawer of the chest and the dresser, but except for a few slips and some pantyhose, all are empty.

He moves to her closet and gasps slightly when he opens it to find all the suits he's ever seen her wear. He sees no jeans, T-shirts or sweaters. Only suits. There must be at least fifteen of them, most black or gray but with a few browns and navies thrown in. They hang patiently under clear plastic dry cleaning bags, one to each suit. Beneath them, assorted pumps and sling backs are lined up like soldiers on the hardwood floor.

At the end of the row, he spots the mint green suit he always liked. She called it her "lucky suit." Even bringing up the rear, it stands out among the more somber colors, refusing to blend in. No one but Jenny, with her striking black hair, her dark skin and long legs, could pull it off. He wonders if he'll ever see her wear it again.

He looks up at the shelf and notices the family photo album she showed him is gone, too.

The desolation of the room suddenly saddens him and causes him to reconsider all of his conclusions about her. Despite his suspicions about her failure to show him the fourth letter, he begins to think she really didn't leave of her own accord. She was run out of town and forced to leave the largest chunk of who she is behind. She was convicted of nothing, but she was punished nevertheless. She'd loved the law as much as he did—for different reasons, he knows—but the law had let her down.

Had he let her down, too? And with his relentless doubts, is he continuing to do so?

"*What does it mean?*" he'd asked.

"*What does what mean?*"

"*The name. Ayanna. What does it mean?*"

She hadn't blinked.

"*Innocent.*"

The bed creaks when he sits on the end. He resists the desire to lie back and let his memories take him even deeper, to a place he might not be able to leave. Instead, he looks around the room. His gaze rests for a moment on the large casement windows, and then, on the piggy bank again. If she was worried about money, why didn't she take the change inside?

He jumps up and grabs the bank. Turning it over, he tugs at the rubber stopper until it pops out. Coins trickle from the hole onto the bed and he shakes it to help them along. Once it empties, he paws through the pile. His efforts are quickly rewarded. Hidden among the pennies, nickels, dimes and quarters is a small silver key. He inspects it. From the cuts he suspects it's the key to a safe deposit box; the box number on one side of the head confirms his suspicion. On the other side the letters SG—for the manufacturer Sargent Greenleaf, he knows—are imprinted above a seven-digit code of numbers and letters.

He pockets the key, scoops the coins back into the bank, and replaces it on the dresser in the exact spot he found it. He quickly leaves the bedroom, but on the stairs he hesitates. He returns to retrieve one more thing.

He's about to call Dog to ask if there's any way to trace the key code when his cell phone rings with an unknown number.

"Hi, Jack."

His pulse speeds up at hearing Jenny's voice for the first time in three months, but when he speaks, he tries to disguise his sense of urgency. "I'm surprised to hear from you."

"Brian said you were looking for me."

"I am. But you knew that from my call. The one you didn't answer."

"I didn't get any call from you." Silence, then, "Oh, you mean to my other phone." She laughs lightly. "That phone's at the bottom of the Mississippi River."

It takes only a moment for Jack to understand her meaning. *Under the Poplar Street Bridge.*

"Where are you?" he asks.

"Why?"

"I want to see you. I know who sent the letters."

"So you finally believe it wasn't me, sending them to myself?"

"I finally believe you." *About that, at least.*

"Maybe I don't believe *you*. Maybe you're just saying that, to convince me to tell you where I am. For all I know, you'll show up accompanied by a squad car. You told me if you contacted me again, it would be at their behest."

He glances at his watch and sees it's nearing three. "I doubt it, seeing as they're probably looking for me right now, too."

"What do you—?"

"I cut out of court." *And Earl won't be happy about it.*

"The trial was recessed until Monday. That's what the news said, at least."

This surprises Jack, but he's relieved.

He needs to take a different approach if he wants her to agree. "Jenny, please. I believe you. If you trust me to tell me where you are, I'll believe everything you tell me from now on."

She laughs bitterly. "The words of a desperate man. What's changed, Jack?"

"I told you. I know who sent the letters, and I know it wasn't you."

"So tell me who it was."

He decides to take a chance. "Celeste. I need to get the originals from you, for fingerprints. We want it to be airtight when we take it to the judge." When she doesn't speak, he says, "Jenny?"

Finally, in a voice choked with relief, she folds.

"I'm back at the motel. Come on over."

She surprises him by laughing as she opens the door, and by her playful comment, "This time you're the wet one," an obvious reference to their run-in at Mark's house. Her mood is a hundred times lighter, and it causes mixed emotions in him. He's missed that laugh, which once came so easily, and her fearlessness, but the return of both confirms his suspicions. She has, in fact, been withholding some sort of information from him, and now that she's learned the letters were a hoax and assumes Jack doesn't know about a fourth one, she no longer fears disclosure.

Until he has the original letters in hand, he doesn't intend to correct her.

She takes his overcoat and then grabs a hand towel and tosses it to him. He hastily wipes his face and dries his hair, feeling her watching him the whole time.

"Here, sit." Her open suitcase has reclaimed its spot on the extra bed, and she drags it to one end to make room for him. He notices it's packed.

"I can't believe you came back here, of all places."

She waves his concern away. "Once they checked and didn't find me here, I knew they wouldn't come back. And if they did, a hundred dollar bill to the night clerk goes a long way." She sits on the opposite bed across from him, her hands tucked between her knees. "So, tell me, how'd you figure out it was Celeste?"

"Michael admitted it." He explains how he first saw mention of a "juris doctor" plan in Michael and Celeste's text messages, but didn't connect it to Jenny until, during Michael's testimony, Earl wrote the initials "JD" on a note to Jack. "He was asking me if it was okay to ask Mike about you, but when I saw the letters on the note, I thought 'juris doctor' and it dawned on me that the words might have been their code for Jenny Dodson. At the break, I confronted Mike, and he confessed."

"So that's why you thought you saw me on those tapes you mentioned."

He nods. "From the post office where the letters were mailed." She doesn't need to know he never actually saw the tapes.

"How would she have known where to mail them?"

"Mike said she researched everything online. It's not hard to find an address. I guess she took a chance on them being forwarded. It's not like she had anything to lose if they weren't."

Jenny rises and crosses to the suitcase. She stands mere inches from him as she carefully digs through the neatly folded clothes. Her movements release the familiar fragrance. She pulls out the plastic bag containing the letters and hands it to him. "All yours." Their fingers touch as he takes it. "How will you explain how you got them?"

He holds her gaze as he tucks the bag into the inside pocket of his suit coat. "Are you going somewhere?" He tilts his head slightly toward the suitcase.

He sees wariness cloud her eyes as if she's dropped a veil over them. "I may go home soon."

"'Home' being Chicago?"

"For now."

"Why don't you come forward, tell them you didn't know about Maxine until after your arrest?" The question, he sees, catches her off-guard. Brian apparently didn't mention to her he'd told Jack. "Wouldn't you like to return to your real home?" he adds.

"They wouldn't believe me. And the timing wouldn't be great for you, would it?"

He ignores the second half of her answer. "You could take another lie detector test."

"Why do you care, Jack?" The tone hints at her irritation at being questioned.

"I guess I don't understand why you wouldn't want to be cleared, once and for all."

She smirks. "I thought I was cleared."

"Except you don't act like it, do you?"

She whirls to turn away from him, but he grabs her wrist. A mistake. The line separating his competing urges is much too fine.

She tugs, but he holds tight. "Do you remember our agreement?" he asks.

"Yes."

"Remind me. What was our agreement, Jenny?"

"That I'd tell you everything."

"Yeah. Except you've told me virtually nothing. I risked my neck, I helped you when you asked me to, I got the information you wanted, and yet all you've done is lie to me. Why?"

"I haven't."

"You have. You let me believe you were in Chicago when you weren't. You didn't tell me you'd gone to Mark's house. You didn't tell me you were meeting with Rebecca Chambers." At the name *Rebecca Chambers*, her eyes flicker toward her suitcase. The action was almost imperceptible, but he caught it. If she wonders how he knows the name, she doesn't ask.

He pulls her closer, back to where she started. He flips her hand to reveal the scarred wrist.

"You never told me why you did this."

"I didn't answer when you asked because it's none of your business, but I didn't lie to you."

She tugs again, and this time he releases her.

"Why won't you tell me?"

"What? You think I did it because I murdered Maxine? Is that what you really think?"

His anger begins to yield to her questions. It isn't what he thinks. At least, it's never been what he *wanted* to think, but she's given him too many reasons to doubt her and not near enough to trust her. Would Claire say the same about him?

"I don't know what to think." His voice softens. "You've kept so many secrets from me."

She drops onto the other bed and lowers her head into her hands. Her hair falls forward, blocking her face. He almost reaches over to touch it, to see if his memories of the texture are accurate; other memories stop him. He thinks again of Brian's comment. *She's protecting you from a lot of things.* What burden does she refuse to share?

He slips the key from his pocket and hides it in his closed hand. He has no idea if the key has anything to do with the fourth letter, but he's about to find out.

"Why'd you come back, Jen?"

She whips her head up. "For exactly the reason I told you!" she pleads.

"The letters?"

"Yes."

He holds up the key. "Then why didn't you show me the fourth one?"

The passion in her expression slips away, her cheeks go pale. She stares at the key, he sees her swallow. She blurts, "I think I'm going to be sick," and springs from the bed toward the bathroom. He follows, thinking only to help her somehow, but she slams the door and locks it.

Although she might pretend otherwise, there's nothing she wants more than to be able to tell you, and for you to be strong enough to listen.

He returns to the bed to wait, and to ready himself to listen.

She sits on the toilet lid with her head hanging between her legs, trying to slow her rapid breathing and racing mind. She should simply demand he leave. She should threaten to call the cops and see if he calls her bluff. She doubts he would, not in the middle of his trial. He'd leave and come back later unannounced to try again. By then, she could be in Chicago. She tells herself she owes him nothing, but she knows that isn't true. If not for his willingness four years ago to take a fall for her, she might be sitting on death row next to Alex. Or instead of Alex. Jack could argue Jenny owes him her life. Brian would argue she owes him more than that.

Take your chances and tell him.

Brian has always felt the secret was not Jenny's to keep. He believed Jack was entitled to know everything, regardless of the consequences to him, to his marriage, to Jenny. Any decisions Jack made, Brian argued, should be based on a full knowledge of the facts. Jenny, on the other hand, believed Brian's opinion to be clouded by his desire to protect her. To her way of thinking, she had no right to cause further pain to a family that has already had enough. On that she and Brian agreed: full knowledge would equal pain. Much more pain, to everyone involved. When she pointed this out to him, he shrugged and said, "What did C.S. Lewis say? The happiness I feel now is the pain I had before?" She never bothered to tell him he had it backwards.

She hears the exterior door open and close, and she lifts her head. Has he given up and left? She waits until she's sure. When the door opens and closes once more, she curses herself for not going out the first time to lock it.

After a few more minutes of careful listening, she opens the bathroom door and braces herself for the inevitable confrontation. He may hold the key, but she holds the power over the box and its contents. The bank will never allow him access without her at his side. Perhaps, someday, that time will come. But not today.

He waits in the same spot she left him, but something is different. Her suitcase. The lid has been flipped closed.

"I brought you a present," he says.

She approaches hesitantly until she sees it. Her mint suit, the one he used to tease her about, peeks out from the gap between the lid and the base. He called it her "Crest toothpaste suit" to make her laugh. She lifts the lid and sees he folded the suit carefully and set each piece, the skirt and then the jacket, on top of the other clothes she had already packed. She smiles as she lifts the jacket, but her smile fades quickly when she sees what he placed underneath. The manila envelope. He searched her suitcase and found it.

He stands, and suddenly her face is cupped in his hands. His hold on her is stronger than it needs to be. "Jenny, I didn't open it, and I won't force you to tell me anything you don't want to tell me. But please, just tell me why you won't trust me anymore." Without releasing her, he uses a thumb to wipe a tear about to fall. "You used to trust me with anything."

She closes her eyes, willing him to just leave, but he whispers, "Please look at me," and she can't deny him. "Why don't you trust me anymore?"

All the things she wants to say catch in her throat. She wonders what happened to the woman who waited for him to wake up that morning four years ago. She gave the best argument of her career that morning, when she convinced him they'd done nothing more the night before than satiate their sexual appetites. She ridiculed all his talk of soul mates and love, and sent him away confused and broken. She didn't believe her own words, but he did, and the verdict was hers. But now, on appeal, she's forgotten how to do it.

She looks into his eyes and understands why the juries love him. He's always argued from the heart. "Say something," she says quietly, "just one thing, I can trust in."

His confusion at her request is fleeting; she sees recognition dawn on his face, followed quickly by regret. He can't give her what she wants. Not now. Probably never.

But then he surprises her by echoing the words he overheard her speak at Mark's house.

"Okay. This: if there's one thing you know, it's how I feel about you."

She nods, over and over. It's the best he can do, and it'll have to be enough.

"Do you trust me, then?" he asks.

"It's not about trust."

"Tell me then. What is it about?" When she doesn't respond, he says, "I'd like to know what's in the envelope, what you're so afraid for me to know."

Suddenly, she realizes that he thinks whatever was in the safe deposit box is now in the envelope. In that instant, she decides if giving him the envelope will keep him at bay, she's prepared to do it. Even though it, too, will hurt him. "Be careful what you wish for," she says.

"What's in it?" he repeats as if he hasn't heard her warning.

"Nothing you want to see. Believe me."

"Do you remember what I said to you when I first visited you at the jail?

"You said a lot of things."

"I told you I could never hate you, even if you'd murdered Maxine."

"You think the envelope has evidence I murdered Maxine?"

"I don't know. Does it?"

She shakes her head, laughs sadly at the irony. He might not hate her once he sees the contents, but he still might want to kill the messenger.

"Okay, Jack. You win." He drops his hands from her face. "But I don't want to be with you when you open it. I think you'll want to be alone when you see what's inside."

At the door, he stops as if he wants to say something more. She stands stoically with one hand on the doorknob. Now that she's made the decision, she can't get him out fast enough. Her palms sweat and her stomach feels as if it's in her throat.

She knows what he thinks he will find. She knows what everyone believed about her back then. That she's a liar, that she's manipulative. That she planned everything from the very beginning. He tried not to believe it, she knows he did, but he always had his doubts, too.

"Thank you," he says, lifting the envelope. "For this. For trusting me."

"You may want to reserve your gratitude until after you open it."

He studies her, taking his time as if he's afraid to leave. His sad eyes say what his lips don't: he knows a big change is coming. She wonders if she'll ever see him again.

"I'm sorry," she says. "I am so, so sorry."

"Tell me why, Jen. What are you so sorry about? Why don't you want me to know what's inside?"

She hesitates. "Because what's inside that envelope is going to break your heart."

At that she leans close, and with the palm of one hand on his cheek, kisses him on the mouth. He closes his eyes. She feels the battle taking place inside him as his lips part slightly, but in the end, they remain frozen, refusing to return the affection.

Even after he's secure in his car, her scent lingers on his coat. In his hair. On the envelope.

And her taste. Her taste lingers on his lips.

He tries desperately to remember how Claire smells, how she tastes, and when he can't, he curses Jenny. *She's like a drug to you.* No matter how many times he denies it, he can't change facts. He craves Jenny and despises the fact of her existence at the same time. He knows what he's about to find. He knows that he's probably the closest he's ever been to knowing the truth, to seeing the evidence of her guilt revealed. And yet, he can't stop the thoughts running wild through his head. The thoughts that tell him to knock on her door, and when she lets him back in—because she will let him back in, he knows that, too—to lie down with her one more time. One more time before he destroys her with the information she's given him. Because, above all, Jack knows he will have to destroy Jenny to save himself.

CHAPTER TWENTY-SEVEN

IT MIGHT HAVE taken him forty-five minutes to get to the law school; it might have taken three hours. He has no idea. He doesn't remember the drive. He doesn't even remember making a conscious decision to go there. But he must have, because here he now sits, in his car in the parking lot just across from the school. It's rare to find an open space so close, especially on such a wet day. It's as if someone saved it for him, as if this moment was inevitable.

He looks at the new building through the cascade of rain. It's beautiful, and majestic, in a way. Gothic, resplendent in Missouri Red Granite. The law school finally has a home befitting its noble purpose, and one that matches in style and, in some opinions, surpasses in beauty, the other buildings on campus. It's nothing like the old Mudd Hall, the boxy building in which he and Claire first met, with its exposed concrete walls inside and out, the rust marks that dripped from the rebar, and the unnatural green hue that trimmed the exterior of the structure. Inside, the carpet was frayed and stained in many spots. Even the library and professors' offices on the upper levels felt as if they were in the basement because of the concrete walls and the stained carpet. Both the old law school, and the matching Eliot Hall next door, looked to be someone's 1970's contemporary architecture project gone horribly wrong.

And yet, he longs for that ugly building. In the same way his throat closed watching the first wrecking ball attack the old Busch Stadium, he felt an acute sense of loss when the university chancellor announced plans to tear down the old law school and build a new one on the opposite side of the campus.

The new school *is* beautiful. Claire's office is beautiful, too. But he can't help but think that something more than walls and carpet was permanently lost the day they brought down the old school. He didn't see it happen like he did the stadium. He'd been in trial.

He steps from the car, envelope in hand. He's not sure why he thinks she'll be in her office, or what he'll do if she's not. Will he have the strength to wait for her? And what if she's there, but someone is with her? Another professor, or a student?

He walks by reception without stopping to say hello as he usually does. He takes the stairs to the fourth floor. He doesn't have the patience to wait for the elevator.

His concerns are unfounded. He reaches Claire's office and finds her alone behind her desk. Red pen in hand, she's engrossed in grading the contents of a blue book and doesn't even notice him. He stands in her open doorway and waits for her to look up.

At some point she must sense a presence. She slowly raises her head, her eyes trailing behind as if she's reluctant to stop her activity. She startles when she sees him.

"Jack."

Later, when he looks back on everything and remembers this moment, he'll understand that she knew the reason for his surprise visit the instant she saw him in her doorway. But just then, even though he sees the clues on her face, he's still in shock and can't interpret them. He thinks he has to tell her. He thinks he has to show her the evidence of her betrayal so she'll know why he came.

"Earl has been looking for you," she says. "The trial was recessed until Monday, so I thought I'd catch up here." He stares at her, unresponsive. Her comments are nothing more than a delay tactic.

He steps in without invitation and walks between the two guest chairs. Leaving the photos in the envelope, he pulls out the papers and places them face up on the desk. They cover the blue book.

She doesn't look down. "You're soaking wet."

"Read them."

She continues to meet his stare. "Jack," she says again.

"Read them."

Her lips part as if she wants to speak again, but after a moment she lowers her eyes and begins to read. One hand rests on her lap, but the one holding the pen, the right one, trembles violently.

Like the ride over, he has no concept of how much time passes. By the time she raises her eyes to him again, thirty seconds might have elapsed, or twenty minutes. He might have been standing there an hour. He simply doesn't know.

He does know from the look on her face that none of the information comes as a surprise. She knew all along. She probably knew within minutes of her father knowing, and the date on the report from Lee Randolph to her father made clear that Harley Lambert knew almost immediately. For all Jack knows, she's had copies of the photos and report hidden all these years in a drawer at home.

He remembers her hysterical reaction when she first learned the truth. Or so he thought. Turns out it was Claire, not Jenny, who was the real actress.

"I wish you'd sit down."

"Would you have let her die?"

She rises and comes to his side of the desk, walks behind him and shuts the door. She approaches him, but he takes a small step away. She understands not to touch him.

"Will you *please* sit down?" she asks.

"Answer my question." He still stares at the papers on the desk as he talks. "Would you have let her die? If they hadn't believed I was her alibi, and they'd convicted her, would you have let them execute her?"

"Of course not," she whispers. "I would have come forward."

"How do I know that?"

"Jack."

"How do I know that, Claire?"

"Because I'm telling you."

He closes his eyes and shakes his head. When he opens them, he sees students through her large window streaming across campus. For an instant, he remembers doing the same with her, hand in hand, so many years ago. Both innocently unaware of how much pain they would inflict on each other.

"You've told me a lot of things," he says. "Not all, I know now, were true."

"How can you say that to me?" Her voice flares with anger. "After everything you—"

"Don't. Don't try to say what I did somehow justifies your withholding exculpatory evidence. You *knew* she was innocent."

"No! I didn't *know* she was innocent. And neither do you. Just because she was there with you the whole time doesn't mean she wasn't involved."

"Do you hear yourself, Claire? Fine, you want to call it *potentially* exculpatory evidence? Does that make you feel better? You had *potentially* exculpatory evidence and yet you didn't tell me, you didn't tell Earl. You didn't tell anyone."

"Why would I? You got her off all on your own, remember?"

"But what if I hadn't? What if I'd denied it? What if I'd agreed with her insistence that I would hurt you less if I continued with the lie?"

She drops like a ragdoll into a guest chair. "What do you mean? What are you talking about?"

"She didn't want me to confess to being her alibi, did you know that? She tried to talk me into keeping my mouth shut. You know why?"

Claire simply stares up at him, waiting. Skeptical.

"Because she didn't want to hurt you, or the kids. She knew what the truth would do to our family."

"Oh, please." She grunts with disgust. "I'm supposed to somehow think better of her for that? She fooled you then, and she's fooling you now if you believe that."

"You think so? Look at the date of the cover note to her. She's known of this for over four years." He picks up the papers and waves them inches from her face, causing her to lean back and turn her head. "All this time, she's known. She knew your father had proof of her innocence—which also meant you probably did, too—and she kept it to herself. She left town to get out of our lives. She gave up everything so that we had a chance. Even as recently as today, she was doing everything in her power to keep me from knowing what he did."

"Is that the story she's feeding you?"

"No, it's the truth I've finally come to understand on my own. Everything she's done since the morning I woke up in her bed has been geared toward protecting our family."

Claire winces at the image he just portrayed. "You really expect me to believe that? If she cared about our family you wouldn't have *been* in her bed!"

"I don't care anymore what you believe. Think whatever you want. But the fact is, she was willing to risk prison, even death, to protect me, to protect you. Whereas *you* were willing to keep evidence to yourself that supported her innocence. Even knowing what might happen to her. That's despicable."

"How dare you! How dare you say that to me after what you did!"

"You can't compare what I did with this." He gives the papers another shake before dropping them on the desk. "I didn't set out to hurt you. *She* didn't set out to hurt you."

"Well, like I said, if that's true, maybe you shouldn't have slept with each other."

Her sarcasm only fuels his anger. "She *knows* that, Claire. *I* know that. Okay? We both know what we did was wrong. No one's trying to say that—"

"But you still did it, didn't you?"

"Yes. Yes. I've admitted that a million times. And you'll never let me forget it, will you? But you know what? The motivation was different. It was wrong, yes. It was so, so wrong. But we did it because of our feelings for each other, not to hurt you. Can you say the same for what you've done?"

She looks up at him, stunned. It's the first time he's acknowledged to her his feelings for Jenny. He didn't use the word, but she heard it nevertheless. It's been firmly wedged between them for four years, an invisible barrier, though both tried to ignore it. Her expression softens as her fury deflates. "I didn't do it to hurt you," she says quietly. "I—"

"You did it to hurt *her.* To get back at her for what we'd done."

"No." Her next words come out in a whisper. "I did it so I wouldn't lose you."

He laughs at that. "You'd let her die so you wouldn't lose me. Brilliant. But then you turned around and kicked me out of the house. Where's the logic in that?"

"I wouldn't have let her die, Jack. And I was hurt. Can't you understand that?" She starts to cry but it has no effect on him. "I was so hurt."

Shaking his head, he says, "Let me ask you one more thing, Claire. How long were you going to let me think she'd done it?"

She stares up at him helplessly.

"Forever. Right? Even after all this time, you're so hurt that you would have let me go to my grave thinking she was a murderer."

She makes no effort to deny his allegation, and he knows for certain it's true. "Yeah, that's what I thought.'"

He grabs the report from the desk and shoves it into the envelope. When he turns around to leave, he runs into the empty chair. He shoves it aside and heads for the door.

"Jack, please. . ."

He grips the door handle, but before he presses down to open it, he turns to look at her one more time. As improbable as it is, he keeps hoping she'll say something, anything, to convince him it's all a mistake.

"Jack," she tries again. "Don't leave like this." She speaks so softly he barely hears her. But it doesn't matter. She could have screamed it, and it wouldn't have mattered.

"I'll see you in court," he says, and he walks out of her office for the last time.

He turns his phone off first thing. He drives away from the city just as he did the day after his arrest, but this time he heads southwest on I-44. He stops at Lion's Choice for a roast beef sandwich, fries and a Coke, at a liquor store for whiskey, and at the pharmacy for Tylenol PM. He then finds a hotel off the highway where he can spend the night undisturbed and, hopefully, unrecognized.

He takes a shower and sits on the end of the bed. *What now?*

He thinks about the day Michael was born. Claire woke in the middle of the night with labor pains. She cried out in her sleep, and the sound woke both of them at the same time. She laughed about that. She laughed right through the pain, and he loved it. He loved how he was married to a woman who could see the humor in her own pain, even as she knew it would soon get exponentially worse.

How does one walk away from that?

It had been raining when they went to bed the night before and it was still raining when they woke. A steady spring rain, just like today's, punctuated by distant thunder. By the time they left for the hospital at 5:12 a.m.—for some reason, he remembers the exact time—she claimed to be hungry and insisted they stop by Dierberg's to buy a box of yogurt popsicles.

"They won't let you eat them," he said, reminding her of one of the many warnings they received in the childbirth classes.

"Oh, I'll eat them, all right," she said, and fifteen minutes later they stood in an empty aisle of the brightly lit grocery store, slightly wet and shivering in front of the freezer case as she decided which brand of popsicles she wanted. Every few minutes she gasped and her right hand flew to the base of her belly, as if by putting it there, she could hold Michael inside a bit longer. Once, a stock boy stopped and asked if she was okay.

"Fine," she said, suppressing a smile, "I simply wanted some popsicles before I have my baby."

The stock boy's face paled, and once he'd turned the corner, Jack and Claire burst into laughter. Tears rolled down her cheeks and it wasn't until she gasped again—louder this time—and her eyes got wider than he'd ever seen them, that he knew the tears were no longer from laughter.

How does one walk away from that?

They brought Michael home from the hospital two days after his birth. They placed him in his new crib with the Peter Rabbit sheets and matching mobile above his head—a theme Jack had complained was girlie—and watched as he quickly fell asleep. It was much too easy. They tiptoed into the family room and sat on the couch. Jack said to Claire, "What now?" They'd had nine months to prepare, but only then did they appreciate the full measure of how much their life had changed, that nothing would ever be the same again.

He can't imagine moving forward, and yet he knows they can't go back.

He thinks of all the times he jogged through the park near their house and saw the divorced dads desperately trying to entertain kids who would have rather been with their friends or in front of a computer screen. "How do you know they were divorced?" Claire asked once when he returned home and mentioned it to her. "Maybe they're just giving their wives a break." But he knew better. Even without the empty ring fingers to give them away, he knew. A man with an intact marriage, having no fear of the yawn of space before the next time he'd see his kids, would simply let them go with their friends or play on the computer. Time is less precious to those who have more of it.

Later, he turns his phone back on to call Earl. The phone plays a symphony of tones to signal the receipt of backed-up voicemail and texts.

"What the hell happened to you?" Earl asks angrily, but Jack hears his relief, too.

"Are they looking for me?"

"No, but only because the sick juror got sicker, and the judge decided to recess for the weekend. You're a lucky son of bitch."

He remembers Mark's comment. *You know, I almost envy you. If you had any balls, I would envy you. Some people never have that connection with another.*

"Yeah, that's me, all right."

"Claire called me, frantic. What's going on?"

Jack closes his eyes and lies back. The Tylenol is starting to have its effect. Or perhaps it's the whiskey. Or both. That was the plan. "She didn't tell you?" Of course she didn't. She'd have to admit she withheld exculpatory evidence that would have exonerated his client.

"Tell me what? She asked if I knew where you were. What's going on, Jack?"

"She had proof that Jenny is innocent."

"*What?*"

"Her dad, apparently, hired a PI to follow me after the first election. The night I stayed at Jenny's? The whole time I was under surveillance. And Jenny, too, by extension. Two unbiased witnesses, the PI and his assistant, knew Jenny never left her house. That's the one piece of information I was never able to testify to, not with certainty, not once I admitted that I'd slept part of the time."

"Holy shit. How long has Claire known?"

"Long enough. When I confronted her, she didn't deny that she's known all this time. I presume as soon as they reported to her dad, he reported to Claire."

"Why was her dad having you followed?"

Jack laughs bitterly at this. "I guess he knew what I didn't." Earl is quiet, and Jack imagines one silver eyebrow furrowing in confusion. "I remember him grilling me about Jenny the day after the election. Claire and I had stopped by her parents' house to pick up the kids and we ended up staying for dinner. He asked a lot of questions about my friendship with Jenny, when Claire was out of earshot, of course. I guess he suspected something between us and wanted to prove it to Claire."

"How did you find this out?"

Jack doesn't answer. Earl doesn't need to know.

Earl's next words surprise Jack, not for their content, but for how quickly he jumped ahead to the thought. He senses where Jack's head is, and it's the last place he wants it to go. He loves Jack like a son, but he also loves Claire like a daughter. "She forgave you, Jack." His stern tone alone speaks the rest. *Now it's your turn.*

"I thought so." He thinks of how she's still never told him she knows he didn't assault Celeste. How she wanted him to take the plea. She thought admitting guilt and serving two years was preferable to being wrongly convicted. She should be a court administrator, he thinks; she'd have the docket cleared in no time. He needs to tell Earl that Jenny didn't know about Maxine until after her arrest. He can't remember how he knows this. He needs to tell him about the letters, too, how Celeste sent them. Tomorrow is Saturday. Maybe he'll take Jamie and join the other dads at the park. Maybe he has a hat and some shades in the car that will help disguise him. He laughs again when he realizes he has a real buzz going. With the heel of his hand he wipes the single tear that slips from the corner of his eye. "I really thought so."

At some point in the night his beeping phone wakes him and through bleary eyes he sees Jenny has texted him.

U ok?

He takes a mental inventory. By what standard? he wants to ask.

It takes all the effort he can muster to text her back.

I'm ok, thx

He takes two more pills and they knock him out good. He wakes ten hours later unsure of where he is or why he's there. At once he remembers, and when he does, the fight in him returns. He refuses to spend the rest of the trial sleeping in a hotel room. He won't even spend it sleeping at Mark's. Possession is nine tenths of the law. He's going home.

The fight in Claire has returned, too, because she's waiting in the laundry room, arms crossed, when he comes in from the garage. She must have heard his car. The other door at the far end of the short, narrow room leading into the kitchen is shut. The air is much too close.

"Where have you been?" she asks.

He walks by her in the direction of the kitchen, but she grabs his arm.

"You're not going to do this, Jack. You're not going to run off to her every time you're pissed at me and then wander home when the mood strikes you. You can go to hell if you think I'll put up with that."

He almost laughs. "Damn, you caught me again." He snaps his finger in mock disbelief. "Yep, that's exactly what I did. I left your office and I went straight to her, and we fucked each other all night." He can't believe he said it. He can't believe it's come to this. He's never spoken to Claire like that, and in all the years he's known her, she's never been what he thinks of now as shrill and spiteful. But he can't stop himself, and he suspects she can't either. "And this time you didn't even need your dad's help. Here, I'm sure he'll want the evidence." He pulls out the receipts from the pitiful night before—the hotel, the pharmacy, the liquor store, Lion's Choice—and slams them onto the dryer. He glares at her. "You're fuckin' crazy, you know that?"

She stands, stunned, without looking at the crumpled papers.

"I spent the night alone in a fuckin' hotel, okay? Trying to figure out what the hell happened to us, because God knows a marriage isn't supposed to be the nightmare ours has become."

"I'll tell you what happened! You—"

"I *know*. You don't have to repeat it for the hundredth time. It's my fault. I know that. I really do know that. And I'm sorry. I'm sorry, I'm sorry, I'm sorry. I can't say it enough. But I also can't go back and change things, and you, apparently, require that in order to forgive me. So I guess we're stuck."

"What's that supposed to mean?"

"It means when the trial is over, you and I need to figure out the best way to do this without hurting the kids more than we already have. I guess if I'm convicted, it'll be figured out for us. If not . . . " He shrugs. "I don't know."

"What's *this*, Jack?"

He sighs. "Claire . . ." Is he suggesting they split up? "I don't know. I don't know."

A wave of tears swells in her eyes. He forces himself to look, to acknowledge the pain he's causing her. But he's still so angry at what she did and that she hasn't even begun to accept responsibility for it. The words "I'm sorry" haven't crossed her lips.

She plants her hands on her hips. "I guess it's easier when there's someone waiting in the wings, isn't it? Well, let me ask you this: What happens when you wake up one day and realize life's not perfect with her, either?"

"What are you talking about? What *life* with her?"

But it's as if she didn't even hear the question. She's made her assumptions and she won't hear otherwise. "What happens when the attraction wears off? Because it will. When the things you think are so *sexy and charming* are outweighed by the things you find irritating? When you see her at her worst, when she's angry about something but taking it out on you because you're the nearest target? Or when she's angry at *you* because it's your day to see the kids but she has other plans for you and you tell her, sorry, my kids come first. Or will you trade them in, too?"

"Stop it. You sound ridiculous."

"It's easy to think so highly of her, isn't it, when she's not the one who yells at the kids, when she's not the one who's crabby when she gets home from work because she knows she still has to cook dinner, and clean the house, and do the laundry—" She suddenly spots the supplies on the shelf above the washing machine. She yanks at a box of fabric softener sheets and flings it at him. He dodges and the box grazes his shoulder and falls forgotten to the floor. "You wait and see how attracted to her you are when she's doing load after load of your stinking laundry! You wait. What happens when all of a sudden another woman looks good to you and you can't figure out why? When, *once again*, you can't keep it in your pants? You think she'll react differently than I have? You think she won't care when you cheat on *her*?"

He reaches for her arm above the elbow, tries to pull her close. "Claire, don't do this."

"Let *go*!" She wriggles to pull away, but he locks his arms around her and holds tight.

"Don't do this to yourself. It's about us, not her."

She attempts to push against his chest but can't get leverage. "Of *course* it's about her!"

"No, not in the way you're thinking. If she evaporated into air tomorrow, we'd still be having this conversation. You know that."

"No I don't."

"Yes. You do."

And like a defenseless animal making a last ditch effort to ward off a ring of predators, she makes a guttural noise, part scream, part growl, and tries to break free. He tightens his grip, and she finally surrenders with a small cry, and then crumbles, sobbing, into his arms.

CHAPTER TWENTY-EIGHT

A SOFT GASP rises from the gallery when Walker calls Claire to the stand on Monday morning. Jack forces himself to watch as she enters with the bailiff through the rear doors and walks purposefully up the center aisle. He forces himself to watch her climb the single step into the witness box, all the while trying to maintain a look that says he's perfectly okay with his wife testifying as a witness for the prosecution.

Once Claire takes her seat on the stand, she surprises Jack by meeting his eye. On Saturday, after she extricated herself from his embrace, she left the house and stayed away the rest of the weekend. He assumed she went to her parents' house, but just like her assumption that he'd gone to Jenny, he could have been entirely wrong. Once she pulled out of the drive, Jack went in search of his sons. Jamie, thankfully, was nowhere to be found; Jack learned later he'd gone downtown with Billy's family to the Soulard Farmer's Market. He found Michael upstairs in his bedroom. As soon as Jack saw his son's vacant eyes, he knew Michael had heard the fighting, if not the specific words exchanged.

Now, Claire looks away from him only when the bailiff asks her to raise her right hand for the oath. She answers so quietly, he has to ask her to repeat her affirmation.

The judge nods to Walker that he may proceed.

"Can you state your name for the record?"

She turns to the jury for her response. "Claire Hilliard."

"You're married to the defendant in this case, Jack Hilliard?"

"Yes."

"How long have you been married?"

"Almost eighteen years."

"Do you consider your marriage a happy one?"

Claire blinks slowly. *You're an asshole, Walker,* her look says. She knows, of course, that Walker considers her an adverse witness even though he's the one who subpoenaed her. Even so, they all thought he'd pretend otherwise for the benefit of the jury.

Jack glances at the jury box; all twelve faces are aimed at Claire, anxious for her answer. He hears whispers and titters from the gallery. They've been trained by the media to rally for the wife, to cheer when she leaves the scoundrel, and to shake their heads in disbelief, even sometimes disgust, when she stands by his side. For four years they've hungered for the answer to this question and many more like it, yet Claire always refused to take her private life public. Now, thanks to a sixteen-year-old girl, that choice has been taken away from her.

"Like most marriages, we've had our ups and downs, but overall, yes, I've considered it a happy one."

Jack closes his eyes. She walked right into Walker's trap.

"What types of ups and downs?"

Earl draws a large question mark on his legal pad, meaning *Want me to object?* Jack shakes his head. The judge made it clear during pretrial motions that he'd allow questioning about Jack's past with Jenny, and since they touched on it already during Michael's testimony, it'd be useless to object now. If it has to be discussed, Jack can't think of anyone more capable of handling the topic than Claire. By the time she finishes, Walker will regret asking the question.

"My husband had a brief affair, Mr. Walker. He was genuinely repentant and asked for my forgiveness. I gave it to him."

Walker stills. In the same way Claire thought Walker would allow her to warm up before firing off the uncomfortable questions, he most likely expected Claire to dance around the issue and was prepared to ask follow-up questions to pin her down. Now that she has given him such a blunt answer, he has to jump forward in his questioning.

"Most wives wouldn't be so magnanimous."

Claire remains silent, and Jack smiles slightly, pleased that she noticed Walker didn't ask a question. Walker continues when he realizes she won't be easily riled.

"With whom did he have this 'brief affair'?"

"A woman named Jennifer Dodson. A fellow lawyer."

Walker retrieves something from a folder on his table and crosses over to show it to Earl. It's an 8 x 10 color photo of Jenny, one of the shots used by the media four years ago. Earl nods, and Walker approaches Claire. She glances at Jack before looking down at the photo.

Despite her best efforts to maintain a neutral face, Jack sees she's shaken. Her hand trembles as she holds the photo. Jenny might have been an ever-present force in both Jack and Claire's lives for a long time, but for Claire, once Jenny left town, and even after her return, she was merely an intangible idea, a concept. The other woman. "Jenny" was merely the label attached to the concept. Now, the photo forces Claire to acknowledge the actual woman.

"Is that Jennifer Dodson in the photo?"

"Yes." Claire hands the photo back to Walker as if it's covered in germs.

Walker motions to the jury and says, "May I, Your Honor?" With the judge's permission he hands it to the juror at the front, left end of the box. One by one, each juror looks and then passes it on. A few of the braver ones study Jack afterward.

"When did Mr. Hilliard have this brief affair?" Walker asks the question as he retrieves the photo from the last juror. He smiles and nods at the juror as if they're the best of friends.

"About four and a half years ago, just after his first election as DA."

"Am I correct that shortly after his affair with Ms. Dodson, authorities charged her with the murder of a client, but the charge was subsequently dropped after the DA admitted to being with her on the night of the murder? Indeed, he *spent* the night with her, thus providing an alibi?"

"Yes, you're correct."

"And it's believed that shortly thereafter, Ms. Dodson left St. Louis?"

"Yes, many believe that."

"Do you?"

"Yes."

Earl rises calmly. "Objection. I'm losing sight of the relevancy of this line of questioning."

Judge Simmons looks at Walker over the top of his glasses. "Mr. Walker?"

"Judge, I was hoping to lay a foundation for my later questions, but I'm happy to jump ahead to help Your Honor understand the relevancy now."

"Please do."

Earl returns to his seat, and Jack leans close to his ear. "Relevancy? Seriously?"

He was about to ask whether you'd been in contact with J since, Earl writes on the legal pad.

Jack sits back in his chair, stunned that he missed the obvious direction of Walker's questions. He wonders if Claire understood, and whether she would have perjured herself on the stand. There was a time when he thought he knew the answer, but now he's not so sure.

Walker resumes his questions. "Mrs. Hilliard, the victim in this case is the girlfriend of your son Michael, is that correct?

"The alleged victim, you mean? Yes, she is."

"I presume, therefore, you are quite familiar with her physical appearance?" he asks, glossing over her clarification.

"Yes, I am."

"Can you describe her?"

"She bears a striking resemblance to Jennifer Dodson." Once again, Claire surprises him with her candor.

"In what way?"

"In every way." Claire's voice trips. "Except, of course, she is much younger."

Walker addresses the judge, then. "Your Honor, I'd like to ask the bailiff to escort Ms. Del Toro into the courtroom."

The volume of chatter from the gallery escalates quickly as excitement and speculation run rampant. Anyone who followed the case knows that Celeste is rumored to look like the DA's former mistress, but because of Celeste's age, no pictures of her have been publicized. This is the first glimpse of the girl who supposedly caused Jack not only to stray once again, but to commit rape and violate the very laws he swore to uphold.

Jack doesn't turn around to see the rear door open, but he knows it has by the crowd's collective gasp. He hears the bailiff, "Everyone stay seated." He watches Claire, who watches Celeste. Any moment Celeste will stand only a few feet away, and he has to decide if he's going to look at her. If he doesn't, he'll appear guilty. If he does, he'll look as if he's trying to bully her.

He sneaks another peek at the jury, and sure enough, their gazes volley back and forth from Celeste to Jack, Jack to Celeste. Whatever he decides, they're poised to form a judgment about his decision.

And then she's there, in the periphery of his vision. He sees her shoes— black pumps. He sees her pants—black dress slacks. She's not dressed like a teenager; she's dressed like a lawyer. And suddenly Jack understands what Walker has done. Jack knows he must look right at Celeste if he is to have any chance of being acquitted. He has to show no emotion, no reaction to Walker's stunt. He lifts his eyes to take in the rest of her—a black suit coat to match the slacks, a red silk blouse almost identical to the one Jenny wore in the picture—just as Earl objects.

"Your Honor, I strenuously object to this performance. What is the point of this, except to inflame the jurors' emotions? If Ms. Del Toro is testifying, the jurors will see her then. She shouldn't be in the courtroom."

"Counsel, approach the bench," the judge says.

As they argue in muted whispers, Celeste takes a seat in the chair next to Walker's empty one. Her hair has been cut to better match Jenny's style, even the necklace at her collarbone bears a striking similarity to the one in the picture. Yet, for all Walker's efforts to make her a twin of Jenny, she's still a child in adult clothing. She stares at her hands in her lap as if willing them to be still, but she can't stop kneading them together nervously. If she's not kneading, she's using one hand and then the other to tuck her hair behind her ears. Her frightened eyes seem to be held open permanently with invisible toothpicks.

Jack wonders if Michael told her that Jack knows about the letters, despite Jack's order not to. Earl plans to confront her with them when she takes the stand, but if she denies sending them, he'll recall Michael to the stand during the defense case. "The jury needs to understand this girl has major issues," Earl said, "and they have nothing to do with you, at least not in the way she claims they do."

But seeing Celeste now, Jack knows the last thing she needs is to take the witness stand. Her fear is palpable and Jack is certain it's not stage fright. The girl huddled at the prosecution table is an exaggerated version of the girl who sat in his car and begged him to keep her secrets. While they all sit in the courtroom playing this game, the real source of her fear still walks the streets.   Earl returns to the table and reports to Jack. "She has to leave now, but he won't cut off questioning. As we suspected, Walker intends to argue you simply couldn't keep your paws off Celeste because of her resemblance to Jenny."

"Yeah, that's it," Jack mutters. "Just line up a bunch of clones and I can't help myself."

The chatter increases as the bailiff escorts Celeste from the room, but it dies down as soon as the doors close behind her.

"Mrs. Hilliard?" Walker resumes. "Four and a half years have passed since your husband had his affair with Ms. Dodson, is that correct?"

"Approximately."

"Has he seen her, between—"

Earl begins to stand, but Jack touches his arm to stop him. He knows Walker might word the question in a way that won't matter.

"—the time she allegedly left St. Louis and the night he took Ms. Del Toro home?"

But Claire goes mute, and Jack worries that she doesn't understand she can answer truthfully without revealing Jack's recent interactions with Jenny. "Can you please repeat the question?" she asks.

She just gave it away, Earl writes. Jack nods.

"Certainly." Walker realizes it, too. Even if he doesn't reword the question, he'll follow it with more pointed ones. "Has your husband seen Ms. Dodson between the time she allegedly left town four years ago and the night he drove Ms. Del Toro home?"

Claire leans forward, squints as if thinking hard. "I don't know."

With those three words, Claire wipes Walker's smug expression from his face. She caught the question, all right. She simply took the time to parse it in her brain and ensure she answered it correctly. Walker didn't expect an "I don't know"—he was hoping for an unqualified "no" to bolster his later argument. He made the classic mistake: asking a question for which he didn't know the answer.

Walker rubs his chin. He obviously understood from Claire's sudden nervousness that Jack had, indeed, seen Jenny at some point since she left town, but by limiting his question to a certain period of time, he not only diminished his motive argument, he lost his chance to expose Jack. Walker knows Earl will now object as irrelevant to testimony about Jack's possible contact with Jenny *since* the night with Celeste, and the judge, most likely, will sustain the objection.

Sure enough, Walker leaves the subject of Jennifer Dodson behind and decides to focus on Jack's more recent lies.

"Mrs. Hilliard, on the night in question, you were at home, asleep in your bed, is that right?"

After Walker and Claire move through a series of questions and answers in which Claire explains what happened from her point of view—beginning with her coming down the stairs to find Jack and Michael in the living room, and ending with her admission that yes, she only finally learned she'd been lied to when Jack was arrested—Walker turns her over to Earl.

Earl rises briefly. "Can Your Honor give us one moment? I'll be quick."

At the judge's assent, he leans over and whispers in Jack's ear. "I'm going to ask her point blank if she thinks you did it. Are you okay with that?"

"And if she says yes?"

"She won't."

Earl leaves Jack's side and takes a spot near the jury box. He nods politely to Claire, and she subtly returns the gesture. Jack can barely watch the nascent exchange. He hates that Earl, who is so fond of Claire, has to do this.

"I have only a few but very pointed questions for you," Earl begins, and then stands a good, long time without speaking. The delay reflects his reluctance to treat her as an adverse witness, but Jack knows it also ensures he has the rapt attention of every man and woman in the courtroom. He sighs, looks solemnly at Jack one more time, and then turns back to Claire.

"Mrs. Hilliard, do you think your husband committed the crimes he's accused of?"

"Objection," Walker says quickly. He smirks to show how ridiculous he thinks the question is. "Calls for speculation, Your Honor. And what Mrs. Hilliard thinks is irrelevant."

Earl calmly crosses his hands low and waits for the judge's ruling. Even though Walker asked the same question of Michael, Earl still expected the objection. Judge Simmons, who probably wants to hear the answer himself, doesn't even bother to look at Walker. "I'll allow it." He smiles at Claire. "Go on, ma'am."

"Your Honor," Walker says quickly, before Claire answers. "Will you please remind the witness she's under oath, then?"

Walker must anticipate the glare he gets from the judge, but clearly he doesn't care. The request alone accomplished his goal: to remind the jury that a wife may very well lie to protect her husband.

"I think you just did that, Mr. Walker. Now, why don't we let her answer? That is, if she remembers the question." He turns to Claire. "Would you like the question repeated, ma'am?"

"No, Your Honor. I remember the question."

Claire then, in her infinite wisdom, looks not at Earl, not at the jury, but directly at Jack. The moment before she answers stretches, and he holds his breath. He thinks everyone in the courtroom might be holding their breath, too.

The courtroom is quiet except for the creak of the benches as spectators try to unobtrusively shift positions. And even though he looks back at her—her stare leaves him no other choice—in his peripheral vision he can see the court reporter's hands hovering above her machine.

"No, I don't think Jack committed the crimes he's accused of. Indeed, I know he didn't."

Jack can only blink. He's otherwise paralyzed by her gaze.

"Even though he lied to you on the night in question?" Earl asks.

She nods, but she doesn't release her hold on Jack. "Yes, even though he lied to me."

"Even though, in the past, he committed adultery?" Earl persists, his tone aggressive.

One tear falls down her right cheek as if forcefully pushed over the edge. Another follows on the left side. She still continues to stare at Jack, and he finally manages to raise a hand to wipe at his own eyes before they betray him.

"Yes, even though he committed adultery."

Earl looks down at the floor. "Mrs. Hilliard, I have one more question for you."

She looks from Jack to Earl, slowly, as if he just woke her from a deep sleep. "Why?"

She scrunches her brow, and he adds, "Why do you think—excuse me, you said you know, didn't you?—how do you *know* Jack didn't commit the crimes he's accused of."

She lowers her head, then, as if studying her hands in her lap. She breathes in and finally looks to the jury box to give her answer.

"I've known Jack Hilliard for nineteen years. One of his best qualities, and one that made me fall in love with him, is, ironically, the same quality that caused him to commit adultery. It's this same quality that convinces me he didn't do what Celeste says he did."

"I don't understand."

"Let me finish, Mr. Scanlon." She chastises him kindly, the way a mother might chastise a toddler for a minor offense.

"I'm sorry, go on."

"Jack is an idealist, a romantic. He lives his life trying to do what's right." A few skeptical murmurs rise from the audience. Claire sits up straighter and raises her voice as if she's talking not just to Earl, not just to the jury, but to an entire community. "I imagine that sounds strange to some of you. How can someone who strives to do right cheat on his wife? Right? That's what you're all thinking, isn't it? I know because that's what I kept asking myself, too, for a long time. But it's true. He went to law school because he's an idealist, he got a job at the prosecutor's office because he's an idealist. He devotes long hours to helping the victims of crimes by bringing the perpetrators of those crimes to justice. And yet, because he's an idealist, he also believes most criminals can be rehabilitated, and he does what he can to make rehabilitation a reality for those who are willing to work for it. Some of you are probably thinking, *but didn't he go to one of the big silk stocking firms after law school?* He did. But he did that, too, because he's an idealist. He graduated from law school with $35,000 in student loans, and back then, that was a lot of money to owe at graduation. The right thing to do when you owe money is to pay it back. The fastest way to pay it back is to work at a high paying job, no matter how much you hate it. And trust me, he did hate it. He won't appreciate me saying this, but he also got fired from that firm for trying to do the right thing. He refused to do something he believed was unethical."

"Your Honor," Walkers says. *Come on*, his tone says. "She's giving a narrative, much of it is hearsay, and frankly, I also don't see how any of this is relevant."

"Would you prefer I lead the witness, Mr. Walker?" Earl's question gets a snicker from a few attorneys in the audience.

"Well, it *is* a cross-examination," Walker shoots back.

"Mr. Walker," Judge Simmons interrupts their bickering, "I'll allow it. She's giving a narrative, yes, but some questions call for a narrative. Mr. Scanlon asked her why she believes Mr. Hilliard didn't commit the crimes. She obviously feels she can't answer that question in one sentence. As for your hearsay objection, I've not heard anything in her testimony wherein she repeats statements made by others. Where's the hearsay?"

"She's testifying as to why he was fired from a job. She's testifying why he hated that job. These are not things of which she had direct knowledge. They're based on what he, or someone, has told her."

"But the testimony is offered not to prove its truth, but rather to explain her opinion."

"Exactly, Your Honor. And that leads me to my third ground for the objection. Her opinion, as I argued when I originally objected to the question, is not relevant. The point of this trial is to decide Mr. Hilliard's guilt or innocence. That's the jury's job, not his wife's. Her lay opinion isn't appropriate."

Jack scribbles on Earl's pad, *He's right.* Earl writes back, *Not our problem, the judge would rather err on the side of the defendant.* Jack knows this is true. By giving a defendant's attorney more leeway at trial, the judge effectively limits the grounds for appeal after conviction.

"Well, as judge, I have wide discretion in these matters, and I do think her testimony goes to Mr. Hilliard's intent somewhat, so I'm overruling the objection. *Again.*" The judge peers down at Claire. "Ma'am, were you finished answering Mr. Scanlon's question?"

"No, Judge, but this time, I'm afraid, I don't remember where I was." She laughs a little, though everyone sees she doesn't think it's funny. The judge asks the court reporter to read back the last few lines of Claire's testimony. She listens, breathes deep, as if reloading her nerve. "I was about to say, even the decisions he made that night, he made to help Celeste. At the risk to his reputation, I might add. Did he show poor judgment? Perhaps, by some standards. Many men, in this day and age, wouldn't dare be alone with a young girl for fear of being falsely accused of something, anything. But Jack doesn't think like that. He simply tries to do what's right. And that night, he thought it was right to drive a drunk girl home. He thought—"

"Your Honor!" Walker's frustration is palpable. "I apologize, but now she's testifying to Mr. Hilliard's thoughts. I have to object."

"I *will* sustain that objection," Judge Simmons says. "Mr. Scanlon, your client may testify about his own thoughts"—a few more laughs from the gallery—"if he decides to take the stand." The judge then smiles down at Claire as if in apology. "Mrs. Hilliard, you'll need to limit your testimony to your own thoughts."

"Yes, Your Honor." She turns back to Earl. "My point is merely that I know Jack couldn't have committed the crimes he's accused of because it's not *in him* to do something like that. His whole career has been about *stopping* people who do such things. I've watched him shed tears for the victims in child abuse and sexual abuse cases. *It's just not in him.*"

Her voice breaks with the last sentence. She's clearly frustrated with her inability to express her thoughts without drawing an objection.

Earl lets the jury absorb her testimony, and then he quietly thanks Claire. As he walks back to the table, his body radiates the same frustration. *It's okay,* Jack writes. *They care about emotion, not objections.* Earl ignores the note, poised for redirect.

Walker stands even before the judge motions to him. "Ma'am, I don't quite understand your testimony. You stated that Mr. Hilliard's idealism made you fall in love with him, and yet his idealism also caused him to commit adultery?"

"Yes."

"If an idealist is ruled by the principle of always wanting to do right, how can that be? Surely you don't mean to say that Mr. Hilliard thought it right to have sex with a woman who wasn't his wife."

Claire's nostrils flare. Jack and Earl exchange a look. Walker should have let it lie and then used it in his closing. Now, not only has he angered Claire with his blunt language, he's also given her free rein to fix the inconsistencies he pointed out in her testimony.

"No, Mr. Walker. I am quite sure he knew it was wrong. What I mean to say is that idealists aren't perfect, just like the rest of us. And just like the rest of us, they sometimes do things that violate their code. The difference, though, is that while most people accept they made a mistake and move on with their life, an idealist has a hard time forgiving himself. No one, I mean *no one*, beat up Jack Hilliard more for what he'd done than Jack Hilliard. Not even me."

"Who's to say he didn't violate his code by raping Celeste Del Toro?" He says the word "code" with obvious disdain.

Claire ignores his sarcasm. "Because raping a child would be more than wrong, it would be evil. There's a difference. An idealist's mind can rationalize doing something wrong. But evil? It's simply not in an idealist's DNA to do anything evil."

"Adultery's not evil?"

Jack can't believe Walker continues to pursue this. Anything she says now can only hurt his case. Has it become personal for Walker, too?

"I suppose that depends on the reason for it. In most cases, I'd say no."

"Well, then, why do you think Mr. Hilliard committed adultery?"

Claire's mouth opens slightly but no words come out. She blinks several times as if the question has left her dumbfounded. She shifts her gaze to Jack again, helplessly, as if searching for the answer in his eyes.

Claire once told Jack she'd made a promise to herself never to ask him the question Walker just asked. "I told myself that it was the one question I'd never let myself ask, because I knew—no matter what you said—it would never satisfy me, never justify what you'd done."

She kept the promise to herself. Not once did she ask him why, and he was grateful, because he didn't have an answer. Not one, at least, that either of them was ready to accept. It took more than four years for that to happen.

"Mrs. Hilliard?" Walker persists. "Please answer the question. In your opinion, why did Mr. Hilliard commit adultery?"

She reluctantly looks away from Jack and sits taller. For courage, Jack thinks.

"Based upon everything I know about Jack Hilliard, only one thing could have compelled him to do what he did."

Holding its collective breath, the courtroom waits. Jack stares at the blank lines of his legal pad. He knows what she's about to say, and he can't bear to look at her as she says it.

"Love."

CHAPTER TWENTY-NINE

WHEN JACK ARRIVES home around four, reporters clog the street in front of his house. This time, they're there for Claire. Inside the house, silence reigns. He knows she left the boys with her parents that morning after receiving a commitment from Ruth that she wouldn't let Harley badmouth Jack in front of them. When he doesn't find her in the kitchen or the family room, he wonders if she joined them after leaving the courthouse. Her minivan, though, is in the garage.

He climbs the stairs to their bedroom. Except for the suit she wore to court hanging on the closet door, there's no sign of her up there, either.

It's not until he enters the office downstairs to get online and check the day's accumulated emails that he finds her. She's curled up asleep in the corner chair, a forgotten book open and turned upside down on the armrest. She let her hair down; except for a few strands on her cheek, the loose curls splay against the cushion behind her head. She exchanged the suit for a fleece sweatshirt and shorts. Her pale legs are bent, her bare feet are tucked to the side underneath. He's still drawn to her delicate features, and the knowledge he always will be doesn't make any of this easier.

He pulls the French doors shut, but through the glass panes he sees her eyes open at the click of the latch. She lifts her head and spots him.

"Jack."

He reopens one door slightly. "I'm sorry. I didn't mean to wake you."

"It's okay."

They regard each other tentatively.

"Thanks for today," he says. "I mean, for what you said on the stand."

After another awkward silence, he says, "Well, I guess I'll go find something to eat. Do you want me to shut this?"

"No, it's okay." As he turns, she calls his name again to stop him. "I wanted you to know, I didn't perjure myself. I meant every word." He waits, unsure what part she thinks he might believe was perjury. "I know you didn't do anything to Celeste."

He looks at the floor because if he continues to look at her, he'll be tempted to say what's on his mind. *Why did you wait so long? Why didn't you tell me that a long time ago?* If she had, he thinks they might have had a chance.

In the kitchen he stands before the open refrigerator but doesn't see the ample contents. Instead, he sees himself a few months into the future, standing before a refrigerator in a small apartment somewhere, maybe in the city closer to the courthouse. The refrigerator will be empty except for the basics—milk, eggs, maybe some lunch meat. Even the loaf of bread will be kept there because it would mold quickly if left on the counter. He wouldn't need more because he can't imagine bothering to cook for one or having the time. He'll become one of those attorneys who always works late into the night because he'll have nothing to come home to.

And even though Claire would never poison Michael or Jamie against him, he'll still become the interloper, always on the periphery of his sons' lives. He imagines the various milestones—graduations, weddings, the birth of grandchildren—where the role of host will default to Claire, and Jack will be just another guest. He thinks about holidays, Michael and Jamie crowded around a table with Claire and her parents, her aunts and uncles, and eventually their own kids. Thanksgiving or Christmas with Jack will be nothing more than a pity visit to be endured until they politely move on to their mom's house. Given Mark's affection for Claire, Jack thinks even his own brother might defect.

He can't imagine moving forward, and yet he knows they can't go back.

He shuts the refrigerator, as empty-handed as when he opened it. He can't seem to take a deep breath. His eyes fill again for the second time that day and he tells himself to get a grip.

He turns for the stairs and startles when he sees Claire at the end of the island, watching him.

"I guess I'm not very hungry," he says. It's a lame attempt to disguise what almost happened, but she saw, and she mistakes its meaning.

"We could open a bottle of wine," she suggests. "Mom said she'll keep the boys all night if we want. We could talk."

Earl once told Jack that a marriage can survive infidelity. Jack believed him. After all, Earl's did. Jack thought his and Claire's would, too. He wanted it to. He really wanted it to.

"I don't think so."

She moves closer and stands on her tiptoes to reach two wine goblets from the cabinet. He wants to grab them from her hands, fling them so they shatter against the wall, and ask her if she heard him. Instead, he watches her uncork a bottle of red. Her small hand is strong as it twists the corkscrew. He notices her nails are painted, rare for her, and it makes him look down at her toes, too. They're painted a blush pink color that always reminds him of the beaches on Cat Island, where they celebrated their tenth anniversary.

She pours the wine and he accepts it without meeting her eye. He can't think of a time they didn't toast, no matter the occasion or lack thereof. But he knows there will be no toasting tonight. He lifts the glass and swallows more than a sip. Hers remains on the counter, untouched.

She stands in front of him and her hands go for his tie. She gives him a look that asks, *May I?* When he fails to respond either way, she picks at the knot and loosens it for him. Next she starts on the button at his collar. He calmly but decisively pushes her arm away.

"Don't."

"I'm just—"

"I can unbutton my shirt if I want it unbuttoned."

She steps away and raises her hands in surrender. "Fine. Sorry."

"What did you want to talk about?"

"Seriously?"

He sighs and places his glass down, starts to leave. She grabs his arm.

"I want to talk about us." She pauses, perhaps anticipating a protest. "I want us to start fresh. I'd like to put everything behind us and start over. Can we talk about that?"

"I think we tried that once and failed."

"We'll try again. We were doing fine until this mess with Celeste."

Fine. Not quite how he wants to spend the rest of his life. Simply *doing fine.* He also can't help but notice she doesn't mention Jenny this time.

"You'll be acquitted and we'll put it behind us."

"And if I'm convicted?"

She steps closer again and he feels like a caged animal. "You won't be."

"I might. You said so yourself. Celeste might give an Oscar-worthy performance tomorrow."

"Then we'll fight it."

He shakes his head. How can she not get it? "I *have* been fighting it, Claire, even if you weren't. Even as you were still deciding whether you thought I was guilty."

Her cheeks redden. "I never thought you were guilty."

"You know what? I think I believe you. And that's the problem. Even though you always believed in my innocence, you couldn't bring yourself to tell me. Instead, you withheld it as some sort of punishment. You've been punishing me from the moment I was arrested. Christ, Claire, you actually suggested I take the plea." He shakes his head, still unable to believe it. "You did perjure yourself today—"

"What?" she cries. "I didn't—"

"—when you said you forgave me for what happened with Jenny. You haven't."

"I have."

"You haven't. You tried. I know you tried, but you haven't been able to. And if you couldn't forgive me after four years, you never will. I don't blame you. I won't stand here and profess to know how it felt when you found out what I'd done. And I don't know whether I would forgive you, either, for the same thing. It doesn't matter."

"Jack, it matters," she says softly. "It matters. We have a family. We have Michael and Jamie." She places her palm on his cheek, and he closes his eyes to ward off the attack. She knows his weak spot and won't be shy about going after it. "If I've been punishing you, I'm sorry. But don't make the same mistake. Don't punish me now for not telling you about the PI. Don't punish *us*."

He's already been through all this in his head. He's done the mental gymnastics and thought about whether his decision is merely his own way of striking back at her. He doesn't think so. It hurts too much.

It occurs to him that they're both making their way through the five stages of grief. He just happens to be further along, somewhere between depression and acceptance. She's stalled at bargaining.

She gently touches her lips to his. He doesn't resist. He even tries to reciprocate, but he feels nothing but sadness.

He pulls away and wonders if he just kissed his wife for the last time.

"Just say you'll try," she whispers. Her cheeks are wet from silent tears. "We'll both try."

"Claire . . ." The rest—*I can't*—sticks in his throat.

"Do you still love me?"

"You know I do. You know I'll always love you."

"Then we can—"

"It's not enough."

"Would it have been enough if she hadn't come back?"

There it is, finally. He knew in the end, for Claire, it would come down to this question, and he made himself think a lot about this, too, so no matter his answer, it would be honest.

"No."

"But—"

"If she hadn't come back, would that have made a difference in your ability to forgive me?" He asks the question as if he already knows the answer, because he does. Her silence and the devastation on her face convince him he's right. She knows she can't honestly answer and save the marriage both.

"It might have taken longer for us to reach this point if she hadn't come back," he says, "but we would have reached it, one way or another. The damage was already done."

Later, after the boys are home and everyone has gone to bed, Jack climbs the stairs in the dark and waits a moment outside the master bedroom. He listens for the page of a book turning, the toilet flushing, the setting of the alarm clock, any sounds indicating Claire might still be awake.

He offered to sleep in the spare bedroom, but she refused. They can't shield Michael, who already suspects what has happened even if neither Jack nor Claire has told him outright, but Claire wants Jamie to remain ignorant about the impending split until they know Jack's fate. Jack assured her that Jamie wouldn't have to know—he could retire long after Jamie falls asleep and rise before he wakes—but, perhaps fearing he may soon spend his nights on a prison cot, she insisted Jack sleep in their bed as long as he remains in the house. He reluctantly agreed even as he already dreaded the oppressive tension he knew would accompany this nightly façade.

He thinks she's asleep and is about to attempt a stealth entrance when he hears her voice through the door. At first he thinks she might be talking in her sleep, but then he makes out the next words—"I don't think so, Mom. I think he means it."—and knows she's not. He has a sudden urge to barge in, tell her he didn't mean it, that he's willing to try again, he's willing to do anything if it would get them back to the place they were before he walked a drunken Jenny to her car so long ago.

Instead, he steps away from the door and plants himself at the top of the stairs, elbows on knees, chin in hands, to wait for the call to end and for sweeter dreams to claim her.

Jack wakes later to a soft knock on the bedroom door and then an urgent but gentle whisper.

"Dad?" The voice belongs to Michael, but Jack must be dreaming because Michael hasn't spoken to him like that since before his arrest. He rises up on his elbows and listens for the voice to repeat itself.

"Dad? Wake up." The tone has escalated from urgent to desperate.

Something's wrong. Jack shoots out of bed and opens the bedroom door. Michael shoves his phone at him. "It's Celeste," he says breathlessly, and in the small white glow from the screen, Jack sees panic on his son's face.

Disoriented, Jack looks at the phone. Celeste wants to talk to *me?* he thinks. "What—"

Exasperated, Michael grabs Jack's hand and twists it so the screen faces him. "She's in trouble," he says. "We have to do something!"

Jack blinks and squints to focus on the tiny text. He reads I will, txt me back soon and glances up at Michael for an explanation.

"Read it all. From the beginning."

"Jack?" Claire's sleepy voice joins the confusion. "What's going on?"

"I don't know." He scrolls up to see the messages that came before.

Mike u up?
Yeah
I dont no what 2 do
R u scared about cort 2morow?

My mom pickd me up 2nite
??
Im on way 2 FL

"What?" Jack mutters, not quite comprehending what he just read.
"Dad, *read.*"

Ur not home?
No, tha came 2 take me back
Y did u go?
It wasnt a choice!
?
My dad called her, told her 2 come get me
?
He was mad after ur testimony
Shit
Im scared
Is he w/ her?
Yah
Y didnt u tell ur dad?
U no i cant!
Wher r u rite now?
bathrm in hotel
r tha asleep?
Yah i dont have long 2 tlk, im really sorry, b sure 2 tell ur dad 2, k?
What about 2morrow?
Idk i guess my dad will tell judge or lawyer

At that sentence, Jack suddenly understands he's about to be a free man. He
briefly looks up again at Michael, who's oblivious to the line Jack just read. He's
bouncing like a jumping bean waiting for Jack to finish.

U cant go back thr
I no
Call police
yah right
I mean it!
U dont understand
Where r u exactly?
Told u
what state, city?
Idk TN?
U need 2 find out
Y
I'll come get u
U dont understand, u cant
Yes I can
He's not like people u no

?
Just keep ur fone on, k?
Find out whr u r
I'll try, I luv u, k?
I luv u 2. Can u call me?
Not now, mybe l8tr, I hve 2 go
Let me tell ur dad
No! u promised me!
But y not???
I told u!
U cant go back thr
I alrdy am
What should I do?
Just keep ur fone on
Im gonna get my dad
No!
He can help
He hates me
He will help trust me
Just tell him im sorry, k? I will take care of it
?
I gotta go, luv u
Luv u 2
Dont 4get keep fone on
I will, txt me back soon

"How long ago was all this?" Jack asks just as Claire flips on a light and joins them near the door.

"Just a few minutes ago. Dad, you don't understand! We gotta do something." He looks from Jack to Claire to Jack again. "He's sending her back to Florida."

"What's going on?" Claire asks again, this time more insistently.

"What's so bad about her going to Florida?" Jack asks Michael as he hands her the phone. "I mean, other than the obvious fact of skipping out of a trial she instigated." He thinks he can guess the answer, and judging from the way Michael grunts with stubborn exasperation, he's pretty sure he's guessed right. "Mike, I can't help if you don't tell me what I need to know."

"She's afraid of her mom's boyfriend."

Claire looks up from reading the texts, and she and Jack exchange a worried look.

"What do you mean?"

"Dad . . ."

"Michael, *what do you mean?*"

"He raped her." His teenage voice cracks and his eyes grow wet with tears. "More than once. I mean, like a lot."

"She told you this?"

He nods shamefully, as if he's the one who did it.

"Neither her mom or dad knows?"

"Her mom's a stupid whore," he says angrily. "When Celeste told her, she blamed Celeste. That's why she started living with her dad."

"So her dad knows? I don't get it." Jack looks at Claire to share his confusion, but then he remembers she wasn't in court for Del Toro's testimony.

"No, he doesn't know. Her mom told him Celeste was getting too *wild*"—he says "wild" with disgust—"and that she couldn't handle her anymore. And you know what her dad is like, how strict he is. That's all he needed to hear."

"Why didn't she tell him?" Jack asks, although he knows the answer in the same way he knew about the boyfriend. He's heard this story too many times at work.

"They threatened her. She was too afraid to tell anyone, Dad."

Over Claire's shoulder, Jack reads the last few lines again.

> Just tell him im sorry, k? I will take care of it
> ?
> I gotta go, luv u
> Luv u 2
> Dont 4get keep fone on
> I will, txt me back soon

What does I will take care of it mean? Michael seemed to ask the same question, but Celeste never said outright what her plans are.

"Text her again and ask what hotel they're at. Ask if she can look for the address on the phone in the room without waking them up."

Michael grabs the phone from Claire and frantically taps out a new text.

"We need to call her dad, Jack," Claire says.

"No!" Michael pleads to Jack. "No! That'll make it worse."

Jack studies his son's reaction. "In what way?"

"It'll just make it worse. She made me promise not to tell him. I just know her dad can't find out." Michael won't look him in the eye; Jack knows he's not getting the full story.

"Mike, she's in a hotel room with a guy who raped her repeatedly, according to you. Or according to her, I guess. How much worse can it get?"

"Can't we just go get her, Dad? Please?"

"*What?*" Claire says. "Are you out of your mind?"

Michael finally addresses his mother directly, as if he just noticed she's standing in the hallway with them. "She can't go back to Florida with them. It'll just happen again."

"We understand that," Jack says, "but it's either call her dad or call 911 to get Child Protective Services involved. Or both, really."

"Why can't it be *you?*" he cries. "You're a prosecutor!"

"That's not the same. You know that." Jack looks to Claire as if to say *Can you help me here?*

"In case you forgot," she says, "there's a restraining order against your dad. He's not supposed to be anywhere near Celeste. And he's also not allowed to leave the state."

Not quite what Jack hoped for, but at least she made valid points.

Michael grunts and turns back to Jack as if Claire isn't even worth arguing with. "Why can't we—" His phone vibrates and he quickly redirects his attention to the screen. "She says they're at a Red Roof Inn." He continues to read. "She says it may be a while before she can see the phone because when she went over to the nightstand to look, he woke up and asked her why she wasn't sleeping. She has to be sure he's sound asleep again." With his fingers moving at warp speed, he sends a message back.

"What did you say?" Jack asks. Claire moves down the hall and gently closes Jamie's bedroom door.

"I asked her if he's done anything to her." The answer comes back before he finishes his sentence. He pushes the phone toward Jack's face as if to say, *See?*

He said if I dont bhav he mite giv us rufies at the red ruf inn then he laughed

"Us?" Jack says aloud before the meaning of her word choice fully registers. The question causes Michael to lose his already waning patience.

"For both of them! For her mom, to knock her out, and—"

"Mike," Jack grabs his shoulders, "calm down. Okay? I understand."

"You don't! We need to get her out of there before he does it again."

"We will. Okay. Just calm down." When Claire rejoins them, he asks, "What do you think?"

She answers as if Michael is no longer in the hallway with them. "If he really thinks she's in imminent danger, we need to call 911, and then we need to call her dad and let him know."

"No, Mom!" Michael begins to cry. Embarrassed, he swipes his eyes to erase the tears. "Please," he begs. "I promised her! If you bring all these people into it, that'll just make it worse! She says it'll just set him off again."

"Again?" Jack asks.

He's not like people u no. Was this her way of warning Michael away? Of telling him that her mom's boyfriend is capable of much worse than rape?

"Mike?" Jack persists. Michael looks at Jack helplessly. The "again" was clearly an unintentional slip. "What did he do?"

Michael grunts. "You know her finger? Her pinky?"

"Where she's missing the tip?"

Michael nods.

Oh, Jesus.

"Jack," Claire touches his arm, drawing his attention back to her appeal, "they're trained for this stuff. You know that."

"What would we say? We don't even know where she is."

"That's right, and they're much better at finding people than we are. Or call her dad. He might know where they stopped."

"The man's a lunatic, Claire."

"Only if the stuff she's told Mike about him is true."

"I heard him myself in court. I'd rather err on the side of caution."

"*Which is why you should call 911.* Let someone else handle this."

Maybe it's everything that's happened between them, maybe it's because he no longer views her through the same lens he once did, but he can't help but think her protest is less about helping Celeste and more about washing her hands of the problem.

Jack sighs and glances at Michael, who has returned to feverish texting. *The guy cut off part of her finger.* When he looks back at Claire, she shakes her head. She can read him, she always could, and she knows he's considering a drive to Tennessee. She yanks him into their bedroom, shuts the door halfway. "Don't make another mistake like this," she whispers. "Stop trying to be Mike's hero."

Her accusation stings, but he buries the familiar impulse to react. "I think he might be right. I think the mistake might be bringing all these others into it."

"How can you say that? *They're trained.* They'll know how to handle it."

"You saw how she kept asking him to tell me she's sorry."

"So?"

Jack shrugs. It's nothing more than a hunch. "I don't know. I just think that maybe if she knows it's okay, that I'll forgive her and she won't lose us, then she'll trust me. I think I'll be able to get her out of that room without Torpedo knowing something's up."

"Torpedo?"

"The boyfriend."

"Jack, if you so much as cross the river to chase after Celeste *you—will—be—violating—two—court—orders.*"

"I don't care about the damn court orders, okay? This is her life we're talking about."

"Which is why you should let professionals handle it! If you don't, if you take matters into your own hands and she gets hurt, you'll have to live with it."

"I'll also have to live with it if I call 911 and Mike's right, if it causes that guy to do something desperate. You know how they do things. Remember what happened with that South County case? When they tried to rescue that girl who'd been abused? I don't want to risk something similar. They'll either show up with guns blazing, or they'll knock on the door, ask if everything is okay, and leave when he says yes. Either way, it'll probably set him off."

Claire fixes her hands on her hips. "So you're going to risk her life, and yours too, by the way, by taking the advice of an immature sixteen-year-old boy."

"He knows her situation better than anyone else."

"He's sixteen, Jack! I can't believe this. Are you losing it?"

No, actually, I'm getting it back. "I'd rather get close and then decide if I need backup." He swings the door open wide. "Put on some clothes, Mike. We're going together this time."

Michael starts for his room, but Jack catches his arm. "But on the way, you're filling me in about what the hell's been going on, got it?"

Michael nods guiltily.

"From the beginning," Jack adds before releasing him. He weaves around an incredulous Claire to get dressed.

CHAPTER THIRTY

"WHAT WILL WE do when we get there?" Michael asks as they pull out of the driveway. It's almost one a.m., and the few media stragglers who have haunted the street outside their house each night during the trial are long gone.

"I'm not sure. I guess that depends on what the situation is and what you tell me." He glances at his son to see if he gets the message. From the way he shrinks against the passenger door, he does. "We first have to find her."

"What if Mom calls 911 anyway?"

Jack asked himself the same question. "She'll do what she thinks is best."

Michael tilts his head back against the headrest and closes his eyes. Jack can tell he's thinking, not sleeping, but he waits until they pass the lights of the city and are halfway across the Mississippi toward Illinois before he pesters him.

"Hey."

Michael looks around to get his bearings. He spots the Arch out the rear window and relaxes.

"We've got about four hours to the Tennessee state line. Start talking."

"I'm not sure where to begin."

Jack wants to ask him to begin with his decision to cover for Celeste no matter the cost to his dad, but he knows this isn't the information that will help them help Celeste. So instead he says, "How about if you explain why she decided to accuse me of raping her?" *And why you went along with it?*

Michael shifts in his seat. His knee bounces up and down from the Morse code jitter of his left leg.

"Three hours, fifty-eight minutes."

Michael huffs a sigh. "It wasn't like she decided."

"What was it like, then?"

His son keeps his eyes trained outside his window.

"Mike, I know this is hard for you, but you really need to just spit it out."

"She did one of those at-home tests to see if she was pregnant, and her dad found out."

"That's funny, since you testified you didn't know she thought she might be pregnant."

Michael lowers his eyes. Jack lets him squirm a bit and then says, "Go on."

"He went through the trash in her bathroom. She didn't leave the test in there or anything, but I guess she'd ripped up the instructions and one or two pieces got left behind."

"Why did she do an at-home pregnancy test?"

"She was late . . . you know."

"Did she think she might be pregnant from previous times you two were together? Because those tests wouldn't tell her anything the very next day."

"Yeah." He mumbles so quietly Jack barely hears him.

"Does she realize that?"

"Yeah, she knows."

"Forgive me for harping on this, Mike" —Jack's tone makes clear he couldn't care less if Michael forgives him on this next point— "but if she was so worried about getting pregnant, why the hell weren't you guys using birth control?" He knows it's useless to ask the question now, but his frustration over the whole situation makes him ask it anyway.

Michael simply stares at his phone and shrugs.

"When did her dad find out?" Because of Del Toro's testimony, Jack already knows the answers to many of his questions, but Michael doesn't know that.

"Sometime that day, that Sunday. That's when he searched her trash."

"He actually searches her trash?" After seeing the instant messages on the computer about checking her underwear, this shouldn't faze Jack.

"He wouldn't admit it. He said he was just emptying it. But she knows what he does."

Maybe, then, she should be more careful about what she leaves behind.

"And he confronted her?"

"Yeah. He barged in her room holding up the piece of paper he found and yelling at her to explain and she just made something up." Jack shakes his head, grips the steering wheel tighter. His jaw is clenched so hard it aches. He's torn between feeling sorry for Michael and wanting to shake him. Michael must sense his reaction; he starts crying again. "She had to have some excuse, Dad!" he says, his voice higher. "She just panicked!"

"She panicked and threw me under the bus."

"It wasn't like that. He would have killed her! She knew if he found out about us that he'd send her back to Florida. You don't understand what he's like." He snorts to stop his nose from running and his face is a wet mess, so Jack reaches over and opens the glove box to show him where Claire keeps a packet of tissues. Michael pulls it out without comment.

"I think I have a good idea. If you recall, I came home that night trying to find out what was up with him. You told me I was crazy, remember?"

As if this spurs Michael on, he says, "Because she always made me promise not to tell anyone the stuff she told me! I knew if I told you, you'd go to him. Or to the cops. Or someone. You always think your laws can fix everything!"

The last comment stuns Jack. *His* laws? Is this what all his years as a prosecutor has meant to his kids? Is that how Michael thinks of Jack's faith in the legal system? Not that Jack is sure he has such faith anymore, not after everything that's happened with his case, and with Jenny's. He doesn't know whether to deny his son's accusation or to say *Is that so bad?* Michael, obviously, thinks it is.

"I don't think I'd be out here on the highway with you in the middle of the night if I thought laws could fix everything," he says quietly.

Michael simply lowers his eyes again, as if he, too, realizes he just mocked his father's life work.

An uneasy silence settles inside the car. Traffic on the Illinois interstate is light at this hour, and Jack has to fight against the hypnotic effect of the reflective lane markers that fly by at a fast, rhythmic pace. He starts to watch for road signs indicating somewhere to buy a cup of coffee.

Michael's phone vibrates. "She says she remembers the room number on the door. 224."

So they're on a second floor. Jack has to think about whether that will make things easier or more difficult. He almost wishes Celeste would go to sleep instead of risking her mom or Torpedo waking to see her texting.

"You didn't tell her we're on our way, did you?"

"No. Should I?"

"No, not yet. If one of them happened to wake up, we wouldn't want them to see that in her text history." Although what's already there is damning enough.

The interruption provides Jack the opening back into their previous conversation. "So tell me the rest," he prods. "What happened after Celeste lied to her dad about why she'd taken the test? Didn't he find it odd that she would be taking a test the very next day after the supposed rape?"

"Yeah, but she just played dumb, like she didn't know it couldn't tell her so soon. He always thinks she's so naive, anyway. She guessed he'd buy it, and he did."

Jack's not so sure. According to the police reports, Celeste's dad never mentioned the pregnancy test when the cops interviewed him. Was he trying to protect himself by not bringing up a topic that would lead to his habit of searching his daughter's trash? It came out for the first time on the stand, but Jack is starting to think that was a slip on Del Toro's part, especially since Walker seemed surprised by the testimony. But how could Del Toro not realize that Celeste's story didn't quite jive? Or maybe he did, but they were all so far down the road that he didn't want anyone else to realize it, too? Or maybe he was simply in denial, as so many parents are.

"Keep talking," Jack says. "Tell me how we got from there to here."

"She never thought he'd make her report it. She thought he might come to you, and you'd deny it, and he'd back off, you know, because of who you are and stuff."

Instead, *who Jack is* gave her father all the more reason to report it. Jack can't fault the man; he would have done the same.

"But that didn't happen. He made her go to the police, and then it just snowballed from there. She even thought the police would brush it off, that they'd assume she was lying and wouldn't do anything about it. But that's not what happened."

"No, that's not what happened, all right," Jack says bitterly.

"Dad, I didn't know at first," he says. "She wouldn't talk to me, she wouldn't answer my texts or my messages. When you came home that day after they held you overnight, all I knew is what I'd heard on the news and from Mom."

Jack has to assume Claire told him the charges were ridiculous, but if she didn't, he doesn't want to know. "And you believed what you heard on the news."

"I didn't know who to believe! Not after—" He stops as if his mouth was ahead of his brain.

"After what?" He glances over and sees that the old anger has encroached on Michael's more recent shame. "After what? After what happened with Jenny?"

Michael nods.

"Mike, it's okay that you didn't know what to think. All right? It's okay. It was wrong, what I did. I hurt Mom, I hurt you and Jamie, I hurt a lot of people. It was horrible, and I understand why you could hate me for it. But . . ." He sighs, and Michael sneaks a look at him. ". . . you realize how different that was from what Celeste accused me of, don't you?"

"Yeah, I do now. I mean, I did then, too, once I thought about it. But when I first heard, I don't know . . . It took Celeste a while to admit to me what really happened, and at school everyone . . ." He lets out a small, helpless grunt. "I was just mad, and upset."

For the first time it occurs to Jack that Michael might have suffered at school the same things Jack suffered at work and around town—the dirty looks, the whispers, the snickers. He assumed that since Celeste was the purported victim, Michael, as her boyfriend, would garner the same sympathy. He realizes now how wrong this might have been.

"Okay, I get that. I do. But here's what I don't get: At some point you knew she made it all up, and yet you just let everything happen to me? To all of us, really, not just me. I mean, haven't you paid any attention to what's been going on outside our house? Haven't you watched the news? Haven't you noticed what it's done to—" He catches himself, because no matter what, the last thing he wants is for Michael to blame himself for what's happened to his parents. "—my career? Why didn't you come to me? I don't understand what you thought would happen. You had to know I could go to prison."

Michael sniffles and Jack thinks he might be about to start crying all over again. "I don't know! I didn't know what to do. She was terrified of being sent back. And she was even more afraid to tell someone *why* she didn't want to go back because he told her—"

"Who?"

"Her mom's boyfriend. He told her that if she ever told anyone, he'd hurt her, and he'd hurt her dad and her grandma."

"But Mike, if she told someone, or if *you'd* told *me*, even, do you really think anyone would let him hurt her again?" Jack wonders briefly if Celeste was afraid of not being believed.

"You're not listening! You don't understand! She did try to tell someone and look what happened!"

"What do you mean?"

"Her finger. Her pinky, like I told you. When her mom was released, she tried to tell her what he'd done, but he claimed she came on to him, and her mom believed him, so nothing changed. A little bit after that, he did that to her finger and made her tell everyone that it happened accidentally when they were fixing dinner."

None of this should surprise Jack—he's prosecuted so many cases just like it and worse—but nothing has ever hit so close to home. He's starting to sympathize with Claire's desire to stay out of the fray.

"He told her it was her punishment for talking."

"She told you all this?"

"Yeah."

"Mike, don't get mad at me for asking this, okay, but how do you know it's true? How do you know she's not making it up?" *Like she's made up so many other things.*

Michael looks over at him. In the red glow of the dashboard, Jack sees the wet remnants of tears on his cheeks. His lips contort as if he just ate something foul tasting, and his brows sit low over the blue eyes that match Jack's own. He regards Jack warily, as if he's not sure whether the man next to him is really his father.

"Because I *know* her, Dad," he says, and his quiet voice sounds so young and innocent, and yet so wise. Jack suddenly understands that he and Claire had it wrong. Jenny or no Jenny, Michael would have fallen for Celeste either way. "I know her, so I believe her."

As they drive through the night, past cornfields and pastures whose existences are marked at this late hour by nothing more than distant farmhouse porch lights or barbed wire fences alongside the road, Jack thinks about everything Michael told him. As a prosecutor, he and his family have always been exposed to threats from the criminals he prosecutes. Both he and Claire knew from the start it came with the package and they accepted it as one of the prices they'd have to pay for Jack to pursue a career he loved. They took the standard precautions: having an unlisted number, keeping their address out of the neighborhood and school buzz books, and once Jack was elected as DA, keeping the kids out of the spotlight. They received a few threats over the years, but none ever rose to a level that required genuine concern for their safety.

Now some guy from halfway across the country comes along, with a tie to Jack so tenuous that Jack shouldn't have to worry about whether he poses a danger to his family. And yet he does, and the danger is a very real and distinct one, but instead of doing what Claire suggested, Jack barrels closer and closer to making himself—and Michael—the bull's-eye for Torpedo's target practice. What the hell is he thinking?

And then he looks at Michael, dozing restlessly in the seat next to him, his mussed hair clinging to his sweaty forehead and his right hand clutching his phone, the only lifeline he has to a girl he loves, and he knows.

"Are you going to move out?"

Michael's question startles Jack, more for its content than the way it pierces the bubble of his thoughts. Thoughts that surface only when you're alone in the middle of the night.

He looks over. Michael's still curled against the door, his head still rests on the pillow he brought, but his eyes are open and staring at Jack. "You're awake."

"Are you?"

"I don't know. I mean, yeah, eventually, but not until my case gets worked out." He's not even sure what that means.

"Are you going to live with Jenny?"

The question feels like a punch to the chest. "No. I—"

"That's why you're leaving Mom, right? Because of Jenny?" He's relentless. Very matter of fact, but relentless.

"No, not because of Jenny . . . I mean, I'm not leaving to live with Jenny." Nothing is coming out right. "I'm not *leaving*, okay? Yes, I'll be living somewhere else, but not with Jenny. And I'm not abandoning you or Jamie. I don't want you to think that."

"You will no longer live at our house because you're splitting up with Mom. That's *leaving*."

Jack sighs. An attorney in the making. "Okay. Yeah, okay. But I'm not leaving to live with Jenny. In fact, wherever I end up, you and Jamie can spend as much time with me there as you want, as much time as Mom is comfortable with."

"Then why are you moving out?"

"Mike . . ." Jack isn't so naïve to think Michael doesn't understand on some level. "What happened with Jenny really hurt Mom, and we haven't been able to get past it. We tried, but we haven't. I don't know how else to explain it. Your mom deserves to be happy, and—"

"But she doesn't want you to leave."

"No, you're right, she doesn't. Not now. She's scared, you know? But I think, with time, she'll understand, and she'll be happier."

"Or you will be."

The dig hits Jack just as Michael intended. His first instinct is to defend his decision, but no defense he might raise would placate Michael. Nor should it.

Instead, he breathes deep, tries to beat back the pain that's just as relentless as his son, and quietly acknowledges the truth. "I hope so. I hope we both are."

Michael falls silent and closes his eyes.

Just outside of Eddyville, Kentucky, Michael stirs. He sits up, disoriented, and looks around. The phone in his palm reminds him.

"Did I get any more texts?" he asks Jack.

"I don't think so. I didn't hear it vibrate or see it light up." He's relieved they're back to talking about the task at hand.

"Where are we?"

"About to hit Eddyville, in Kentucky. We're about an hour away from the Tennessee line. We need to figure out what town they're in. She said Tennessee but that can mean a lot of things, even if our assumption they took the most direct route is the right one. It could mean Nashville, it could mean Chattanooga. It could mean any dot on the map in between. If it means Chattanooga, we still have a long drive ahead of us."

"What if they didn't take the most direct route?"

"Then we're fucked." He feels Michael's stare and looks over. "Screwed, I mean."

"What if they left already?"

"I don't know, Mike. We'll worry about that problem if and when we come to it. Anyway, I think she would have texted you about that, don't you?"

"What will we do when we get there?"

He asked the same question when they first climbed in the car, and Jack is no closer to having an answer. "We'll take her back home with us." It's all he has for now.

"I think I should text her."

"Go ahead. Just be careful what you say. I wouldn't mention we're coming, not yet."

"Why not?"

"Just wait until we're within striking distance."

Michael begins his rapid-fire tapping. "I'll ask if she's still awake."

"That's good. It's benign."

Jack reaches in the cup holder for his own phone and hits the speed dial for

Dog. When Dog answers, sputtering expletives about the time—"Fuckin' a, it's four in the morning!"—Jack tells him to get into the office ASAP, get the file Jack's been keeping on his own case and dig out Torpedo's real name. He remembers Celeste's mom's name—Lillian Del Toro—and he could have called Earl for Torpedo's, but then he'd have to explain himself. When he hangs up, he calls ATT and after cursing the automated help system, interrogates the live woman who finally answers until he learns that unless Wi-Fi is available, text messages get routed in the same way as phone calls, and that the most recent messages between Michael and Celeste were routed through Clarksville. Bingo.

"Call Information and get the number for the Red Roof Inn in Clarksville," he says to Michael.

But Michael doesn't respond, causing Jack to look over. He's staring wide-eyed at his phone screen. "Oh, God."

"What?" Jack asks.

"They know."

"What do you mean? How do you know?"

"The text back says Mike everything is fine now don't worry I'll call you when I get to Florida. She didn't write that. I know she didn't write that. She wouldn't spell everything out."

"Listen up. Do what I said. Get the number for the hotel and call it. Make sure they give you the front desk, and then describe Celeste to them and ask if they remember someone like her checking in last night with her parents. Or anyone named Del Toro."

"What if they say yes?"

"Then ask if they've checked out yet. Or better yet, if they say yes, hand me the phone."

The man Michael speaks to in Clarksville informs him that no one by the name of Del Toro is registered, and since he just came on duty at eleven, he's seen only a few check-ins and none fit the description.

Frustrated, Jack can only wait for Dog to get back to him. The twenty minutes it takes feels like hours. Finally, Dog texts him: Torrence Nash, u o me boss.

"I love you, Dog," Jack says to the screen, and Michael just looks at him curiously. He gives him the phone and says, "Dial the Clarksville number again, then hand it back to me."

The clerk at the front office informs Jack that the Nashes have already checked out.

"Do you know when?" he asks, trying to disguise any sense of urgency.

"This morning."

Well, no shit, he thinks. But he forces a pleasant and non-threatening tone. "Oh, could you tell me what time?"

There's a silence at the other end as the clerk checks his records. "Looks like a few minutes ago." His tone, in contrast to Jack's, is one of being put upon. "Maybe twenty minutes."

Jack closes his phone and signals the answer to Michael with a shake of his head.

"What are we gonna do?" Michael cries. "They know!"

"First, you're going to calm down, okay? You've gotta calm down." Michael presses his back against the seat, which Jack supposes is the equivalent of *I'm calm*. He checks the clock on the dash. "We're less than thirty miles from the exit. They have no reason to think we're heading their way. All they know from your texts is that she told you she's going back to Florida. We—"

"Yeah, and that I was trying to figure out exactly where they are. And that I know what he's done to her."

"True. But as far as they know, you have no clue where they are, and you never mentioned you're already on the way. Let's just get there and find out more, and we'll take it from there."

Michael grunts, but gives up the fight.

The first thing Jack notices as he circles the parking lot is a large freight truck with Florida plates. The truck is parked just below the entrance to Room 224, which faces the highway at the rear of the building. The words "Southern Freight" fight for attention with layers of dirt and cinders splattered on the side. Underneath the name is a website and phone number.

"You wouldn't happen to know if the boyfriend is a truck driver, would you?" Jack asks.

"I don't know."

He circles the lot again to see if any other cars have Florida plates. They don't. He parks close to the lobby but on the street side, out of sight of the room. "Stay here."

"But I—"

"I said stay here. I'll be right back." Before he gets out, he adds, "While you're waiting for me, get on the internet with your phone and find out what you can from that website listed on the truck. But keep your eyes open."

Except for the clerk behind the desk, the lobby is empty. Jack isn't surprised, given the early hour. The clerk, a skinny kid in a black T-shirt, well-worn jeans, and tattoos covering both emaciated arms, once again claims that they checked out, though he can't describe any of them. His attitude is even larger than on the phone, and it pisses off Jack.

"I would think it'd be unusual for guests to check out so early. How could you not remember them if they're the only ones who've been in the lobby this morning?" With his elbows on the counter, Jack leans closer to the punk. A small, aluminum ashtray rests on the desk and a half-smoked cigarette smolders at the ashtray's edge. He can't be older than twenty-one, twenty-two, but Jack sees he's lived hard. "Isn't this a non-smoking hotel?"

"Who the fuck are you?"

"I'm someone who might want to rent a room. Can't imagine your boss would appreciate you talking to me like that."

"They checked out remotely, using the TV," he says, apparently deciding to now answer Jack's earlier question.

"What kind of vehicle did they have?"

"I don't know, man. I told you, I didn't see them leave."

"Maybe not. But your records know, don't they." Jack's tone makes clear he's not asking.

After reaching for the cigarette, the guy pushes at the desk to roll his chair out. He rocks the chair and looks at Jack with narrowed eyes as he takes a long drag. "Dude, you look familiar."

"Yeah, a lot of people tell me that." Jack slaps a twenty dollar bill down on the counter. "This is important. One of them is in danger."

"No, seriously, man. Where do I know you from?" He slides the bill off the counter and down onto the desk as he questions Jack.

Fuck him. "I'm the DA." Jack flashes his credentials so fast that the clerk can't read that Jack doesn't mean the local DA. *This is becoming a bad habit.* "And you're this close"—he holds up his index finger and thumb to demonstrate—"to being charged with obstruction of justice."

The guy stares at Jack, thinking, and Jack sees a slow wave of recognition travel his face. One side of his mouth rises in a smart-ass grin. He reaches for the cigarette that still dangles from his lips on the other side and holds it over the ashtray, pushes down a few times to extinguish it. "You're not shitting me, are you? I know now. You're that guy who's been on the news, the one who's on trial for nailing that high school girl."

Jack swipes hard at everything on the counter separating them. The grin slips from the kid's face as he watches items scatter—brochures, a bowl of candy, some sort of hotelier award in a small frame. Some land on the floor, some land on the desk in front of him. The clerk stands, and Jack reaches across, clutches a bundle of the T-shirt in his fist, and pulls him so close he smells the stale cigarette breath. "Listen, you little prick! Answer my questions or I'll come over this counter and make you eat that fuckin' cigarette. What were they driving?"

"I told you, man! I don't know! We have a space on the registration form for vehicle information, but no one ever bothers to fill it out. I'll check, but I'm telling you, it won't be there. Last I saw'em, the mom came in here asking where the nearest twenty-four hour drug store was. Something about her husband having a migraine. That's the last I've seen of them. I swear."

"Before or after they checked out?"

"Just a few minutes ago. Maybe five minutes before you came in."

"You're not making sense. When I called earlier, you said it had been twenty minutes since they checked out. It took me another twenty or twenty-five minutes to get here. If she asked about the drug store only five minutes before I came in, that means they were still here for forty minutes or so after they checked out. Why would that be?"

The clerk shakes his head in confusion, trying to do the math. "I don't know! You'd have to ask them, man." He squirms, but Jack holds tight to the T-shirt. "Let go of me and I'll pull up the records and you can see for yourself!"

Jack lets go but not without a strong shove, which causes the clerk to fall backwards onto the chair.

"Christ, dude!" the guy hollers, flapping his arms to regain his balance before the chair tips over. With a glare at Jack, he rolls back to the desk, grabs the computer mouse and starts clicking.

"How far is the drugstore?"

"We don't have any in town that stay open all night. We always send people to the Walgreens in Madison, a little north of Nashville. It's about a 45 minute drive south." He turns his computer monitor so Jack can see the screen. "See, they checked out at 4:11."

Jack glances at his watch and sees it's now 5:06. He and Michael pulled in the parking lot ten minutes ago, at most, which means Lillian Del Toro asked about the drug store around 4:50. *What's going on?* "Did she go alone?"

"Dude, I told you. *I didn't see them leave.*"

"Who drives the truck? The Southern Freight truck?"

"What? Oh, that's Walt. He's a regular, every Monday night like clockwork."

So it's not Torpedo's truck. "Have you been in the room since they checked out?"

"No. The cleaning lady will clean it when she comes on duty at seven."

"So you really don't know if anyone's in there or not, do you?"

Like Celeste. Alone. With Torpedo. The clerk gives Jack a blank look.

"I need to get in that room. Right now."

"I can't—"

Jack leans close again. "You unlock that room right now or I'll break the window to let myself in. You got it?"

"But—"

Jack leaves the lobby. He hears the guy yell, "Wait!"

Outside, the sky is still dark but the walkways are dimly lit. The fertile, humid scent of the spring morning overpowers even the exhaust fumes of vehicles on the nearby interstate. He weaves his way to the rear of the building, the clerk on his tail. He catches up to Jack on the stairs. "You can't just barge in if somebody's inside! At least let me knock and make sure no one's in there and then I'll let you in."

"You don't get it. I want in *if* someone's in there." But the clerk's words reach one part of Jack's brain even as another part causes his feet to continue forward. **He's not like people u no.** The clerk's right. If Jack barges in, it's not likely Torpedo will go down without a fight, and he might take everyone else down with him. Jack may be capable of battling the guy in a courtroom, but he has no idea what awaits him, physically, behind the door to Room 224. Flashing credentials won't cut it with a guy like Torpedo. "Look, I won't barge in, but I need you to get in there and find out what's going on while I call the cops."

"Oh, trust me, dude," the clerk looks Jack up and down as if he's an escapee from an insane asylum, "I already did that."

On the balcony at the top of the steps, Jack sees Michael running across the parking lot in their direction. Unable to shout for fear of being overheard, Jack waves to warn him away. Michael stubbornly ignores him.

"I want you to knock on the door and pretend like you're housekeeping or maintenance or something. I need to know if anyone's in there."

"And if there is?"

"Try to get in. I don't care what pretext you use. Just try to get in without setting off any alarms. Act like there's a plumbing emergency. Anything. And then stall. Don't let them know I'm out here."

"What the fuck are you trying to send me into? I ain't going in there if there's some sort of shit going down."

"Look, the only *shit* that might be *going down* is a rape. I'm trying to prevent it before it happens, or if I'm too late for that, I need to stop it in progress. Got it? You gonna help me? Or you want that on your conscience?"

"You serious?"

Michael appears at Jack's side, breathless. Jack puts his arm out to stop him from going any farther. "I'm serious. I suspect the guy in there sent the mom on an errand for a reason."

The clerk stares at Jack, and Jack sees he's scared.

"You have nothing to worry about as long as you stick to your hotel role. If you see it's a guy alone with a girl, just stall, okay? Whatever you do, don't let him close the door on you."

"Is she still here?" Michael asks, panting.

"We're about to find out."

The clerk looks down at the master key card in his hand. "If you don't want them to know you're here, maybe you should stay on the steps until I'm in the room. He may come out."

Jack nods. "Just hurry." He pulls Michael back with him. "I told you to stay in the car." When Michael doesn't respond, he adds, "Stay behind me, and *do not* leave this landing unless I give you explicit instructions to. Okay?" Michael nods. "And keep an eye out for the cops."

"I called them."

"What?"

"I called the cops and told them what was happening. I overheard what you said to Mom about guns blazing, so I told them to try to arrive without anyone knowing about it."

As soon as the words are out of his mouth, Jack hears the clerk's knock on Room 224 and his yell, "Maintenance! Anyone in here?" He puts his fingers at his lips again to remind Michael not to speak anymore, but with the hand closest to his son, squeezes his arm to tell him he's proud of him for what he just revealed.

Jack grows more nervous when the clerk repeats his call, which is followed by the sound of the door opening but then abruptly stopped by the security chain. He can't hear if anyone speaks on the other side of the door, but someone must have finally shown himself because the clerk says, "Sorry, dude. The computer showed you checked out already."

"Yeah, we did." The voice Jack assumes belongs to Torpedo has the low rasp of someone who smokes two packs a day. "But that was before I got hit by a migraine. We'll be leaving as soon as my wife gets back with some medicine and I get some relief. You're gonna have to come back later. We have 'til noon, right?"

Michael's frantic eyes go wide, and Jack raises a hand. *Just hold on.*

"Sure, but I first gotta get in there to check on some pipes. We had a report of a gas leak and we think the problem's originating from this room. I need you to wait on the balcony."

"I haven't smelled anything. Look, I'm in massive pain here." The fake friendliness has given way to a more threatening tone. "I need to lie down and close my eyes."

Jack hears a voice from inside the room that he thinks is Celeste, but he can't make out what was said.

"She's right, it may be the gas causing your migraine," the clerk says. "Sorry, man, I don't have a choice. State law." Jack suddenly loves the guy for how well he's playing the part.

"Come on, Cee," Torpedo says angrily. To the clerk, "We'll be out in a second." He must try to shut the door because Jack hears a thud—the clerk's palm hitting the door?—followed by, "Sorry, dude, you gotta keep the door open."

Michael taps Jack on the shoulder to point out two police officers quietly making their way along the wall near the front office to the stairwell. *Perfect timing.* Jack repositions himself so he can see the balcony outside the door. He watches as Celeste comes out first, Torpedo right on her heel. She wears purple pajama pants and a white thermal shirt with long sleeves, an odd choice for the warm, muggy weather. Her hair is frizzy from the humidity, and tangled from what Jack hopes is just sleep. She's tall like Jenny, but she looks tiny next to Torpedo, who towers over her with the wide, bare-chested muscles of a body-builder. A barbed wire tattoo circles his large left bicep; a snake design curls around the other. His stringy brown hair is pulled back in a ponytail, revealing a pockmarked but incongruently boyish face.

As soon as the clerk disappears into the room, Torpedo leans against the railing with his arm around Celeste. She visibly tenses when he pulls her close, and her reaction alone convinces Jack that everything she told Michael is true. Torpedo bends close to her ear, his lips touching her hair, and whispers something as he casually brushes his free hand against her breast. Celeste lowers her eyes, her mouth screws up in fear and revulsion, but otherwise she doesn't move.

"What's happening?" Michael whispers. The first cop reaches the landing just as Jack turns to shush Michael.

"Mr. Hilliard?" the cop asks. "Jack Hilliard?" Jack nods and moves toward him. He silently signals with one hand as he reaches for his credentials with the other, but the cop stuns Jack when he grabs his wrist and executes a maneuver that spins him so quickly he doesn't have time to object. He advises Jack that he's under arrest for contempt of court and begins to recite Miranda as the second cop grabs hold of the other arm and together the two men cuff him. Jack doesn't try to verbalize their mistake for fear of being overheard by Torpedo, but Michael, whether lacking the same restraint or perhaps foresight, cries, "He's not the one! He's trying to help her!" Jack hears Celeste cry, "Mike?" just as the first cop pushes Michael against the wall and shouts, "You need to stay quiet, son, until we tell you to speak!" The second cop abandons Jack and starts in the direction of Celeste's voice while Jack starts talking at the first cop, just tries to get as much of the story out so the man will move to assist his partner. His prayers are answered when the second cop issues an order—"Step away from her"—and then shouts, "Morris, I need back-up!"

Michael, hearing *Step away from her*, assumes the worst and takes off to follow Officer Morris. Jack yells "*Michael, stop!*" in a tone he's heard come out of his own mouth only one other time, when a four-year-old Jamie came within seconds of propelling himself off an icy hill of plowed snow into the path of an approaching SUV. It works. Michael halts, and Jack exhales his relief.

He hears Celeste crying as the second cop again orders Torpedo to step away from her.

"Whoa, officers, slow down there," Torpedo says. "You're scaring her. I'm just a guy trying to get some rest before driving my family home to Florida."

With his arms still trapped behind him, Jack edges back to his former viewing spot and sees Celeste is now standing slightly in front of Torpedo as insurance against the cops, who both have their guns trained on him. He grips her shoulders in a casual, fatherly stance. The frightened clerk stands with his back pressed against the doorframe. Jack hears helicopter rotors in the distance and knows the media is about to descend upon them. Morris knows it, too; he glances at the sky and mutters, "Damn it!" When a curious guest opens the door to the room at the end of the balcony, he orders her back into her room. To Torpedo, he says, "Step away from her and then we'll sort this out."

"I will, I will. Just lower the guns, will ya? You got the wrong guy." Torpedo spots Jack. "There he is, Cee." He squeezes her shoulders. "Tell 'em, cupcake. Tell them who really hurt you."

Celeste keeps her eyes aimed at the ground.

"Cee?" the second cops says gently, using the name he heard Torpedo use, "is this man your father?"

She shakes her head. Torpedo says, "I'm her mom's boyfriend. She's known me for years. Her mom will be back any minute and she'll tell you. She just went to find some medicine for my migraine."

"Is that right, Cee?"

This time she nods, still refusing to look at anyone. Jack can't stand it anymore. "Celeste, tell them what you told Mike. Tell them what he's done to you." But she pretends not to hear. "He raped her," he tells the cops. "Repeatedly."

Torpedo laughs and say, "Hey, man, *I'm* not wearing the cuffs," just as the clerk says to the cops, "Dudes, I think you should listen to the lawyer." He nods at Jack in case they don't realize who he means. "There's something in this room you might want to see."

His last comment cracks Torpedo's shell. "You have no fuckin' right to search our room."

Officer Morris starts to speak but Jack quickly cuts him off. "What did you see?" he asks the clerk. Jack knows he might say something to convince the cops that a crime, if not already occurring, was about to be committed. If so, they'll have no obstacles to a warrantless search.

The clerk looks from Jack to the cops, his mouth open in doubt, as if afraid to answer anyone except them. "*What'd you see?*" Jack asks again, insistently. Torpedo snickers and pivots Celeste to face the door. "Go on in, cupcake. These officers can come back when they get a warrant." His hands still resting nonchalantly on her shoulders, he tries to push her forward.

A helicopter appears from over the top of the hotel, and as the bird's spotlight sweeps the balcony, the officers order Torpedo to stop, but the noise drowns out their commands. In the chaos created by the noise and wind, Celeste ducks and slips free of Torpedo's unsuspecting grip. He shouts her name, but she ignores him and sprints down the balcony past the cops, who immediately descend upon a resistant Torpedo and within seconds have him Tasered and on the ground. Celeste crashes into Jack and sinks against his chest, sobbing, her arms flung around his waist. Without the use of his own arms, he loses his balance and stumbles against the stair rail behind him.

"Hey, hey, it's okay. It's okay. It's over," he whispers to the top of Celeste's head, but either she can't hear him over the commotion or she's simply hiding from it. He catches Michael's eye and motions him over with a tilt of the head. Michael approaches hesitantly, as if uncertain whether this wild-haired creature hugging his dad is the same girl he last saw in St. Louis. "Celeste," Jack hollers to get her attention. She lifts her head, emerging from behind the veil of black hairs clinging to her wet cheek, and spots Michael. With nothing more than an impulsive "Oh!" she releases Jack and falls uninhibited into Michael's welcome arms.

They learn later from the clerk—whose name, they also learn, is Danny—that he began to believe Jack as soon as he cracked open the door to Room 224 and glimpsed Torpedo working furiously to untie a rope from Celeste's wrist. Once he got inside, he found two separate, short pieces of rope kicked behind the dresser and a bottle of lubricant on top of it. "I mean, it wasn't much. I see kinky stuff all the time, you know? But she didn't look like a willing participant to me." His dry manner of reporting what he saw belied the malice behind the scene he stumbled upon.

The cops found even more—a gun and eight grams of cocaine. No Rohypnol, though.

Celeste insisted nothing happened, that Torpedo didn't get far in his plans, and the rape kit, which this time she consented to, backed her up. She claimed it was the first time he had tried to restrain her; she also claimed it was only the second time she physically resisted, the first being the first time he assaulted her. After that, she knew better than to fight. Jack wasn't sure he believed either claim, he felt sure she downplayed what had happened to her, but he knew the full truth would come when she was ready. He only hoped she'd be ready by the time the Florida authorities interviewed her.

His own situation wasn't so straightforward. Despite a full report from the Tennessee authorities to Judge Simmons, Walker and Chief Matthews, the judge refused to dismiss the rape charges against him until both Jack and Celeste could appear before him in person. He did, however, agree to look the other way with respect to Jack violating both the bond and the restraining order. This favor allowed Jack to drive home in his own car instead of in the back of a cruiser. After a nap in a back room of the Clarksville police department and permission from Celeste's father, Jack pulled back onto Interstate 24 toward St. Louis at half past six that evening, Michael and Celeste curled together like newborn pups in the back seat.

News trucks followed them the whole way.

EARLY FALL

CHAPTER THIRTY-ONE

WHEN EARL FIRST called Jenny on a Thursday afternoon in early September and asked her to meet for breakfast the next morning, she assumed he had good news about his discussions with Alan Sterling, the DA from Franklin County who had handled the murder case against her. Earl had met with Sterling months ago to present the new evidence supporting Jenny's innocence and to seek assurances that he no longer considered her a person of interest. The new evidence included the PI's report and Brian's affidavit that Jenny didn't know Maxine Shepard had been their father's mistress until after her arrest. To strengthen the affidavit, Jack located the ancient injunction order Brian had mentioned. The existence of the injunction further bolstered Earl's argument that Jenny wouldn't have ever discovered, absent Brian telling her, the identity of their father's mistress.

But what gave Jenny the most hope was Alex's decision to accept a plea bargain. Jeff McCarthy, the prosecutor from Jack's office who had handled the case against Alex, turned over a copy of the PI report to Alex's attorney along with an offer of life without parole in exchange for a guilty plea. To everyone's delight, he took it. Jenny hoped to reap the benefit of the general consensus that no man accepts a life sentence unless he's guilty.

But justice moves slowly, and Jenny and Earl had been waiting patiently for Sterling to review the information and get back to Earl with his decision.

Now, as Earl takes a seat across from her, it occurs to her that he could have easily shared good news over the phone. She braces herself for the worst. She calculates her next step, whether to stay in St. Louis despite the cloud over her head, or sell her house, return to Chicago for good, and hope they file her away as a question that will never be answered. Earl surprises her when, first thing, he slides an envelope across the table.

"What's this?" she asks.

"Your retainer. Congratulations. You're officially off the hook." He says it with such little fanfare that it takes a moment for her nerves to believe the announcement. "Sterling is confident the right man is already in jail."

"Thank you." She slips the envelope into her purse. "You could have mailed it."

"My wanting to meet is only tangentially related to you being cleared."
"Oh?"

The waitress appears and Earl turns over his coffee cup for her to fill it. "What's your pleasure?" he asks Jenny, nodding to the menu.

She waves the idea of food away. "I'll stick with coffee for now. I tend not to have an appetite when I'm anxious. How long will you keep me in suspense?"

"You have nothing to be anxious about." He places his own order. When the waitress leaves the table, he says, "Have you talked to Jack lately?"

She almost laughs. Is he serious? "No."

"This is still under wraps, but I'm starting a practice and I've asked him to join me."

Jenny sets her cup into its saucer a little too hard. "Wow."

"So you really haven't talked to him."

"No, Earl, I haven't talked to him. Anything I know about Jack's life over the past few months, I learned from the news."

In fact, except for the two text messages, they've had nothing to do with each other since he showed up at her motel asking for the original letters.

"Did he say yes?" She's incredulous.

"You know he and Claire have split?"

Not quite an answer to her question. "So it's been reported. I wasn't sure." *Since he hasn't called to tell me himself.* "I guess if you're telling me, it must be true."

Earl explains that Jack made the decision to end his marriage during his trial. "They continued to share the same physical space for the rest of the trial, but he moved out not long after the Tennessee incident, once the charges were dropped."

Jenny knows Earl isn't relaying this information for her benefit. To the contrary, she feels the full weight of his disapproval. But she puts up no defense to Earl's obvious belief that she bears a large part of the responsibility for the break-up. Like it or not, she knows he's right, even if he doesn't fully understand why. Jack had given Earl a copy of the PI report knowing he could use it to persuade Sterling to clear Jenny. When Earl showed it to her, she realized right away Earl didn't know how Jack had first come into possession of it.

"It's interesting, though," Earl says. "He found out about the surveillance on the same day he met with *you* to get the originals of Celeste's letters." He raises one gray eyebrow.

"You think something happened when he saw me that day to cause him to go home and end his marriage?"

"Coincidence, then?"

"Except for a three word text he sent, I've not heard from him since." She raises her right hand. "I'd swear on the Bible."

He stares at her as if she's a puzzle he can't solve. It occurs to her that Earl thinks the three word text is something entirely different than the actual message sent.

"It said 'I'm okay, thanks,'" she adds. "Not quite a marriage breaker."

"No, it doesn't sound like it. But then, why would he be telling you he's okay?"

She takes it as a rhetorical question. If it's not, she's saved from answering when the waitress delivers Earl's omelet and potatoes. He takes his time placing his napkin on his lap, seasoning the food. She still has no idea why he asked to meet with her.

"My goal is to put together a criminal defense team that will deliver a level of service unrivaled by any other firm in St. Louis," he says, segueing back to his new venture. "I plan to keep it small, personal. I'm thinking somewhere between three to five attorneys max, but the team I put together will be the best of the best."

"Sounds impressive," she says to humor him. "You and Jack have always made a good team."

"I'd like you to be a part of it."

His statement shocks her into silence. When she finds her voice, she speaks one word. "Why?"

"Because you're a damn good lawyer, and I suspect you have no desire to return to Newman."

"I *was* a damn good lawyer, a *corporate bankruptcy* lawyer, and I'm not even sure I'm that anymore, it's been so long. Criminal law is a foreign language to me. And—"

"You can learn to speak the language. I'm not concerned."

"Jack won't want me there. You know that. Neither, for that matter, will Claire. There's no way she'll like this idea."

"First, you're wrong about Jack. And I didn't say Claire *would* like it, but she accepts it. I've spoken with her. I even gave her veto power over the idea. She understands you're not going away, and that she'll have to live with you unless she goes away herself." He takes a bite of his omelet, chews leisurely, and dabs his mouth with the napkin before continuing his thought. "And I assure you, she has no intention of going anywhere. She won't hurt her kids to spite you or Jack. If there's anyone who will handle the situation with class, it's Claire. I have no doubt she'll emerge from all this stronger than ever."

Jenny wants so badly to ask him if he thinks withholding evidence is classy. She wishes she could knock Claire right off her pedestal of perfection while all of St. Louis watches. She almost laughs at the irony, because she never had such desires before Jack knew the truth. She didn't care about hurting Claire then; she only cared about not hurting Jack. But with the reason for that motivation gone, so too is any empathy she had for Claire.

"Maybe she's wrong. Maybe I *am* going away."

"Well, then, it's my turn to ask, why? Didn't you come back for a reason?"

"What's that supposed to mean?"

"It means, Ms. Dodson, that you finally have Jack exactly where you want him. So why on Earth would you leave now?"

Jenny places her own napkin next to her cup. She pulls a twenty dollar bill from her purse, slaps it on the table, and stands. "Go to hell, *Mr.* Scanlon. I'm not the horrible person you seem to think I am."

"Did I say that?"

"Let me make something clear. Jack came to *me* the night Maxine was murdered. Go back and check the transcript from Alex's trial and I think you'll find he admitted it under oath." She points her finger at Earl, and the volume of her voice escalates. "So don't act like I'm some evil witch who somehow manipulated him with my black magic. Because that's bullshit. You and everyone else in this city would like to believe that, wouldn't you, because then it's easier to forgive your beloved DA. Blame it all on the other woman, right? The home wrecker?"

"I think plenty of folks blamed him, too."

"Except he didn't feel compelled to leave town, did he? He kept his job, didn't he? Even his wife took him back. I willingly accept much of the blame for what happened, and I always have, but I didn't finagle events to break up his marriage, that's for sure. I know I could have told him no and I should have, but let's get one thing straight—he's as much to blame as I am, if not more. He came to me; I didn't go to him. He was married; I wasn't. And after it all happened? I'm the one who pushed him away and told him to go home where he belonged. He never told you that, did he? And then I got out of his way so he *could* go home and have a chance to repair the damage we'd caused. Oh, and just in case you're wondering, I didn't hire Celeste to become his son's girlfriend and then accuse him of assault. I didn't ask her to send me threatening notes. I wasn't there when Jack made the decision to drive her home and lie to his wife about it. So your little comment about 'having Jack exactly where I want him' is a crock of shit. Got it?"

During the course of her rant she leaned closer to Earl without noticing, arms straight and palms flat on the table as she hovered in front of him. She straightens back up and takes a step away to put distance between them. Only then does she realize she's shaking. A few diners stare at her. *Tough shit.* She's tired of hiding.

Earl crosses his arms and the slightest grin breaks on his face. "You can sit down now, Jenny. Interview over. The job's yours if you want it."

"Fuck your job."

He laughs, and the sound makes her even angrier. "You'll have to clean up your language, though."

She gives him her back and starts for the entrance.

"I wondered how long it would take the Jenny Dodson we all know and love

to reemerge," he calls to her. "I never imagined it would take almost five years."
Another customer crosses in front of her, briefly blocking her passage. She takes
the opportunity to turn around and glare at Earl. "Why don't you let yourself
come home for good?" he asks. "I think you're finally ready."

His words puncture her resolve. He has no idea how often she's asked
herself the same question. She knows something changed in her after she let Jack
into her bed. She remembers making him promise not to treat her differently. He
gave his promise, but her metamorphosis from intrepid warrior to spineless
weakling made it virtually impossible for him to keep it. She ran away and in the
process, gave up so much that mattered to her. Too much.

"And what makes you think he's ready? How come I haven't heard from
him?"

"Because he's still punishing himself. He's accepted that his marriage is over,
but he hasn't accepted that he's allowed to be anything but guilt-ridden and
devastated about it."

"And is he?"

"What?"

"Guilt-ridden and devastated by it?"

"Absolutely."

She lowers herself back onto the edge of the chair she abandoned, poised to
bolt again if she chooses, and sighs.

"You didn't think it'd be easy, did you?" he asks.

"And you think bringing me into your partnership will help him?" She
scoffs. "You might want to run that by him first."

"Since you mention it, I *have* talked to him about you. Not in the context of
the firm, mind you. He's noncommittal, which is easy to be when you're not
around, but I've seen the two of you in a room together. It's only a matter of
time."

"I'm not sure he *wants* to be in a room with me."

"Why don't we find out?" He pulls a piece of paper from his breast pocket
and hands it across the table. "That's the address of the new offices. They're
being built out as we speak. Show up tonight a little bit before five, and I'll bring
Jack by to talk about it."

She reads the Clayton address written on the paper. "I don't think so, Earl.
He won't like it. If he wanted to talk to me, he would have called."

"Why don't you let me worry about that? If he doesn't like it, he can be
angry at me."

The waitress stops by and tops off Jenny's coffee without asking. After
considering her options, she relents and adds cream. Earl half-smiles.

"You two are more alike than you realize, or want to admit," he says.

"Oh, yeah? Why's that?"

"You're both incredibly stubborn."

Jenny lowers her eyes, tries not to laugh, but does anyway when she realizes her reaction proved Earl's observation.

"Tell me, what's in it for you?" she asks, stirring slowly. "Why are you so anxious to play matchmaker, especially since you seem to think I'm just a step up from the devil?"

"I wouldn't offer you a job if I thought that."

"You haven't answered the question."

"What's in it for me? A contented partner, I suppose. He loves you, Jenny."

She stares at a crumb near his plate and then, at an elderly couple who just entered the restaurant and are waiting at the hostess stand to be seated. They hold hands.

"There are so many reasons why this is wrong." *And some you're not even aware of.*

"Maybe." He shrugs. "But there are even more why it's right."

She spends the afternoon fighting a panic attack. Her fears subside slightly when she slips on the green suit and regards herself in the mirror. It still fits well. A woman she used to know and admire looks back at her.

She eyes the lingerie she laid out on her bed, considers whether wearing it is some sort of admission of a desire she should resist. Warrior or weakling? She wore such things under this suit long before Jack, though. They were part of her arsenal, even if she was the only person who ever knew they were there.

She undresses and starts over with her own version of chain mail.

She waits alone in what will eventually be the lobby of Earl's new offices. As Earl promised, the construction workers expected her arrival a few minutes before they finished for the day. After ten minutes of flirting and trying to convince her to stop for a beer at Krueger's after her meeting, they leave her with only the sawhorse and the construction dust to keep her company. Once their trucks pull away from the curb, she gives herself a short tour.

Although the floors are stripped to the foundation and the interior walls still display studs, she easily envisions the purpose of each room once the renovation is complete. Downstairs will be the lobby, three individual offices, a small conference room, a half bath, and a short galley kitchen. Upstairs, walls have been knocked down for what she guesses will house a modest library. Another bathroom and two more offices fill out the top floor.

Back downstairs, she sits on a stack of drywall panels. The workers left the windows cracked and the first cool breeze of autumn waltzes across the room, but she still perspires. Her mouth is dry. She licks her lips and wishes she brought a water bottle. She's sure the kitchen faucet isn't turned on yet.

She takes in the space and tries to imagine the three of them working here together. The square footage is miniscule when measured against a firm like

Newman, Norton & Levine, but she knows Earl intends his new venture to be a boutique firm, and the small house on the tree-lined street a few blocks away from downtown Clayton epitomizes boutique.

She tells herself that it wouldn't be so strange; she and Jack worked at the same firm once before. Yet with the meeting imminent, she can't bury her anxiety. The last time they stood in the same room, he was a man with an intact, albeit unstable, marriage. She was, in large part, the woman to blame. He's made no effort to contact her. Despite what Earl claims, she takes this as the clearest signal yet that Jack would rather she disappear from his life, not become further entrenched in it. Perhaps he simply believes she's done enough damage already. She can't imagine he will welcome Earl's bright idea to invite her to join their firm.

She stands when she hears voices just outside the door, a key in the lock. Why did she lock it? She brushes the dust from the back of her skirt.

The door swings in and Earl comes through first, Jack just behind him. They're talking, something innocuous from their easy tone, and she suddenly knows that Earl didn't tell Jack she'd be here. *Damn him.*

Earl moves farther into the room and sets his briefcase on the drywall next to her, but Jack stops short just past the threshold and stares at her. Something is different about him. His expression is unreadable but intense, so intense she finds herself trying to remember if the house has a back door through which to escape.

"Jenny."

She stands taller and tries to meet his gaze without withering. She tries to summon the woman from the mirror. She tries to remember the warrior who railed at Earl in the coffee shop. She glares at Earl now to show her displeasure at his stunt.

"What's going on?" Jack asks.

"This is the prospect I told you about. I think she'd make a perfect fit, don't you?"

"*What's going on?*" Louder, stronger. Still unreadable. Still staring at her.

"Just what I said. An interview. And everything I told you about the candidate is accurate."

"But incomplete. You left out a few minor details, starting with a name."

"Hmm, that's true. I did."

"Are you suggesting you want her to join your firm?"

Her. Jenny stifles a wince, feeling exposed and invisible all at once. "Jack, I'm sorry, I didn't—"

"*Our firm,*" Earl says in answer to Jack as if Jenny wasn't speaking. "Yes, but only if you agree."

If this is how it will be, with the two of them ignoring her, Earl can take his idea and shove it. "Hey, I—"

"I'd like to speak with her alone," Jack says.

Earl looks to Jenny for agreement, and even though she's fuming, she nods slightly. He picks up his briefcase to leave.

"I'll call you when we're done," Jack adds.

"You'll take care of locking up?"

"I'll call you when we're done," he repeats. Not once does he look away from her.

Jenny glances at Earl, hoping for a hint to Jack's mood, or *something*, but Earl simply winks at her. As if she's supposed to know what that means.

Jenny gets relief from Jack's penetrating stare when he moves to lock the door behind Earl.

"I guess the suit came in handy." He loosens his tie as he talks, but even so, she sees the slight tremble of his hands.

She looks down at herself as if she forgot she's wearing the green suit. "Yes." She's about to tell him that she's back home in Lafayette Square and purposely picked this suit from many, but instead says quietly, "Thank you. For bringing it to me, I mean." When he simply stands there, hands in pockets, she says, "The offices will be nice when they're finished."

"Did Earl give you a tour?"

"I gave myself one, while I waited. I hope that was okay."

"Pick out an office?"

She thinks she detected sarcasm, not good-natured teasing. She pretends not to notice.

"So," she says, sweeping her arm to gesture at the offices, "which one will be yours?"

He tilts his head, motioning her to follow him. He leads her to one of the two rooms at the front of the house, in the southwest corner. Late day sunlight shoots through the two west-facing front windows and captures the dust motes hanging weightlessly in the air. She crosses through the beams to look out the bay window on the south wall. A large oak shades a small side garden and brick path leading to the rear yard. The path is lined with ivy and flowering shrubs.

She laughs a bit. "How fitting."

He comes closer, so close their shoulders touch, and looks out with her. "What?"

She sits on the wide sill and points at a shrub that drips with an abundance of hot pink flowers. "See the little heart-shaped flowers? They're called Bleeding Heart." She sneaks a glance at him to see if he gets her ribbing about his left-leaning tendencies, and that's when she realizes what's different about him. He's letting his facial hair grow in again. She hopes this time it's intentional.

She fears he misunderstood the comment, but he finally cracks a reluctant grin.

"It'll be lovely," she says. "Your office, I mean. It's got good light."

"I thought so, too. Earl preferred the cooler north side, so it worked out."

He keeps his eyes aimed on the scene outside the window, but she knows he's aware of her studied gaze.

"How have you been, Jack?"

He swallows, and just when she thinks he's going to ignore the question, he says, "I've been better."

"Earl said you're living at Mark's."

He nods. "I figured I'd wait until after I announce my resignation before finding some place permanent. After that, Wolfe and the rest of them will be on to the next thing and won't pay attention to where I go." He laughs softly, but it's tinged with bitterness. "He's not there much, anyway."

"Who?"

"Mark. He spends a lot of time with Claire."

Jenny's shock must have been evident from her expression, because he quickly adds, "No, it's not what you're thinking. He wouldn't do that, not unless he made sure I was okay with it. He's just being a friend to her right now. He's always had a soft spot for her, and she for him. It's a good thing he's doing."

Despite defending his brother, Jack's adding of "right now" to his explanation suggests to Jenny that he believes the relationship might later change. She can't tell how he feels about that.

Turning back to the window, she hears children playing in a distant yard, and she wonders if it will be hard for him to hear that sound every day.

"Do you regret your decision?" she asks.

"Which one?"

She looks up at him in surprise. "Jack—"

He shakes his head. "I know what you're asking." He meets her eye. "No. I miss my kids, not seeing them every day, and . . ." He hesitates, as if he's weighing whether to say the rest of what's on his mind. "I have this unrelenting sadness because we couldn't manage to keep it together, but no, I don't regret the decision. It was the right one."

She wants to tell him she's sorry, but she knows coming from her, the sentiment will only sound self-serving. She thought she knew what Earl meant when he accused her of having Jack exactly where she wanted him, and she doesn't think this was it.

"I should have called you," he says. "I owe you an apology."

"For what?"

"For ever doubting you."

"No, you don't—"

"But it wasn't just that . . ."

He stops talking and her stomach twists with dread. "I'm listening."

"I wanted it to be for the right reasons."

She stands and faces him. "I don't understand." He reaches up and pushes a loose strand of hair off her cheek in the same gentle manner he once used to. She grips his hand before it drops. "Please tell me what you mean."

"I'm not sure how."

"Try."

He breathes deep. "I didn't want to make the mistake of coming to you for comfort while I licked my wounds. I wanted to be fair to you, by waiting to make sure I had my head on straight and I *was* coming to you for the right reasons."

Her eyes tear up. She tries to turn so he won't see, but he catches her by the arm. "I'm sorry. I know it doesn't make sense."

"But it does. I just wish you'd called and told me. I didn't know what to think. I gave you that report, and I thought you'd hate me after you read it. And then I saw the news online about what Claire said on the stand, and I was so confused. How could your own wife say something like that, and yet from you, silence?" The tears come anyway. She slumps back onto the window sill. "God, Jack, I'm sorry. I really didn't want to do this. I don't mean to sound like I expect anything from you. And I *really* didn't want to become a blubbering idiot, either."

This gets a genuine laugh from him.

He squats so that he's level with her. "Jen, look at me." He waits until she reluctantly complies and then hands her a handkerchief. Now she laughs, too, because he did the same thing when she was first arrested for Maxine's murder and he visited her at the jail. "You truly have no idea what you do to me, do you?" he asks. "I was a mess that night after seeing the report. If I'd called you, do you think I would have been able to stay away from you? The better part of me realized how pathetic that would have been."

"I wouldn't have thought you were pathetic."

"Maybe not then. But at some point you would have wondered whether you were just a substitute."

Would she have? She can't honestly say.

"Even after Alex took the plea bargain, I was afraid to call you. I knew if I so much as made a move in your direction, you'd be skewered. I didn't want you to have to hide anymore. Until I get off the radar, they'll be watching everything I do."

"You think I care about that?"

"I care about that. I saw what they did to Claire. Even though they saw her as a victim, they still used her when it served their purposes. Just imagine what they'll do to you."

She hands the handkerchief back to him. "I don't get it. What, exactly, do you care about? What 'they' think? Who *are* 'they', anyway?"

"I care about *you*, and what they'll do to you."

"*Who are 'they'*, Jack? Tell me."

"I'm talking about the press. And everyone. This town."

"The *press*? What more can the press do to me? Have you forgotten what they put me through a few years ago?"

"No. That's why—"

"Do I look that delicate?"

As soon as she speaks the words, she understands. His hands hold hers and his thumb rubs her wrist the way it did when he first asked to see the scar. She's not sure he even realizes he's doing it. She quickly stands, but he rises with her.

"Jenny." He holds tight to her hands.

"Please tell me this isn't the reason you're resigning. I hope you don't feel forced to give up something you love in some misguided attempt to protect me, because I don't need protection. I almost wanted Alex to turn down the deal so I could finally get on the stand and tell the world my side of the story."

"I'm resigning for the same reason you think those flowers are so fitting."

She scoffs. "You really think you'll be able to represent the other side and feel good about it?"

"When the other side is a defendant like you or me, yeah, I do."

"And when they're not? Because most times, they're not. You know that."

He shrugs. "Even the guilty are entitled to a lawyer."

"Yeah? What will you do when the guy who raped and murdered the little girl down the street wants to hire you?"

"I guess I'll try and keep him off death row."

She can't help but laugh. They've slipped right back into their old arguments, the same ones that sparked their attraction to each other and kept it going for so many years. "You really are a bleeding heart, you know that?"

"So I've been told." A rogue grin sprouts on his face.

"I was so afraid you hated me."

He frowns. When he realizes she's referring to the PI report again, he says, "Why would I hate you for something you had nothing to do with?"

"I don't know. Kill the messenger, I guess."

He steps closer, and she has nowhere to go but against the window frame. "Look. You're right. I should have called you. Maybe I was being stupid, but I didn't want us to start something that way."

"Are we starting something?"

"I hope so." He reaches around and pulls the pin that holds her hair in a twist. The hair falls but is still bound at the nape of her neck with a hair band. He tugs to remove this, too. She closes her eyes for a moment as he combs his fingers through.

"Why, because Earl put in a rush order?"

"Because sometimes Earl knows me better than I know myself."

She wants to be skeptical, but she can't stop a small smile. As if that's the only cue he needs, he kisses her, at first gently, but harder when she returns it. Like an octopus, his hands seem to be everywhere at once—in her hair, behind her neck, at the small of her back as he tries to press her closer and then closer still. She responds eagerly, weaving a leg around his ankle as her hands brush against the stubble on his face before finding their way to his shoulders and down his back. She hears a rumble from deep in his throat, and she understands. They can't get to each other fast enough now that they've given themselves permission. Everything else—their clothes, the empty room with only nails and random tools strewn dangerously across the foundation, even his grief and her fear of telling him what she knows she must tell him—all will be dispensed with quickly or dealt with another time.

One by one, he unfastens the silk-covered buttons of her jacket. Only then does his mouth finally leave hers and move down to the side of her neck, into her hair, brushing her jaw and ear along the way. He meets the camisole underneath and mumbles, "too many layers," and all at once he hoists her up and carries her, laughing and legs wrapped around him, back into the lobby. Somehow he sets her down at the end of the drywall without dropping her.

"Such strength, Mr. Hilliard."

"You have no idea," he says, and she laughs again.

He removes his coat and tosses it over the sawhorse. The tie follows. She lies back when he moves to join her, and for a moment his kisses are gentler as he hovers over her. When he stops and with an earnest expression says, "You are so beautiful," all she can do is try not to cry. She knows he's not referring to her appearance.

He hikes up her skirt and sees the thigh-high stockings, the garters. "Sweet Jesus, do you always dress like this under your skirts?"

"Only when I wear the green suit."

He leans close to her ear and whispers, "Then you should wear it more often."

She wants this so badly, but she also knows they're being as reckless now as they were the night that started it all. "We can't do this."

"Are you uncomfortable?"

"No." She laughs a little at his genuine concern and reaches to feel the bristles on his jaw again. "It's not the most comfortable place I've ever been seduced, but that's okay."

"What is it?" he asks. She feels the tension grip his back muscles. "What's wrong? Tell me."

"I'm not using anything."

He relaxes as if to say *Is that all?* He strokes the hair near her face. "Then we'll wait." The mischievous grin returns. "But I can still make you feel good, can't I?"

Her eyes close as his lips graze the inside of her thigh. She thinks, *I love this man.*

"But for the record," he whispers, causing her to open them again, "I'd be okay with taking our chances."

"What do you—"

He props himself up to see her face. "Jen, if that's the worst thing that could happen . . . I don't know. I'm not saying it would be the best thing right now, or it wouldn't be difficult, but still, I'd consider myself lucky to have a little Jenny running around."

She sees the honesty in his eyes, but still she says, "Don't say things like that unless you mean them."

He kisses a tear away. "I mean every word."

It's all she needed to hear.

CHAPTER THIRTY-TWO

HE SMELLS THE scent.

It's happened before. The first time, when he and Claire cut through the cosmetics department at the mall, his heartbeat soared with such trepidation that he clutched at his chest, startling Claire. Another time, alone in line at a coffee shop near their house, it came up behind him like a wind on a blustery day. Both times he experienced the same physical sensation, the fleeting but intense pounding of his heart. It ended as soon as it began, after the mistake in his assumption quickly (and with much relief) became apparent.

Those other times, no touch came on the heels of the scent. Neither the girl at the cosmetics counter nor the woman who stood behind him in line at the coffee shop knew him intimately enough to touch him.

This time is different. This time the scent wakes him. He opens his eyes and takes in his surroundings. The four posts at each corner of the bed, the tall casement windows cracked open to let in the fresh air, the gentle flutter of the sheers. He hears a dog bark in the park across the street. He dares to roll over and make sure she's lying there next to him.

This time the scent calms him.

She faces the windows. The white sheet bunched at her waist exposes her bare back to him. Her hair spills like strips of black satin across the pillow. He thinks of the morning, now almost five years ago, when he woke in the same spot to find a different woman in the bed with him. Safe in his belief that no surprises await him this time, he scoots closer and molds his body against hers. She reinforces this belief when, with a sleepy moan, she gropes for his arm and pulls it tighter around her.

He inhales the scent and falls back asleep.

She wakes him with coffee and warm gooey butter cake. She wears only his shirt with the sleeves rolled up and one button fastened in the middle.

"Wow." He'll let her decide what motivated the comment.

"Don't get too excited. It's store bought. I simply warmed it for a moment in the oven."

She sits at the edge of the bed and places a hand on his. Her expression is serious. Too serious. "Is there anywhere you need to be today?" she asks.

The question causes a bittersweet tightening in his chest. Weekends used to mean Claire, and kids. Now they mean only kids, and only half the time. This weekend is an empty half.

He shakes his head.

"I'd like you to take a drive with me."

"Where?"

"Up to Champaign. There's something I need to show you before . . ."

"Before what?"

Her eyes fill, and he sits up. "Hey, hey. What's going on, Jen? What's the matter?"

She lowers her head and her hair falls forward. He reaches over and tucks each side behind her ears. He doesn't think he'll ever grow tired of touching her hair. "There's something you need to show me before *what?* Just tell me. There's nothing you can't tell me, okay?" Even as he says it, the old fear returns, the fear that maybe she still hides something. Something big.

"Before you love me, I guess."

The dread feels like a stone in his throat. Yet, when he lifts her chin to meet her eye, he speaks the truth.

"I think it's already too late for that."

It's a long drive. For almost three hours, they barely talk. In the driver's seat, she appears to be on the verge of tears. She spends the first hour switching the radio from station to station whenever a song comes on she doesn't like. She finally settles on a classical station and he realizes it wasn't the songs, per se, that she didn't like on the other stations; it was their lyrics. Too many tales of lost loves and broken hearts. He almost offers to drive for her, but he thinks her concentration on the road might be the only thing preventing a full-fledged breakdown.

When they pull off I-57, he says, "We're going to the university?"

She nods. "To a park near the campus. A good friend of mine from Yale teaches at the law school here. I want you to meet her and her family."

"Okay." He doesn't ask why. He assumes the explanation will come when she's ready to give it.

A sign on the corner reads Hessel Park. The park is several residential blocks long on each side and surrounded by homes of varying sizes and ages. A typical Midwestern university neighborhood. She pulls into a parking lot shaded by trees. A pavilion stands at the back of the lot and he sees tennis courts to the right.

"We'll meet them at the playground—it's down that path," she says, pointing to the left, "but I want to say something first."

She doesn't look at him. She just sits there with one hand at the top of the steering wheel and the other resting on her thigh as she stares out the front windshield.

"No matter what you think of me after today, I want you to remember two things."

She finally turns to him, and he blinks slightly, a slow blink to say, *go on.*

"I've always loved you. You've told me more than once that you loved me, but I've never let myself speak those words to you. I thought it was wrong to have those feelings. But it really wasn't the sentiment that was wrong. It was that we acted on it. So I'm telling you now, I *do* love you. More than you know."

A door slams somewhere in the parking lot and they both turn to look. A mother, just emerged from her minivan, slides the side door open to release her toddler from a car seat. The child, a red-headed girl in pigtails, waves her arms and kicks her legs in eager anticipation of the afternoon ahead of her. The windows in Jenny's car are up and they can't hear the mother's voice, but they see her smile and they watch her animated pantomime. Jack can't help but think of Claire and the many times this scene played out in parks near their home. He glances at Jenny and knows she must suspect the thoughts in his head. If so, she accepts them.

"The other thing is, I hope you understand why I never told you what I'm about to show you. I hope you're able to put yourself in my shoes and realize I didn't know what else to do."

"*What* are you talking about?"

"Come with me and I'll show you."

She grips his hand as they follow the path through the trees until it leads to a clearing with a playground and splash pool. Summer's warmth has returned and children screech with delight as they take turns covering the fountain spouts with their feet. Others dart between the swing set and the jungle gym. She leads him to a shaded bench set back far from the playground but within easy view of it. He watches her for some hint of what's happening; she watches the playground as if searching for someone. He knows she found her target when the sides of her mouth lift in a smile. He turns to look just as she lets go of his hand and waves. A man and woman near the slide both wave back. Both appear to be of Indian descent. The woman leans over and speaks at the ear of a child at the top of the slide, points in the direction of Jack and Jenny. The little girl breaks into a smile and waves wildly at them. Or rather, at Jenny. She launches herself down the slide and takes off across the mulch.

If Jack didn't know better, he'd think Jenny's little sister, Andrea, has come back to life. The child coming at them reminds him of the young girl in the photo Jenny used to keep on her dresser, and in the photo albums she showed him after she told him about her family's murders. Her sister was six years old at the time of the murders, and this child is younger, but she shares the same amber hair as Andrea and the same brown skin of both sisters.

"Ayanna Mausi!" She flings herself into Jenny's arms and the two hug tightly. Jenny takes a quick swipe at the corner of her eye while the child's face is against her breast.

"Hey, little one." Jenny presses a hard kiss onto her small forehead and ends it with an exaggerated smacking sound that causes the child to giggle. "How are you?"

"Good!" She quickly lifts her dress to display a skinny wisp of a body and a yellow gingham bathing suit with an abundance of ruffles. "Mataji and Pitaji said I can go in the fountain today. Will you come?"

Jack laughs at her brashness. He decides she also shares Jenny's easy confidence.

Jenny laughs, too, and says, "Well, I'll have to check to see if my bathing suit's still in the car from last time. But first, will you meet my friend?"

At the mention of meeting someone new, she moves back in close against Jenny and stands between her legs. Her thumb promptly goes into her mouth. She nods and for the first time turns her face straight in Jack's direction.

He reels when he sees his own cobalt blue eyes staring back at him.

Even as Jenny makes introductions, "Jack, this is Andrea, Andrea, this is my friend Jack," even as he forces a smile and reaches out to shake her miniature hand, he starts to do the calculations. If Jenny conceived two weeks after the election, she would have come to term the following August, and a baby born then would now be just over four years old. The child in front of him—named after Jenny's sister, apparently—easily qualifies.

He glances across the playground at the putative parents. Without a doubt, both are Indian. It's not impossible, but what are the chances both of them have the blue eye gene?

"Tell your mom I'll be over in a minute, okay?" he hears Jenny say.

"Bye, Mr. Jack."

Numb, he looks back down at the child. She's staring up at him warily and he thinks *Jesus, I'm scaring my own kid.* "Bye, Andrea," he manages, but his voice sounds unnatural even to his ears.

"Is it that obvious?" Jenny asks quietly when she's out of earshot. When *his daughter* is out of earshot.

He watches as she skips back to her parents. *Who are these people?* The woman squats to eye level and listens to whatever Andrea has decided to share. Something about the fountain and Jenny, apparently, because Andrea points in their direction and begins to strip off her dress.

"Jack, please say something."

But how does he choose from the barrage of words attacking him at that moment? So many words fighting for attention in his head.

"Please. Please say something. Anything."

He finally plucks two from the ether. "She's ours."

"Yes."

The girl darts for the fountain and the woman stands straight again, calling for her to take it slow. *Who is this woman pretending to be her mother?* "But she's not."

This time, Jenny doesn't answer so quickly. "No."

"She's theirs."

"Yes, she's theirs." She barely gets the words out without choking on suppressed tears. He grasps her hand and pulls it onto his lap to tell her what he's unable to speak aloud just yet. *I understand.*

He starts thinking of the legal arguments he might make to wrestle her away from these people he assumes are her adoptive parents. Just as quickly he dismisses the idea as ridiculous and wrong and hates himself for how easily he went there.

More collateral damage. All because of one reckless, stupid, selfish decision. He thinks of what it will be like to tell Michael he has a half-sister, even as he questions the oddness of having such a thought just then. Michael, who took so much crap from his father for not using birth control.

"I'm sorry," Jenny says. "I'm so sorry."

"Who does she think you are?" He's grateful the words are coming now, although he's still having trouble injecting them with anything other than shock.

"She calls me her aunt, but it's just a term of endearment. She knows I'm not a sister to either of her parents. I'm a close friend."

"And *are* you?"

"Yes. What I told you in the car is true. I went to school with Pari. We were very close, and have continued to be since we graduated. She started dating Rajat in our last year, so I've known him a long time, too. They're good people. But they couldn't have children, which, until I found out I was pregnant, was nothing more to me than an unfortunate fact about two friends. Even then, it was a while before I came up with the idea."

He looks down at her hand in his, turns it so he can see the scar. He now thinks he understands the *why*. The *when* will come in time, he guesses.

"It's legal?" he asks numbly.

"Yes. An open adoption, of sorts. I wouldn't have done it without the right to be in her life."

"Even if she never knows who you are."

"It wouldn't have been fair to them, Jack." He doesn't disagree; he was simply wrapping his head around the fact of it. "There's something else you need to know." He feels dizzy. How much more can there be? "I didn't list you as the father on the birth certificate. I left it blank. I can show you, in the safe deposit box. You'd moved back home by then and—"

He squeezes her hand. "You don't need to explain. I understand."

"If you want, I'm sure they'd allow us to do a DNA test—"

"Jenny, *stop.* I believe you. I don't doubt for a second she's mine."

She nods, and he pulls her closer, guides her head onto his shoulder. Together they watch Andrea cavort in the plumes of water that shoot from holes in the padded, multicolored ground below her feet. She begins to sing a nonsensical song whose meaning is known only to her, and it makes the adults nearby laugh. Her joy is contagious, and before long, other children—those in the fountain and some from the playground—follow her lead. Parents can't help but stare. Like Jenny, she possesses an innate talent for turning heads that goes so far beyond her physical beauty.

He thinks of what he said to her yesterday—*I'd consider myself lucky to have a little Jenny running around.* He couldn't imagine it would ever happen or, if it did, that it would happen so quickly. But then, he couldn't imagine a lot of things.

A ladybug lands on Jenny's hair and he reaches up.

"What is it?"

"Be still." He lets it crawl onto his finger and then shows it to her. When she looks up at him and searches his face, he gently kisses her. Her lips are soft against his. "Do you want to change into your bathing suit now?"

She gazes at him. He sees the slow dawning in her eyes.

"Our bathing suits," she says.

"*Our* bathing suits?"

She shrugs. "I brought one for you, just in case."

I'd consider myself lucky to have a little Jenny running around. He might not have been able to imagine it, but he meant it nevertheless. He meant it.

"Let's go change, then."

He still does.

BOOK CLUB DISCUSSION QUESTIONS

1. Jack drives Celeste home after he discovers Michael and Celeste drunk and fooling around in the family room of their home. Did this show poor judgment on his part, or was it a natural response once he realized his son couldn't drive Celeste home? Is there any reason he should have feared being alone in the car with her? Have you ever been in a similar situation? (For example, a husband and wife deciding who should drive the babysitter home . . .) If so, how did you handle it?

2. Jack makes three decisions at the very start of the novel that ultimately come back to haunt him: he lets Celeste sober up before arriving at her house; he decides not to tell her father about the drinking and about Michael and Celeste's sexual activities, and he lies to Claire on Michael's behalf when she asks why they're up so late. Why does Jack make each of these decisions? Without the benefit of hindsight, were they reasonable decisions? Logical, even? Why or why not?

3. The novel takes place four and a half years after Jack cheated on Claire, and at the start of the story, he believes she has forgiven him. Claire, on the other hand, "thinks" she has. Later, their views reverse: Jack believes she hasn't forgiven him and never will; Claire argues that she has. Do you think Claire has forgiven him? Why or why not?

4. Why does Claire agree to Jack helping Jenny? Is there more to her reasoning than she lets on to Jack?

5. Does Jenny do the right thing by coming back to tell Jack "her secret" before he finds out from someone else? When Jack eventually learns what the secret is, he tells Jenny he understands why she made the decisions she did. Do you agree? Were her decisions the best ones she could have made at the time, given the circumstances? Why or why not?

6. Even if Jack was not legally required to report Jenny's return to town, should he have done so anyway? Why or why not?

7. Why is it so important to Jack for Claire to tell him she believes he didn't molest Celeste? Do you think she believed all along that he was innocent? Or do

you think she doubted him? If you were married to Jack, would you have believed him?

8. Jack thinks Celeste's journal entry is evidence that someone molested her, but because he knows a jury will believe the evidence points to him, he steals the page out of the journal. What would you do if you were charged with a crime you didn't commit, but came across evidence that would almost certainly lead authorities to believe you were guilty?

9. Jack's brother Mark suggests that it might be better for all involved if Jack and Claire split up. Is he right? At what point does someone stop trying to save a marriage, and how does one know when he or she has reached that point?

10. What do you think Claire would have preferred—that Jack's one-night-stand with Jenny was a meaningless fling? Or that it happened because he was in love with her (as Claire concluded)? In situations of infidelity, which do you think is worse? Why? Is one more forgivable than the other?

11. Jenny's brother Brian thinks Jack "deserves" to know Jenny's secret. Do you agree? Why or why not? Near the end, Jenny says to Jack, "I hope you're able to put yourself in my shoes and realize I didn't know what else to do." Did she have other, better options? Do you believe the choice she made when she first discovered the "secret" was reasonable, given the circumstances?

12. Jack thinks Claire's withholding of the information to exonerate Jenny is a larger crime than his infidelity. Do you agree? Why or why not? Is Jack's view on this issue influenced by his profession?

13. Why does Jack disregard the restraining order and terms of his bail to go after Celeste?

14. After Jack and Claire split up, do you think Jack would have eventually gone to Jenny even if Earl hadn't arranged to get them together? Why or why not?

15. For a couple to recover from a betrayal such as Jack's, which is more important, trust or forgiveness? Why? Discuss other instances in the novel where trust and forgiveness were at issue.

ACKNOWLEDGMENTS

Although only my name appears on the front cover of this book, so many generous and supportive people lent a hand along the way and deserve recognition.

Jamie Morris believed in this one from the beginning and encouraged me to follow my heart instead of the market. I'm so fortunate to have met such an amazing writing mentor not long after arriving in Florida (and I gained a great friend to boot).

Pam Ahearn also believed in this one—and in me—*despite* the fact that I followed my heart instead of the market. Agents like Pam don't come along too often.

I owe a huge debt of gratitude to Linda Dunlap for her keen editor's eye and tireless attention to detail. She combed through every line of the manuscript and made so many valuable suggestions for improvement. It's a leaner, smoother novel thanks to Linda.

My first readers—Carla Buckley, Margaret Reyes Dempsey, and Melanie Tamsky—gave the early feedback that every writer needs and ignores at her peril. Melanie deserves an additional thanks for once again helping with my medical questions.

I credit my sisters-in-law Shannon and Wendy Combs for the genesis of the story idea. Their discussion at a family Christmas Eve gathering some years back about "who drives the babysitter home" sparked an idea that eventually turned into this *Tell No Lies* sequel, something I never thought I'd write.

Alison Hicks and the folks at Philadelphia Stories supported me at the start by publishing an early excerpt and giving me priceless exposure. Alison has been a mentor for many years. Back when I was lucky to write something longer than twenty pages, she encouraged me to persist, giving me the confidence to eventually make the move from lawyer to novelist.

Thanks to Terri-Lynne DeFino and all of my VAB Dollbabies for their friendship and for sharing an inspiring space to write without distraction for one week of every year. Geri Throne, thank you for inviting me into the fold.

No acknowledgment would be complete without mention of the many readers whose enthusiasm for my work makes it pure joy to sit down at the keyboard each day.

My daughters Jessie and Sally provided the usual (but oh so important) family support, but Jessie deserves special thanks for the long hours she devoted to cover design, and Sally for her tutorials on teen texting habits.

And Rick, of course, for everything. There are no words.

JULIE COMPTON was born and raised in St. Louis, Missouri, where she attended Washington University for both undergraduate and law school. She began her legal career in St. Louis, but last practiced in Wilmington, Delaware as a trial attorney for the U.S. Department of Justice. When her family moved to Florida in 2003, she gave up law to pursue writing full-time. She lives near Orlando with her husband and two daughters. *Keep No Secrets* is her third novel. Julie is available for book club meetings and other appearances both in-person and via Skype. To contact Julie, sign up for her mailing list, or for more information about her other books, please visit www.julie-compton.com.

If you enjoyed *Keep No Secrets*, won't you please tell your friends and consider posting an online review? In an increasingly competitive book market, your opinion matters.

Thank you for your support!